Names of the Dead

Mark Leggatt

All the best,

Mark Leggatt

Author image courtesy of Chris Close Photography

Published by:
Fledgling Press Ltd,
7 Lennox St.,
Edinburgh,
EH4 1QB

www.fledglingpress.co.uk

ISBN 9781905916979

Printed and bound by:
Bell & Bain Ltd, Glasgow

ACKNOWLEDGEMENTS

My thanks to Eric Nelson for his invaluable guidance and advice. It made all the difference.

Pour Caroline

CHAPTER 1

This is it. Right here.

Beyond the lights, the traffic on the Via Crescenzio streamed past. The evening rush hour in Rome was easing. Montrose edged the hood of the car closer to the rear of the Mercedes, and watched the exhaust smoke curl up over the lip, then lifted his head and stared through the windshield.

The men in the front of the Mercedes sat motionless, facing the line of cars, waiting for the lights.

He shifted in the seat where the Glock was wedged under his groin. The stench of the exhaust from the Mercedes drifted into the Fiat. To his left he saw a side street before the junction. The line of traffic shuffled towards the lights. The Mercedes crawled forward.

He slid the Fiat close behind until he was level with the side street then wound the steering around until the wheels pointed left. Badly parked cars lined the street.

The lights changed to red. The Mercedes rolled a few yards, closing up to the line in front.

They could be through the lights on the next sequence. And then they're gone. He rubbed his eyes. The red traffic light seemed to burn into his retina. He wiped his palms on his jeans until the skin began to burn, then pulled the Glock from between his legs and hauled back the slide to chamber a round.

The Mercedes drew to a car length behind the Fiat.

Where are they going? He stuck his head out of the window and saw a drop in the curb, just before a hotel on the corner. The foyer came into view, with several limos parked outside. *That's it. That's where it's going down.*

The Mercedes pulled in and stopped behind a limo, the rear of the car jutting out onto the road.

The skinny tires squealed as he spun the Fiat right and pulled past, running the lights. As soon as the foyer was out of view he swerved onto a crosswalk and brought the Fiat to a halt then hit the hazard lights. Tucking the Glock deeper into his sweatshirt pocket, he jumped out and headed for the hotel. *Slow down. This isn't a bust.*

At the entrance of the hotel the Mercedes edged forward as the limo pulled away. The two men got out and the doorman stepped towards them. The driver tried to hand him the key, but the doorman nodded to a bellboy.

The driver stood for a moment as the doorman tried to explain. Montrose headed for the doorway. *Sweatshirt and jeans in a fancy hotel. Yeah, looking good. Wear the face.* Sticking his chin out, he nodded to the concierge as he entered, "Good evening." He didn't wait for a reply and headed over to a large board showing the dinner menu.

With his back to the foyer, he pulled out his iPhone

then reversed the camera. The recording icon flashed red. He twisted it in his hand until the screen showed the front door and he watched the two men stride through the lobby. *They're not going to the desk. This ain't no vacation. They have a meeting. This is where it happens. And I'm right here.*

The two men ignored the main elevators and walked straight to a single elevator at the side of the foyer. One man took out a piece of paper, and slowly typed into a keypad at the side of the door.

Top right, top left and two at the bottom. Got it.

The two men stepped into the elevator.

Do the right thing. He held the phone in his hand. *Call it in.* As he turned, the elevator door was closing. *Jeez, it could be all over by the time the cavalry get here. Langley must have a team in Rome. Or Interpol can call in the Italian cops. And do what?*

Weaving past a businessman and a wheeled suitcase, he stepped over to the elevator. *Cops need a search warrant. And if the main man is up there, he's probably bought them off. Yeah, this is Rome. But I could check it out. Get a face. The one that's buying all the shit.*

Lifting a finger to the keypad of the elevator, he traced the number in the air then turned away. *No, that's a crap idea.*

He stood in the middle of the foyer. *You don't know what's up there.* He twisted his shoulders and stared at the elevator door. *And all you've got is a bad attitude and a 9mm.*

CHAPTER 2

Particles of dust danced in the air as they crossed a pencil-thin shaft of light, streaming through a gap in the shutters holding back the morning sun that had baked Rome for weeks. The hum of the traffic around the Coliseum drifted into the room.

Control your breathing. Montrose caught the scent of old wood and paper in the dry air. *Relax. Give nothing away. You did the right thing. The forensics in the hotel will back you up.* For a moment he remembered standing in front of the school principal. *For smoking? Some crap like that. Though this time it's gonna be more than detention.*

"Do you know why you're here?"

Montrose tried to read the old guy's expression, but the face was tighter than a Puritan's collar. *Sure, you party with a 9 mm Glock and you win a free trip to the shrink every time.* "Yeah, I know."

The old guy slid a pair of half-moon spectacles onto his nose then opened a buff folder on his desk. "My name is Doctor Richmond. Following the events of last night, I have been assigned by the CIA in Rome to assess the results of your psychological examination. Standard procedure."

To his right a desk fan slowly rotated, gently stirring the warm air. Montrose resisted the urge to loosen his tie. *Just play the game.* His mouth began to dry, and he imagined an ice-cold Pepsi from the gelato vendor he had passed on the way in. *Tell them what they need to know. That's all.*

Richmond pulled the papers from the folder and spread them across the desk. "CIA Technology Support in Langley. Then an incident where you exceeded your system security level. After which, you were downgraded and seconded to Interpol for six months." He pursed his lips. "And now this. Very interesting. Professionally speaking, of course."

Montrose scratched his ear. *Yeah, and you're a real pain in the ass, professionally speaking.*

"So, why Interpol?"

"I majored in Languages and Technology. Interpol were looking for a Technical Liaison officer. I assist on cases and report back to Langley."

"And your role on this particular mission was to provide technical support. What is that?"

"Face recognition software, tracking, bugging, and accessing computer systems."

Richmond glanced at the screen for a moment. "Why were you issued a weapon?"

"I'm weapons trained. If I think I need one, I draw a weapon."

"Did Interpol issue you one, or did you request it?"
What the hell does it matter? "I requested it."

"And is there any operation you have been on where you have not requested a weapon?"

"I've got no idea. Maybe." *Stupid question.*

Richmond nodded slowly then began tapping on his keyboard.

What are you writing? "Look, this wasn't a stakeout, sitting in a van with fat guys wearing headphones and eating pizza. We were in Indian country." *You were justified. 100%. Don't make it sound like an excuse.*

"Naples?"

"Yeah. Where Mr. Cosa Nostra lives, you know? The nice old Italian guy that sells drugs to half the kids in Europe."

"I am aware of the Cosa Nostra's activities, Mr. Montrose. I have lived in Italy for over twenty years."

"Well, you haven't lost your accent." *You're still an Ivy League asshole.*

"Let's talk about the incident in Langley. You were disciplined for accessing a restricted database."

It wasn't restricted. The firewall was wide open.

"A database containing a record of private jet flight records. Is that correct?"

Montrose licked his dry lips and wiped the sweat from his cheeks. "If you know that, why are you asking me? What are you driving at?"

"We're here to examine your intentions, Mr. Montrose, not mine. I want to hear it from you."

"Hey, if you know that then it's no secret. Yeah, I was looking at flight records. And I came across something I shouldn't have seen."

"Assuming this was highly confidential information, and considering the reason we are here today, was there anything in the nature of the flights you discovered that I should perhaps know about?"

Oh yeah, you should know about it. But you won't hear it from me. "Nah. Routine stuff. They just didn't like me sticking my nose into their database." *You're getting clumsy, my friend. You just want to know if I'm gonna tell anybody. That ain't gonna happen.*

"These private jets you were looking for . . ."

He folded his arms.

" . . . they were centered on flights to one particular country, am I correct?"

Montrose shrugged. "What can I say? It's confidential."

Richmond squinted down at a printout. The spectacles slipped down his nose as he looked up. "You didn't blink."

"I fired my weapon in self-defense. It's what I'm trained to do."

"Self-defense, yes. We'll come to that later. But that's not what I'm talking about."

He watched Richmond draw his finger over a row of figures.

"In one of the psychometric tests this morning, we showed you photos of atrocities. Women and children butchered. Unbelievable carnage from every corner of the globe."

The way of the world. The way it's always been. "How could I forget?"

"According to these figures, you showed a slight increase in heart rate and blood pressure. All normal reactions."

Five shots of espresso always do the trick.

"But you didn't blink."

Montrose shifted in his seat.

"Everybody blinks faster." Richmond ran his finger

down a column on the report. "It's a normal reaction. The higher the stress, the higher the blink rate. But not you." He looked up. "Why?"

"Maybe I'm professionally detached. Might be Post Traumatic Stress."

"Might be. But this concerns last night. It's a bit soon for PTS. Do you feel traumatized?"

I couldn't give a damn. "I'm not sure how I feel."

"Well, that's what we're here to find out."

Yeah, find out if I'm nuttier than squirrel shit.

Richmond rolled a pen between his thumb and forefinger. "Tell me, why were you in the hotel?"

Montrose cleared his throat. "That's where the suspects led me. I was right behind them."

"All the way from Naples?" Richmond glanced up at a yellowing map of Italy framed on the wall. "That's about a hundred and fifty miles. All the way to the hotel?"

"All roads lead to Rome." *Two hours in a one-liter Fiat, trying to tail a Mercedes. I can still hear the engine screaming in my ear.*

"You could have handed this to the Italian police at any time. What made these two suspects so special?"

"You want to know?" Montrose pushed himself up in the chair. "For the past four months the deaths of heroin addicts in Italy have skyrocketed. All from accidental overdoses. Someone is bringing in a ton of very high-grade heroin into Italy and dumping it on the market. Interpol suspected Naples. They were right on the money."

"Pure heroin?"

"Pretty much. The Mafia cut it down, but not enough. It's a damn sight purer than the shit they usually deal with. It has to be someone new to the market. And it has to be through Naples."

"Naples is not the only port in the Mediterranean, Mr. Montrose. The heroin could be coming from anywhere."

"Have you ever been to Naples?"

"Of course, but . . ."

"Naples docks are over two hundred acres, spread along the coast. At the last official count seventy per cent of cargo that goes through the port is unchecked. One hundred and fifty thousand containers pass through the docks every year. It takes about thirty minutes from a ship docking to a rig and container hitting the interstate. And they're gone. All over Europe." Montrose sat back in his chair. "And tracking the containers? We haven't got a chance. The Mafia have got the place running like clockwork. The guys we found were Pakistani organized crime. Very organized."

Richmond held out his hands. "This is all fascinating, Mr. Montrose, but it is difficult to say that it is anything other than complete conjecture."

Montrose tapped his forehead. "Think like a cop. The only place that kinda heroin could come from is the Golden Crescent, and that's Pakistan or Afghanistan. These guys were watching a container ship. Intelligence confirmed a ship was due to dock. The last port of call was Port Bin Qasim. In Pakistan."

"A container full of heroin? That seems a major risk, Mr. Montrose. All your eggs in one basket. Would they risk losing it all?"

Montrose looked down and shook his head. "Not in Naples. Besides, they're experts in risk management. And logistics. Pakistani heroin normally follows the ancient Silk Road, through Russia then into Turkey. But it's thousands of miles over rough terrain. It gets cut down along the way to make a few bucks more. It never arrives pure. Even if it comes through Iran, and they're closing down the routes. The smugglers the Iranians catch are dangling from a crane by the end of the day. The Ayatollahs are doing something right. But by container ship, it can be right in the heart of Europe in a week. So we waited, and watched."

"Indeed. *Were* watching them is what I was told. Past tense. The surveillance operation was cancelled."

"Yeah." *At the last minute.*

"I understand that your superiors in Interpol were unimpressed with your lack of results."

Superiors? More like weasels in suits. "That's what I heard."

"My notes tell me that the order to cancel the surveillance operation caused a serious disagreement with your boss, Jack Morgan."

Who's been telling tales? "Sure. We spent eight weeks in a two room apartment, breathing in our own stink, and then they pull the op when we're close to a result."

"He sees it somewhat differently. You refused to cancel the operation."

"I was making my thoughts known. And yeah, in no uncertain terms."

"The conversation is described as 'intense'."

"Just blowing off steam. Morgan knows that."

"And did you at any point intimate that you were 'going to sort it out yourself'?"

Has he got this verbatim? "I wasn't being serious. Things said in the heat of the moment, you know. I was pretty pissed off. So were the team. What can you do?"

"But the team went home, Mr. Montrose. That is the difference."

"Hey, I'm CIA, not some flatfoot from Interpol. What I do makes a difference. There are people on the streets, or kids in school, who won't be able to get their hands on the shit those guys are selling. That's the difference." He realized he was jabbing his finger at Richmond. *Ah, what the hell. I've had enough of this crap. Get the message.* "Sometimes people die. And you know what? The world is a better place."

"And you have no regrets?"

Montrose turned away for a moment and blinked as his eye caught a sliver of sunshine from the window shutters. *It's a beautiful day.* He rubbed his forehead, exhaling through his nose. "First phrase I ever learned in French. *Je ne regrette rien.*"

"Indeed."

"Shit happens. Game over."

Richmond folded his hands together as if in prayer, then rested his chin on the tips of his fingers. His cell phone buzzed on his desk and a text message flashed on the screen. He scanned it for a moment then picked up his pen. "You'll excuse me for a moment while I make some notes?" Richmond began to write in a slow, fluent manner at the bottom of a page. He looked up. "Mr. Montrose, I want you to think very carefully about what happened in the hotel. This game is far from over."

A surge of adrenalin made his neck stiffen and before he could stop himself, he brought up a hand to rub the back of his head. He could still smell the acrid tang of cordite on his hands. *No. It ended in the hotel. A dead end. But not for me.*

*

The elevator doors had closed by the time he turned around. A faint whine came from above when the motors engaged, but the movement was barely perceptible. In front was a black panel where the buttons should have been.

Montrose pushed his hands through his hair and looked up at the ceiling, listening to the sound of his own breathing. The muscles were tight in his chest and he threw his shoulders back then rummaged in his pocket for the Interpol ID. A camera blinked above the door. *That ain't good.*

The Glock hung heavy in his pocket as he shoved his hand into the sweatshirt and wrapped it around the pistol grip. *I come in peace.* He thumbed off the safety. *Mostly.*

A loud ping rang in his ears and his hand trembled on the Glock. The elevator bumped to a halt and the doors slid open.

Facing him was a full length mirror, built into the corridor wall. He stood, gazing at his reflection. *Boots, jeans, a grubby sweatshirt. I look like a hood. Or a cop.* The doors began to close and he stuck his boot into the gap. The doors clattered into his boot then slammed back. He stepped forward. *Oh yeah, fucking good entrance.*

He began to pull the ID free from his pocket. A movement to the left caught his eye.

A man came around a corner and stopped dead. His mouth dropped open.

Who the fu . . .?

The man's face twitched and he looked past Montrose, down the corridor.

Montrose turned and saw one of the Pakistanis, eyes wide open, staring at the shape of the Glock through his sweatshirt pocket. *Shit.*

The elevator door closed.

The Pakistani's hand dived into his jacket and brought up the butt of a machine pistol. The cocking handle caught against his shirt and he tried to wrestle it free.

Shit shit shit! Montrose tried to take out his ID, but it flew from his hand and bounced across the corridor.

The Pakistani tugged his pistol free and racked back the cocking handle.

Montrose dived to the floor, pulled out the Glock and snatched at the trigger. The butt of the gun bounced on the carpet and the first round flew wild, splintering the Pakistani's shin.

The machine pistol waved wildly in the Pakistani's hands as he roared and stumbled against the wall then leveled the stubby barrel towards the floor.

Montrose pushed his arms forward and pulled the trigger twice.

The rounds burst into the Pakistani's chest. He flew backwards, his hand tight on the trigger as he emptied the magazine into the roof.

The second Pakistani lifted his hands.

Montrose jerked the sights of the Glock to the right and fired. The round left a neat hole in the Pakistani's face as a gout of blood blasted out behind him and shards of bone punctured the wall.

The other guy. A shrill whine pierced his ears as he tried to roll over, but his arms were locked, stretched out in front of him. Curling into a ball, he tumbled to the side and twisted his shoulders.

There was no one there.

He spun back and watched a cloud of plaster drift down, settling into a pink scum on the pool of blood. The voice of a man screamed in his head. He realized it was his own.

CHAPTER 3

"Take me back to Naples, Mr. Montrose. You continued the surveillance alone. Why?"

Man, change the record. "Why not? It was Friday night. The Interpol guys went home to Lyon. We had the apartment for another month. I had nothing else to do that weekend."

"I take it your superiors in both the CIA and Interpol were unaware of this?"

"What do you mean?" Montrose let his hands consciously droop over the edge of the armrests.

"Interpol in Lyon tell me you're supposed to be on vacation. In fact, they strongly recommended you take some time off."

"I cancelled."

"Not according to them."

"I didn't get around to telling them. Anyway, it was on my own time. Going the extra mile, you know?" *Don't fold your arms.*

"Let's be very clear, they ordered you to end the surveillance and take a vacation."

"Well, I just decided to hang on a bit."

"For two days. And what did you see, Mr. Montrose, that led us here today?"

A couple of crims waiting for their boat to come in. "Two guys in fancy suits. Pakistani or Pashtun. You can't walk about the docks without knowing someone. They were allowed in. Then they met a guy walking from the truck park."

"Did you report this?"

"No, I was off the case."

"You didn't follow them?"

"On foot against three guys, in two different directions? I'm not Jack Bauer." *That was a joke, tightass.*

"Then who did you follow?"

"The suits. There were maybe two hundred rigs parked up. Coming and going all the time. So I tagged the suits."

"Did you then inform your superiors?"

Where's he going with this? "No, like I say, I was on my own time. Just to satisfy my curiosity, you know?"

"Or perhaps you realized you would have been disciplined for disobeying orders?"

Montrose tried to shrug, but it came across as if he'd been poked in the eye. "Maybe. But Interpol don't pay my wages." *Jeez, stay still.*

Richmond seemed to consider this for a moment, nodding almost imperceptibly. "So you followed them to the hotel."

"They went straight there."

"Even at this point, you didn't think to inform Interpol? Or the CIA?"

"All I had was two suspects."

"Yes, the suspects. One man with two rounds to the chest." Richmond checked his cell phone. "The other with a round to the head. One of whom is now dead."

Yeah, dead. Unless he's a freakin' vampire. "He was the last time I saw him." He looked down at Richmond's cell phone and felt the skin tighten across his scalp. "What do you mean one dead?"

Richmond nodded slowly. "It seems one of the men is still with us, though the prognosis is poor."

"Who?"

"The man you shot in the face."

Montrose felt his mouth drop open. "No, he couldn't survive that . . . head wound." *I saw parts of his skull spray across the corridor.*

"It seems the bullet entered the cheekbone and passed under the cerebellum, then blew out a large hole behind his ear."

"Cerebellum? Are you saying I missed his fucking brain?"

"I wouldn't put it quite like that, but that certainly seems to be the case."

Holy shit. "Can he talk?"

Richmond tapped the pen against his lips.

I am so gonna shove that pen right up your . . .

"Would that be a good thing, Mr. Montrose? If he could talk?"

You piece of . . . "Yeah. That would be a good thing. Especially before a judge."

"It's not for me to deal with the legal fallout, so we'll skip that particular problem."

That interview was next. Some internal affairs lawyer looking to tear my balls off. It would make an interview with a psychiatrist look like a clumsy speed date.

"Three weeks in an apartment overlooking the docks," said Richmond. "That's a pretty boring job, no?"

Montrose blinked. *He's playing the game. Stay with him. The guy with the hole in his head can wait.* "Well, not recently." *Wise-ass.*

Richmond's face betrayed no emotion. "You're an IT specialist, basic training as an agent, and yet they keep you busy on stakeouts. Why is that?"

Wasn't much goddam' choice. "Maybe my boss doesn't like me."

"Perhaps." Richmond flicked through some papers then pushed on his spectacles. "Or is it because they thought you may be emotionally unstable after your recent bereavement?"

Montrose heard the blood pumping in his ears. *He knows what he's doing.* He wiped his damp hands on his suit. The heavy wool was fine for Lyon, but it was damn hot for Rome. *Relax. Don't let him get to you. Everything I do, everything I say, this guy can read like a book.* "I'm a professional. I was given the job, just like any other."

"Really?" Richmond leaned forward on the desk. The spectacles slipped down his nose. "You're sure you had no say in the matter?"

What the hell does he mean by that? Montrose tried to swallow, but his throat was dry. "Maybe. I don't recall." He had an urge to rip the spectacles from Richmond's face and smash them into pieces. *Be cool. Go along with the ride. He'll get tired before you do.*

Richmond filed the sheet of paper back into the folder. "You followed the two suspects into a palazzo. The Hotel Versailles. Is that standard operating procedure?"

He tapped the folder with the leg of the spectacles.

Montrose shrugged. "Sure. I wanted to know what they were up to." *Could I kill a man with his own spectacles? Got to be a first.*

Richmond flicked through the papers until he found the one he wanted. "Then you took the elevator."

"Yeah."

"When you stopped at the Executive Suite did you have your weapon ready?"

You mean was I going to kill them? "No. I did not."

"At exactly what point did you draw your weapon?"

"When one of the goons drew out a machine pistol. The elevator door closed behind me. I had no choice."

"Did these men identify you as a CIA agent?"

"I was wearing a hood. It was raining." *Was it raining?*

"They may have taken you for a terrorist."

"Maybe. Or a cop."

Richmond pushed his hands through his graying hair. He took off the spectacles, carefully folded the legs and then placed them in his breast pocket.

About time. Montrose felt the tension slacken in his chest. *Any more crap and this guy might find out his own reaction when a gun is pointed at him.* He pushed his arms out to lever himself up. *If the Italian cops give me it back.*

Richmond leaned back in the chair. "Tell me about your sister."

Montrose felt his hands ball into a fist. *None of your fucking business.* "You know about my sister. It's in my file."

"I want to hear it from you."

"It's not relevant."

"With respect, Mr. Montrose, I'll decide that."

Go to hell. "I just did. Move on."

Richmond spread his fingers over the buff folder. "One man dead. The other perhaps fatally injured."

Helluva good shooting. Still, got to give some credit to Mr. Machine-Pistol. He really got the party started.

"Tell me again why you started shooting?"

"Because the guy pulled a gun on me."

"You could have surrendered."

"It wasn't the OK Corral. These guys don't take prisoners."

"You can't know that."

"Would you have preferred if I'd taken the chance? Is a dead agent less hassle for you?"

Richmond held out his hands. "Mr. Montrose, such flippancy . . ."

"It's my job to know if the guy was going to shoot me. And he was."

"Did you identify yourself prior to opening fire?"

My ass I did. "Yeah. I have Interpol ID. Works better than my CIA badge."

"What did you say?"

"Armed Police. Drop your weapon."

"And did he?"

"He might still be alive if he did."

"Did you repeat the warning?"

"I didn't get the opportunity. I was face down on the carpet."

"But you're not police."

Montrose threw a hand into the air. "Hey, you're way ahead of me. Next time I'll say 'Hi! I'm an armed agent of the Central Intelligence Agency, seconded to Interpol in Lyon, France, so please don't point a gun at me', by which time he'll have blown my freakin' head off."

Richmond turned to the desk fan. "Are you warm, Mr. Montrose? Shall I turn up the fan?"

How about I shove your shiny face in it? "Whatever."

Richmond leaned over and hit a switch. The noise of the fan increased with no discernible effect. He looked up at the ceiling. "Why would the first man pull a gun on you?"

Montrose scoffed. "What do you think? Something to do with drugs?"

"Not all Pakistani visitors to Rome or Naples docks are drug runners."

"Maybe, but they're not immune to terrorists. They've got plenty enemies. The Taliban for one."

"That's reasonable. They may say they were defending themselves. Of course, that's unlikely to be confirmed, given the survivor's precarious state of health.'

The blood rushed to his head, and Montrose resisted the urge to pull at his shirt collar.

"I'm on your side, Mr. Montrose."

Like hell you are.

"I need to be sure that your reaction was a reasonable one. That you have good reason to do what you did. You have to help me on that."

You're fishing, but I ain't biting. "It went down just like I said."

"Did you suspect you were walking into a drug deal?"

What do you think, Einstein? "You're not listening. I track them on suspicion and I convict them on evidence. There was none. All I had was a stack of dead junkies, a container ship from Pakistan, and two guys from the

Golden Crescent in an expensive hire car to Rome. If I get something concrete, then I phone it in. Like you say, standard procedure."

"Phone it in, yes. But you could have done that before. You know how this could look?"

It looked like a butcher shop by the time the shooting had stopped. "It looks like a drug dealer is dead and the other ain't far behind him. That's what it looks like."

Richmond shook his head. "It's really not as simple as that, so we're gonna start getting real."

Montrose forced himself to breathe slowly. *Chill. This guy could be a big problem.*

"Let me play devil's advocate." Richmond closed the folder. "You followed two suspects and suddenly there's one in the morgue and the other on life support. Why?"

"Not everyone. One suspect got away." *Shit happens.*

Richmond stopped and opened the folder while fumbling for his spectacles.

You ain't looking so clever now, Professor.

Richmond looked quickly across the papers. "Two men confirmed shot. You're saying a man escaped?"

Try to keep up. "He came around the corner when the shooting started."

"Just another hotel guest?"

"Wrong place, wrong time? I don't think so."

"Did you get a good look at him?"

"No. About six feet, blond hair, dark suit."

"Is that all?"

"It was only a glance. When the party started he turned and ran."

"You didn't try to pursue him?"

I was face down on the floor breathing in carpet cleaner and cordite. "Once I made sure that the two men were no longer a threat, he was gone."

"And there's no trace of this man?"

"Not yet."

"I have a note here saying that the hotel staff confirmed the arrival of yourself and the two men. No mention of anyone else."

"Drug dealers."

Richmond looked up. "Excuse me?"

"They're not just two men. They're drug dealers."

"Let's focus on this third man. From what I can see, the only person who says he exists is you. There is no trace of him. No other witnesses."

"He took the fire exit. I followed the stairs down to the alley at the rear of the hotel, but he was gone."

Richmond drummed his fingers on the desk. "Is it not convenient that your witness cannot be traced?"

Montrose shot forward in the chair. "You think it's convenient? I will find him!"

"May I remind you, Mr. Montrose, you are here on a professional basis. This man may be the only person who can back up your story."

"It's not a goddam' story! I nearly got my ass shot off!"

Richmond returned to the folder. "Two men shot. One dead. One clinging to life. And of course, the mystery man." He closed the file and looked up. "We should consider the worst case scenario."

Montrose leaned back. *Here we go. I've just plugged two guys in a Rome hotel and CIA Internal Affairs are going nuts. I'll spend the rest of my career in Antarctica, up to my ass in penguins. What could be worse?*

Richmond cleared his throat and closed his eyes for a moment. "Let me tell you how it could have been."

Montrose held out his hands. "Why don't we just talk about how it was?"

"Bear with me on this. You followed your targets and when the opportunity arose, you assassinated them. And then you say that there is a mystery man who can prove you didn't."

He felt the beads of sweat pooling in the small of his back. "You're freakin' crazy."

Richmond pointed to the wall. "I've got a lot of fancy paper up there says I'm not. What I have in front of me is a story that has no corroboration, no drugs, no cash, a witness that doesn't exist, and a psychologically damaged agent who uses his vacation to kill two men."

Montrose slammed his hand on the desk. "It didn't happen like that and you damn well know it! Why would I do that?"

Richmond didn't look at him. He slipped a photograph from the folder. "I think you know why."

CHAPTER 4

The button popped as Montrose tugged at his collar. He dropped onto the park bench and drank greedily from the bottle of Pepsi. A girl approached in high heels, tight shorts and a green t-shirt emblazoned with the name of an oil company. Wearing a fixed smile, she thrust forward a leaflet and a small stuffed polar bear in her outstretched hand, then pulled it back sharply when she saw Montrose's face.

I must look like shit.

He pulled out his iPhone and thumbed the power button. He caught his reflection in the screen. *What if the old guy was right? Maybe I'm a psycho.* Lifting his head, he watched two pretty girls sitting on a bench opposite, their knees touching when they leaned towards each other in giggling conversation. *They're safer for what happened. Not much, maybe, but . . . I guess that doesn't count anymore.*

He reached into his pocket and pulled out a gold lighter, stained and scored with age. He could barely make out the word 'Cartier' where the metal had worn away. His grandfather's lighter that he brought from Berlin. *She didn't sell it.* The coroner had found it sewn into the pocket of her jeans. He closed his eyes and slowly rubbed his thumb back and forth across the metal. *Everything she went through and she didn't sell it.*

He last saw her when her emaciated china-white body lay on a slab. Somewhere, deep in the sunken eyes and tightly drawn skin around her cheeks, was the smiling face of their childhood.

He remembered she didn't look peaceful. She looked dead.

He tipped his head back and drained the bottle, ignoring the insistent beep from the iPhone. *The Pakistanis had it coming. The look in the guy's eyes when I squeezed the trigger. Was he trying to surrender? Like that was gonna work.*

The iPhone rang in his hand. *Morgan. Be good to me, you Washington ass-licker. Tell me what I want to hear.* He jammed it to his ear. "Have you found him?"

"Who?" said Morgan.

"Who do you think? The bastard that got away!" Montrose jumped to his feet, kicking the Pepsi bottle across the sidewalk. The two girls on the bench grabbed their bags and scurried away. "Who's looking for him? We need a CIA team, not some coffee-shop cops from Interpol."

"Listen, Montrose, you just step back. Right now I've got something bigger to worry about. Rome is full of European Trade Ministers and there are some very important people on the way from Washington. Langley are going crazy. The Italian police can take care of your mystery man."

"They couldn't find their own ass with a map and a mirror. This is our case. It's got nothing to do with the Italian cops. We have to find this guy!"

"I'm looking at the bigger picture. This guy's a sideshow. If he exists."

"If he exists? Are you calling me . . ?" He squeezed the phone in his hand. "Okay . . . Has the hotel been dabbed for prints?"

"Montrose, you've got other things to think about. The first one is the shrink. What did he say?"

Play the game. Give him the right answers. "He wants to see me again. Run further tests before he makes his recommendation."

"Maybe that's for the best."

"Whadaya mean for the best? Sounded like he was trying to prove I'm a nutjob. Are you saying the same? I've turned into some kinda vigilante, all 'cos of Sandie? My sister has got nothing to do with this. I thought you knew me better, Boss. Maybe not, eh?"

"Wind your neck in. You just shot two guys, you got no drugs, no witnesses, and I'm trying to keep Internal Affairs from sticking your ass in an Italian jail!"

Montrose heard the venom in his voice. *There's no way I'm going to find this guy unless Morgan is on my side.* "Boss, I think we are close to finding a fuck-ton of heroin. These guys were using a container ship."

"Listen to me, you've got nothing on these guys. Nothing."

"The dealers I dropped weren't some hillbilly rag-heads. They were clean-shaven, shiny shoes and styled hair. They wore Armani and IWC watches."

"Yeah, and your only lead is some guy in a nice suit. In Rome. That doesn't really narrow it down. This guy could be just a businessman, or a tourist. You got nothing on him. You don't even have a description."

"He came around the corner of the hotel corridor just before the shooting started. Six foot, maybe, blond hair. But they recognized him, Boss. The two guys I dropped. I'm sure of it. One look, but I know. He was no stranger. We've got to find him."

"Yeah, yeah, we'll think about it. Look, you're a tech specialist, leave this to the cops at Interpol. Just get yourself back over to the office. The CIA European Director is in town. He wants to make sure you're onside."

Wrong answer. He felt the iPhone slip against the sweat on his face and relaxed his grip before it shot out of his hand like a bar of soap. "Yeah. I'm on my way."

He cut the call and turned east, lifting his hand to shade his eyes against the morning sun. In front of the Coliseum a row of green flags from an oil company hung lazily in the warm air as students handed out stuffed toys to the tourists. From the Via Labincana, two motorcycle cops swung to a halt in front of the junction of Via Celio Libenna, holding up the traffic as a line of blacked-out SUVs swept towards the centre of Rome. Montrose wiped the iPhone on his jacket and watched the motorcade. Cadillac Escalades for the US, with the Stars and Stripes, and Range Rovers for the Brits, the Union Jack fluttering in the slipstream. They disappeared towards the Via Dei Fori Imperiali and the Italian motorcycle cops looked back nervously, as though waiting for stragglers.

Just then a white Maserati sedan appeared, curving smoothly around the Coliseum. A small Norwegian flag was fixed to the windshield with scotch tape.

The windows were open and the occupants sat in shirtsleeves, eating ice cream cones as they pointed towards the Coliseum. An Italian Army jeep was right behind it, the driver hunched over the dashboard, one hand gripping the wheel and the other waving wildly. The traffic cops motioned to the Maserati, to hurry them up, but the Norwegian driver ignored them, resting his elbow on the door and adjusting his shades as he headed towards the centre of Rome.

Nothing to do with me. But the big bad CIA boss wants me in front of his desk. Ain't no such thing as coincidence. They're all NATO countries. Maybe the spooks in Langley want to make sure that they ain't got a crazy running around. They want to know if I'm a good little doggy. And if they think I've gone fruit loops, they'll stick me in a kennel.

He picked up the empty Pepsi bottle. *There were four nine-millimeter rounds waiting to be picked out of the plaster on a hotel wall. The fire pattern would back me up. The CSU team can track all the shots and they'll see it happened just like I said.*

He slipped off his jacket. *The third guy. Someone must have seen him. A deal was going down. Ain't no doubt. And I will find him.* He turned and looked east towards the CIA office. *Maybe ten blocks away. Fuck 'em, they can wait.*

Tucking his chin to his chest, he spun around and headed west.

Agent Ferguson stood before the desk, watching a bright carmine flush spreading across the Director's face as he listened to the call. He watched the Director's eye squeeze tight shut, the voluminous crow's feet around his eyes turning from red to white, and the folds of fat enveloping his chin as he buried his head on his chest.

Behind them the office door was open and CIA operatives barked orders down the phone as they monitored the motorcade heading towards the airport. Ferguson glanced back and a few faces looked his way. They'd warned him about European Director Spinks, or 'Cartman' as he was known, but not to his face. Ferguson checked a thin piece of paper in his hand for the third time. The Secretary of State was arriving from Washington in the next thirty minutes and had asked for an immediate report on the shootings. The US Ambassador to Italy was waiting on line two. The shitstorm had started.

Spinks slammed down the phone and shot to his feet, his gut brushing the coffee cup on the desk, spilling some of its contents. He pointed a chubby finger at Ferguson. "Who the fuck is Montrose?"

The phone rang and Spinks grabbed the receiver. "Yeah? Hi, Mr. Ambassador. Did you phone me up to tell me something I already know? Damage limitation? What do you think I'm doing? Do you think the CIA employ me to add some glamour to the team? No. So why don't you get off the goddam' phone and let me do my job!" Spinks dropped the phone and shuffled from behind his desk, advancing towards Ferguson. He grabbed the piece of paper and held it up to the light. "Who is this prick?"

"Connor Montrose, sir. He's a Langley IT support technician attached to Interpol. I asked for the complete file but it's classified."

"Of course it is, or dicks like you would see it. Send a request with my clearance. What else?"

"All we know is that he was disciplined for accessing a secure database, then seconded to Interpol."

"So what? Where is he?"

"He's been sent for psychological analysis. Standard procedure. He's been told to report here immediately afterwards. Interpol said he's supposed to be on vacation, but . . ."

Spinks grabbed his jacket from the chair. "When Montrose walks in the door, get security to chain him to a goddam' radiator until we get back, so I can kick his ass down the corridor." Spinks struggled into his suit jacket. "No, just send him to the farthest CIA station and take his passport. We can deal with him later. Then get me a car. You're coming too."

Ferguson turned towards the door. "Where are we going?"

"The hotel. I want to see where Mr. IT Geek shot those ragheads."

"The specialist teams are already there, sir. I'm waiting for a message to say they have completed their . . ."

"Shut up. My ass is on the line for this and if we don't sort this out right now, they'll be looking for someone to hang out to dry." He screwed up the paper and threw it at Ferguson. "And that's you."

CHAPTER 5

The blaring of horns as he rounded the corner told him he had arrived. TV news vans, adorned with satellite dishes, lined the street on both sides, squeezing the traffic to a standstill. Italian cops seemed to be walking about, waving their hands in every direction, shouting at reporters and then at each other. *Helluva big show for two drug dealers. Whatever, it's the perfect distraction. But too many cameras.*

Montrose brought up the Google Maps satellite picture on his iPhone. There was a concreted area behind the hotel. *Service entrance.* He ducked down a side street then turned into an alley at the rear of the hotel.

A cop stepped out in front of him, resplendent in mirrored sunglasses, designer stubble and shiny leather jacket, waving his hand dismissively back down the alley.

Montrose stuffed his CIA ID deep into his pocket and flipped out a badge.

The cop squinted at the photo. "Interpol?"

"Yeah. Call it in if you've got a problem."

The cop stuck out his chin.

"You've seen an Interpol badge before, right?"

"*Si,*" shrugged the cop. "We have to be careful. The press, they get everywhere."

"They sure do. Is this the only other entrance?"

"That's all. One front, one back, and a fire escape."

"Thanks. You've saved me some time." Montrose walked down a line of expensive German automobiles and low-slung Maseratis with blacked-out windows. The dumpsters were hidden behind a wooden fence and the concrete area was free from litter. *It's cleaner than most European streets*. He could see why the Pakistanis had chosen this place. *Rear entrance and exit for those who don't want to be seen. Maybe it was a specialty of the hotel. It would explain the lack of CCTV*. He looked up at the door and saw a security camera blinking. *Maybe not*. To the right were the steel doors of the fire exit. He checked the concrete step and spotted a faint score where the steel door had scraped the surface. There was no powdered stone beside the scratch. *If the door had been opened recently it would have left a trail. Only one other way out.*

The thick wooden door to the hotel was adorned with gleaming brasswork. A small square framed window sat to the side. Montrose peeked in, but saw only his reflection. *Mirrored glass. Very discreet*. He hammered on the door and held up his pass to the window.

The door opened with a click. Montrose stepped inside to a small corridor, lined with polished wood panels. *Not your average service entrance*. To his right he saw the fire exit. It was chained shut. *Security over safety. Way to go.*

To his left there was an office door with a frosted glass partition. Through the glass he could see the outline of a figure. He had just brought up his hand to knock when he heard a voice at the end of the corridor.

"Nobody gets in! I want this place locked down!"

Montrose spun around. *The Langley circus was in town. Shit, it's the last thing I need.* He saw elevator doors halfway down the corridor. *Service elevator.* He ran forward and jabbed the button. The doors opened to reveal a clutter of buckets and tools. He kicked them aside and pushed the button for the Executive floor. The doors clanked shut behind him and the elevator lurched upwards.

I'm about to step into a crime scene. The place will be crawling with specialists. He flipped his badge open. *Might buy me a few minutes.* The elevator shuddered to a halt and the doors opened.

A cleaning maid holding a bucket and mop stood facing him.

He checked the floor indicator. *Executive Floor.* He looked over the head of the bemused maid. *No crime scene tape?*

"Scusi." He held up his badge and squeezed past, but the maid ignored it and stepped into the elevator. He looked down the corridor. To his right was the fire exit and steps down to the rear entrance. *That's the way he came.*

The corridor carpet felt wet and stank of chemicals. He turned at the end and stared blankly. *What the fuck?*

The place was spotless.

He ran his fingers across the wallpaper. It was damp to the touch. He could smell the paste.

"Get the hell out of here!"

Montrose turned. *Harry Ferguson. CIA Europe's number one asshole.* "Well, Mr. Ferguson. Langley's favorite janitor. You must have licked this place clean. What the hell is going on?"

"This is our party now, Montrose. You know the rules."

"Yeah, the rules that say you can take over a crime scene and clean it like your mother-in-law is about to arrive? Those rules?"

Ferguson strode straight towards him and thrust a finger into Montrose's chest. "This town is packed with US Government HVPs. You go around wasting people and think we don't care?"

Montrose brushed Ferguson's arm aside then stepped forward until their faces were almost touching. "You do that again and I'll rip your fucking arm off and shove it up your ass."

"Back off, Montrose. You're way out of your league. You're just a neckbeard IT geek. Basic training don't make you a hotshot hero. And you've got a reputation for sticking your nose where it's not wanted."

Montrose looked down at the carpet. *The blood must have soaked through, but they'd probably taken up the floor. They'd done it before.* "Yeah, and you're a janitor, that's all. Don't matter what your badge says, Agent Ferguson. Hey, what's that on your nose?"

Ferguson began to lift his hand.

"Don't bother. It's shit. You must have been talking to your boss."

Ferguson pushed his jacket aside to reveal a revolver. "You're coming with me. And don't think you've got any backup. The Italian cops have your gun, and I got the word about you. You're a crazy. They'll send you to the nutty farm. You'll be eating your steak with a fucking spoon."

A door opened at the end of the corridor and a voice came from the room.

"Ferguson! Get in here!"

Montrose froze. *The whining Brooklyn accent. Joe Spinks. Head of CIA in Europe. That guy would lock me up without a second thought.* "Your boss is looking for you, asshole."

"I swear you're going to Langley chained to the floor of a Lear Jet."

"Yeah, you'd love that, wouldn't you? Strapping down guys, is that your thing?"

"Ferguson!"

Time to go. "Fuck you, and the big fat fucking horse you rode in on." Montrose headed for the fire exit. *If Spinks hears I'm on the premises, he's gonna go ballistic.*

"Montrose! You stay right there!"

He turned the corner and kicked open the fire exit. *Ferguson would be coming back with his friends. He didn't have the balls to do it on his own. Reckon I've got five minutes.* He ran down the stairs and into the small corridor. Behind the frosted glass he could make out a face.

The wooden paneling rattled on its dry hinges as Montrose rapped on the door. The glass slid aside and the porter looked up. His face seemed to have been freeze-dried. They dug three thousand year-old bodies out of glaciers that looked healthier. "You speak English?" said Montrose.

The porter thought about it, his pale watery eyes distracted for a second. "*No.*"

Montrose pulled a fifty euro bill from his wallet. "Or maybe you understand English?"

The rheumy eyes fixed on the money. He shrugged again. The bones under his thin shirt seemed to pierce his skin. "*Si.*"

"The CCTV from last night. Where is it?"

The old guy nodded toward a flickering black and white screen at the corner of his desk.

"That's it? How many cameras?"

He thought for a moment then shrugged again, this time pursing his lips.

The effort must be killing him.

"*Una.*"

Montrose checked the screen. The camera didn't cover the door. *No surprise. Minimum security for maximum discreetness.* "Wind it back to eight o'clock last night."

The porter looked down at the trackball and keyboard as if they'd just landed on his desk out of thin air.

"Look, Pops, there's a guy coming in the next few minutes who's going to take that system away. For that, you'll get nothing. But from me, you'll get another one of these." Montrose slid out another fifty.

A quivering hand wavered over the keys before it plunged down and rolled the trackball back.

Montrose watched the clock on the screen wind backwards. "Stop." The timer read 19:58. "Play."

The porter jabbed the keyboard with a talon-like finger and the picture jerked into action.

Montrose heard voices behind him. Just then, a long black shape slipped across the screen. *A taxi.*

"Stop!"

The picture shuddered to a halt. A figure slipped from

the rear door of the taxi and headed towards the hotel. *Blondie. It had to be him.*

"Go forward one minute."

For a moment the picture sped past in a blur. The taxi was still there. Then a figure darted across the screen and dived into the rear seat of the taxi. The taxi sped off.

Montrose glanced back down the corridor. *Ferguson will be on me in seconds.*

"Listen, Pops, you see everything that happens here. Who comes and who goes."

The porter said nothing.

"The taxi had a license plate on the trunk. If someone needs a taxi, you know who to call, yeah?"

The porter expanded his reactions to a wet sniff and a long blink of his rheumy eyes.

"So, I bet you one hundred euros you could phone up the firm, find out the name of that customer and where he was headed. Safe bet, yeah?" Montrose pressed a hundred euro bill against the glass.

The eyes grew sharper.

"This bet won't last forever. Remember the guys right behind me are gonna want this for free. This way you get to win a bet. It's down to you." Montrose dropped the bill on the desk.

Pinning it down with his finger, the old guy pulled it towards him then picked up a phone. A short conversation took place in wheezing, guttural Italian. He scrawled down a few words in thin, spider-like writing, then held it up. "No name."

Montrose grabbed the paper. "72 Via Nableone." He heard the voices behind him become louder. "Thanks, Pops."

The old guy pocketed the money. "For what? This did not happen." He slid the glass shut.

CHAPTER 6

The gleaming white stone façade stretched down both sides of the avenue. Montrose shaded his eyes against the glare as he approached the polished black door of a town house. There was no name plate. *Maybe Blondie likes his privacy. Or he's left town. That's what I'd do.*

He crossed to the other side of the street, and stood before a shop window. In its reflection he gazed up at the shutters of the house behind him. The Google satellite map showed a steep metal roof. *No air con vents. No back alley. One way in, one way out.* He heard one of the shutters open and watched as an old woman in a floral apron shook a small carpet out of the window. *I'm guessing she's not the lady of the house, but she'll do.*

He pulled an old Blackberry from his pocket. *A hundred bucks for this piece of crap. Ten hours on the pay card. That would be more than enough.* He crossed the street, glancing up at the apartment. *It don't matter if I'm seen. They'll get to know me pretty soon.*

Hurrying across the street, he stood before the door. *No warrant. No lawyer. Everything that happens now would be deniable.* He rapped on the door then pulled the Blackberry from his pocket and fired up the Snooper app. *Not quite.*

After a few moments the old lady's head appeared around the door, nervously holding a brush close to her stained apron.

Montrose flipped open his ID and flashed it in front of her face. "Police."

She opened her mouth to reply, but Montrose shoved open the door. "What was that? I can come in and have a look around? Thanks very much. Well, I think that's what you said. My Italian ain't that good."

Facing him was a long, spacious corridor. Sunlight streamed down from a cupola high in the roof and splashed across a marble floor, inlaid with a Roman mosaic. The walls were lined with ancient statues. *Is this shit real? They should be in a museum.* At the end of the corridor, an ornately carved double door lay ajar. He stepped forward, his rubber-soled shoes squeaking on the marble.

The room was shaded and cool. Beside an empty, blackened fireplace, carved with Bacchanalian figures, sat a stooping, grey-haired man whose sallow skin heightened his aquiline features. He sat perfectly still, save a gnarled hand dotted with liver spots which trembled where it rested on a silver-topped cane. He was dressed in a sober, dark suit that had fitted when he was in his sixties, but now hung loose on his frame. He fixed his grey eyes on Montrose for a moment. "And you are?"

"Montrose." He flipped out his badge. "Interpol."

The old man let out a small wheezing laugh. "Interpol? God save us from civil servants."

Yeah. I'll save the CIA surprise for later. Our house calls are a little more dramatic. Montrose gazed around the room, trying to fix the old man's accent. *Not Italian. Middle European. Swiss or German.* The walls were lined with heavy wooden bookcases. Framed photos adorned a dark oak bureau. But there was none of a young man and the others seem to have been hastily rearranged. *You were expecting a visit. Nice try, old fella.* "So, what's your name?"

"That is not your concern. State your business."

Go for it. See how he reacts. "Your son." He saw a tremor in the old man's hand though the face gave nothing away. *Cool customer. Any other father might have shown some concern. Not this guy. What was going down wasn't news to him.* "Your son was seen in the immediate vicinity of a fatal drugs bust last night."

The old man scoffed. "Immediate vicinity? Drugs bust? You sound like a cheap cop show. I heard of the incident at the hotel. That area is full of marvelous restaurants. There are many reasons why my son would be there."

Bad move. Now I know he was there. "A drug dealer is dead. Another is clinging to life."

"I take it you are enquiring as to whether my son has anything to do with this?"

"You got it, Sherlock."

"My son is a successful businessman and would never be involved in something so sordid. I assume you're scrabbling around for information. Otherwise the police would be here and not some Interpol office boy, desperately looking for clues."

"Yeah, whatever. Where is he?"

"I couldn't say. He leads his own life."

"I'll find him." Montrose slipped off his jacket and holding it across his arm, palmed the Blackberry behind the frame of a photograph. "So what's your business then? Fancy art, ancient Roman statues?" He nodded towards the old man's dark blue overcoat as it hung on the arm of the chair, exposing the red silk lining, "And fancy clothes, too. Where does all this come from?" He pulled a wooden chair from the side of the room, dragging the feet across the floor, and sat in front of the fireplace.

The old man smirked. "Life has been good to me."

"Yeah, I'll bet. Running heroin can be very lucrative. And the accent? You've got the nose, but you're as Roman as sauerkraut."

"I am a Swiss citizen. And that is the end of this conversation."

He heard the creak of a hinge. Two men stood in the doorway. One moved towards the fireplace while the other covered the door. *Good move. One to protect the old man and one for the exit.* They wore loosely cut Armani suits. It was impossible to see if they were armed.

"Well, Mr. Grey Suit and Mr. Black Suit have arrived. Fashion show over, is it?" *These ain't thugs. They're relaxed. Professional.* "Don't tell me, time for me to leave with my head held high and my feet held higher?"

The old man pointed the tip of his cane at the door. "Correct. You will leave now, Mr. Montrose."

"Yeah, sure. But like Inspector Colombo used to say, one last thing. What's an ordinary businessman like you got to do with these goons?"

Grey Suit walked directly towards Montrose, placed his hands on each arm of his chair and leaned in until their faces almost touched.

Montrose caught the smell of expensive cologne then edged his face even closer. "You fancy me, big boy?"

The voice was low and calm. "You'll leave now, or I'll snap your neck like a fucking twig."

A Brit? Probably ex-special forces. And they don't come cheap. "I bet you say that to all the boys. But first, you'll have to stop the man-love and get out of my way."

Grey Suit smiled and stood back.

Montrose picked up his jacket. "I've enjoyed our time together." He nodded towards Grey Suit. "Just one tip, sweetheart. Your mouthwash ain't cutting it."

He pushed the doors further aside and strolled into the corridor. At the end he could see his reflection in the polished front door, and the outline of the goons behind him. He scanned the artwork lining the corridor. *Give me something I can use.* To the left of an armless statue of Juno stood a small brass horse. *That would do some damage. If they get too close.* He pulled open the door and glanced around.

"Hey, dickhead," said Grey Suit, "you forgot something." He threw the Blackberry down the corridor.

Montrose ducked. The Blackberry skimmed past his scalp and bounced on the sidewalk.

Ferguson stood framed in the doorway.

Spinks shot him a look from behind his desk. "Have you found him?"

"No, sir . . ."

'Then what the fuck do you want?"

Ferguson advanced slowly, holding a buff folder in front of him. "I have Montrose's file, sir. There's a lot missing."

"Missing?"

"It's highly classified. Way above my security level, sir." Ferguson placed the thin folder on the desk.

"Paper?" Spinks picked up the folder and emptied the contents onto the desk. "Two sheets? Is that all there is?"

"The whole file was marked 'Not To Be Transmitted'. That's all I could get from Personnel in Langley. They really didn't want to give it to me. All it's saying is that he was caught looking at flight databases."

"Did they say why?"

"His sister. Seems she had some boyfriend with a private jet, who took her on trips south of the border. Then she disappeared."

"So? Happens all the time. She's probably shacked up in some hacienda with a rich Cheech, living the high life."

"Sir, Montrose was searching all the private jet flights to South America."

Spinks looked up. "South America? All of them?"

"It seems certain classified information was, uh, not as secure as it should have been. Montrose is a tech, he knew how to get around the firewall."

"You're saying his sister goes missing and Montrose was using a secure CIA database to find her? Is he crazy? The FBI take care of missing persons."

"No, sir. She wasn't missing. They found her body in Mexico, near the docks at Ensenada, sixty miles from the border. She'd been trying to hitch back home. No passport, no papers, no purse. Just an old cigarette lighter. Her UCLA tattoo and blond hair meant the Mexicans called the border cops."

"Yeah? Too bad."

"That's why Montrose was snooping around for flights. The report says he was trying to track the boyfriend who took her there."

"That's a long shot. Maybe got nothing to do with him."

"She's not the first, sir. It seems the guy has a rep. The report says it's probable she was forced into drug dependency and prostitution. Talks about porn movies in Mexico. Not, uh, the big budget kind. Looks like she was trying to get back to the US when she died."

Spinks shrugged and held out his arms. "You know what? It's a goddam' shame. She shouldn't have been so stupid. But with what I've got in front of me right now, I couldn't give a fuck." He jabbed a fat finger down on the paper. "I want to find out what's missing here and why Langley put up the shutters. We have to evaluate the risk. Get me a call to the Director. With full encryption. Let's see what this asshole Montrose really knows."

CHAPTER 7

Threading his way past the customers of the coffee shop, Montrose took a seat under an awning. He turned a metal chair to face the house. The door opened.

A stretch Mercedes pulled up at the curb and the old man edged down the steps. The goons watched from the doorway of the house, waiting until the old man was in the car, then closed the door.

On his own? Where the hell is he going? He thumbed the iPhone. *It don't matter. This is gonna take time. And manpower. I'd better call out the troops. They can shake that place down and find out who the hell that guy was in the hotel. The old man knows. But he ain't telling. His son? Or the British goon. No, got to be the son. Unless he keeps photos of his security guards alongside his wife. That's just weird. Whoever Blondie is, he's about to become very popular. And the Boss can stop giving me shit about a mystery man. Blondie will have to turn up some time. And I'll be right here when he does.*

"Boss? It's Montrose."

"Where the hell are you?"

"Via Nableone. I got an address. Where the mystery man took a taxi after the shooting." He thought he heard a sharp intake of breath at the other end. *Yeah, I'm good.*

"Montrose, I told you to . . . I want you to listen to me very carefully."

"Hey, I know where Blondie lives, don't I get a hug?"

"You have no idea . . . Listen to me, or I will instruct the Italian police to take you off the streets. Do you understand?"

What the hell was up with him? "Yeah. I'm all ears."

"I want you to report to the CIA office in Rome. Go straight to Director Spinks. He's waiting for you. Talk to no one else. Go now."

No way. "Boss, this is our gig. We've busted a . . ."

"Have you any idea what's at stake here? Let me paint you a picture of where your drugs deal fits in. Rome is playing host to a major trade conference. The Secretary of State is on the way from Washington and the press is running a story on how an American agent is shooting people in hotels."

"Aw, that's just a crock of . . ."

"You think so? The foreign press are going to have a field day. Let me make this clear. You will talk to no one else. Not any mystery man, local cops or hotel porters. If you want to keep your job and stay out of an Italian jail, you keep your mouth shut and get your ass over to the CIA office. Right now!"

Montrose squeezed the phone so hard he heard the plastic squeak. *Fuck you.* He cut the call and closed his eyes, taking slow, deep breaths, resisting the temptation to throw the phone across the street. *Trade conference? And the Secretary of State? Jeez, follow the money, that's what they say. And it goes all the way back to the good old US of A. God knows what we're selling, but businessmen will get their bonus and new BMWs, and Mr. White Collar can afford the latest Chevy. And if I have to take a step back while a shitload of poison hits the streets of Europe, it's SEP. Someone else's problem.* He closed his eyes and rubbed the muscles in his neck. *So, the Boss had heard about the visit to the hotel. Bet that cheered him up. Now Spinks wants me off the streets and as far away as possible. Shit, if they want me, they can come and find me.*

He looked up and saw the old man sitting motionless in the back of the limo. *What's he waiting for?* He brought up the camera on the iPhone. *One for the record. Before Spinks shuts me down.*

An airport taxi pulled up beside him, blocking his view. The rear door swung open and a pair of stockinged legs with killer heels clicked onto the sidewalk, and an expensively dressed woman in a clinging business suit emerged.

She stood facing him and smoothed down her short skirt. "Mr. Montrose. What are you doing with that phone? I do hope that photo isn't going to appear on the internet."

He looked down at the phone pointing towards her crotch. "Jeez, does everybody in this town know me?" *Probably one of Spinks' little ladies. He had a fondness for empty heads and full blouses. Pretty fast work, though. And I'll bet she's got a van full of CIA goons at each end of the street with handcuffs and leg restraints. What, they think I'm less likely to punch a chick?*

"So, who might you be? And what the hell do you want?"

She sauntered over and sat down at his table. "I want you to buy me a coffee."

The taxi remained idling at the curb, blocking his view. *Spinks' goons will be closing in while they think I'm staring at her tits. But I want that old bastard's face. If the Boss won't tell me, the system will.*

"Out of my way." The metal legs of the table squealed on the stone as he stood.

She grabbed his arm and gently pulled him back, pushing her thumb into his clenched fist. "Relax, Connor. The gentleman in the limo isn't going anywhere. For the moment."

"Yeah? Thanks for letting me know." *She's smooth, got to give her that. And she has a hand in her pocket. 9mm or stun gun?* "So, how about that coffee. Latte?"

"Espresso. Nobody in Italy drinks latte after breakfast. Except tourists. Your first time in Rome, Connor?"

"You got me bang to rights. How's my friend, Mr. Spinks?"

She smiled and shook a perfectly manicured finger at him, then began tapping on her cell phone. "I don't work for Spinks. And before you ask, I'm not at liberty to tell you who I work for, but there are things you need to know. Firstly, I'm Gabrielle." She looked up and ran the tip of her tongue along the edge of her bright red lips. "You can call me Gabby."

The bitter coffee coated his tongue and stuck to his palate. Montrose signaled to the waiter for a glass of water.

"You've really pissed off some serious people." Gabrielle smiled and checked her phone. "Time to give you the bigger picture." She crossed her legs, allowing Montrose a glimpse of her stocking tops before she straightened her skirt.

"You mean the trade deal? I'm guessing the Pakistanis are involved, otherwise why would everyone be so pissed about a couple of dealers? They've got connections, right?" *Just spit it out, sweetheart. The striptease ain't doing it for me. Not right now, anyway.* "I heard all about it. I stop shooting drug dealers and some Joe in Idaho can make his mortgage payments. That's not my style." He took a sip from the cup. "So, what are we selling? Drones armed with missiles that can take out a farmer from five thousand feet who doesn't worship the same god?"

She tilted her head to one side, and was about to speak when her phone beeped. "I think it's buying, rather than selling, and it's not . . ."

"Yeah? What have the Pakistanis got that we want, other than a million acres of opium poppies?"

She looked up quizzically, but her phone beeped again. She checked the screen. "If I was a fortune teller, I'd say you were about to get an invitation from someone who will whisk you away."

"That'll be Spinks. Bet he's already booked my flight on Langley Airways. I'll be lucky if I get a seat."

"I take it Mr. Spinks is not your best friend?"

"I haven't got enough middle fingers to tell you what I think of Spinks."

She tossed her hair back and laughed, and stroked her neck as she spoke. "Well, your visitor will not be tall, dark or handsome. Rather, he'll be ancient, wizened and Teutonic, if I'm not mistaken." She straightened one of her legs then wiggled the toe of her high heel, pointing towards the stretch Mercedes. "Someone wants a word."

Montrose caught the bright red sole of her shoe. *She's wearing Louboutins. This chick ain't on government pay. So who's pulling her strings?* He looked up at the Mercedes.

The tinted rear window lowered and the old man fixed his gaze on Montrose then beckoned him over to the limo.

"You'd better go." Gabrielle dropped the phone into her purse. She placed a ten euro bill on to the table. "I'll get this, you can make it up to me by buying dinner."

"What the hell does he want?" Montrose got to his feet.

"I suggest you go and find out." She stood close and smoothed down his coat, picking a few threads from his collar. "Got to look your best. And be a good boy. You can save the bad boy for me." She patted his butt. "Off you go."

His eyes locked with hers. *Save the bad . . . yeah, later.* He glanced up and down the road as he crossed over towards the limo. No one stepped out of a doorway. No vehicles moved into position. Montrose stood before the open door of the limo and looked in. *No goons?*

The old man sat low in the seat, his frail figure enveloped in the deep leather, his hands atop the cane between his knees. "Mr. Montrose, I believe I owe you an explanation."

A thick glass window separated them from the driver. Montrose stepped inside, and the door closed. The silence struck him. "So, you've been checking up on me."

The old man lifted his cane and rapped on the privacy

window. The limo pulled off smoothly into the street. "Let me say, I admire you, Mr. Montrose."

"Really?" Montrose settled back and stretched his legs. "Well, I don't think that's gonna last. Not when I tell you what I've got planned." The door locks clunked. *Relax, it's automatic.* "The blond guy in the hotel. He escaped and took a taxi to your address. Your son. You can't protect him."

"My . . . The gentleman in the hotel?" He waved his hand dismissively. "He is nothing in this. But first, I want to apologize for my earlier reticence. You must understand, there are issues of national importance involved here. For your nation, I should say, not mine."

You'd be shit at poker. Now I know he's your son. The missing photo gave it away.

"National importance? I don't think we've included drug dealing in our balance of exports. That's private enterprise. Or an illegal, vicious and murderous trade that preys on millions of people." Montrose thrust a finger towards the old man. "That's your son. Not my country."

"Please, let me be clear. My son only plays a bit part in this drama. Yes, he was in the hotel, and he was meeting the men you shot. But this is not about drugs. I'm afraid that this is, rather sordidly, all about money."

"Tell me something I don't know. Like, what's his name? And where is he?"

"I suggest you put that thought from your mind, Mr. Montrose. Let us deal with the more important issue at hand. I have been authorized to impart certain information, to give you an understanding of what happened last night." The old man slowly cleared his throat, closing his eyes with the effort, then composed himself. "You are aware that the heads of government in Europe, and your Secretary of State, are involved in a major trade deal. One of the men you killed was a senior representative at the trade conference."

"You're shitting me." *This has got to be the mother of all excuses.* "Go on, I can't wait to hear this."

"I understand you followed these men from Naples to Rome, after a surveillance operation was cancelled."

Was that why they cancelled the Naples gig? Trade delegates? "Who told you all this?"

"I am party to quite sensitive information, Mr. Montrose. But let's be clear. The cancellation of your surveillance in Naples had nothing to do with drugs. The man you injured is an importer of entirely legal goods. The surveillance was cancelled to stop anyone witnessing the Government of the United States paying a bribe to a trade delegate. It's as simple as that. My son was at the hotel in Rome to facilitate the transfer of funds. Once we have them under control then these people will be sidelined. But for now . . ." He shook his head. "They still hold the whip hand."

Some dead Pakistanis wouldn't stop them. They'd just bribe the next one in line. Waiting with their hands out for some fat greenbacks.

The old man brought out a linen handkerchief and dabbed away tiny bubbles of spittle at the corner of his pale lips. "There is a window of opportunity to have the US achieve unparalleled control in Afghanistan. One they could not hope to achieve through military means."

Afghanistan? What the fuck?

"The potential for wealth is huge. I must declare an interest, of course, as I am a major investor, which is why I am involved. We can bring peace to the Afghans through capitalism, rather than the end of a rifle. I often think it's your country's greatest export. You can bring their country into the twenty-first century. And they will have no need for opium when the oil is flowing. Think of it as a fifty-first state. The US will build industrial bases there and fight the drug war at its source, with American hardware. Empire building, possibly, but the benefits in trade and winning the drug war will be immense for the US."

Holy shit. The suits in DC must be licking their lips. The Europeans have been trying to control Afghanistan for the last century. And got their asses kicked every time.

"The oil and mineral reserves in Afghanistan make Alaska look like loose change. There is a multi-billion dollar oil deal underway between your country and Afghanistan. And my son was the conduit for a bribe. Kickback, I believe is the colloquial term."

Montrose let his head rest back against the leather. *Jesus, all the soldiers. And all the civilians. Was that what the war on terror was all about? Destroy the Taliban and then let the oil companies roll in? Hell, why not? We did it in Iraq with Saddam.* "And you're saying your son was organizing a kickback?"

"The Afghans are, to be polite, slightly backward in their business practices. My personal opinion is that the country is run by thugs. Their Government is controlled and funded by drugs. But that is about to change."

"Really? With one sack of cash? I don't think so. That would be business as usual."

"In a way, yes. Washington has been forced to play their game. Bribes are unavoidable. It's how the

Afghans do business. Of course, it would be better for a foreign national to pass on the bribe, in case Washington was compromised. I understand the foreign corrupt practices in your country are especially harsh. In this case, since I have friends in your government, they asked us to provide a service. It's what we do, Mr. Montrose. We are the middlemen. We keep the wheels of industry rolling for your government when they cannot be seen doing it themselves. We are your allies."

And Spinks is the circus master. No wonder the hotel was cleaned down. The press would have had a field day if they found out about a bribe.

The old man cleared his throat. "Afghanistan and the US are on the brink of a historic agreement. Do you see the potential here? You see the scope of what's involved? Control of one of the world's biggest oil fields. One that the Chinese are desperate to get their hands on. This is about the future wealth of the United States. There is an economic war raging, Mr. Montrose, and you're losing it. Your country is twelve trillion dollars in debt. Ten percent of that is owed to the Chinese. And China is in ascendancy. They are buying up even more US Government debt. If their growth is not checked you'll soon be dancing to their tune. The picture does not get much bigger than this. If they are not stopped then you will be taking your fiscal policy from Beijing. That is the future of your country."

"The Chinese? You've got to be kidding me."

"I am deadly serious. China has a lust for oil. Their whole economic plan is dictated by it. They scour the world for deals. Angola, Nigeria, the Gulf. The US are promising the Afghans the technology to deliver huge wealth in their country, something that the Chinese cannot match. But for the moment the Afghanis are wondering whether it's such a good idea after all. One of their trade delegates, and a close relative of several Afghan Government ministers, is mown down in a hotel by an American agent."

Guess that's my pay rise fucked. "Yeah. Shit happens. Let's get back to your son. What's his name again?"

"As I said, my son was merely a simple courier. I admire your tenacity, Mr. Montrose. It is a quality of your countrymen that will see you win the economic war with the Chinese. But you have the wrong target. It is not my son. You may find these bribes immoral, but we are dealing with a corrupt regime. You have to do what it takes. It was described to me as 'pay to play'. Now, please, leave us to get on with it. We hold the future of the US economy in our hands."

I need a little bit more than this, my friend. I have a nagging feeling you're blowing smoke up my ass. Montrose slipped the old Blackberry from his pocket.

"Hey, I think we can survive without any Afghan oil. We've got enough of our own." He fired up the Snooper app and let his hand drop towards the door pocket.

"Certainly, you could survive without the oil. But you cannot hope to survive if the Chinese have it. You would be handing them the rope to slowly strangle your economy. I give it twenty years, Mr. Montrose, and then you will no longer be in control of the dollar."

I've always hated economics. This could be a ton of horseshit and I'd never know. One way to find out. "I want to see him. Your son. I want to hear what he's got to say."

"I can ask, Mr. Montrose, but you must understand, my son is rather nervous after your last encounter. He believes you would have arrested him."

Arrested? I was going to shoot him in the face. Turns out he was Spinks' bitch.

"I'm aware of exactly who you are, Mr. Montrose. If you were a simple policeman, I'd have you dealt with out of hand. But, as you are someone whose organization is an integral part of this deal, I'm sure we can have confidence in your discretion."

You mean you're telling me stuff that I could find out for myself, or spinning me a line and passing it off as a big secret? Montrose grinned. "You sure about that?" *What can they do? Kick my ass out of the CIA?*

The old man nodded slowly. "May I say the alternatives do not bear thinking about. You would be exposing yourself to grave danger."

Montrose sat forward in the seat. "Is that a threat?" The car rumbled over cobblestones and turned into a main boulevard.

"There are many ways to skin a cat, Mr. Montrose. My advice to you, if you will accept it, is to do exactly what Mr. Spinks says. To the letter."

Out the window, he glimpsed the Tiber, shards of sunlight dancing on the dark water.

"May I rely on you, Mr. Montrose? Can I tell the powers-that-be you are on our side?"

They must be crapping themselves. "Yeah."

"I understand your cooperation will be very valuable to your career. Men who appreciate the importance of these operations are trusted with more challenging roles."

Are you gonna give me a reference? You fu . . .

"Where would you like the driver to take you?"

I need to think. Montrose slumped in the seat. *The old guy's son was luckier than he could ever imagine. Christ, I nearly killed him.* "Wherever. Here's fine."

The old man rapped on the driver's privacy window with his cane. "We appreciate your cooperation, Mr. Montrose. I understand the difficulties the shooting has caused you. I wish I could help in some way, but there is nothing I can do. There will be no record of the incident at the hotel."

Plus ça change. But there's a big fat record on my personal file from a trick cyclist. "Oh, you can still help. Your son. I want to see him and I want him to meet someone."

"Mr. Montrose, outside of the negotiations team, only you are party to this information. We cannot . . ."

"It's a psychiatrist." *The guy who thinks I'm making all this shit up. And the guy who could ruin my career.* "He's CIA affiliated. He knows what happened in the hotel."

"Mr. Montrose, the intentions of your country would be best served by you returning to the US. Perhaps when all this has blown over . . ."

No chance. If I step away now, I'll never get near them again. Spinks will make sure of that. "You could say this is kinda important to me, yeah? Quid pro quo. That's all it would take. Then I'm outta your life forever."

The old man nodded as the car slowed to a halt. "I think it will be very unlikely, but I will see what I can do."

*

Deputy Director Spinks sat wedged behind his desk, one hand wiping his face with a stained handkerchief and the other feeding peanuts into his wet fleshy lips. He hit the refresh button on his email, but there was nothing. The office chair strained under his bulk as he leaned back to find a stream of air from the air-conditioning vent above.

There was no news from Langley. He closed his eyes for a moment and let the cool air drift over his face. If it took this long, the authorization request was going higher than God. Why the hell had Montrose been bundled over to Europe? What did he find?

The door swung open. Spinks stood up and pointed a fat finger towards Ferguson. "Tell me you've got him."

Ferguson closed to the door and hurried over to the desk. "He was talking to a woman, sir."

Spinks advanced from behind the desk. "Have you got him?"

The words tumbled out of Ferguson's mouth. "A car pulled up at the house, sir. Montrose got in and we lost him."

Spinks stood open-mouthed. "You lost him?"

"Yes, he talked to a woman on the street, outside a cafe, then took off in the back of a car."

"A woman? Real good-looking chick? Reddish hair, short skirt?"

"Uh, yes, sir. We have her under surveillance and we're looking . . ."

"Jeez, no! Leave her alone. She'll rip you apart like a rag doll and the rest of the pussies in your team."

"You know who she is, sir? If she's a threat to Montrose, we can . . ."

"A threat to Montrose? Ferguson, you are thicker than

shit sticking to a bear's ass. If he's gonna start wasting people in hotels then he's gonna make some enemies and these guys . . ." He tilted his head back around and held out his palms, his features relaxing. "Hell, I don't need to do this. Why didn't I think of this before? You say he left in a car?"

"Yes, sir, a stretch Mercedes, then the team lost him."

"Who cares? That asshole Montrose has just dug his own grave." He punched a fist into the air. "You know, there might be a day when I get concerned about a nosey, do-gooder IT neckbeard disappearing off the face of the earth. But let me tell you, today ain't that day."

"But sir, we should . . ."

"Shut up." Spinks picked up the thin folder from the desk. "Shred this. Cancel the call to the Director, then get me the Ambassador. And forget Montrose. He no longer exists."

CHAPTER 8

Where the hell am I?

He strode towards the fast traffic at the end of the street, his chin tucked onto his chest, and stepped onto a broad boulevard bordering the Tiber. In the distance rose the dome of the ancient papal fortress of the Castel Sant' Angelo. Behind would be Saint Peter's, and the Vatican. He brought up the map on his iPhone. *Via Giuseppe Zanardelli.*

The CIA office was about twenty minutes west, across the river. *Time to check in. The boss would be ecstatic. They've got me lined up for a trip stateside and the Langley Funny Farm to get me out of the way. No wonder they didn't want anyone to know why Blondie was at the hotel. And without that, the damn psychiatrist thinks I'm just a crazy shooter. Langley were going to let me hang. Unless the old guy tells the psychiatrist that his son Blondie was the third man. That's all it would take. That's all he had to know. This is gonna be fun. Damn, I could call him. Tell him I've got a meeting with a ghost. Nah, that pleasure can wait. I want to see the look on his shiny face.*

He turned west and joined the tourists heading for the bridge. His grin widened. *Blondie was a go-between? Spinks figured he could use some patsy rather than a CIA spook. He didn't figure it turning out like the Alamo. Blondie must have damn near crapped himself when it kicked off in the hotel. I'll bet his old dad is calling him now, trying to coax him out of his bedroom. Telling him no bad men are coming to take him away.*

He dialed the number of the old Blackberry, hoping it wouldn't make too much noise rattling around in the door pocket of the limo. *Time to be a fly on the wall. Maybe he's giving the good news to Spinks.* He heard the road noise of the limo, then a voice.

"I think we can draw this to a conclusion, Herr Kessler."

The old man. So who's Kessler?

"The Americans are always stupidly sentimental. They think life is one Hollywood soap opera, each outdoing themselves to prove their patriotism. You only have to mention that they can help their country, and they become all misty-eyed. It makes me sick."

He can't be talking to Spinks. Who the hell was he talking to?

"Your security staff have been very helpful, Wolfgang, they passed on your message, and I'm sure we no longer have to be concerned about Montrose. He did want to meet my son, though I'm loath to indulge Montrose's fantasy. Whatever we do, we must ensure Kurt is out of the country before the Cosa Nostra come calling for their money. Once he has the merchandise from your bank, he can bring the funds back to Rome."

A cold shock ran through his spine. *The Cosa Nostra? This has nothing to do with an oil deal, the lying piece of shit. They're just drug-dealing scum.*

The rasping noise of a scooter came towards him. *Dammit, I'm broadcasting.* He frantically searched for the mute button. The line popped and fizzed and then cut. His fingers shook as he searched the contacts list of the iPhone. *Kurt − the son? And Wolfgang Kessler? Maybe the money man.*

"Interpol Crime Desk, who's calling?"

"This is Connor Montrose. You know who I am." *Time to kick over the hornet's nest.*

"Of course, Good morning, Mr. Mont . . ."

"Listen to me. I want a European Arrest Warrant for . . ." *Dammit, I can't send out a warrant for some guy called Kurt.* "For Wolfgang Kessler. He's in Rome, right now. He's owns a bank. Check the name. Charges are major narcotics and money laundering. Get it sent to the top. Call me back."

The old guy wanted me away from the apartment so that his son could head for the border. He felt the anger surge through him. *I need a gun. They better hope Interpol find Kessler the banker before I do.*

Spinks eased the his waistband down and wiped the sweat from his forehead. He checked the map on his screen. Everything was in place. The Afghans were on their way to the conference. The VP was secure and waiting for the arrival of the money men. A beep sounded and an email flashed up on his computer.

Fwd: European Arrest Warrant – Wolfgang Kessler

He launched himself forward, slamming down his fist and scattering the nuts across the desk. He grabbed the phone and punched a button. "Get in here!"

A moment later Ferguson entered the room and stood in front of the desk.

"You know what he's done? Your friend Montrose?" He pointed a finger at the screen. "There's an arrest warrant out for Kessler!"

"Who? Sir, I . . ."

"You had one chance to bring Montrose in and you let him go!"

Ferguson shuffled from one foot to another. "But sir, you said the woman . . . I tried an armed arrest in the hotel and he ignored me. I can't just shoot him!"

"Then beat the shit out of him! This whole affair is rapidly turning into a clusterfuck. I've got an Afghan trade delegate on a life support machine while that prick is running around playing detective! If they link those drug-dealing ragheads to us, we're fucked. Get Interpol on the phone. I want that arrest warrant cancelled. Right now!"

"Yes, sir."

Spinks held his head in his hands as Ferguson scurried from the room. The Afghans were already going crazy. If the press knew that Washington and shady middlemen were trying to buy some Afghan drug dealers there would be a feeding frenzy. The President could fall. It could unravel a plan that had been ten years in the making.

And it wouldn't stop there. There'd be a line of liberal asswipes waiting to buttfuck anyone involved in the operation. But once the deal was signed with the ragheads then Langley would be calling the shots.

He brought up a file on the screen and checked the updates. Montrose took off with someone in a car. But it couldn't have been Kessler. Or what would have been left of Montrose could be mopped up with a sponge. It was Kessler calling the shots. Spinks stopped for a moment and looked at the cell phone in his hand. The sooner this shit was over, the better. He tapped in a message.

Interpol Arrest Warrant has been sent out for Kessler.

Kessler was the 'go to' guy for the oil companies. The master at sanctions-busting and shady deals. He had form for fixing deals for everyone from Serbian warlords to Saddam. He was tied into the network of 'fixers' who had connections that Langley could only dream about. He would know what to do.

Time to force the issue. He picked up the desk phone. "Get me a print out of Montrose's profile. And the psychiatrist's report. On plain paper."

I'm not using email, he thought, that was about as secure as a chocolate fireguard. "And get a message to all agents in Rome. Extraordinary Rendition Order. I want Montrose bound, gagged and face fucking down on the floor of a jet to Langley in one hour."

The cars and taxis flew past as Montrose stood at the edge of the sidewalk on Corso Vittorio Emanuele. *A diversion. And I fell for it. But what about that chick, Gabby? Who's she working for?*

He stuck his hand in the air, but the taxis ignored

him. *What have you got to do to get a taxi in this town? Throw yourself in the road?*

On the far side of the street two Carabinieri leaned against an Alfa Romeo, cigarettes hanging from their mouths and machine pistols dangling from their sides.

Cops. They can take me straight to the Interpol office. I'll let the CIA thank me later. No point in going back to the old man's house, sonny-boy would be long gone.

He scanned the approaching traffic, readying himself for a dash between the cars. *This reeked of Spinks. I'll bet the CIA knew about the heroin all along. That's why they cancelled the gig in Naples. They cut a deal with the Afghans. One of them gets to sell his heavy hand luggage and the rest of the gang take a sack of dollars and sign up to the oil deal. They probably all took a cut. Shit, they probably owned all the poppy fields. It must have been a helluva surprise when I turned up with Dr. Glock and his patented cure for drug dealers.*

Bouncing on his toes, he steadied himself and then darted for a gap in the traffic, accompanied by a blast of horns. He stopped on the other side and grinned at the cops. He began to pull out his Interpol badge when the iPhone rang. *Jeez, not now, Boss, I don't need this.*

"Yeah?"

"Mr. Montrose, I have done as you asked."

His breath caught in his throat. *The old guy?*

The cops ground out their cigarettes and stood up.

Montrose struggled for words. "You . . . You've done what?"

"My son. You wanted to meet him, is that not correct?"

Is he crazy? What the hell is he doing?

"Are you there, Mr. Montrose?"

"Yeah, yeah, I'm all ears."

"I understand, Mr. Montrose, that the sole reason for this meeting is to provide a witness to the psychiatrist who examined you, to prove you were acting in a reasonable manner when faced with a threat."

"Absolutely. That's all I need." *Holy crap, he's going to drop right into my hands.*

"Then we are happy to oblige. My son will also confirm that he was there to meet the Afghans. The bribe will not be referred to in any way. Though I also expect quid pro quo. You will confirm with your superiors that my son is no longer a suspect. Is that clear?"

It's clear you have no idea of the shit that's heading your way. "That works for me. Let's do it."

"Then my son will meet you at the psychiatrist's office in ten minutes."

He's mine. "Yeah, that's great. Listen, what's his full name? I got to make sure they let him in."

"You don't need to know that. You just need him to talk to your psychiatrist. How far away are you, Mr. Montrose?"

He looked down the river as it curved gracefully south towards the Coliseum. "Ten minutes, or less."

"My son will be waiting for you."

"Maybe, but let me make one thing crystal fucking clear. I need only your son. I don't want your Armani monkeys turning up."

"I assure you he will be alone. You have nothing to fear."

"I'm on my way. Looking forward to it." *More than you will ever know.* He stared at the phone then punched a fist in the air. He looked up to see the cops pulling off their sunglasses. *Maybe this wasn't such a good idea. The old guy could be lying about the goons. They'd have lookouts. If they see me turning up in a meat wagon they'd get Blondie away and make sure he wasn't found, arrest warrant or not.*

He spun on his heel and looked south, bringing up the map on the iPhone. *Could make for a short career. The CIA will kick my ass right back to the US of A. Yeah, whatever. At least I'll get a decent cup of coffee.*

He tapped in the psychiatrist's address. The map showed all the roads marked with one-way arrows, in every direction except south. And all the traffic was heading the wrong way. A deadened thump and tinkle of glass came from the Vittorio Emanuele Bridge and the traffic squealed to a halt, accompanied by a cacophony of horns. *It's gonna be quicker by foot.* He dodged between the stationary cars, peeling off his jacket.

When I haul this bastard in Spinks can kiss my ass. The Italian Police and Interpol will have to process the Arrest Warrant, and there will be nothing Spinks can do about it. Once it was on the system, everybody would know. He checked the screen. *If one bridge traffic flow goes west, the next bridge has gotta go east.*

He slid to a halt and shielded his eyes against the sun as he looked down the river, then he ran for the Principe Amedeo Bridge.

CHAPTER 9

Montrose checked the street and the lines of parked cars. *No goons. No one hiding in alleyways. No one walking about with a finger in their ear, talking to their cuffs.* He stood before the door and was about to lift his hand to the buzzer when he noticed it was ajar. *They're expecting me.* He stood in the cool hall for a moment, then turned and threw the bolts. *If any goons are coming behind me they'll have to knock.*

He ran up the steps and stopped just outside the psychiatrist's office. *No voices. No movement.* He twisted the handle and stepped in.

The secretary's desk was empty. He took a pace forward. Her chair was lying on its side.

What the hell? On the desk, he saw a spray of blood and saliva glistening on fragments of teeth. *Oh, sweet Jesus, no . . .*

He jerked his head from side to side, searching around for a weapon, and grabbed a metal paperweight from the desk. The sweat chilled on his face as he turned to Richmond's office.

The door was open. Edging forwards he saw a pool of dark, red blood spreading towards him. His heart thumped against his chest as he nudged open the door with his foot.

The secretary lay across the chair, her neck twisted to a sharp angle and her head hung limp, blood caked across her swollen face.

Montrose tore his gaze from her staring, lifeless eyes and looked over the desk to where Richmond lay slumped, his head caved in, pieces of skull sticking from the wound, exposing the grey, shining matter, flecked with red. On the desk beside him an ancient metal typewriter lay broken, the keys matted with hair and gore. The only sound was the dripping of thick blood from the desk.

Montrose gasped in a lungful of air and could smell a sweet stench. *Beaten to death.*

The desk fan rotated slowly, gently ruffling the secretary's skirt.

Why?

He stared down at the blood. It slowed as it coagulated. *Why didn't they shoot them?* He felt the paperweight slip from his hand.

Because I haven't got a gun.

He jolted at the sounds of distant sirens. *My prints are all over this room.* He looked down at his hands and searched frantically around for a cloth, then stopped. *You're fucked,*

He ran, kicking open the door, and hit the stairs, sliding on the polished stone. He fumbled at the bolts on the door and glanced out onto the street. The sirens were louder. *Walk away. Just walk away.*

The gelato vendor smiled as he stepped out into the street.

Positive ID. They have me by the balls. Keep walking. He turned into the first side street and picked up the pace.

His iPhone beeped in his pocket. He brought up a text message. *What the hell is that?* He stared down at a picture of a USB memory stick. The phone rang in his hand. Blocked Number. He lifted it to his ear.

"You've been a bad boy, Connor. You should have walked away," said Gabby.

The chick at the café?

"We heard about the arrest warrant. I thought we had an agreement? Oh, and you shouldn't have killed . . ."

"I didn't kill him. You know that." He ducked into a piss-stained doorway. "You're a lying, drug-dealing scumbag. The old guy has got fuck all to do with the trade negotiations. And you've killed two innocent people."

"You can be sure I have no idea what you're talking about."

"No way can you pin this on me."

"Oh really? That's not what it looks like, I'm afraid. I understand that there is a great deal of evidence against you. But I know of something that may interest you. You remember a certain aged gentleman, the one you chatted to in the car. The one that gave you a way out? The way out you didn't take?"

The old bastard.

"Well, his friend was very upset when he heard about an arrest warrant."

"Kessler?"

"Yes, you found his name. You are so clever. Anyway, Herr Kessler has a USB memory stick with a recording of the security camera at the psychiatrist's office.

Apparently it's very revealing. Have you checked your text messages recently? He's sent you a photo."

"Yeah, I got it. So what?"

"The memory stick contains a video recording. From the security camera at Doctor Richmond's office. It shows the murders being committed. More importantly, not being committed by you."

"There's no video. That's the worse bluff I've ever heard. You know where you can shove your memory stick."

"Check your email. A more technologically astute colleague of mine has sent you a little video clip. If you want to see the remainder, you'll do what you're told. It isn't difficult, Connor."

"I'm coming for you, and when I . . ."

"Oh, you are sweet, but you'll have to keep your pecker in your pants for a little while longer. So, listen to me very carefully, because I think your balls are getting in the way of your brain."

"Spit it out. What do you want?"

"I want you to disappear, Connor. I want you to vanish from the face of the earth. Just for a month. Although with the CIA and the Italian police on your cute little tail, I suspect you had that in mind already. It's just for a month. Then you can come and see me. Clothes are optional. You can take me to dinner and I might give you a present." She laughed. "I might give you the USB stick, too. Depends if you're nice to me."

"You're crazy. They'll never believe I did this."

"Connor, I've just read your psychiatrist's report. Not the original, this is a fresh copy. And judging by the blood stains, it's very fresh. Between you and me, it doesn't make for good reading. I mean, according to this . . . Well, let's say you're not the kinda guy I would take home to my folks."

"There's no way . . ."

"Just be a good boy, Connor. Get out of town. Don't talk to anyone. No emails, no press, no cops, no CIA. Switch your phone on exactly one month from now. I'll call you."

He stared at the phone as the call ended. The email icon flashed. He brought up the message, and hit a Vine link. A grainy black and white picture showed a man facing Richmond's secretary before he pulled her across the desk and smashed her face down. *That could be anyone. It's too fuzzy. But what about the rest of it?* The video ended. He stared at the phone in his hand and saw a dark stain smeared across the cuff of his jacket.

He was rubbing at the sticky bloodstain when her words popped into his head, 'Got to look your best!' as she picked fibers from his coat. *Shit, they had it all. They'd be stuck into Richmond's . . .* He gagged, and bitter bile flooded into his mouth. *Fingerprints, fibers, motive. The report? They must have had Richmond write it before they killed him.*

The sirens were closer. They stopped. *They'll be waiting for backup. What did that bitch say? Dangerous psychotic? If the cops catch me, Kessler will destroy the video. It's not as if he owes me any favors.*

He spat into the doorway. The plan was simple. *Get the fuck out of Dodge.*

He headed down the alley, the iPhone shaking in his hand as he glanced at the map. *I have to find them or I'm a dead man. They won't let me near Kessler. And the psycho that killed Richmond will be guarding him. The old man. Get the old man. But I'll bet he's not at home. Or his son. The old bastard will be laughing his wrinkly face off.* He let out a few slow breaths. *Focus. Find him. But where?* He pictured him on the seat of the Mercedes. *Snappy dresser. Wait. The coat he was wearing. Yeah, I know where I remember it. The TV show. Doctor Who wears one. High class British coat. Velvet collar. Burberry? No. Crombie! And there can't be many dealers in Rome. You think so? I'm in Italy. Even the goddam' yappy mutts carried in handbags wear Louis Vuitton.*

At the end of the alley was a small hotel. And a taxi. Two fat tourists got out. Montrose quickened his pace, waving a hand towards the driver, then punched "Crombie dealer Rome" into Google.

The tourists fumbled with their bags, examining their cash and handing over each bill in turn. Montrose slipped into the back seat. *Jesus, hurry up!*

The search results came up on his iPhone. *Yeah, that'll work.*

He looked down at his suit. It had to go. He had to blend in. Look like an Italian. But asking an Italian taxi driver for the best suit shop in town was an invitation to a two day conversation. At the end he'd be invited home for dinner to meet his daughter and he'd be married by Christmas.

The tourists turned away and the driver caught his eye in the rear view mirror. "Where to, signore?"

"Brooks Brothers, Via San Pietro." The iPhone rang in his hand. He recognized the number.

"Connor?"

"Hi, Boss." *He never calls me Connor. He knew. He goddam' knew.* "So, what's up?"

"Connor, I'll get straight to the point. I've got a report in front of me. It's not good reading."

"Really? Something to do with me?" *Straight from Richmond. Before they beat his fucking brains in.*

"Yeah, it's about you."

"What's it say?"

"He says, well . . . He says a lot of things, but also that you threatened him."

"I what?"

"Threatened him, Connor. Did you do that?"

"Boss, there's no way . . . this is just . . ." *He doesn't know yet. But they'll find the bodies. Kessler will make sure of that. And then we won't be on first name terms any more.*

"The police are looking for you, Connor. We got to get you safe. Back to the US. They can't touch you there."

Yeah, they want me safe. "Boss, you're right. Listen, tell me a bit more, what else did he . . .?"

"This ain't the time, Connor. We'll get you home. Report like this, we have to follow procedure. Look, I'm not suspending you."

Yeah, that's the first thing you should do. You really are scared. "Let me guess, psychotic, immediate danger, on the verge, that kind of thing?"

"I can't . . ."

"You don't have to tell me, I can guess." *Kessler had done a great job.*

"Tell me where you are and we'll come and pick you up."

"Yeah, about that . . ." *They'll be all over me like a rash.* "Don't worry, I'll come straight back to the office. See ya."

The only place I'll be headed is straight to a CIA cell.

And the only way I'll be coming out is folded up in a packing crate with my name on it.

The taxi pulled into the curb. He stepped out and leaned into the window. "Wait here." *There's only two chances of them giving me that video. None, and fuck all.*

CHAPTER 10

Montrose walked through the ornate brass and glass entrance.

An assistant appeared at his side. "Welcome to Brookes Brothers, sir. How can I help you?"

"I'm in a big hurry. I have to get to a meeting and I need something better than this." He glanced down at the suit and swept back the jacket to hide the blood stain. "Eating spaghetti. It should come with a bib. I'll need a complete outfit. Suit and shirts. Plus a bag to carry it all. Tell me, do you sell Crombie coats?"

"Of course, sir, was there a particular style you wanted to try?"

"Uh, just the classic type. You're the only dealer for these coats in Rome, no?"

"Indeed, sir, one of the very few outlets in the whole of Italy."

"Yeah, thought so. A colleague of mine recommended them. It was the type with the felt collar, long, black wool, bright red lining. It looked fantastic. He's an old guy, can't remember his name. Has a son called Kurt, tall blond guy. Not sure if he shops here too."

The assistant thought for a moment. "It doesn't ring a bell, sir."

"Really old guy, lives in Via Nableone. German accent, silver hair. Thin, coughs a lot, looks like he's being followed around by a guy in a big black robe and a scythe."

The assistant smiled. "Perhaps you mean Mr. Reinhard, sir. And I believe his son is also a customer."

"Reinhard. Yeah, that's the fella. Old Mr. Reinhard."

The assistant looked down for a moment.

Montrose glanced towards his shoes. *Blood.* "And a pair of black brogues, if you have them."

"Yes, sir." The assistant clicked his fingers and pulled out a measuring tape. "One of my colleagues will fetch the requisite items and check the stock for a Crombie in your size. Please step to the rear, sir. I'll be with you in a moment."

Montrose marched past the cash desk to the fitting area. *Kurt Reinhard and your wrinkly old bastard of a father. I got your number. I'm coming for you.*

"You imbecile!" Reinhard launched his cane across the room. It ricocheted off an ancient alabaster figurine, sending a spray of powder into the air, then bounced off the parquet floor. It came to rest at the feet of his son. "The Mafia? And you led Interpol straight to my door!"

Kurt Reinhard held out his hands as he approached. "I had no idea . . ."

"What in the name of God did you think you were doing?"

"Father, it was a simple exchange. The Afghans tell me where the drugs are hidden. I tell them where the cash is hidden. We have a man at each location and they both simply confirm and collect. The Mafia put up the money and they make over three million euros in profit when they sell it on. My commission for the deal was one hundred thousand euros. The set up was perfect!"

"Perfect? You think so? Then why am I scrabbling around trying to find three million euros to pay off the Mafia?"

"They can't do this! The deal is off, how can they expect their profit?"

"Oh, so you deal with murderers, pimps and drug dealers, and suddenly you're surprised they're not playing the game?"

"Father, what am I supposed to do? You never give me anything. I have to make my own business. Take my own risks. I never wanted you involved. This was not how it was . . ."

"With Mafia scum? You listen to me, Kurt. This is the last time. I have given you free rein and this is how you repay me." He bent forward to get his breath back then lifted his head. "You are my son and I will get you out of this. But from now on you work for me. No questions."

"Father, stocks and shares, it's so dry, you're just a businessman. I need to do something more . . ."

Reinhard threw his head back, his vertebrae clicking loudly. "Just a businessman! You think that's all I'm worth?" He jabbed a bony finger across the room. "Bring me my cane." He fished a dull metal key from his pocket. Grabbing the cane from Kurt's hand, he gestured towards the corner of the room. "Open that door."

"The store cupboard?"

"Yes. Where I keep my files." He waved the cane under Kurt's nose. "The files of a businessman."

Kurt took the key and turned to the cupboard door as his father shuffled across the room behind him.

"Businessman!" Reinhard stopped for a moment to let a bronchial cough subside.

Kurt pushed the door open to a small, windowless room. "What is all this stuff?" Basic shelving lined the walls, stacked with dusty document boxes.

Reinhard shoved past him and reached over to the drawer of an unvarnished desk. He pulled out a silver framed black-and-white photograph, examined it for a moment then held it up. "Look carefully. Tell me who you see."

Kurt took the photograph and lifted it up to the single low-watt light bulb. It was the figure of a young man. The uniform was unmistakable. *Wehrmacht*. So was the face. It was his father. "My God! It's you. A soldier?"

"Lieutenant Reinhard, to be precise. Taken in Antwerp during the war."

Kurt threw him a look of astonishment. "In the Wehrmacht?"

"Don't be so surprised. I always told you there was more German than Swiss blood in the family. In fact, there's no Swiss blood whatsoever."

Kurt shook his head. "Why didn't you tell me?"

"You didn't need to know. It was safer that way." Reinhard lowered himself onto a plain wooden chair. "Our family are from a long line of Saxon nobility and can be traced back over a thousand years. Your blood is German, Kurt."

"But I . . . What about our name? It is Reinhard?"

"Yes, though I was not born in Zurich, no matter what my passport says. I was born and schooled in Dresden. Our family had been part of the regiment for eight generations. We were soldiers, and proud. But the Nazis robbed our army of any honor. When we saw what was to become of Europe, powerful friends made sure we were in the right place at the right time. There were many opportunities if you knew where to look. In 1940, when we marched through Belgium, we helped ourselves in the diamond quarter of Antwerp."

"Diamonds?"

"Yes. Spoils of war. Of course, I handed over large quantities to the Nazis, but a significant amount of the very finest stones, notably the blue diamonds, I kept for myself. Most of them are flawless. The largest would be worth a million dollars apiece on today's market. And there are hundreds of them. Once we had achieved our aims, I traveled directly to Zurich and deposited them in our family vault. Your grandfather arranged for me to be listed as missing, presumed dead. A Swiss passport gave me all the access I required to sympathetic clergy in the Vatican. They found a place for me in Rome in return for contributions to their *charities*. And here I stayed. There was nothing left to return to."

"Nothing? What about our family?"

"Not even ashes. When the British firebombed Dresden the whole city was obliterated. Twenty five thousand people, including our entire family. They perished in a firestorm so intense that their bones melted into the stone. A war crime that wasn't mentioned at Nuremberg."

"I had no idea." Kurt stared down at the photograph.

"No, that is often the case. From now on, you will do

what you are damn well told. This was supposed to be your inheritance. Now it will buy you out of this mess. I have no choice. I have allocated all of my available funds to the oil deal."

"Buy me out . . . with diamonds?"

"We have a buyer. More importantly, a buyer with a cash surplus which will pay off the Cosa Nostra. No doubt some dealer wanting to launder his cash. I don't care." He lifted the cane and placed the tip on Kurt's chin. "So, just a businessman?"

Kurt placed the photo carefully on the desk and stood up straight. "What do you want me to do?"

"An old friend in Zurich will help us. Wolfgang Kessler owns a private bank, where our vault is kept, and looks after my affairs. I want you to collect the diamonds from the vault. Herr Kessler has arranged a buyer in Zurich. I have much more to explain, but it can wait."

"I'll be ready, Father."

Reinhard gazed around the cramped room. "Do you know what these files contain?"

"Are they from the war?"

"Yes." His eyes lost focus for a moment. "War stories, you might say. Though all the authors are dead."

"Soldiers? In the Wehrmacht?"

"No, Kurt." Reinhard shook his head. "Not soldiers." He pulled a small silver box from his pocket, took out a pill, placed it under his tongue and sat back for a moment. "The diamond merchants and wealthy burghers of Antwerp. We interviewed them prior to their departure to the camps. They were very helpful. Eventually. We gave them no choice."

"The death camps?"

Reinhard tugged at his collar. "Yes. It was an appalling time, Kurt. Untold misery. We didn't all believe the lies of the Nazis, but there was no point in missing such an opportunity. Besides, once the Jews were transferred to the SS it was out of our hands."

Kurt stared at the boxes. "They're all dead?"

"Of course. Don't get the wrong idea. The Jews mean nothing to me."

"But the diamonds? Does anyone know?"

"No. Except Kessler. Remember, I died in the war. And so did the Jews who owned them." Reinhard's mouth twisted into a sneer. "They are remembered. Some days we hear of nothing else. But what of the millions of Germans who perished? I don't see the historians weeping over their graves." He shook his head. "The flower of our nation. Cut down by communists and the dregs of the British Empire. That's all the Americans are. It was war. Filthy and vile. But Germany was to fulfill its destiny. We should have ruled Europe, over the . . ." Reinhard's eyes narrowed. "*Untermenschen* surrounding us. Does this shock you?"

Kurt puffed out his chest. "No, Father. My bloodline, I feel . . ."

"This is your last chance, Kurt."

"I know. I won't let you down. There are so many questions. I want to know everything."

"You will. In happier times, perhaps you would have made a fine soldier. You remind me of my father. A magnificent man, utterly ruthless in battle, but impetuous."

Kurt stuck his chin in the air. "Whatever you want me to do, I'm ready."

"In a few years you'll be running everything. I have

amassed a great deal, though what I'm about to tell you will be the source of our wealth for generations to come." Reinhard leaned over on the desk. "But first, the bag containing the diamonds has been in Kessler's bank since I placed it there more than seventy years ago. At the bottom of that bag is a large envelope. It contains some information I compiled during my time in Antwerp and a file taken from the office of Heinrich Himmler. It is, shall we say, a list."

"Himmler? A list of what? The diamonds?"

"That and other things." Reinhard pushed back the chair. "Kessler must never find out. Make sure when you deliver the diamonds to the Embassy that you keep that envelope. It is for your eyes only."

"I will, Father."

Reinhard levered himself up from the chair and straightened his jacket. "This wasn't the plan. Another few years would have been safer. Now we have no choice. Mossad agents have been searching for the diamonds since the end of the war, but they're old men now." His lips tightened into a thin smile. "And no one listens to old men." He waved a hand at the haphazardly stacked boxes. "Look around you, Kurt. The diamonds are worth a fortune, but what those files contain is beyond the dreams of avarice."

"But how . . .?"

"We will talk later." He motioned Kurt towards the door, then placed the silver framed photo on the desk. He took small, careful steps back into the room and turned the key in the lock. "Do not fail me."

"I'm ready, Father."

"Pack a bag. You will take the next flight to Zurich."

CHAPTER 11

Nothing. Not even the sound of the engine. Montrose cut the call to the Blackberry.

An assistant was waiting for him. "If you could face the mirror, sir?" He moved the measuring tape expertly over Montrose's body. "Perhaps a suit in blue or grey?"

"Blue. Dark blue, and two shirts, one white, the other a blue check. Remove any packaging and place them in the bag."

"Very good, sir. Perhaps a few ties?"

"Yeah, match them to the shirts, I'll go with your expert judgment."

"Thank you, sir. Warm or temperate climate?"

Montrose was about to ask him what the hell he was talking about, then thought of the suit. "Temperate. It might be cold where I'm going." *Or red fucking hot.*

"Shoes, sir?" An assistant held out a pair of shiny black English brogues.

"Ah, yes." He sat down on a nearby chair and kicked off his sneakers to reveal a toe sticking out of one of his grey socks. "Throw in a few pairs of socks. I'll change later." The assistant lifted his foot and slipped on the brogue with the help of a silver shoe horn. "These will be fine. No need to try on the other." *The last time I bought new brogues they ripped the crap out of my feet.* "Can you get me a pair of sneakers, too? Any color."

Another assistant appeared holding a polished leather bag and two long, black wool overcoats. "We have the double-breasted, sir, or the classic retro Crombie, as you requested."

The scarlet lining of the retro Crombie caught his eye. It was the best-looking coat he'd ever seen.

"Do you have a preference, sir?"

"That one." He pointed to the retro.

"We also have a matching suit in exactly your size, sir. Would you care to try it on?"

"I'm pushed for time. I'll wear it now. Pass everything to me in the changing booth." He pulled a pair of sunglasses from a store dummy and ducked behind the booth door. "Ring all this up and I'll meet you at the cash desk." He took his Amex card from his wallet and shoved it through the slats in the door.

"As you wish, sir."

He checked the iPhone. *No calls. That won't last. I keep this switched on and I'm gonna light up on the grid like a Christmas tree at a bar mitzvah.* He switched the ring to silent and tugged off his jacket. He ripped at the buttons of the shirt, then stopped. *The phone. They'd follow the phone. That would work. Spinks goes one way. I go the other. He stuck his head out of the booth.* "Can you put the other stuff in the leather bag and get me a store bag for my dirty clothes?"

"Of course, sir."

Montrose connected the iPhone headphones. *Let's see what the old bastard is up to.* He hit redial for the old Blackberry and heard a brief ring tone as he kicked off his pants.

"There will be no second chance, Kurt. I want you to listen very carefully."

Jeez, they're in the car. Old Reinhard and his son.

"I understand, Father."

What the hell are they up to? No second chance for what? He stuck his head out of the changing booth. "You got a pen?"

"I beg your pardon, sir?

Montrose caught the assistant's look. A guy in a changing booth with his pants around his ankles, shirt half-unbuttoned and listening to his iPhone. "A pen. I've got a voice mail."

"Of course, sir," replied the assistant, holding out a Mont Blanc.

Man, what do they pay these guys here? "Thanks." He pulled the door closed on the booth as he heard the voice speak again.

"A car will be waiting for you. It will take you directly to the bank. You will meet Jacques Kessler, Wolfgang Kessler's son. He will require proof of identity."

Montrose scribbled 'Jacques Kessler' on the wall of the booth.

"Use my Wehrmacht pass. These six digits are the combination to our safe deposit box. Take the merchandise to the South African Embassy where a specialist will be waiting for you. He will verify the quality and price, then separate the required amount and return the remainder to you. When this is done, Kessler's client will arrive with three million in cash."

"Euros?"

"Yes. Count the money. There will be exactly one hundred bundles in high denomination bills. Total, three million. Do you understand?

"I understand."

What the hell? The merchandise? Yeah, I can guess. A fuck-ton of dope. He kept scribbling.

"Who's the buyer?"

Yeah, who's the buyer, old man?

"Herr Kessler is being rather coy. I suspect it's someone who wants to launder some cash. Kessler knows many important people. His discreet services are much in demand among the ruling elite in political and financial circles. This is an opportunity to make a name for yourself, Kurt, as a businessman, just like me. Not a runner for the Mafia."

"I've told them I'll be returning tonight with the money."

"What time is your flight?"

"13:00. We're here."

"Everything okay in there, sir?"

"Yeah, yeah, I'll be out in a moment." He heard the doors close on Reinhard's car. *I've got to go.* He hauled on the new shirt and pants and scanned the scribbles on the wall.

Zurich - Kessler - Wolfgang or Jacques - army pass - six digits - pick up merchandise - 3 mill - SA Embassy - swap for cash - pay off Cosa Nostra.

He slipped on the new shoes and shoved his old clothes into the store bag. *Holy shit. Kurt Reinhard owes the Cosa Nostra three million and the old man's emptying the family vault to pay up.*

He pulled on the jacket, hastily tucking in his shirt,

and took a last look at the wall. He grabbed his old shirt from the floor of the booth, then spat on the writing and rubbed it hard with the shirt cuff. The ink smudged blue across the wall. *Yeah, that worked. Good job.*

Slipping the Crombie over his arm, he stood for a moment in front of the mirror. *Looking good. In a 'psychotic wanted for murder' kinda way. Get with the program.* He stuffed the remaining clothes into the store bag then smoothed down his suit.

The assistant was waiting as Montrose pushed open the door and slipped on the sunglasses. *By the look on your face, buddy, you're gonna look to see who else was in that booth.* "Thanks for the pen."

The assistant regarded the powdered plaster compacted around the end of his Mont Blanc, then blew it off and returned it to his pocket.

"Yeah, my bad. Tell you what, stick a new one on my check."

"That won't be necessary, sir, I . . ."

"I insist." *A free pen from the CIA.* "It might bring me luck." *And any time starting now would be good.* "Where's the cash desk? I gotta go."

"This way, sir."

He followed the assistant to the desk at the centre of the store. "Is everything ready?"

"Yes sir, I've placed your sneakers in the leather bag. Please sign here."

Damn sunglasses, I can't see a thing. He pushed them onto his head and scribbled on the receipt. "Thanks for everything." He grabbed the bags and made for the door, then remembered the phone. He looked down at the store bag. *They don't need the suit for evidence.*

They got enough of that already. He turned back to the assistant. "Can you call me a cab?"

The assistant looked past Montrose to the waiting taxi. "But there is one waiting . . ."

"Yeah, but he ripped me off. I want another. Took me the tourist route, you know?"

"Of course, sir. Where to?"

"Maybe the Coliseum." *Why not?* "Yeah, the Coliseum."

"Of course, sir," replied the assistant, but Montrose was already heading for the exit.

The store bag swung in his hand as he stood before the waiting taxi. The driver looked expectantly as Montrose checked his iPhone was set to silent, then lifted it to his ear.

Listen carefully, buddy, this call is only for you. "Yeah, I'm in Rome. What? Lyon?" He pulled open the door and dropped onto the rear seat. "The bag? You got to be serious, I can't get to Lyon today. I'm in a taxi on the way to headquarters. And I'm not putting this bag on a flight. If we lose this, the whole case could go under. We've been chasing them for months! Those damn bankers are going down for this, one way or another." He caught the driver's eye in the rear view mirror, and began nodding vigorously. "Yeah, yeah. What? The taxi? Yeah, that could work. It's got to be the fastest way. It'll be eight hours by road. The judge ain't gonna wait." He leaned forward and read out the taxi number from the license plate on the dashboard. "Rome. CO50702. It has to work − we can't lose this. Yeah, I'll send it direct to you."

The taxi driver began to turn around.

If you're looking for your fare, you're in for a big surprise. "Okay, hold on. Driver, you take Visa, yeah?"

The driver looked relieved. "Of course, we take Visa, MasterCard, Amex. This is Rome, signore, we're ahead of the times."

"Yeah, very good." *Spinks was gonna love this. If it worked.* He pulled out his Interpol badge and held it up in front of the driver. "Write down my name and number. You're gonna need it."

The driver squinted at the badge then began scribbling on a pad.

"Listen, I need this bag delivered to Interpol Headquarters in Lyon, France. Address is 200 Quai Charles de Gaulle. Write that down too."

"Lyon? France?" The diver scribbled down the address. "You want to go there now?"

"Not me, the bag." He held up the Brookes Brothers' store bag stuffed full of his old clothes.

"Just the bag, signore?"

He ain't looking convinced. No surprise. "This is Interpol business. I could get another taxi?"

"Signore, that's going to be very expen . . ."

"Whatever. Tell me how much. I'll pay for it now." The driver's eyes lit up and he grabbed his phone.

Thought you'd like that. He pulled the Visa card from his wallet as the driver spoke fast Italian into the phone. Montrose leaned over and tapped his watch.

"*Si, si,* Lyon." The driver held the phone to his chest. "They say two thousand euros, signore."

Robbing bastards, it's nowhere near that. "Fine, let's do it."

The driver grabbed the Visa card and slotted it into the machine. "I will have to call my wife, and tell . . ."

"Do it later. This is crucial evidence. Interpol are counting on you. Don't let them down."

"*Si, si, importante.*" He handed over the machine.

Montrose keyed in his PIN code. "I'll need the receipt."

"Of course, signore." He tore the ticket from the machine and read the price to make sure.

Enjoy, it buddy. "One more thing." Montrose patted the store bag. "You can look inside the bag, but don't touch anything. You don't want to get your prints on this stuff. Understand?"

"*Si.* I won't touch it."

Yeah, let's make sure, my friend. "You ever been in trouble with the police? Had your fingerprints taken?"

The driver shrugged and held out his hands.

"I'll take that as a yes. Don't worry about it. Remember, you can look but don't touch. Your prints come up on these clothes then the Carabinieri will be around to kick your door down. They won't be there for coffee and cake. Do you understand the mission?"

"Mission! Yes, but this one is possible, no?" The driver grinned.

For the right price, anything is possible. Even buying Afghanistan. "Yeah, you're Tom Cruise. Only taller." Montrose slipped the iPhone between the cushions of the back seat and felt it drop into the trunk. "And don't get stopped for speeding. No delays, okay?"

"You can rely on me, signore."

"Go for it." Montrose laid the store bag flat on the seat and stepped out on to the street. The driver waved and sped off into the traffic.

"Mr. Montrose?" The shop assistant stood in the doorway. "Your taxi is here, sir."

He looked up as a taxi pulled into the curb. The assistant opened the door and Montrose got into the rear seat. "Thanks."

The driver looked around. "The Coliseum?"

"No." Montrose slid down in the seat and tugged up the velvet collar of the Crombie. "Airport. Fast as you can."

CHAPTER 12

The doors of the First Class lounge were mirrored and he stopped to admire the Crombie. He looked like a million dollars but felt like shit.

The receptionist smiled as he approached. "Good evening, sir."

Montrose handed over his ticket. He caught a row of clocks behind the desk. *The cops will be tracking a phone to Lyon, running up and down the autoroute looking for me. But I ain't there. They'd work it out, but not yet. Not just yet.*

"Your boarding begins in ten minutes, sir. Enjoy your flight."

"Thanks."

It was too dark in the lounge to wear sunglasses without looking like a dick. He slipped them into his pocket and walked slowly through the lounge. *Six foot, maybe. Fair hair.* He stopped to pour himself a coffee from a free bar. Some of the occupants of the room busied themselves with papers, others dozed in their seats or chatted with colleagues around low tables.

I can't picture the face. The face in the corridor when it all went to shit.

He scanned the lounge. Around him some passengers dozed in their chairs, others chatted in groups. *Fifty people, tops. Forget the groups. He'll be on his own.* A few businessmen sat apart, reading papers or working on laptops. Montrose let his eyes rest on each one for a second. *Too fat. Too old. Too small. He's got to be here.*

A row of high-backed recliners faced the windows. Above one was a crop of fair hair, just visible over the edge of the headrest. Montrose approached, checking his reflection to make sure the passenger couldn't see him coming. There was a flight case beside the chair. Closer now, the reflection in the window sharpened. Well dressed. Yuppie clothes that looked old but cost more than a working man's monthly salary. The kind of guy women love to be with, and the kind of guy that men would never tire of punching in the face.

It's got to be him. Old Reinhard's identity pass. That was the key. The son must have it. But where? Only one way to find out.

He turned back to the lounge. A phone booth was set into the wall at a corner of the room where he could get a view of the reception desk. Pulling a few coins from his pocket, he opened the door of the booth and ran a finger down the numbers printed on the wall. He grabbed the handset and dialed, shoving in coins when the voice spoke.

"Aeroporti di Roma, Sicurezza."

Shit, my Italian ain't that good. "Hi, this is, uh, Bobby Spinks, Interpol Rome. Do you mind if I speak English?"

"Yes, this is Airport Security, how can I help you?"

"Thanks, I'm calling with some security information. We've got a tip off that a gang of pickpockets is working the departure lounges. Could you put out a warning to the passengers? We're still trying to track the guys down."

"Of course, I'll do it right now."

"*Grazie*. We'll be in touch when we have more information." He had to see what happened next and pulled open the door of the booth. *Bet they start with First Class.*

The receptionist picked up a phone and listened to a short conversation, then leaned over to the PA microphone. "Ladies and gentlemen, we have a message from Airport Security. There are pickpockets operating in the airport, please be careful with your belongings. Thank you."

Everyone started jumping up and down like Pavlov's dogs. *But just one doggy will do.* The figure at the window stood up like the others, patted his hip pocket and shoved a hand inside his overcoat. Montrose moved to the side to get a better view as the man opened a paper ticket wallet and took out a faded piece of card.

Around him, passengers checked their pockets and bags. He scanned the faces. *Some six footers, but no fair hair. It has to be him.* Montrose took a chair behind the man and watched him pick up some travel brochures from a nearby stand. Montrose squinted at the covers. They were for Ireland, like the ones at the reception desk. The man tucked the card into a brochure then slipped it into the zipper pocket at the side of his flight case. *It's him.*

The hotel trick. Montrose tightened his grip on the leather bag. *It was the only way.* He'd tried it in training, but not for real. The best chance to steal a briefcase was in a hotel, just as the target was checking in. They had observed a businessman walk to the reception desk, then place his briefcase at his feet, out of his line of sight. It was a simple trick to walk up quietly behind the sucker and pick up the briefcase while he was busy writing down his details or trying to catch the eye of an attractive receptionist. Some criminals made an industry out of it, but all he needed was the contents of the zipper pocket.

He's on edge. Got to be. He's not going to fool easily. Unless he's distracted. Montrose checked his watch, and reckoned there was about five minutes before they were called for boarding. *If it didn't work there might not be another chance until the flight. But I'll know for sure.*

He opened the phone booth and lifted the handset, glancing back through the glass panel. The receptionist was engrossed in her Nintendo, holding it in front of her burgeoning chest. Her breasts jiggled as she thumbed the controls hard, straining the buttons on her silk shirt. *Sweet Jesus, that chick is stacked. Super Mario would have a big smile on his face. She couldn't be more perfect.* He hit redial on the phone.

"Security?"

"This is Spinks, from Interpol, I called a few minutes ago. I need to speak to a colleague in the first class lounge, I think we may be on to something. Can you put me through?"

"Of course."

"I'll let you know if we find them. But if I don't call back, it's a dead end."

"Do you want me to send a security team?"

"Nah, we're not sure yet. But when we are, you can come and take them down. What's your name?"

"Paola Cabrelli, Security Officer."

She sounds sweet. "Thanks, Paola. If we nail them, I'll buy you dinner to celebrate."

"*Grazie*, Mr. Spinks. I'll think about it."

"My pleasure. So, can you put me through to the First Class Lounge? I need to speak to . . . "

"Oh, of course. One moment."

The line buzzed and clicked. He watched the receptionist drop the Nintendo and pick up the phone. *Apologies, Mario.*

"*Sala d'attesa Prima Classe?*"

"I have an urgent call for Mr. Reinhard, who's in your lounge. Can you bring him to the phone?"

"One moment, sir." The receptionist flicked the button on the PA. "Telephone call for Mr. Reinhard. Reception desk, please."

Montrose pressed his face against the glass.

The blond guy stood up with a puzzled look, checked his Blackberry and then hurried to the desk. He took the phone from the receptionist and dropped his bag on the floor. "Reinhard speaking."

You freak, I'm going to put a bullet in your heart. "Mr. Reinhard," said Montrose. "I have an urgent call for you, please wait while I connect."

This has to be damn quick. Reinhard didn't look like the patient type. Montrose laid the receiver on a ledge, then pulled open the door and crossed to the reception desk. "Hi! Say, can I change my seat to an aisle? I like to stretch my legs. Gotta get my shut-eye!" He placed his leather bag beside Reinhard's flight case, then picked up a travel brochure from the desk and grinned at Reinhard. "How are ya doing, buddy?"

Reinhard turned away with barely concealed irritation, leaning on the desk and pressing the phone to his ear.

Don't you remember me? Maybe if I was wearing a hooded top and carrying a Glock? How 'bout then, asshole?

The receptionist held out a perfectly manicured hand. "May I see your ticket, sir?"

"Sure, yeah." Montrose patted his pockets. "Hold on a moment, it's here somewhere." He bent down to the leather bag and stole a glance at Reinhard, who was listening intently to the call and trying to catch a glimpse of the receptionist's impressive décolletage. *Couldn't be better, just keep an eye on those sweater puppies.* Montrose slipped back the zipper on the travel pocket of Reinhard's case, pulled out the brochure and slid in his own. He stood up, exasperated.

"I can't seem to find . . . Ah, here it is!" he said and palmed Reinhard's brochure into the Crombie then pulled out his own boarding pass.

The receptionist scanned the details. "This is an aisle seat, sir."

"Really? Great! Hey, my bad, I thought that was a centre seat."

"Not in First Class, sir, it's all aisles and windows."

"Even better, more legroom for me!"

She gave him her best professional smile for dealing with idiots. "Glad to be of help, sir. I hope you enjoy your flight."

"I think I will." He hurried back to the phone booth, kicked the door closed and grabbed the receiver. "Kevin!"

"What?"

"One of my buddies spotted your name at check-in. There's only one K. Reinhard who goes whoring in Rome!" Montrose turned his head just enough to peer through the glass, and saw the face of Reinhard crease in disgust.

"You have the wrong Reinhard," he replied and almost threw the phone back to the receptionist.

"I don't think I did, buddy," Montrose murmured and took a small notebook from his wallet. It was time to give Zurich Customs a call.

CHAPTER 13

First class was starting to fill up. Montrose gave his overcoat to the stewardess, threw his leather bag in the overhead locker and settled into the seat. He stood with his back to the aisle and pulled out the travel brochure, holding it inside his jacket. He thumbed the pages and they fell open to reveal a faded brown card. His breath caught in his throat when he saw the eagle and swastika stamped on the cover. He felt someone behind him pushing past. He clamped the brochure to his chest and dropped his gaze for a moment as Reinhard passed by.

Old man Reinhard was about as Swiss as Osama Bin Laden's ass.

Glancing over his shoulder, Montrose caught Reinhard sitting a few seats behind and watched a businessman attempt to make conversation, but with little success. *Good news. That would keep the bastard quiet. Reinhard wouldn't go looking for a Nazi pass with a nosy neighbor sitting next to him. That would make for a very interesting conversation piece.*

"Nervous flyer, sir?"

He jerked his head around to see the stewardess looking concerned.

Jeez, wear the face, you're just a tired businessman.
"Only a little. Once take-off is over, I'll be okay."

"We're approaching the runway so it won't be long before we're in the air. Perhaps you could read a magazine? It would help pass the time."

"Thanks." In the seat pocket was a well-thumbed copy of *Time* magazine. The cover was emblazoned with "The Poppy Fields. The Harvest of Death." He dropped the magazine and rubbed his face to mask the tension. *Now the Taliban were weaker, the poppy fields were back at full strength. Production had doubled since the first GI boots had hit the ground. Maybe that's part of the deal. Makes sense. Wikileaks had already published the emails, alleging President Karzai's brother was an international opium dealer. And the DEA had been told to back off while US soldiers patrolled the poppy fields, keeping the Taliban at bay.*

He stuffed the magazine back into the pocket and tightened his seat belt. *Holy shit. They think I'll go to Wikileaks and tell them about the flights and . . . Christ, they're never going to let me live.* A burst of energy made his skin prickle as the thrust from the engines pushed him back in the seat. *Whatever happens, I'm saying nothing.* He rubbed his wet hands on his pants and felt the shape of the lighter in his pocket. *I have to do this.* He tugged at the seatbelt as his chest tightened and pushed his head back. *Focus. It will be over in a few hours. One way or another.*

*

The hotel window stretched the length of the room. Wolfgang Kessler gazed down at the heat haze nestling between the seven hills of Rome. He looked out to the street and watched a black Mercedes pull up at the curb. The security guard held out a hand, but a tall, stooped figure thrust his cane from the back seat and knocked it aside. Erwin Reinhard stepped slowly out onto the sidewalk, his chin stuck in the air.

Kessler closed his eyes and pressed his forehead against the cool glass of the window. Montrose was history. He felt the blood pressure building in his neck and moved his head so that his cheeks pressed against the glass. In the old days Erwin Reinhard would have dealt with Montrose. No one would have been left alive. But the old man had come running to him.

In the near distance he could make out the Via Nableone and Reinhard's apartment. There was no point waiting any longer for the old man to die. The Russian and Chinese markets were now open. Glasnost and the rise of the yen had seen to that. And the networks and contacts were ready. The oil deal with the Afghans would bring in hundreds of millions of dollars. But Reinhard held access to wealth beyond the dreams of ordinary men. And his idiot of a son had provided the key.

He dabbed his face with a silk handkerchief then straightened his back and smoothed down his suit. He smiled at the thought of Kurt Reinhard on his knees before his father, pleading for the money to pay off the Cosa Nostra, who were expecting a quick return. With interest, to cover the loss of heroin to their market. Kurt Reinhard would find the money or his body parts would be feeding whatever fish managed to survive in the Tiber. Upsetting the Cosa Nostra made for a very short career.

And there was only one way that Erwin Reinhard could cover his son's loss at such short notice. His vault in Zurich.

He turned his back to the window. There would be no greater chance than this. The door opened. "*Ja?*"

The PA stood in the doorway, a shorthand notepad in her hand. "Herr Reinhard is here."

"Bring a hard chair." Kessler strode across the room as Reinhard shuffled through the doorway. "Erwin. Good to see you again."

"You too, my friend," replied Reinhard. "If only it was under better circumstances."

Kessler shook Reinhard's hand. The steely grip was gone. The old man was fading. "I'm honored you came to me. The old bonds still hold tight."

"I'm not a young man any more. I have no one else to turn to."

Kessler waved a hand dismissively. "You are my oldest customer, Erwin. My father spoke warmly of you until the day he died."

The PA entered with a dining chair and placed it in front of Kessler's desk.

Reinhard took her hand and lowered himself onto the chair. "He was a great man. He passed his bank to you and now I must pass my affairs to my son."

Kessler motioned the PA away and she headed for the doorway.

Reinhard waited until the door had closed, then spoke through gritted teeth. "Though this is not the way I wanted it to happen."

"I understand. Montrose is history. But let us be absolutely sure. Tell me again what he said."

"He was fishing, I'm sure of it. If they had proof . . ." Reinhard shook his head.

Kessler sat behind a long walnut desk. "First we must establish the facts. Kurt said the only man who saw him in the hotel corridor, however briefly, was Montrose."

"That is correct."

"And there was no CCTV?"

"Kurt said there was a way to avoid it. He is quite sure."

"But Montrose found his way to you very quickly."

"He traced the taxi that Kurt used. Straight to my apartment. Sometimes I despair of that boy."

"He'll make you proud, Erwin, one day. But for the moment . . ."

"For the moment we have the Cosa Nostra demanding three million euros."

Kessler shrugged. "Mere spending money for a man of your wealth."

"Perhaps. But you know everything I have is tied up in the oil deal. And the Mafia want their money in twenty four hours."

Kessler had no doubt. He had informed his Cosa Nostra contact to accept nothing less, or the son would face the consequences. "Ah, that is more of a problem. Let us deal with that first."

The mottled skin of Reinhard's knuckles became transparent as he squeezed the top of the cane to stop his hand from shaking. "It would take me weeks to liquidate my assets. In the current market I would lose a fortune. It's impossible. They know it's impossible!"

"They are not reasonable men, Erwin. But I'm sure we can come to some arrangement."

"You said you had a buyer? At such short notice?"

Kessler shrugged. "There are always ways to do these things. The contents of your Zurich vault will always attract buyers. The trick is in finding the right one. How long has it been now? Sixty years?"

"Or more. I think of it every day. But we cannot . . ."

Kessler recognized the bluff. Reinhard's vault had lay untouched for over seventy years, deep in the rock under his own private bank. They both knew there was no other choice. "I have been working on the options for your property for some time, for when the day eventually came. A specialist valuer is available. Then a simple trade. I was hoping to tell you soon, but we can bring things forward."

Reinhard let out a low, bitter laugh. "I should have known you'd be one step ahead. That was supposed to be Kurt's legacy. And to think it will be used to pay off some filthy tribesmen. And the three million euros?"

"When the valuation is complete, the money will be ready. The buyer is a customer of mine, who is, shall we say, cash rich."

Reinhard leaned forward on his cane, nodding vigorously. "It will work. But is it safe? If they appear on the market . . ."

"Times have changed, Erwin. China has an insatiable need for gems. The Russian market is wide open. Not only do they both understand confidentiality, they care very little for provenance."

"Of course, provenance." Reinhard gave him a wry smile. "That's something best avoided." He stuck out a hand. "Then we do it. Kurt will be landing in Zurich very soon."

Kessler felt the handshake firmer. The old man was

desperate enough to believe anything. All these years Kessler had been waiting for him to die, and what was about to happen might kill him after all.

CHAPTER 14

The remains of the in-flight meal lay on the tray.
All he'd done was push it around the plate and the
coffee had gone cold. The target was clear. That meant
there was only one plan.

*Zurich. Then Reinhard would be dancing to a
different tune.*

*But the Kesslers? Father and son? Where the hell do
they fit in? Just bankers? It doesn't matter. All I need
to know is that old Kessler is in Rome and the son,
Jacques, has never met Kurt Reinhard.*

Instinctively, he made to turn his head and look down
the aisle, then stopped himself for what felt like the
hundredth time. If Reinhard recognized his face from
the airport, he didn't want him making any connections.
Especially when Reinhard discovered that the pass was
missing.

The stewardess appeared by his side. "Shall I take
that away, sir?"

"Thanks. Say, are we landing soon?"

"On time for 14:30. Starting the approach now, sir."

He adjusted his watch to the correct hour and added five minutes. The old watch always ran a little slow and he gave it a rub for luck. It had seen his grandfather through the beaches of Normandy. A few bars of GI chocolate and a box of silk stockings had had some serious buying power when his Liberty ship sailed into Liverpool. He'd swapped the lot for a new British Army Omega wrist watch, made in Switzerland and stamped with the Broad Arrow of the War Office. The lighter and the watch were the only heirlooms his grandfather had passed on. Anything else was abandoned in the flight from Berlin.

He reached into his pocket and held the lighter in his fist, rubbing his thumb over the metal for a moment, then pulled out his wallet. In the clear plastic ID flap was a passport photo of a blond girl. He slipped the photo from the plastic and held it in his hands. A crease in the photo spread across her face. *Her 21st birthday. The day before the bus to the West Coast.*

He remembered the excitement in her voice. She'd met some guy with a private jet. Some hotshot businessman. He took good care of her, she said. He had connections in the modeling industry. No more money worries. She didn't say his name.

But the LA detective had told a different story. They find a good-looking girl, no ties. Promise her a modeling career, go to the right parties, take the right drugs, then reel her in. They were feeding her, the detective had said, and when she got hungry, she knew where to go. He'd seen it before. As soon as she was out of the country, they'd take her passport. Cocaine turned to smack. Smack cost more. More than she had. She was sliding. Wasn't long before her hotshot boyfriend became her pimp. Just the occasional john to start, and then more as the addiction deepened. Forced into porn movies in the Mexican suburbs and when the needle tracks started to show, the boyfriend sold her down the line.

Seems that the dealers at the bottom of the food chain were cutting their goods with animal tranquilizer. One night, one fix, and her heart had slowed to a halt. They found her on a bench near the docks. Someone had stolen her shoes.

You should have called. I would have come running. But pride was always your weakness. He tried to flatten the crease on the photo. *The last time I saw your pretty face.* Flakes of colored plastic fell from the crease onto his lap. *No. It wasn't the last time. That was in a morgue.*

A voice came over the P.A. "Please return to your seats and fasten your seatbelts."

The tension was tight in his chest as he buckled the seatbelt. A sudden panic made him catch his breath. *Maybe Richmond was right. Maybe I can't stop. No. Fuck them. Fuck every goddamn one of them, the scum-sucking dealers and the politicians who kiss their ass for power. I will not stop. This is over when it's over.*

He forced himself to exhale slowly then checked his watch and counted back the hours. *The CIA would know for sure when I didn't turn up at Lyon. Maybe they'd already organized a reception party. No, they couldn't know about Reinhard and Zurich. All I need is a little more time.* He tucked his thumbs into the seatbelt and screwed his eyes shut. *If they were waiting, there's not much I could do. Maybe say I was following Reinhard on my own initiative. Like the dead Afghans. Yeah, that'll go down like a burning Messerschmitt.*

And then tell them how I was set up? Against all the evidence? They wouldn't swallow it for a second. I'm a psychotic killer. They'd want to bury this operation deeper than hell. No. Spinks would personally dig my grave and bury me head first.

The plane shook as the wheels bumped and squealed on the asphalt. *I might make it out of Switzerland, but what the hell then?* He pulled a hand from the belt and rubbed his face. *They'll never stop looking for me.*

The plane stopped and turned to taxi to the terminal. *Unless I get the video. Reinhard started this. I'll finish it.* He peered out of the window to catch any waiting cars or police on the apron, but there was nothing.

"Welcome to Zurich," said the stewardess over the P.A. "Please keep your seatbelts fastened until we have come to a complete halt at the terminal."

The engines whined as they wound down and the plane stopped at the gate. The stewardesses came along the aisle holding the overcoats for First Class. Montrose took his Crombie and folded it across his lap then busied himself with his seatbelt. Reinhard grabbed his overcoat and pushed forward. Montrose stood up and lifted his leather bag from the overhead locker. Over his shoulder he saw Reinhard hurry out of the door, brushing past the stewardess and ignoring her smile.

Don't lose him. He stepped out onto the air bridge and began to match Reinhard's pace, then forced himself to slow down. *My cover is just another tired businessman. Time to start behaving like one.*

They emerged into a large passport control room, already busy with incoming flights from all over the world. There was no separate line for US citizens, but then there was no line for Europeans. *It looks like everyone is a foreigner to the Swiss, even their neighbors.* He spotted Reinhard in a line and joined right behind, wondering how they would make the mark.

Reinhard marched forward and presented his passport. The Customs Control Officer glanced briefly at his face, stamped the open page and called for the next passenger.

Shit, was that it? So much for the tip off. Reinhard was through.

"Next!"

Montrose placed his passport on the desk.

"Your business in Zurich?"

"Just a few days," replied Montrose.

"No, sir, your business in Zurich. What will you be doing here?"

"Excuse me, I'm a bit sleepy. Too many airports and flights." He rubbed his eyes for a moment, stealing time to think. "Just some business meetings."

"Very good, sir." The officer stamped his passport.

"Thanks." Adrenalin was starting to kick in.

Reinhard was heading for the line to the customs channels. Montrose's heart started to race and he stopped himself from wiping his damp hands on his Crombie. *If Reinhard got out of the airport, the deal would be on. Nazi pass or not.*

Relax. Looking nervous in a customs area wasn't a good move, and I'm in enough trouble already. Be cool. Yeah, it's not easy when you're walking into the lion's den and asking the big furry bastard for a fight.

Montrose turned into the 'Nothing to Declare'

channel then stopped dead just before he walked into the back of a man in a black overcoat.

Shit. It's him. Montrose hurried past the desk and bent down to check his shoelaces. He could hear the conversation. It didn't sound friendly.

"Your passport may have been checked, sir," said the customs officer. "But I am required to check it again. You are Mr. Reinhard of Rome?"

"You're damn well wasting my time," said Reinhard.

"Put your bag on the table, sir, and open it. Remove everything and place it to the side."

"Look, I haven't got time for this. I have a very important business meeting with one of the most senior bankers in Zurich."

"Yes, but I have plenty of time, and so do my colleagues. You will come with us."

"This is ridiculous! Your government will hear of this!" Reinhard pulled out his Blackberry.

The guard snatched it from Reinhard's grasp. "I'm sure they will. I'm not asking you, sir. We have been informed of an outstanding arrest warrant. I'm *instructing* you to come with us."

The blood pulsed in Montrose's neck as he fumbled with his shoelace. Two burly figures carrying latex gloves walked past. He stood up and hurried forward. The corridor turned into the main airside terminal. *Where the hell was the exit?*

He looked down the concourse past a line of duty free shops. *Yeah, like every other modern terminal, they make you walk through the shops before they let you out.*

Striding forward, he dodged around passengers, glancing at the displays as he passed. *One thing they don't stock is a nine millimeter and a case of ammo. I don't know what kind of situation you have to be in before you need a liter of Scotch and a ten pound bar of weird-shaped chocolate, but sure as shit, this isn't it.*

He quickened his pace. The illuminated sign for the taxi stand was dead ahead, but he only had euros. *If I use the company Amex card to buy Swiss francs, Interpol will know exactly where I am once they've checked the records. And they would.* To his right was a small boutique selling Swiss specialties, and in a rotating glass case, a display of Swiss Army penknives. *Better than nothing.*

"Hi, do you accept euros?"

"Of course, sir."

"I'd like one of those knives."

The assistant opened the glass case. "Which one, sir?"

Montrose glanced down the shelves. Some of them looked like they had enough gadgets and tools to strip down the Space Shuttle. "That one."

"The Explorer. Very good, sir. It has the screwdriver, scissors, a tool for removing stones from a horse's . . ."

"I'd love to know, but I'm in a big rush." He dropped a fifty euro bill on the counter, and grabbed the penknife. "Thanks for your help. Keep the change."

He turned into the main terminal and scanned the line of expectant relatives and chauffeurs holding name cards. Two men stood apart from the crowd, in the corner, one holding a large piece of card with 'Reinhard' clearly written in thick black pen.

One man held a chauffeur's hat and the other guy was the size of a house.

Montrose walked over and fixed his face hard. "I'm Reinhard. I take it you're from Kessler."

"I am Herr Shechter," said the big guy. "Head of Security for Herr Kessler."

Kessler. The Banker.

Shechter adopted a professional bearing, but his sheer bulk was menacing. He looked like he could stop a meteorite.

"Shall I take your luggage, sir?" asked the chauffeur.

"That won't be necessary." Montrose tightened his grip on the leather bag. "Let's go."

"This way, please, Herr Reinhard." The chauffeur headed towards the exit.

Montrose followed, noticing Shechter falling in behind. *Man Mountain knows what he's doing, which is more than I do.*

They walked in a line out into the bright afternoon sunlight of Zurich. The chauffeur stood before a Mercedes and opened the rear passenger door.

"We should be there in about twenty minutes, sir."

Shechter walked slowly around the car and got into the rear. Montrose stepped in beside him. The Mercedes pulled away smoothly from the curb.

Montrose patted the Nazi pass in his pocket then fixed his gaze straight ahead, searching for the road signs out of town. They soon approached the suburbs, the houses gaining in opulence as they got closer to the city. *Damn, this place could be crammed with wartime loot and no one would ever know.* The official version was to deny everything, but he knew that the Nazis had sold over a billion dollars of gold to the Swiss during the war. Gold stolen from the countries they had plundered, and gold from the teeth of Jews. *The Swiss said nothing, they just did the deal. Bankers to the Holocaust, they deserved that tag. How many other high-ranking Nazis had stashed their loot here? Sure as hell the Swiss weren't going to tell. Especially not the Americans, since they had accidentally bombed the crap out of them a few times. What was the name of the place? Schaffhausen? Some dork in the USAF trying to bomb a Rhineland chemical plant hadn't even managed to get the right country, never mind the right town, though not everyone had been convinced it was such a big deal, considering the Swiss were also selling arms and munitions throughout the war to their Nazi customers. Not much of a price for bankrolling the destruction of Europe.*

He took in the buildings as they flashed past. *This was how southern Germany must have looked before the Allied bombers took up landscape gardening from fifteen thousand feet.*

The broad boulevards soon led to the centre of the city and became a grid of arrow-straight streets, lined with grand facades bordered by medieval passageways. There was an endless array of small, shiny metal plaques on buildings, interspersed with expensive boutiques. Finance companies, international investment companies and sometimes just a name. All very discreet, but the place stank of money.

The Mercedes slowed almost to a halt before it turned left and entered a narrow alley at walking pace. Cobblestones rattled under the tires and medieval walls towered above on each side. The car stopped beside two huge wooden gates. A shiny brass plaque was fixed to the wall. *Kessler and Son.*

The gates swung smoothly open in a very un-medieval fashion, giving the impression they were backed up by something more substantial than wood. The Mercedes pulled into the graveled courtyard of a large town house. The high walls and surrounding buildings shielded it from the sun and Montrose could see bright chandeliers through the windows. A sunny morning and they had all the lights on. A cold chill stabbed his guts.

Holy shit, this is the heart of darkness.

CHAPTER 15

The huge oak gates swung shut as Montrose stepped from the car. A wall of ancient rough-hewn blocks of sandstone surrounded the courtyard. He reckoned they were about two feet thick and maybe fifteen feet high. There was no way out, except through the gates.

"This way, sir," said the chauffeur.

Montrose headed towards the house and up the steps of a grand portico, framed by marble ionic columns. The door was open. He followed the chauffeur into a hall then stopped for a moment, taking in the oak-paneled walls and a large carved fireplace where a log fire burned.

"Herr Reinhard!"

To his left, a tall, young man appeared from a doorway. *Expensive suit, happy smile. This had to be the son of the banker.* Montrose strode forward and offered his hand. "You must be Herr Kessler. A delight to meet you."

"Jacques Kessler, at your service. It's also a delight

for me, to meet the son of one of our most prestigious clients. Our family histories go back together many years. I am told that like myself, you were unaware of this, no?"

Montrose shrugged. "Well, it came as something of a shock, but then again, nothing about my father would surprise me."

"I had no idea he was keeping such a secret. It seems we have had an eventful and prosperous past, so I'm sure that bodes well for the future. Please come into my office." Kessler held out a hand towards the doorway.

"Thanks. You don't mind if we speak English? My German is rather rusty."

"Not at all! I took my degree at Oxford. After all, it's the international language of banking. Can I offer you some lunch?"

"Thanks, but no. I'd like to attend to business immediately." Montrose placed his leather bag on the floor. "I want to get our property over to the South African Embassy, and then perhaps we can sit down to eat. The food on the flight was appalling."

"So let's get this out of the way and we can enjoy a good meal. We'll have plenty to talk about. Do you have the identification?"

"Of course." Montrose pulled the Nazi pass from the inside pocket of his suit and shoved his passport down deeper.

Kessler carefully opened the faded card and examined the yellowing photograph. "I think you have the eyes of your father."

Then you're a fucking idiot. "So I've been told and I would like to think some of his ingenuity as well. We never stop learning from our fathers."

"They are great men. To be able to manage their affairs so effectively during the past troubles of Europe and still maintain a legacy for their sons."

What the hell are you talking about? "Absolutely. Let's hope we make them proud."

"I'm sure we will, Herr Reinhard."

Montrose tried his most convincing smile. The one that Sandie said made him look shiftier than a fox with a feather hanging from its mouth. "Please, call me Kurt."

"Thank you, Kurt. Now, perhaps I can show you to our vaults? I think you'll find them very interesting."

Montrose felt his pulse quicken. *Vaults? Just hand them over, for Christ's sake.*

Kessler crossed to a door in the corner of the room. "The bank has two sets of vaults. One is very modern and contained in another part of the building, for those who are impressed by high technology. However, your family box is contained in the original vault, built over six hundred years ago when the bank was established. It is reserved for our oldest clients."

He took a small key from his pocket, turned it in the lock then pulled open the door to reveal a bookcase. "A precaution from a few hundred years ago, created by one of my more entertaining ancestors. It's full of rare and valuable books to deter the opportunist thief." Kessler curled his fingers around the door frame. With a sharp click the bookcase swung back. "Rather melodramatic, no?"

"Very." Montrose peered into the gloom. A steep flight of worn stone steps led into darkness, tracked by a bronze handrail.

Kessler flicked a switch. Strip lights buzzed into life. "Please descend behind me, but do not touch the handrail at any time. If you do, the roof will collapse. A medieval device, but very effective. It is designed to stop anyone who manages to get past the door. Also, on the way down, there is what we call a 'thief-catcher', an irregular-sized step designed to catch an intruder unawares, causing him to grab the handrail. With obvious results."

"Quite ingenious." Montrose glanced up at the huge granite slabs lining the roof then followed Kessler through the doorway. *Do what you have to do. Play the game.*

"I will be silent until we reach the bottom, Kurt. It's best to stay focused."

With both hands holding the leather bag tight to his chest, Montrose started to descend, stepping carefully over the thief-catcher. Before him was a low stone corridor. He bowed his head.

Kessler turned his head and smiled. "I'm afraid our ancestors were a little smaller in stature, though not in wealth."

Spare me the guided tour. "Are there any more surprises waiting for me? Whirling blades or shark pits?"

"Ah, very good. No, just iron and stone from now on. We can't fool ourselves that any bank is impregnable, but when your vaults are set in solid igneous rock and you own the land for two acres on all sides, you can make breaking in so difficult that it becomes near impossible. But not impossible, you understand, that's when mistakes happen."

Like right now, although it might be me who's making a big mistake.

They stopped in front of an iron gate.

"Combination locks." Kessler spun two dials simultaneously. "Any other lock can be picked, including electrical. No matter what you see in the movies, you cannot hear the tumblers. These have been made by the finest Swiss watchmakers. Any interference and they lock permanently. They are very sensitive."

Tell me about it. Montrose tugged the cuff of the Crombie to cover his old Omega, then followed Kessler through the gate and down another narrow corridor which led to an arch containing a steel door.

Kessler spun a dial on the wall. The door slid silently up into the stone to reveal a small room carved out of solid rock. On each side were the polished steel doors of safe deposit boxes. "Your family box is middle and far right. Number eighteen. Turn the dial clockwise and counter-clockwise alternatively for each number. It will allow three attempts, after which you must wait for several hours."

Number? Montrose stared into the vault. *What fucking number?*

"I shall wait at the top of the stairs to give you some privacy. And remember the handrail. Don't touch it."

"Yeah, right. I'll remember." He pressed the identity pass between his fingers to stop his hand from shaking.

"One last thing." Kessler pointed to a dial on the wall. "This allows you ten minutes. If you are not out by then, the door will close automatically. Is that sufficient time?"

Montrose cleared his throat. "Yeah. Sure. This won't take long."

"Then I shall see you in the office." Kessler turned away through the arch.

Montrose faced door eighteen and held out the Nazi pass.

Spinks sat open-mouthed, scrolling through the police report on his screen. He knew enough Italian to work it out. He looked up from his desk, to see Ferguson standing before him. "You know?"

"I just heard. It's . . ."

"Jesus, I knew Richmond for over twenty years. What the hell are the Italian cops and Interpol doing about this psycho? Listen, whatever happens, we've got to shut this guy down before . . ." He jabbed a fat finger at Ferguson. "Shut him down. With extreme prejudice. You get me?"

"I understand, sir."

"What are you standing about for? Don't tell me you've found the bastard?"

"No, sir, we found his phone. It was in a taxi going to Interpol in Lyon."

Spinks sat bolt upright in the chair. "He's back in Lyon? Call the team. Get him!"

"No, sir. Montrose planted the phone in a taxi in Rome and then sent the driver to Lyon. It was tracked to a motel. We thought we had him. We sent in a SWAT team, tear gas and dogs. All we found was the taxi driver holed up with two Russian whores and an ounce of coke."

Spinks slammed his hand down on the desk. "Holy Christ!" A knock came at the door. "What the hell now?"

An assistant thrust a piece of paper through the door towards Ferguson and disappeared as fast as he could. Ferguson briefly scanned the message. "It's from American Express. He used his Interpol card to pay for a flight to Zurich."

"Give that to me." Spinks tore the message from Ferguson's grasp. "Check if he was actually on the flight. It could be a feint. My guess is he's back in Lyon. Maybe he thinks Interpol will look after him. And once we found the taxi driver, he thinks we'll look elsewhere. Check Zurich, but concentrate on Lyon. Now get out."

"Yes, sir."

"Wait. Have you heard from the director in Langley?"

"They're considering your request for more information. I'm told you can expect a phone call."

Spinks spread his hands on the desk. What the hell did Montrose know? One thing was for sure: when Montrose stopped using his cards he'd be off the grid. Tracking him across Europe would be impossible without mobilizing the entire CIA. The whole operation was supposed to be kept under the radar. Interpol had handed him the mother of all clusterfucks. Why the hell did they keep him on the streets? Montrose following the Afghans all the way to Rome and then shooting one of the bastards in the face should have been a clue.

He grabbed the phone. "Ferguson? Concentrate on Lyon. Leave Zurich to me."

The crime scene photos flashed up on the screen. "You sick fuck," he murmured as he scrolled through the files.

He shook his head in disbelief. Zurich? Would he really go there or was it a feint? The only reason Montrose would go there was to arrest Reinhard. Or beat his brains out to get a confession. And he was crazy enough to do it. But if the Swiss cops found him it could take days to cut through the red tape. Unless someone else got to him first. He scrolled through the on-screen report, looking for a phone number. The call was answered immediately.

"Ja?"

"Mr. Erwin Reinhard?" asked Spinks.

"Speaking. And you are?"

"I am a friend, Mr. Reinhard. I am aware that your son is currently traveling to Zurich, His business there is his own, but you should know that Connor Montrose is still unaccounted for."

"Please identify yourself."

Spinks leaned back in his chair. "As I said, I am a friend. There is some evidence that Montrose bought a ticket to Zurich. Do not approach him. He is now wanted for two vicious murders. Consider him armed and extremely dangerous. If fact, if I were your son, I would disappear until Montrose is off the streets."

"I ask again, who are you?"

"Keep him well away from Montrose. Or your son might be his next victim." Spinks replaced the receiver.

Erwin Reinhard dialed, his hand shaking. Kurt's cell phone wasn't picking up. The flight to Zurich should have landed.

Old Kessler had always dealt swiftly with anyone who got too close, but Kessler's son would know what to do. Montrose would be no exception.

"Kessler and Son."

"This is Erwin Reinhard in Rome. Get me Jacques Kessler."

"Please hold the line."

Reinhard heard a click when the call was transferred.

"Good afternoon, Herr Reinhard, this is Jacques Kessler. How may I help you?"

"Is my son with you?"

"My dear Herr Reinhard, I'm delighted to say that your son arrived a few moments ago and is attending to the matter of your private vault as we speak."

"I need to talk to him immediately."

"I'm afraid he cannot be contacted in the vault, it's too deep for a phone signal. Shall I ask him to call you on his return?"

Reinhard felt a tremor in his hand and pushed his palm flat on the desk. There was no guarantee that Montrose was in Zurich, but the information should come from Kurt. It would earn him some respect. "Yes, make sure that he does. I shall speak to him then. Goodbye, Herr Kessler."

"Goodbye, Herr Reinhard."

A dull ache spread across his chest and he bent forward for a moment until it eased, then took a small white pill from a silver box on the desk. Kurt was safe, he thought. Kessler's security would see to that. If Montrose showed his face, he would join the others at the bottom of Lake Geneva.

CHAPTER 16

The strip lights buzzed and crackled above him. Sweat gathered in beads on his upper lip. Montrose dropped the leather bag on the floor. Old Reinhard had said that only the pass was needed. *A combination number?* He stuck his thumb in the card and opened the fold. The black and white photo of Reinhard stared back at him.

Date of Birth? The handwritten entry was barely legible. But it would translate to numbers. *Dritte November, 1918.*

Six digits? That would be 031118. Make your move. He wiped his hand and placed his fingers around the dial.

Shit. It could be eight digits, if the year was written in full. 03111918.

His mind raced, and he glanced at the Omega. Eight minutes to go. His fingertips trembled where they rested on the dial. *Which one?*

Six digits. Got to be.

He blinked the sweat from his eyes and turned the dial clockwise to the first number, then the others in sequence. He stepped back. *Nothing.* There was a small button below the dial. He jabbed it with his finger. For a brief moment he hoped it wouldn't bring the roof down.

The door didn't move.

Christ, it had to be eight digits. He wiped his hand on the overcoat and tried again. He pressed the button and squeezed his eyes shut.

The door didn't move.

The blood was thumping in his ears. *What else is there?* He scanned the gothic writing. One row of letters and numbers. He knew enough German to work it out. *Army Serial Number. Ignore the letters. Just the numbers in sequence. 24695696.*

The Omega said five minutes to go. *Last shot.* He dialed the numbers. The door clicked and sprang forward a few inches.

He froze. No alarms. No steel shutters slamming to the floor. *Holy shit, it worked.*

The door swung open under its own weight. Montrose saw another handle in the middle of a dull steel plate. He tugged it towards him. The box moved smoothly outwards to reveal a canvas tool bag stamped with a faded *Wehrmacht* eagle. He pulled the drawer fully open and grabbed the bag, lifting it clear of the edge. It was heavier than expected and he placed it carefully on the floor.

Maybe two pounds of dope. Not enough for three mill. What the hell is it?

He knelt, popped the studs on top of the bag and tugged back the flaps. A bead of sweat rolled over his lip and fell amongst the diamonds.

Holy fuck.

There were thousands of them. He shoved his hand deep into the bag and pulled out a handful. Smaller ones trickled through his fingers, others rolled off his wet palm and dropped back into the bag. He chose one and held it up to the light, rolling it between his fingertips, mesmerized by the luminescence.

Get your shit together. It's time to go. He heaved the canvas bag into his own bag, covering it with his old clothes. The box slid silently home. He headed for the stone arch.

The air was still and cool as he stood at the bottom of the staircase. The sweat chilled on his neck. *Don't think about it. Just go.* He wiped the arm of his overcoat across his face and throat and looked up the steps.

Plan A. Shake hands and get the fuck out.

Plan B? Same as Plan A, only a lot faster and no handshake.

"Thief catcher," he murmured. The irregular step was about halfway up and, carrying the leather bag before him, he started the climb. Pausing before the step he threw his head back and exhaled long and slow, then carefully stepped over it and climbed to the top. He ducked his head and emerged from the bookcase.

Kessler stood up behind his desk. "Excellent. Glad to see you made it. I'm happy to report that we haven't had any fatalities in the history of the vault. Well, at least not down there."

Very funny. Let's see who gets the last laugh. "I'm sure. Now, let's get this business out of the way and then we can eat."

"Indeed, I know a bistro near here that serves the most delightful Swiss delicacies. Your car is waiting. I've called our contact at the Embassy and he's expecting you. Also, your father called."

Montrose's heart slammed against his ribcage. *Time for Plan B.* "Really? What did he want?"

"He didn't say, only for you to call him when you returned from the vaults."

The breath stopped in his chest and he felt the urge to run. He pictured the gate and the walls around the courtyard. He wouldn't get far. His grip tightened on the leather bag.

"Parents, huh? They let you go and then you find out you've been on a leash all along. Sometimes the old man can be a real pain in the ass. I reckon we can find the South African Embassy without his help."

Kessler smiled and shrugged. "My father is the same. I can't do a deal without him looking over my shoulder the entire time."

"I know the feeling. I'll call him when I get back. Give him the good news. Then we can visit that bistro you mentioned. I'm looking forward to it." He turned towards the door.

"Kurt, would you mind?' Kessler looked down at the leather bag. "I only found out about this yesterday. I'd love to see them. After all, it's the stuff of dreams, no?"

Shit. I really don't need this. "Of course." Montrose dropped the leather bag onto a nearby chair, pulled back the zip, then popped the studs of the canvas bag.

Kessler made as if to plunge his hand into the diamonds but stopped. "Magnificent!" he said. "Quite magnificent. Shechter! In here!"

Montrose felt his legs start to shake. He shoved a hand in his pocket for the penknife.

Shechter stood in the doorway. His shoulders brushed either side of the frame.

Fumbling in his pocket Montrose tried to flick out the blade, though he reckoned it would be as much use as threatening a killer whale with a cocktail stick.

"Shechter," said Kessler, "accompany Herr Reinhard to the South African Embassy and wait for him there. Kurt, I believe you've met Herr Shechter, our Head of Security."

Montrose let the penknife slip out of his hand. "I'll be back soon, Jacques," he said and closed the bag.

"I'll see you out."

Montrose followed the chauffeur into the courtyard, with Shechter close behind. This was a guy he wanted to keep at a distance. The chauffeur opened the rear door and Montrose threw his bag onto the seat. Shechter walked to the other side. *Dammit, he's going to get in the back again.* Montrose placed one foot inside, then fixed Shechter with a stare. "The hired help rides in the front," he said as he stepped into the car.

Shechter looked towards Kessler, standing between the columns of the porch, then walked around to the front passenger seat. The chauffeur closed Montrose's door.

Stopping himself from grabbing the bag and holding it to his chest, Montrose gradually moved it closer to his side. He watched Shechter get into the front of the car. *Was he armed? Of course he was, he could take that for granted. And now he doesn't like me. And all I've got to stop him is a Swiss Army penknife. Hell, I should have a Masters Degree in Hindsight and the Goddam' Obvious.* He slipped his hand into his pocket and fumbled for the penknife as the words of his CIA tutor came back to him. *If it looks like it's gonna get physical, don't take a knife to a gunfight or you'll need a shitload of chutzpah and a titanium ass.* The oak gates swung open and the chauffeur pulled out into the alley, taking a sharp right. "How far to the Embassy?" asked Montrose.

"Around three kilometers, Herr Reinhard," replied the chauffeur. "It should take around ten minutes."

Ten minutes? That's all? Better break out the chutzpah. Montrose settled back, trying to give the impression that he was relaxed as he braced his feet against the chauffeur's seat. *The fast traffic might be a problem. And Shechter.* The Mercedes reached the end of the alley and pulled into another narrow road with medieval passageways either side. *They would do – the more medieval the better – I could twist and turn and lose him. The guy was big, but maybe not too fast.* He looked down for a moment, remembering his brogues. *Shit. New shoes.*

Jacques Kessler watched from his office window as the gates closed, then sat behind the desk. He opened his father's box of cigars and took out a Cuban Montecristo, drawing it under his nose, savoring the honey and coffee notes.

A doorbell rang in the hallway. He listened for a moment and relaxed. It was too soon for the police to call with the terrible news concerning the death of a wealthy customer and two of his most respected members of staff in an armed robbery. He picked up a gold cutter, clipped the end of the cigar and slowly placed it in his mouth. The phone rang on his desk. "Jacques Kessler."

"This is Reinhard in Rome. Where's my son?"

The cigar dropped from his mouth and he sat bolt upright in the chair. "Ah, Herr Reinhard. Your son is on his way to the Embassy, he said he'll call you on his return."

"I see. Make sure he does."

"Of course, Herr Reinhard." The doorbell to the gate was still ringing. Kessler looked up with irritation as a secretary burst into the room. "One moment, please." He cupped the receiver in his hand. "What's going on? I'm in the middle of an important call!"

"There's a man at the gates, sir. He says he's Kurt Reinhard."

Kessler's mouth opened in surprise. "Where's the car?"

"There's no car, sir."

He jumped up from his seat then remembered the phone. "If you would please hold the line, Herr Reinhard." He handed the phone to the secretary and hurried from the room, ran through the hall and down the steps to the courtyard where a guard stood at the gates. "Let him in!" The gates swung back and a tall figure marched into the courtyard. Kessler folded his arms across his chest. "So, you're Kurt Reinhard?"

The man dropped his bag on the gravel. "Of course I am, you idiot. Why wasn't there a car at the airport? Who the hell are you?"

"You'll find out soon enough." Kessler turned to the guard. "Muller, take him inside. Shut the gates."

Muller pulled a gun from his coat.

The man spun around. "What the fuck is going on?"

"Inside." Kessler flicked his head towards the house and followed them both up the stairs to the front door.

Muller nudged the man into the office with the nose of the gun.

"So, you think you're Kurt Reinhard?" said Kessler. "Then perhaps you can explain to your father why you're late?" He snatched the phone from the startled secretary and thrust it under the man's nose.

"Father? What? No, I've just got here."

Kessler tore the phone from his grasp. "Herr Reinhard? Was that the voice of your son?" The blood drained from his face.

"Give it to me," Reinhard snarled. "Father, what's going on? I was almost arrested at the airport." His features twisted as he turned to Kessler. "Where are the diamonds?"

"They . . . they're on the way to the Embassy. In my car."

"Get them back. Now!" Reinhard jammed the phone to his ear. "Father?" There was no reply, only the sound of crashing furniture and his father struggling for breath. "Father!"

CHAPTER 17

The shoes were a good fit. They'd have to be. Montrose flexed his feet and checked the soles. The leather had hardly been marked and they'd be damn slippery. If the embassy district was like every other one he'd seen, it would be full of big houses and high gates. *Not what I need.*

Whatever. Make it happen. Time to leave these suckers behind. Then Old Reinhard would be like a fish on a hook. When the time was right, just reel him in.

The Mercedes turned into a wide boulevard as they left medieval Zurich behind. *Crap. Now it was open ground.* The traffic lights a few hundred meters ahead showed red. They slowed past a line of cars on the right, blocking Shechter's door. Montrose glanced in the rear view mirror. A taxi pulled up behind them. Shechter's door was only inches from a parked car. *The big bastard would never be able to get out. It had to be now.* He edged forward. To his right, he saw the taxi pull away. *Get ready.*

A phone trilled and Montrose jumped at the sound. He looked up. The traffic lights were green.

"The telephone, sir," said the chauffeur. "It's in the armrest."

Oh shit, maybe they've worked it out . . . The limo began to edge forward. Montrose pulled up the armrest and lifted a slim handset. "Y . . . yes? Kurt Reinhard here."

"Ah, Herr Reinhard. Jacques Kessler speaking. Just to let you know that your father called again and insists you call back immediately. I promised I'd pass on the message."

Bullshit. "Sure, yeah, no worries, I'll call him right away. The old man, eh? What can you do?"

"Of course, I understand completely. Now, if you would be so kind as to pass the phone to Shechter. I'd like a quick word."

I'll bet you do. Montrose glanced at the door handle. "Of course. It's for you, Herr Shechter."

Shechter's huge hand reached behind and took the phone. "*Ja?*"

The limo began to pick up speed. Montrose stared at the back of Shechter's head. *Maybe he's giving Shechter the good news. Maybe not.* Montrose pushed his feet apart and grabbed the door handle. *I'm not hanging around for the answer. Get ready.* He looked out of the windshield for a moment and saw the car in front brake sharply, stopping suddenly. The limo squealed to a halt too late and slammed into the back of the car.

"*Scheisse!*" The chauffeur threw the stick into park and jumped out. The car in front rolled forward a few meters and stopped.

Now! Montrose opened the door, but a car shot past and caught the edge, crashing the door shut again.

Shechter dropped the phone, drawing his weapon as he attempted to spin his huge bulk around in the seat. "Do not move!"

"Nein!"

They both heard the panicked cry of the chauffeur and watched as a man got out of the car in front, holding a silenced pistol. He shot the chauffeur twice in the chest and turned. He stood in front of the car and leveled the pistol at Shechter. Two shots pierced the windshield, hitting Schechter in the face and neck. A thick gout of blood sprayed the windshield from a severed artery, obscuring the shooter's view.

I'm next. Montrose leapt between the seats, grabbed the auto stick and pulled it into drive. Shots pierced the windshield, spraying glass and blood throughout the car. The car leapt forward and caught the shooter, slamming him onto the hood.

Montrose lunged for the door handle and kicked the door open. A car shot past and took the door with it. He dived out and tumbled onto the road, a shower of glass blasting over his head. He grabbed the leather bag and started running, his shoes slipping on the smooth paving stones. He glimpsed an entrance to a shopping arcade and ran over, careering through the door into a passageway. There were shops either side of him but he needed the cover of people. And an exit. He skidded to a halt on the polished floor. *Dead end.* He felt his legs shaking and squeezed them together to keep them still. *Make a move!*

There was a French restaurant opposite him. *It must have a kitchen exit for loading. It's got to.* He forced himself to walk over to the door. *Don't make a scene. You'll leave a trail.* The place was about half full. No one looked his way. *Get to the kitchens.*

He weaved past the tables to the rear of the restaurant but found only a high wall with a gaudily painted frieze. *Where the . . .?* He spun to his left. A white-coated man opened two small wooden hatches set into the wall and removed plates from a dumb waiter.

Downstairs. He saw a narrow staircase set into an alcove and ran down the steps, stumbling into a corridor. A waiter rounded the corner. "I need your help!" said Montrose.

"Monsieur?" replied the waiter. "Ah, the restrooms . . . "

"No, no. Not the restrooms." *Chill. This guy is not going to help if I look like trouble.* "It's a woman."

"A woman, monsieur?"

"Yes, my wife. She's just walked into the restaurant and I'm supposed to be in Berlin, not with the beautiful young lady at table two." Montrose pulled a hundred dollar bill from his pocket. "I need to get out of here."

"Ah, monsieur, of course." The waiter grinned and took the money. "Please follow me." He turned and led Montrose through a swing door to a noisy kitchen. There was an open loading bay at the end of the room and an alleyway beyond.

"*Merci!*" Montrose dodged past the staff and bolted through the doorway. He glanced back, but only the amused face of the waiter was looking his way.

At the end of the alley he emerged into a busy shopping street; cars crawling in the traffic and pedestrians ambling past. *Take a taxi here and I'll be a sitting duck.* Straight ahead there was another alley and a hundred yards down, past a crowd of shoppers, he could see cars speeding by. He crossed the street, pulling the leather bag up to his chest. The walk along the alley seemed to take forever. He'd know if he was seen. There would be a bullet in his back.

Who the hell was the shooter? The Mafia? Trying to take out Reinhard? No, can't be. They'd want their money first. Or maybe they know about the diamonds. But how could they? I only knew when I opened the vault. But someone was trying to take out Reinhard. Spinks? No way. They wouldn't have missed. Spinks would have had a team of goons, not some lone shooter. Or the banker? Kessler? And kill his own staff? He felt the weight of the bag. *No, it's got to be the Mafia. No one else is so fucking crazy. They must have an inside man. Christ, for this amount of ice, any one of them would do it.*

The alley opened into a wide boulevard lined with department stores. A taxi pulled away from the curb and Montrose stuck his arm in the air. "Taxi!" It swerved towards him and he jumped in. "Airport, fast as you can." He pushed the leather bag to the floor and slid down in the seat, pulling up the collar of the Crombie. The taxi swung out onto the street and joined the fast moving traffic.

"He's lost him." Jacques Kessler slammed down the receiver. "Muller, get the Chief of Police. Tell him . . . tell him a messenger has stolen a shipment of diamonds and a two man security team has been murdered. They are to use any force necessary. This criminal is armed and dangerous. I want the city locked down. Tell him that there will be a very substantial reward when the thief is apprehended. Give the necessary information but don't drag this bank into a scandal."

Reinhard advanced upon Kessler's desk. "I don't give a damn about a scandal. If you don't retrieve that bag there will be another murder!"

Kessler hid his trembling hands beneath the desk. "Herr Reinhard, you forget that this bank complied with the identification required. If you have any more threats, please do not repeat them in front of Muller. He is very loyal."

A vein pulsed on Reinhard's temple as he leaned over the desk. "Fuck Muller! Get the bag. Now!"

The secretary entered. "Herr Kessler, your father is on the line from Rome."

Kessler rose, ashen-faced. "I'll take it in the study."

CHAPTER 18

The taxi eased to a halt. It wouldn't be long before the airport was crawling with cops. *The place was ringed with CCTV. Just stroll in like all the other smartly-dressed businessmen. There were enough of those around. Needle in a haystack.*

The driver grunted when Montrose offered him a bunch of dollar bills, but there was enough to cover the fare.

Through the plate glass windows he could see a Bureau de Change. *I need cash, but if I use the Amex card they'll know exactly where I am. What the hell, they'll know soon enough. The transaction would make them concentrate on the airport. The more resources they have tied up looking for me, the better. Might buy a little more time. There is no way I'm flying again today. Sure, I might make it onto a plane, but wherever I land, Spinks would be there, hands extended, waiting to shake me warmly by the neck.*

He closed his eyes and felt a surge of strength. *Just go. Find a safe place. Then Reinhard will do exactly what I want.*

He pushed open the doors and strode across to the Bureau de Change, scanning the hall as he joined a line of Japanese tourists,. There didn't seem to be any unusual activity. *Maybe they hadn't called the cops. They'd have a hard time explaining all those diamonds.* He sneered at the thought. *Not a chance. Kessler's bank would call in the big guns and they'd slam the borders shut. If there was one thing the Swiss did well, it was pull together in a crisis. Their whole history had been one of self protection while surrounded by predatory European countries, so they knew how to look after themselves and tell everyone else to go to hell. After all, they held all the big boys' money.*

A young lady behind the glass beckoned him over. "Can I help you, sir?"

"Hi! Can I buy five hundred Swiss Francs on my American Express card?"

"Certainly, sir. May I have your passport and card, please?"

"Yeah, sure."

She checked the photo and swiped the card. "Excuse me, sir, but this card has been rejected."

"What? Damn, I must have gone over my limit. Never mind, I'll call the office and sort it out."

"No problem, sir." She pushed the card and passport under the glass.

"Thanks." He looked at the card for the benefit of the assistant, then turned back to the exit. *Spinks hadn't wasted any time. It wouldn't be long before some faceless spook in the cellars would work it out. I've got about a hundred bucks left. Once they work out I've been at the airport, they'll spend a good few hours trying to search the whole place and have a nightmare trying to get their hands on the passenger manifests. By which time I'll be gone. Unless they work it out.* He squeezed his eyes shut. *You can't change the past, only the future. Make sure you've got one.*

He pushed through the doors and into the sunlight. *Old Reinhard was still out there. Time to be the puppet-master. We'll see how he likes it when I'm making him dance.*

Above him were the signs to the long term parking lot and in front a waiting shuttle bus stood idling. He took a seat near the front and held the leather bag tight to his chest. The Swiss Army penknife pressed against his leg. He grimaced at the irony. *Might just be the thing to get me out of here.*

It was a short ride and he fell in with the other passengers as they struggled with their suitcases and shuffled into the parking lot. A large glossy map of Europe was mounted on the wall. The roads near the airport had been worn away by fingers, but the nearest border was France or Germany. *It's got to be France. If I have enough gas to get to Paris, I can pick up a train to the coast. That would work. Normandy – the port of Caen – near the D-Day beaches, then the ferry to England.*

But what about MI5? The CIA's favorite bitch. The Cousins would be watching. They'd always be watching. Paris was safe, but London was a different matter. The CIA setup in Grosvenor Square was the biggest outside of the States. It was going to be damn near impossible to stay one step ahead.

The leather bag weighed heavy in his hand. The diamonds could be stashed. *Maybe I should just bury them.*

No. I need them close by. They're my only bargaining chip.

He moved quickly along the line of cars. *Something old. The last thing I need is deadlocks and immobilizers. A French car would be best. The French always had to carry papers. It would work. Three years studying Modern Languages might be useful after all. I could do the mannerisms. Wave my arms and shrug my shoulders. Sandie always said I was a good mimic. More French than the real thing, she said. But this time I won't be trying to make her laugh.* He scanned the license plates. *Nothing. Next floor.*

As he reached the top of the steps, he spotted a yellow headlamp sticking out from behind a BMW. *Didn't the French use yellow?* He squeezed between the cars and saw a Renault sedan with French license plates. The fender and body panels looked as if it had been driven by Stevie Wonder.

He dropped the leather bag. The hood was cold and he prayed for some gas in the tank. He took out the penknife, pulled out the screwdriver attachment, then jammed it into the lock and wrenched it around. The lock popped up. He pulled open the door and threw the leather bag across to the passenger seat. Kneeling down, he made to tear away the plastic cover of the ignition switch and then stopped. *If it worked for the door, maybe I don't need to hot wire it.* He reached for the penknife, then turned the screwdriver to ninety degrees before hammering it into the ignition and twisting it sharply. The lights came on and the fuel gauge showed three quarters full. He jumped into the seat and grabbed a bunch of papers from the glove compartment. On top was a grey wallet with the car registration papers and a service record from a garage in Les Octrois. A map stuck out of the door pocket, folded open at the page showing the border. He found Les Octrois on the map and traced a route back towards the airport. *One hour. Maybe two. But Germany was the nearest border. There was no choice.*

Jacques Kessler stood in the doorway. "Herr Reinhard, would you join me in the study, please?"

"You'd better have some good news."

"That I cannot guarantee. My father wishes to speak to you."

Kurt Reinhard rose from the chair and followed him into a study filled with leather-bound books on shelves that ran from the polished stone floor to the ceiling. A phone with a loudspeaker sat on a long, walnut veneered table.

"This is Kurt Reinhard. Who am I speaking to?"

"Herr Reinhard, this is Wolfgang Kessler in Rome. Jacques has told me of the incident."

"Incident? Someone walks in and steals a fortune in diamonds from your bank and you call it a fucking *incident*?"

Jacques Kessler gestured to a chair. "This will not help the situation. Sit down, Herr Reinhard, my father has some other news."

Reinhard spun around, his eyes ablaze.

"Please, Herr Reinhard. It's about your father."

"What about him?" Reinhard dropped onto the chair.

"Your father," began Wolfgang Kessler, "was found in his apartments a few minutes ago. I'm afraid he is dead. A heart attack. I am so sorry."

Reinhard leant forward and covered his face with his hands. Jacques Kessler opened his mouth but snapped it shut again, suddenly realizing this was not the time for condolences.

"Find him," said Reinhard, without lifting his head. "And when you do, bring him to me."

The parking lot exit was dead ahead. Montrose stopped the Renault at the top of the ramp. He ruffled his hair and pulled his overcoat down at one side, then made a show of searching his pockets. Winding down the window, he drove forward to the booth. The bored young attendant continued to read a paperback. "Do you speak French?"

The attendant looked up. "A little, monsieur."

"I've lost my wallet. Over two hundred euros. I think a pickpocket took it. I just got in from Rome and I've no money or parking ticket. I've spent nearly an hour in the airport trying to sort it out. What can I do? I can't wait any longer, I have to get home. The police said you might know a way I can pay later."

"Do you have any way to pay, monsieur?"

"I only have this American money." Montrose took a hundred dollar bill from his overcoat. "Look, I know it's crazy, but this is all I have. I've got to get home, it's my wedding anniversary. All her family are coming. She'll kill me if I'm late."

The attendant looked at the money. "How long has the car been parked?"

Like you care, now you've seen the cash. "Only a week. Here's my passport and ticket from Rome." He watched the attendant look down at the Renault. *Yeah, who would steal this pile of shit?*

"That won't be necessary," said the attendant, taking the money. "Enjoy your anniversary."

"Thanks, thanks a lot." The barrier lifted, and he drove out into the morning sunlight.

Wolfgang Kessler ignored the view over the streets of Rome, lost in thought. The men in Moscow and London had made their position very clear. Montrose had to be taken out. By any means. Or Kessler's clients would disappear overnight to another bank.

He rubbed his face and turned back to the apartment. The thought of his peers gloating in the private clubs and restaurants around Zurich was insufferable. The network of fixers would put out the word. His reputation would be in tatters. Then they would come for him.

He watched a paramedic lift old Reinhard's body onto a gurney and cover it with a red blanket. His eyes fixed on the plain door in the corner of the room. Behind it was all the information he required. But without the bag from the vault it was useless. He jammed his mouth shut to stop himself from roaring in frustration. He heard the door close, and pounded his fist against the wall. Who was in that car? And where is the bag?

The phone rang on the desk. He snatched up the receiver. "Jacques? Have you found them?"

"Mr. Reinhard?"

"No, Mr. Reinhard is not here. Who is this?"

"This is a friend. I need to speak to him urgently."

Kessler listened to the static bouncing on the line. Whoever was calling was using encryption. "Then I'm sorry to inform you that Mr. Reinhard has just passed away. I believe it was his heart." His hand tightened on the receiver. "Who is this?"

"You know who I am. Just don't say my name, understand? Like I say, think of me as a friend. You might want to know that Connor Montrose is in Zurich. He's used a credit card at a Bureau de . . . "

"Montrose?" No, he thought, it couldn't be possible.

"Yeah, why am I getting the feeling this is news to you? Did Herr Reinhard keep that one to himself?"

"Herr Reinhard did not . . . "

"That's too bad. Really, you need to get on top of this. Montrose is just an IT geek. I'm disappointed, Herr Kessler. Looks like you need some assistance. I'm sending some details through to Reinhard's number."

Kessler heard a click behind him and saw the pages lying in the tray of a fax machine.

"You get them?"

Kessler jaw muscles spasmed as he tried to talk. "Yes. They . . . are here."

"Good. Listen. You're a capable man, Kessler. If you happen to find Montrose, I suggest you deal with him in any way you see fit. For example, if he was to meet with some unfortunate accident, I don't think anybody's gonna be too concerned, yeah? And like, right fucking now would be good."

The line went dead. Kessler dropped the phone and tore the pages from the fax machine. He scanned the details, his grip crushing the paper.

Montrose was an IT geek? The man had evaded every security force in Europe. Robbed his own bank and escaped assassination. No, Montrose was more than some technical assistant. He was a seasoned agent. A killer. And yet Spinks taunts me down the phone.

He scrawled across the first page, *'It was Montrose in the car. I am returning to Zurich. Call all the specialist teams. I want the very best.'* He packed the papers back into the fax and dialed the bank.

Reinhard sat at the table, his hands in his lap and head bowed.

Footsteps came from the hall. Jacques Kessler ran into the study, waving a sheaf of papers. "It was Montrose. Muller is sending his details over to the Chief of Police. We know he returned to the airport. The CCTV is being checked as we speak. Every airline is on alert and all the railroad stations. There's no way out of Switzerland for him. We'll have copies scanned and sent to all units in the city. When he's brought in, he'll tell us everything."

Reinhard stood up and grabbed the papers. The black and white facsimile of Montrose's face stared back at him. Jacques Kessler stood by the window, looking out so that Reinhard could not see his face.

"Montrose must have planned this. He got away, didn't he?" He turned towards Reinhard, confident that that the deception had worked. "Who knew where you were, Herr Reinhard? Who expected you to be in that car? What can you tell us?"

Reinhard jumped to this feet. "I can tell you if I was

in that car, I'd be fucking dead. Only my father and your father knew about the diamonds. Get Montrose!"

"We will. And then he can tell us everything."

"Oh, he'll tell us everything," said Reinhard. "Before I personally cut the bastard into pieces." He glared at Kessler, who looked down at the files on the table." What's wrong? You think I won't do it? Don't underestimate me, just because you don't have the balls."

Kessler shrugged. "I would never do such a thing. I leave that to my staff."

Montrose slammed the gear shift through the grinding cogs and into third. The houses had started to thin out and the rich, green countryside opened up before him. *Switzerland was part of the Schengen agreement. Open borders across Europe. No passport, no controls. But they also had the right to close the border any time they liked and the cops were allowed to pursue fugitives into another country. Reckon this might be one of those times.*

Fourth gear slipped in more smoothly. He scanned the map to his right then stuffed it in the door pocket. A French guy on his way home would have no need for that. The leather bag lay on the seat beside him. Any stop at the border was going to involve a search. A bag of diamonds in the car wasn't going to help. Ten kilometers to go, he'd have to stash them somewhere. On both sides of the road were patches of trees and open fields, leading to the hills. Without a spade, it was going to be difficult. If he was taken at the border, they'd only have to trace his journey. The diamonds would be worth the effort. *There's no time. I need them. The only way is to get out of the country. With the diamonds.*

He dropped the gear shift into third and saw the turning for Sudschwarzald. *The Black Forest. Germany was closest. The autoroute would be crawling with cops and an eye in the sky. It had to be the back roads and the cover of trees.* He took the exit and saw the long stretch of asphalt in front of him heading directly north.

A motorhome was parked at the side of the road. The driver got out and dumped some litter in a roadside bin. Montrose checked his rear view mirror and stood on the brakes. *The garbage cans. They were lined with plastic bags.* The man got into the motorhome, unscrewed a thermos and poured himself a drink.

The last thing I need is a witness.

A sign told him the border was around ten minutes away. Up ahead, a rig pulled into a rest area. Montrose snicked the transmission down the cogs, having finally mastered the stick shift, then swung off the road and parked behind the rig. On the shoulder were three large garbage cans. Walking down the side of the rig, he saw the curtains were drawn across the windows. The driver had gone to sleep. He headed to the garbage cans and opened the first, then stepped back from the acrid stench of stale food and cigarette butts. He tipped the contents into the next can and took the empty plastic sack over to the car and opened the trunk. There was nothing apart from some old newspapers, a bottle of water and a small tool wallet. He unwrapped the tools to reveal a pair of pliers and electrical tape. The tape could make the difference. He pushed aside the flaps on the canvas bag and stuck his hand deep into the diamonds, pulled out a handful and threw them in the stinking sack. He made sure that they were secure in a bubble at the bottom before twisting the bag and sealing it with tape, then moved around to the gas filler cap. There couldn't be any rips in the sack, it had to be smooth. He fed the plastic bubble through the hole, then carefully pulled it out. *It's going to take another sack.*

He worked hard and fast and his shirt stuck to his back despite the breeze. He leaned on the car and bowed his head. *This had to be done right now, before a whole world of shit came down.*

He took off his overcoat and threw it on the rear seat. The first sack was complete, and the long plastic sausage of diamonds lay in the trunk.

The last of the diamonds dropped into the sack. He gagged as he put the end of the sack to his lips to inflate a bubble, before twisting it off and sealing it with tape. They wouldn't lie on the bottom of the tank,with a float and he could hook the damn things out. The last thing he needed to do was block the fuel filter.

The traffic was light. No prying eyes. He carried both plastic sausages around to the filler cap, then fed them in slowly until they slipped down into the tank.

In the trunk the canvas bag was lying folded, its contents gone, and he picked it up and searched inside. A large envelope fell out. He pulled it open, taking out a sheaf of thin, yellow papers. Gothic German script stood out across the top and he scanned what seemed to be a list of names and numbers. It could keep. He slid the papers back into the envelope and threw it into the leather bag. He took a swig from the bottle of water and rinsed his mouth, then poured some onto his hands to wash his lips. He took a last look at the *Wehrmacht* eagle on the empty canvas bag and stuffed it into the bin. A small metal toy car lay in the corner of the trunk. He stood for a moment, staring at the toy car then picked it up. *An old Jaguar XJ-S. I've always wanted one of those.* He made to put it in his pocket, but stopped. *It's not mine.* He carried the toy to the rear of the car and jammed it down between the seats.

The stop had taken twenty minutes, but without it there was no way over the border. The motor rumbled into life and he slotted the gear shift into first. *Ten clicks to Germany.*

Jacques Kessler picked up the fine bone china cup and sipped the lukewarm coffee. The other cup was untouched. Reinhard's face was calm. Only the eyes burned.

All they could do was wait. The entire police force had been mobilized. Kessler stood up at the sound of footsteps running across the parquet of the hall.

Muller burst into the room. "Montrose was last spotted at the Bureau de Change in the airport where he was refused cash. It doesn't mean that he wasn't successful at a ticket desk, but there's no mention of a passenger with his name on any departing flight. All the gate staff have been shown his photo. So far, nothing."

"It's a trick," Reinhard grunted. "He knows the security at airports. And he knew he'd be seen there, so he's left a false trail and moved on."

Muller ignored him and looked directly at Kessler. "We've contacted all the taxi companies. Every driver has been informed by radio to report to a police officer. None have seen him except the taxi that took him to the airport, and he was carrying a bag."

Reinhard stood up. "Then he's taken a car or gone to the railroad station. Even a thief can take the airport bus back into town. Think about it. The last place we would look is Zurich."

Muller turned towards him. "Every hotel is being checked. There are policemen at all the bus and railroad stations and all the taxi stands. CCTV is being monitored in all parts of the city and every train leaving Switzerland has two policemen on board. If he has made it out of Zurich, he will be found. The autoroutes are being patrolled by cars and helicopters and traffic is being stopped at the border. The police are distributing copies of his photo."

"Then we'll find him," said Kessler, as if to convince himself. "It's only a matter of time."

Reinhard stared at him, but said nothing.

CHAPTER 19

The Swiss border post was dead ahead. There were no cars waiting. His grip tightened on the wheel. Two guards emerged from a booth and stood in front of a red and white steel barrier. They had nothing to do but look at him. *Maybe a quiet crossing wasn't such a good idea.* A Swiss Police BMW was parked by the side of the booth. Low slung and fat tires.

That's an M5. Faster than a Ferrari.

The Renault slowed to a halt. One of the guards approached while the second took a good look at the French license plate of the Renault then pulled out a cell phone. Automatic weapons hung at their side. Behind them was Germany and a clear field of fire for about a quarter of a mile. "Don't even think about it," he murmured, and wound down the window.

"*S'il vous plaît, monsieur*, shut off your engine and step out of the car."

"*Certainement.*" The penknife was still in the ignition. Montrose leaned forward and jerked it free, then cupped it in his hand. *The guy with the phone. License plate check.*

"Your papers, please."

"Of course." Montrose slipped the penknife into his pocket and made a search of his jacket. Picking up the overcoat, he stuffed his hands deep into the pockets then dropped it on the driver's seat. He shook his head and walked quickly to the rear of the car and opened the trunk. Boots crunched on the gravel as the guard approached. "Putain de merde!" said Montrose, and rummaged in his leather bag.

"You have a problem, monsieur?" The guard had a thick Germanic accent. His French was good, but not perfect.

"It's my identity card. I must have left it at home. It's probably sitting on my kitchen table. Merde!"

"If you are going to France, why are you taking this road?"

"I heard at the office that the access to the autoroute is completely blocked. Some security alert. I thought I'd save time going through here. It's our anniversary tonight, ten years of blissful marriage. Or not, if I don't make it home in time."

The second guard approached with his cell phone in his hand, checking the screen. "What is your name, monsieur?"

"De Villiers. Luc de Villiers."

"Can you show me the papers of your car, monsieur?"

"One moment." Montrose leant into the car and opened the glove compartment. "They're in here somewhere," he said, rummaging around, then pulling out the papers.

"I have to search your car," said the first guard.

"Of course. What's all this about? Did someone break out of jail? The border barrier is usually wide open."

"Just a security check. We do them from time to time."

Montrose tucked the garage invoices inside the log book and handed them to the guard.

"Where do you live, monsieur?" The guard began to flick through the papers.

"Les Octrois. South of Mulhouse."

"And the address?"

"72 Rue du Duc D'Anjou."

"Open the hood of the car."

"Certainly." The only European car he'd ever driven before was a Mini in London, and he'd never had to lift the hood. Montrose reached under the steering wheel and groped around. "I think it's down here. I never look under the hood myself. I leave that to my garage."

"Do you know a good garage in Les Octrois?"

Nice try, fella. "Yes, Calvert Motors in Rue Barry. They're not bad. Mind you, I think they stiffed me for an oil pump last month. I'm not convinced there was anything wrong with the original."

The second guard tapped the screen of his cell phone.

The first guard flicked through the papers as Montrose's fingers found a lever and he gave it a sharp tug. The guard slipped his hands under the hood and released the catch, then held the hood in the air and looked around the engine bay. Montrose saw the fine layer of oily dust around the engine block and air filter. Anybody trying to hide something would leave fingerprints, but there was nothing. The guard dropped the hood.

Montrose walked to the rear of the car, glancing at

the clipboard of notes that the guard had placed on the roof. One handwritten word stood out. *Montrose*. His guts turned to jelly and he threw out a hand to support himself against the car.

He forced himself to keep on walking, then leaned against the trunk. *Stay cool, cowboy. If they had worked it out, you'd already be face down in the gravel.*

The second guard removed the spare tire and gave it a hard shake.

The passport. If they search the Crombie, I'm done. "Did you discover any contraband?"

"Just normal procedure, monsieur." The guard replaced the tire and closed the trunk. "Do you mind if I lift the seats?"

Montrose glanced at the guard's cell phone screen, and saw he'd Googled the garage. "Be my guest, if you know how. Apologies if stinks a bit, my son gets car sick." He didn't know what to do with his hands so he shoved them in his pockets.

The guards moved to each side of the car. One took his overcoat and gave it a shake, then dropped it on the rear seat and helped the other guard pat the front seats. They leaned into the back and popped the cushions from their mountings, then repeated the procedure, pushing hard into the fabric. The first guard retrieved the toy car from between the seats.

"Very thorough," said Montrose. "I've been through the border many times, but I've never seen a real search. I'll bet you find a lot of stuff that people have lost!"

The guard closed the door and handed over the toy car.

"Thanks. You know, I don't even remember buying this. Kids, eh?"

"That will be all, enjoy your evening."

"Much appreciated." Montrose gathered the papers and shoved them in the glove compartment, then stepped into the car.

The guard leaned into the window. "One last thing. Which road will you be taking to your home? Where was it again?"

"Through Mulhouse to Les Octrois. I'll take the E54 then get back on the autoroute. I should make it home in time for the party to begin." Montrose held the penknife below the door and flicked out the screwdriver.

"Have a safe journey, monsieur."

The barrier lifted.

"Thanks." His fingers found the ignition slot. He pushed the screwdriver in and twisted. The motor rumbled into life and he crunched the gear shift into first.

In the rear-view mirror the border post slipped out of sight and he slammed the stick into third. *There was only one way the Swiss could have got my name. Interpol and the CIA have declared open season on my ass.*

In the distance the Black Forest spread up and over the low hills and stretched to the horizon. He floored the throttle, ramming the stick up through the gears and throwing the car around the bends.

A tight pressure squeezed the breath from his lungs. *What now? I'm on the run from the biggest spook agency on the planet. If Reinhard doesn't play ball, I'll have to hide. For the rest of my life.* "Yeah," he murmured, "Good luck with that, you fucking idiot." His hands tightened on the wheel as it hit home. *Not just Langley. It wouldn't be long before every cop shop in Europe was looking for a psychotic murderer. Yeah, and a diamond thief. If it all went wrong, Reinhard would catch up with me. The CIA would be a picnic compared to those psychos.*

Signs for France appeared in the distance and he swung left for the road to Mulhouse, then dropped a gear and pointed the Renault at the apex of the bend.

It was a long way to Paris.

Spinks replaced the phone, the static from the encryption still buzzing in his ear, and felt the adrenalin thumping through his veins.

Montrose was lucky to be alive. The chair frame squeaked in protest as Spinks' bulk rocked back and forward. Both the Director and the Senior Risk Analyst hadn't taken long to work out the worst case scenario.

He chewed his lip as he worked out the next move. The thought of Montrose standing up in court was unthinkable. The bastard was one of only ten people in the whole of the US who knew the full scope of the black ops flights from Mexico. All the flights from Pakistan, Afghanistan and the Gulf. The Muslim conclaves of Eastern Europe. Or the heart of the EU, the secret facilities in Poland and the UK. There was no Guantanamo for these passengers. Just a black cell in the hills across the border, south of San Diego, and when they had finally given up their secrets, a grave in the desert.

Spinks wiped his face on his shirt sleeve then buried his head in his hands.

What else had Montrose seen? The analyst had spent

all day double-checking the files. How deep did he go? The files had contained the history of the flights from South America in the eighties. The C130s that had landed, full of Argentinean dissidents for interrogation, then flew home with a full human cargo, bound in chains, over the ocean, to land empty. And the Learjets full of cocaine from the Venezuelan Generals to fill their private warehouses in Miami, in support for the putsch on Hugo Chavez. The DEA had been ready to strike when they found out the warehouses were rented by Langley.

The Director had been very clear on what was to happen next.

Ferguson knocked and stuck his head around the door frame.

Spinks stood up. "You better have good news, 'cos I am sick of this shit. Langley wants Montrose shut down. Period."

Ferguson swung the door closed behind him. "There's been a shooting in Zurich."

Spinks jumped to his feet. "Jesus! Who? Did they get Montrose?"

"No. Montrose shot up a bank car from Kessler's bank. Two security men dead. Then the Swiss lost him."

"You fu . . . " Spinks came out fast from behind the desk, advancing towards Ferguson. "You better be joking."

Ferguson held out his hands. "It's straight from our team in Zurich. It looked like a real professional hit. He also stole whatever the guards were carrying. Could be cash or gold. Rumor is that Montrose was targeting Reinhard, but he wasn't in the car."

Spinks held his head in his hands for a moment then

sat on the edge of the desk. "Fuck Reinhard. What about Montrose?"

"They tracked him to the airport, searched the whole place and all the flights, but he wasn't there. Turned out he stole a car and headed for Germany."

"Germany?" Spinks left to his feet. "We've sent the Afghan there for specialist treatment."

"The Afghan?"

"Keep up, you idiot! The guy that survived Montrose's bullet is the brother of the Afghan Oil Minister! Half his skull was left in a hotel corridor and his life is hanging by a thread. We've sent him to the best brain surgeon in Europe. And that's in Berlin. It's no secret. Half the Diplomatic Corps know about it. And now you're telling me that this sick fuck Montrose is in Germany? When did he cross the border?"

"About an hour ago."

"An hour . . . Call the German team and . . . Holy Mother of God, he's going to finish off the Afghan."

"Sir, I'll call Berlin . . . "

"Lock the place down! And get on to the German cops, tell them he's wanted for murder in two countries. Don't mention anything else, understood? He's an hour inside the border. Tell them he's armed and they can shoot on sight. Whatever it takes. Then get me a flight to Berlin. If Montrose makes it to the Afghan or the hospital, there'll be a bloodbath."

CHAPTER 20

The engine started to cough as Montrose passed the Porte d'Orléans. The fuel gauge had been buried in the red for some time. The diamonds would be lying on the bottom of the tank. There had been no point making a float for the sacks, there was nothing left to float on. *The car has to go.*

He glanced down at the ashtray beside the gear stick. There had been no smell of cigarettes when he got in, so perhaps the owner was the only man in France who didn't smoke. He popped open the lid of the ashtray to reveal a handful of coins.

Old Reinhard will do what he's damn well told. The Cosa Nostra will be closing in on sonny-boy. That should focus his mind. He's got too much to lose. Yeah, and I don't? Whatever happens, I've got to stay under the radar until I get to Reinhard.

The Renault slotted into a line of traffic at the lights. He rubbed his face hard and felt the tension slacken in his shoulders. *It's good to be back in Paris.* Worst case scenario, he could hide out for a while then head for the coast. He knew the streets and the cheap hotels around Clichy and the Moulin Rouge where no questions were asked.

The lights changed. The Renault edged forward. *The cops would work out I've made it over the German border. Don't matter. I ain't there.*

The engine spluttered and missed a beat. He turned into the main drag of Boulevard Raspail. The Parisian rush hour had started to kick in. There was a gas station to his left and he slowed down, swung into an alley next to the pumps and pulled over. He took the coins from the ashtray and held them in his hand. Apart from those, all he had was some euros and two hundred dollars, stuffed in the back of his wallet. A trip into town to change the money then get back to the car was out of the question. By that time, the traffic would be solid.

Then what? He cut the engine. *A few hundred bucks won't go far.*

Unless there was a way to get his hands on more cash. He ripped the penknife from the ignition. *I've got a gas tank full of diamonds. Could I sell one? No, I need a pawnbroker. The dodgier the better. They won't ask questions. But word was gonna get out. Damn risky. Yeah, got any better ideas? Just one diamond. That'll get me enough.*

He got out and opened the trunk, then pulled up the liner and rapped his fingers against the bare metal of the gas tank. It must hold about forty liters, and it didn't look like there was anywhere he could get enough water to float them out. He dropped to his knees and stuck his head under the rear of the car. There was nothing to cut through the metal, and he wasn't going to ask a mechanic to use a cutting torch without blowing him and the garage through the roof. The car was going nowhere. The jack and tire lever lay at the side of the trunk. He could hammer away at the tank for hours, but it would be pointless. The muscles in his neck tightened as he stood up and looked over at the gas station. The grass around it was bordered with jagged rocks, dug into the earth. *The rocks. It could work.*

Taking the wheel wrench from the trunk, he loosened the nuts on the offside rear wheel, then pushed the jack under the hoisting point and began to crank hard until the tire was a few inches clear of the road. He undid the nuts from the wheel and rolled it to the curb, then crossed to the gas station and dug the screwdriver around the edge of the sharpest rock. Wrenching it from the turf, he maneuvered it under the car, turning it until the jagged point was below the gas tank.

This is going to be noisy. Pedestrians hurried across the main street without giving him a second glance. He placed his hands firmly on the roof and began to rock the car on the jack, then pushed hard. The car toppled off the jack and crashed onto the road. The jagged rock punched through the gas tank, and the fumes blew out with a *whoosh*. Pulling the jack to the side, he spun the lever to wind it down, then jammed it under the hoisting point and started to crank once more. The metal screeched as the rock tore out from the tank and dropped to the road. He stuck his head under the car and saw a fist-sized hole in the tank. He rolled up his shirt sleeve and shoved his hand inside. The gas stung his arm where it scraped against the ragged metal and spreading his fingers wide, he brushed against wet plastic. He turned and looked under the car to the end of the alley, watching the feet of pedestrians rushing past. *I'm just a guy fixing a car. No one gives a shit.*

Curling his fingertips around the edge of the sack, he moved it towards him and out of the tank. It was untouched. He pushed his hand in again. *Nothing.* Shifting his weight forward, he slipped his arm in past the elbow and reached the second sack, then gently pulled it out onto the road. Both sacks looked intact. Cradling them in his arms, he carried them to the trunk. The gas vapor stung his eyes. He dried off the plastic with some newspaper, but it made little difference. There was no way he was going to blend into the crowd carrying a bag reeking of gas. Wrapping the sacks in the last of the newspaper, he placed them in the leather bag, closed the zipper and laid his Crombie on top, then replaced the wheel. Grabbing the leather bag, he threw the jack in the trunk, slammed it shut and headed for the gas station.

Montrose passed a display of chocolate and cookies on the way to the cash desk and his belly gave a plaintive rumble. He hadn't eaten since he'd picked at his food on the flight in from Rome. Adrenalin wouldn't last for ever.

"Please," Montrose said, barging his way to the front of the line. "I need to use your restroom."

"It's for customers only."

"Look, I have a stomach upset, I really need to go." He caught his reflection in a security mirror at the rear of the cash desk. The face staring back at him was pale and tired.

"Here's the key."

"Thanks."

*

The stench in the tiny room was overpowering. He locked the door and dumped the leather bag on the floor. He jammed the plug in the sink and turned the taps then looked at the stinking hole in the ground. This was a nuclear nation and they still used medieval toilets. He hung his jacket and Crombie on the door and took the plastic sacks and held them under the water. His fingers tore through the plastic. Diamonds spilled out and sparkled at the bottom of the filthy sink and he worked along the sack until there was nothing left. He threw the empty sacks into the hole in the ground and pulled the chain. A measly trickle of water flowed from the stained pipe. Picking up the grimy soap, he washed the gas from his hands and arms then spread his old shirt over the bottom of the leather bag. He scooped handfuls of diamonds onto his fresh shirt, wrapped them up and dumped the sneakers on top.

Taking a few euros from his pocket, he snatched up the leather bag and pulled open the door. In front was a payphone and a tattered phone book hanging by a chain. He dropped the bag at his feet and grabbed the phone book. Half of the pages were torn out. *Guess they run short on toilet paper. What's the word for pawnbroker? Try the pages beginning with 'P'.* He flicked through until he saw adverts accompanied by a motif of three golden balls. *Prêteur.* He scanned through the names. *Adubi– that's got to be Arabic. Paris was full of North Africans. He'll do.*

His back ached as he stood up and he could feel a blister swelling on his heel where the edge of the shoe had started to cut in. It would have to wait. He had an appointment in the Ile Saint-Louis.

*

The train began to pull away and Montrose counted the stops to Saint Michel on the map stretched along the top of the carriage windows. He held the leather bag closer to his chest.

The names. The envelope. He pushed his hand into the leather bag, past his shirt bulging with diamonds and pulled out the envelope from underneath. The thin, yellow sheets crackled with age and became transparent under the harsh lights of the carriage. He scanned the text. It seemed to be a list of Swiss banks with a column of numbers beside them. He flicked over to another page. The heading simply read Antwerp. A list of account holders' names and numbers. Beside them was a column of figures. They were in Swiss francs. Millions of Swiss francs.

It struck him like a knife in the chest. *All the names are Jewish.* He skipped a paragraph of German at the bottom and read the signature.

Heinrich Himmler.

The names of the dead. The diamonds were tarnished by blood.

His hands shook as he slid the papers back into the envelope. The train began to slow. Signs for Saint Michel flashed past the window. He stuffed the envelope deep into the leather bag. *Not just the diamonds. An unbelievable fortune. And the Swiss banks had been hoarding the cash all along. Over forty years of interest. It could make the diamonds look like chicken feed.*

The carriage doors opened and Montrose followed the throng of passengers shuffling out of the station, emerging into the afternoon sunlight. The exit led onto the left bank of the River Seine, the *rive gauche*. Home of artists and intellectuals, bookshops and café life. Climbing the steps, he emerged on to the quay and the breeze from the water brushed his face. He laid his hands on the cold stone wall, staring at the wide ribbon of sluggish brown water. It was just as he remembered, the river leading to the coast and across the sea to England.

He kept a tight grip of the leather bag and stood back against the quay. Stretched in front of him, the quay wall was lined with green, weather-beaten boxes belonging to the booksellers. The racks held a motley collection of old newspapers, magazines and dog-eared books, all wrapped in cracked yellow cellophane to shield them from the sun. Browsing shoppers filled the sidewalk. He glanced at a café across the road where waiters were finishing up and stacking chairs on the terrace.

To his right, a small band of tourists pointed at a large street map. He peered over their shoulders. Rue Lamont was clearly marked on the south bank of the Ile Saint-Louis, but from Saint Michel the view was hidden behind Notre Dame. Keeping a tight grip on the leather bag, he weaved past the tourists and strode down the quay, then crossed to the Quai de Montebello.

The Ile Saint-Louis came into view, and he stopped before the Pont de l'Archevêché. To his left the towers of Notre Dame rose into the sky.

Turning his back on the river, he ran over to the other side of the street. There was a café on the corner where he could keep a lookout across the Seine. He searched in his pocket for the remaining coins. There was enough for a few coffees. He threaded his way through the zinc-topped tables, calling out to the waiter. *"Un espresso, s'il vous plaît."*

The waiter nodded and disappeared inside the café.

Montrose tucked the leather bag between his legs and looked out over the river. Rue Lamont ran along the quayside, lined with expensive terraced apartments facing onto the water. The waiter returned with a small cup and saucer which clattered on the table.

Montrose took a sip of the strong black coffee. Traffic flashed past to a soundtrack of blaring horns. It seemed every control lever in a French car was connected to the horn. He stared down at his cup. *As soon as I use a credit card to buy cash, they'll pinpoint me right away. They'll be all over me like a rash. There's no other way.* He leaned over towards the tourists. "Excuse me, can I have a look at your A to Z?"

"Sure, buddy, you lost?"

"No, I've got an appointment, I want to find the right street." The map was open at the page for the Ile Saint-Louis. Montrose traced his finger along the Rue Lamont. Number 69 was clearly marked at the end of the street. *Just one diamond. That's all I need.* "Thanks, I know where I'm going now."

Dropping a few coins on the table, he squeezed between the parked cars and ran over the crossing, narrowly avoiding becoming roadkill. Parisian drivers didn't stop for pedestrians. They just hit the windshield wipers. These were people who saw traffic laws as vaguely interesting suggestions.

Montrose stopped at the wall facing the Ile Saint-Louis. On the river, a *bateau-mouche* crammed with tourists slid through the murky water, a ripple of flash bulbs popping when they passed Notre Dame. To his left was a telescope mounted on a steel pillar, pointing to the Ile de la Cité. He pulled out a euro from his pocket and slotted it into the machine, then twisted it right and panned across the centre of the island to Rue Lamont. Number 69 was on the corner. He moved the telescope up and saw two windows in the block on the first floor. One was closed and the other open. An old woman holding a cloth appeared at the open window for a moment, then disappeared. He dipped the telescope to the door. Three gold balls hung lopsided above the window. *Mr. Adubi lives above the shop.* A glass door was next to a window, packed with a variety of objects. He swung the telescope to the right, but couldn't see the east side. There had to be more windows, facing on to the street around the corner.

Montrose grabbed the bag and headed for the Pont de l'Archevêché.

Dodging a few tourists, he picked up the pace past the gardens behind Notre Dame, then over the bridge to the Ile Saint-Louis. There was little traffic on Rue Lamont and he hurried past a line of badly parked cars.

A dented trombone, a few scratched violins and a stack of old electric guitars filled the shop window. Along the bottom was a display of cheap jewelry, and china figures. *It's the right place.* A tray of old digital watches lay in the corner of the window. *I had one of those at college. Another few years and they may be worth something.* He pushed open the door. A bell tinkled above him and he saw the figure of an old man in a back office behind the counter. The door closed behind him with a thud and rattled loosely in the frame.

The old man emerged from the office and stood with his hands on the counter as Montrose approached.

"*Bonjour.* I have something I wish to pawn." Montrose rolled the dull diamond between his fingers as he stood before the counter.

The old man's eyes fixed on the diamond.

"I'll be honest, I've no idea if it's valuable."

Pulling out an eye piece, the old man held out his hand.

Montrose placed the diamond in his palm. The skin felt like parchment on the tips of his fingers.

"Very interesting, monsieur." He gripped it between his bony fingers and held it up to the light as he pressed the eye glass close.

"It's been in the family for years, but we've never been sure if it's a real gem or just a semi-precious stone. But, I have a little cash flow problem and I thought I'd ask."

"Hmm, cash flow problems, that's what we're here for." The old man rolled it around in his fingers. "It is indeed a diamond."

"Really? Wow. My grandmother was right. I always thought she was a bit crazy. Maybe not so crazy after all."

"I can say, monsieur, she had very good taste. It is only half cut, and unpolished, but I believe it may be flawless."

Shit. "That's good, yeah?" *You sound like an idiot.*

"It's more than good. It could be very valuable." He removed the eye glass and looked down at the diamond for a moment. "I haven't seen this type of cut for a long time. Very common in the thirties but it's difficult to tell."

"I'm not too worried, as long as it can get me some cash for a few weeks, until I get back on my feet."

The old man nodded. "Just let me check something,

monsieur. I'll have a look at some samples in my catalogues." He placed the diamonds and eye glass on the counter, then turned back in to the small office.

Man, just give me the cash. I couldn't give a damn what cut it is. He stood for a moment and looked around at several ancient clocks hanging on the wall, all ticking at different intervals. *Tempus fugit, old man.*

A dull bell sounded from a grandfather clock behind him. Montrose turned. Through a cracked glass door, he watched the pendulum swing lethargically to and fro, emitting a 'thunk' at every swing. Each movement seemed to be a Herculean effort.

The sound of a muffled voice made him turn back. *Is he on the phone? Who the hell is he calling?.* He glanced through the gap between the hinges of the door, and saw the old man hunched over a desk. *Is he speaking German? No. Yiddish!*

A metallic rumble came from behind. Montrose snapped around and saw the shutters on the window rolling down. He snatched up the leather bag and leapt over the counter, then grabbed the handle to the back office door, wrenching it from the old man's grasp as he tried to slam it shut. "Aw, for fuck's sake!" He seized the phone and slammed it down. "All you needed to do was give me the cash!"

The old man backed into a corner, terror in his eyes. "Get out of here!"

"And how am I going to do that? You just closed the shutters, you old fool."

"I'll call the police!"

Yeah? So, if that wasn't the police on the phone . . . "Just empty the till and I'm gone. You can keep the goddam' diamond."

"I will not take it. I know where it comes from!"

"Yeah, so do I. So that makes you, me and whoever was on the phone." Montrose picked up the cash register and angled it around, then dropped it so it would land on its edge. It crashed to the floor and the cash drawer sprung open. Montrose scooped up the bills, and saw the butt of a small revolver hidden underneath. "That's not smart."

The old man stood up straight. "Kill me. But I will not let you go."

Montrose opened the chamber and emptied the bullets onto the floor. *Got to be a way out of here.* He pulled open a small door at the end of the office.

"No! My wife!"

"Listen, fella, the last thing I'm interested in is your wife. No offense." Montrose stood before a dimly lit corridor. At the end was a narrow wooden staircase to the first floor. He held the bag in front of him as he ran up the stairs. At the top he emerged into a salon crammed with furniture where an old lady stood in the middle of the room clutching her purse. She screamed as Montrose stood before her, looking down at the gun in his hand.

Montrose tossed the revolver onto a chintzy sofa over flowing with different colored cushions. "Is your name Adubi?"

She nodded, her face tight.

Montrose lifted the bag and squeezed past her, around a coffee table then between an overstuffed chair and the sofa. He held the bag high to his chest and shuffled towards the window. "Are you Jewish?"

Her eyes darted from side to side as her husband stepped into the room. He leaned on the door handle his breaths coming in short gasps. She nodded again.

Arab name, huh? When am I gonna roll a seven in this crap shoot? He turned towards the east-facing windows. They looked a damn sight higher from the apartment than they did from the other side of the river, but there was a ledge below the window that would give him a foothold.

He pulled open the window, looped the leather bag around his arm and climbed out. He placed both feet on the ledge and crouched down. His palms were wet and slippery against the window frame. *Just do it.* He pushed his feet away, falling for what seemed an age, then slammed into the sidewalk, absorbing the shock in a crouch.

"Fuck!" The blister on his heel burst and the edge of the shoe stabbed into his Achilles tendon. He leaned forward to run just as a black BMW swung around the corner from the north side. "Slowly, boy," he murmured and began to walk, not daring to look at the passengers. The car rumbled over the cobblestones and turned into Rue Lamont.

The hard leather sliced into his heel as began to run, his shoes slipping on the flagstones. He stopped at the edge of the road leading to the Pont de la Tournelle. *On the run in Paris and carrying two heavy bags. There might be about ten seconds before all hell descended.* The traffic swept past. A cab sped towards him on the other side. Montrose ran into the road and waved a bag. The taxi screeched to a halt. He jumped in, ignoring the blaring horns of the other cars.

The toothless grin of the Algerian driver turned to greet him. "You're in a hurry, monsieur?"

"Take me to the Place des Vosges. I have a date with a very beautiful lady and she won't wait. A hundred euros if you can get me there quick."

"*Allez!*"

The tires of the taxi squealed on the cobblestones and Montrose was thrown back into the seat. The driver made a u-turn, then floored the accelerator and headed for the bridge.

The taxi tore up the traffic and shot down side streets, scattering shoppers. Montrose tried to hold on as they slewed around another corner, the driver blasting his horn through a pedestrian crossing. With one hand on the bag and the other on the seat in front, he peered forward. People, buildings and cars flew past. Another few streets and he'd make it, even if they'd nearly taken out a few tourists on the way. The taxi screeched to a halt in front of the Place des Vosges.

"Fast enough, monsieur?"

Montrose threw the driver a hundred euro bill and jumped onto the sidewalk. He ran into the shade of the colonnades around the square and stopped beside a row of tall pillars, pressing himself against the cold, yellow stone.

Blood ran down his heel and pooled in his shoe. He glanced around. The taxi had gone. Walking fast, he turned into the narrow archway at the end of the square. The road was quiet and he dared to look behind. Nothing.

He had to stay off the main streets. But it had to be around here, somewhere. One of those squares where you find the real Paris, not what they show you in the guides. He took a left into the Rue Saint Antoine and tried to ignore the acute, stabbing pain in his heel. He bent down to ease the edge of his heel away from the wound, but the blood rushed to his head and he stood for a moment until his breathing slowed.

To his left was an alley that looked familiar and he followed it around to a square. The restaurant was still there. On the corner was a frosted glass door and a brass plaque. Stein and Son, Secure Deposits.

This had to work. He ran his hands through his hair, adjusted his overcoat and suit, then pressed the intercom.

"*Oui*?"

"Good afternoon. I wish to enquire about the use of a safe deposit box."

"*Entrez.*" The intercom buzzed and the door opened into a brightly lit stone corridor with a small desk at the end.

Behind it sat a thin, old man, his eyes fixed on Montrose. "You're just in time, monsieur. I was about to close."

"Excellent," he replied. "I don't want to carry this back home."

"How can I help you?"

"I understand you have safe deposit boxes for rent."

The man nodded. "That is correct, monsieur."

"Then I have some family heirlooms I wish to deposit."

"That can be arranged. You do not wish to display them in your fine house?"

"No, my father recently passed away and I want to make sure they are secure before the whole extended family descends upon me. I've just found out about French law and he would rise from the grave if he thought that his most valuable possessions were to be spread amongst his family. They were not always on the best of terms, you see."

"It is often the way, monsieur. As they say, you can choose your friends, but not your family."

"Exactly. Tell me, how long has your firm been established?"

"Well, monsieur," laughed the old man, "give or take a few pogroms and the occasional revolution, about four hundred years."

"That's good enough for me. And the price?"

"That depends on how long you want to keep the box."

"It may be some time. I'm going back to the States."

The old man looked at the bag. "They will be safe, monsieur."

"Let's say ten years. That will give me plenty of time."

"As you wish, monsieur." The old man wrote down a figure on a piece of paper and slid it across the table.

That's about all the cash I have. "Do you do five year terms?"

The man seemed amused. "No, monsieur. Ten year minimum. It deters the lower end of the market, you understand. Perhaps I could recommend somewhere else?"

Yeah, like I have time to shop around. "That's fine. You don't mind cash?"

"I don't mind at all, monsieur, although I shall also require ID."

Montrose pulled out his passport and the wad of bills from his overcoat, then counted the money and pushed it across the table.

"*Bon.*" The old man rose stiffly from the chair and gestured towards a door on his right. "I am Monsieur Stein. At your service. Please, follow me." He produced a ring of keys and unlocked a steel gate, then a tall iron door. It was rough with a hundred coats of paint, but the lock opened silently.

Montrose stepped through the door. Steel boxes lined the wall. Some were old and stained with age, but all looked impregnable.

"You will see the older boxes, monsieur. Some have been there for over two hundred years. When the customer has finished with the box, we replace them. No box is ever used twice. Box 62 is empty, monsieur. Select a combination, then spin the dial to the numbers and press the button. Once it is pressed, the number is set and cannot be changed, so I advise that you take your time. Each number must be at least six digits. These boxes cost two thousand euros each, and breaking in will take days."

"I'll be careful."

"I shall be outside, monsieur."

"Thanks." *Think of a number. The Nazi pass?* The irony made him grimace. Bending down, he took the sneakers from the leather bag and stuffed them deep into the pockets of his overcoat. He was about to pick up the envelope, but stopped. *The accounts had been dormant for over seventy years. The list would be safer here. Another few months wouldn't make a difference.* He pulled back the shirt wrapped around the diamonds and took a last look. They twinkled in the bright overhead lights as he closed the bag and lifted it into the box.

He stood for a moment, staring at the dial. *Got it. All Swiss watches have a unique serial number.* He tugged at the strap of his Omega then turned the watch over and spun the dial to set the combination.

The old man was waiting when Montrose walked back into the corridor. "Guard your number carefully, monsieur."

"I will."

The old man smiled. "Until the next time."

The late afternoon sunshine filtered through the thick glass of the door to the street.

"Until then." Montrose turned and walked towards the light.

Ducking into an alleyway, he pulled the sneakers from his pocket then gently slipped off his brogues where the blood from the wound on his heel had congealed on his sock. The relief was instant. He pushed his feet into the new sneakers and swapped the cash to his pants.

Time to lie low and give Reinhard a call. He took off the Crombie and held it in his hand for a moment, running his fingers down the velvet collar and scarlet silk lining before he stuffed it into a dumpster with the brogues. *Damn shame, that was the best coat I've ever had. But too good for tourists.*

CHAPTER 21

Two hours to Brussels. *What the hell, ten minutes on a train in any direction would be good.* Montrose ran up the steps into the Gare du Nord and pushed through a steady stream of people moving from the platforms to the Métro.

Would old Adubi tell the police the whole story? Nah, he'll just report the cash theft. Sure as shit the cops won't be told about the diamonds. That would be left to whoever Adubi phoned. No prizes for guessing who that would be. He bent down to pull away his sock, stuck against the raw wound on his heel, and glanced across the station concourse. Two gendarmes stood chatting near the far platform. *Not your average coffee-shop cop. Mostly ex-army. You don't start a rumble with those boys. Whatever. I'm ahead of the game. It has to stay that way. If the Swiss police knew my name for the Zurich heist, then maybe they told the French. Yeah, you know how Interpol works.*

The ticket booth was dead ahead. The names of the

Parisian suburbs flashed up on the departures board. At the far end of the platform he could see the big blue Eurostar locos and the signs for international departures. *Time to bid Paris adieu.*

"Two round trip tickets for Brussels. Do you know the time of the next train?"

"In exactly twenty minutes, monsieur. Platform twenty-four," replied the assistant as he handed Montrose his tickets and change.

"*Merci.*" Montrose took the cash and turned towards the exit, then stood for a moment, examining his ticket. He glanced over at the gendarmes. They didn't seem that interested. *Maybe they don't know. They will soon enough. The station wasn't safe. The first thing the police would do was seal the entrance. They'd get a pretty good description from Adubi at Rue Lamont. They could arrive at any moment. I could walk straight into them. Carrying my ID.*

Backing into a corner at the side of the booth, he undid the Omega from his wrist, then pulled out his wallet and the old Cartier lighter. He looked down at the two-inch gap at the bottom of the booth where it stood on the platform. It was thick with dust. *Perfect.* He dropped the train ticket on the floor, then tucked his lighter into the wallet and bent down. He slid the wallet and watch under the edge of the booth, picked up his ticket and headed for the exit.

Stepping into the sunlight, he saw a café across the road. *If the police arrive with all guns blazing, I'll see it from there.* The wallet and watch could wait until the dust had settled. *A change of appearance would be a good idea, but there was no time for anything fancy.* He crossed the Place Napoléon, passed the café and took the Boulevard de Denain. To his left a barber shop was tucked down a side street and he ducked inside. The room was hot, thick with the smell of merguez and couscous. The wail of Arab music coming from a back room assaulted his ears. Montrose hung his jacket on a peg then covered it with an apron.

A bald man appeared from behind a beaded curtain. "Ah, monsieur, how can I help you?" he said, his smile full of gold teeth and gaps.

"A haircut, please. Short. Number two razor."

"Of course, monsieur, please sit, this won't take long."

"Good, I have a train to catch."

The cracked leather chair was hot and uncomfortable against his back. Above the music he could hear a faint police siren, and tried to keep still as the barber tied an apron around his neck. The clock above the mirror said thirteen minutes to go. The station would be getting busy pretty soon. And traffic was starting to build up. Even at weekends Paris was still the slowest racetrack in the world, so getting out by car was not an option. The sirens came closer. *It's only a police car, not every flic in Paris is looking for you.*

He blinked. *On the contrary. If old Adubi called the cops, that's exactly what's going to happen. There was no other way out. It had to be the train and it had to be now.*

The barber tilted Montrose's head forward and the razor buzzed smoothly over his scalp. The scream of sirens became louder. He flinched as a police car sped down the Boulevard de Denain.

The barber released his grip. "Monsieur? Did I hurt you with the razor?"

"No, just a muscle falling asleep. Are we done?"

"One moment." The barber gently touched the razor against the skin above his ear to level the cut. "*Voilà, monsieur.*"

"Thanks." Montrose jumped from the seat and pulled the apron from his throat. "Got to rush," he handed the barber a fifty euro bill. "Keep the change."

With effusive thanks ringing in his ears, he turned back to the station. He looked down at his watch before remembering it was gone. *Maybe ten minutes to go.* He looked up and down the boulevard and saw the sign he needed. *Internet Café.* He ducked into the doorway. The room was full of tourists, all blogging their latest adventures in the City of Light.

"Thirty minutes," said Montrose.

The assistant didn't look at him, just held out his hand for the money and continued chatting to the girl at the end of the counter.

Hurry up, you idiot.

The assistant handed back a pile of coins. Montrose stuffed them in his pocket and headed for a free seat. *I need the video on the USB stick. And a copy sent to a safe place in case Reinhard wants to dick me around. Not the CIA, they might keep the damn thing to themselves and watch me swing in the wind.* He brought up the contacts page for Kessler's bank, then his internet mail. *They'll trace the IP, but it don't matter. I'll be gone.*

FAO Jacques Kessler.

Guess who, sucker? Yeah, I'm still alive and kicking. Kurt Reinhard might be glad of that. Because I've got his bag full of diamonds and if he wants to see them again, this is what he has to do.

I want the memory stick with the security recording of the murders in Rome, plus I want a copy sent to Interpol. Tell Kurt to ask his father.

Let me make myself very clear. Unless I get that video, then old Reinhard won't be seeing his diamonds again. And the Cosa Nostra can eat him and his son alive.

When you're ready to deal, put a clear message on your website home page. Otherwise, I'm gonna be wearing a lot of jewelry.

You've got 24 hours. Any more and the deal is off.

And you're fucked.

When Interpol get the video they can tell the Italian Police. That'll be two monkeys off my back. Montrose weaved past the desks and out into the street. *Then that gorilla Spinks can call off the hunt. I'm not a snitch. I'll keep my mouth shut. Yeah, if they let me live.*

From the corner of Rue Dunkerque the station seemed quiet, just the usual tourists and commuters on their way home. The clock above the station said five minutes to go. A free table stood outside the door of the café and he threaded his way past the chairs, picking up a discarded sports paper. Taking the sunglasses from his pocket, he signaled to the waiter. "*Un espresso, s'il vous plaît.*"

He heard the screech of tires from across the river and saw the flashing blue lights at the end of the street. Two police vans raced down to the front of the station.

That's the CRS. Old Adubi made the call. They've brought in the riot squad. He lifted the paper higher to cover his face then pulled it down again. Everyone else was looking over to check the action, so he'd better do the same.

Heavily armed police raced out of the vans and into the station. *How did they know I was here? No, they don't. It's gonna be like this at every station. Time to disappear. The hotels and brothels behind Gare du Nord should be safe. But I need a little distraction.*

The waiter appeared with his coffee. "Monsieur," said Montrose, "do you have a telephone I could use?"

"It's at the rear of the bar."

Pulling a handful of coins from his pocket, Montrose headed inside. At the end of the long wooden bar, a phone was mounted on a wooden board covered in scrawled numbers. He grabbed the receiver and dialed the operator. "I want to speak to the *Préfecture de Police.*"

"Just putting you through."

The bar looked like it hadn't changed in a hundred years. A dirty wooden fan turned lazily over his head, its only function seemingly a fairground ride for a few lazy flies. To his right was a gleaming brass absinthe faucet, and behind the bar the *patron* stood polishing glasses and scowling at customers.

A voice came down the line. "Bonjour, Préfecture de Police."

Might as well go straight to the top. "I want to talk to the *Préfet de Police.* It concerns the armed robbery of a pawn shop in Rue Lamont."

The voice sounded bored. "Monsieur, the Préfet cannot be contacted . . . "

"If you value your job, I suggest you put me through immediately. This is a security issue." There was a click as the call was transferred.

"Bureau de le Préfet."

"I want to speak to the Préfet immediately."

"The Préfet is not . . . "

"I've heard all that. Tell him I'm from Interpol. I know where an armed robber is hiding. Do it now."

"One moment, please."

To his right, an elderly man sat at a small wooden table, leisurely tucking into a Croque Monsieur. Montrose's stomach rumbled.

"Oui?" The voice was deep.

"Monsieur le Préfet," said Montrose. "This is a friend. The armed robber from the pawnshop in Rue Lamont is at the Gare Montparnasse. He's taking the train to Bordeaux and then Spain. I suggest you stop him. He's an Englishman disguised as an American tourist."

"Who is this? How do you know this man?"

"You have friends in Lyon. Remember, Gare Montparnasse." He hung up. *Let the fun begin.*

Montrose stood for a moment then heard the wail of sirens starting up. *They were off. Give them a few moments and then stroll on over. I'm just a guy catching a train. No drama. If it didn't work, I'll hit the back streets.* He stepped towards the door.

The payphone rang behind him.

He slid to a halt. His mouth went dry. *They've traced the call.* He spun around, but the patron was already lifting the handset to his ear.

"Oui?" said the patron. His eyes narrowed. "What do you mean who have you called? You should know, you dialed the number!"

Don't say it, don't say the name.

"You're the Préfet de la Police?" The patron turned to Montrose with a grin. "Yeah, and I'm Napoleon Bonaparte. Now, fuck off." He slammed down the phone. "Students. I'd send them all to Afghanistan to get their ass shot off."

Walk away. Be cool. He took a deep breath and made for the door. The sunlight in the bar dimmed and he looked up to see the back of a man in a sharp suit blocking the doorway. *Relax, only another rubberneck checking out the action at the station.*

"Pardon, monsieur," Montrose squeezed past.

"Ah, excusez-moi," said the man, stepping aside.

As he walked out onto the terrace, Montrose saw the spooks gather around a police radio then run towards to their car, followed by the CRS. *Two minutes to the train.* Folding the newspaper, he placed some coins in the saucer of his coffee cup. Out of the corner of his eye, he saw the man in the sharp suit cross from the doorway and approach his table.

"Do you mind if I sit here, monsieur?" asked the man.

"Not at all, I'm just leaving," said Montrose.

"I think not, monsieur. Please, sit down."

Montrose turned, and saw the man gesture nonchalantly to the chair.

"Monsieur, there are policemen at every junction but you cannot see them. I think it would be better if you talked to me. Sit down. There is nowhere to go."

Montrose lowered himself into the chair, holding the frame to stop his hands from shaking.

The man called over the waiter. "Deux cafés, s'il vous plaît."

Montrose said nothing.

The man continued. "I suggest you enjoy the coffee, monsieur, while the entire police force chase around the stations of Paris. Besides, it may be the best coffee you taste for some time."

A pulse was thumping in his neck as he pulled down his sunglasses and stared into the man's soft brown eyes. "How did you find me?"

The man shrugged. "Alors, monsieur, it is not so difficult. Your French is very good, but not perfect. You are an American, no? And you have committed a crime. A fashion crime. With all our new CCTV cameras your description was easy to follow. You were spotted near the Latin Quarter, carrying a certain type of bag. Then you disappeared. However, all we had to do was look for a foreigner wearing a suit and an expensive overcoat. After all, it's a pleasant day in Paris, no? We thought you might try to change your appearance, maybe lose the overcoat. Then we are told of a man wearing suit pants and sneakers. An unforgivable crime of fashion. Of course, anyone wearing such clothes had to be an American."

Montrose felt fatigue and despair wash over him. His hands dropped onto his lap. "Is it so obvious?"

"I'm afraid so. Soon, you are spotted again and the bags have vanished. The local police watched all the connecting stations since we guessed you would try to leave Paris immediately. Rush hour is approaching, so your best bet is the train. Then it was simply a matter of choosing a station. I am in luck. I chose the Gare du Nord. It is the quickest way out of France. And if you don't mind, I must say I'm feeling rather pleased with myself."

A waiter appeared with two coffees and the man

sipped from his cup before continuing. "You see, I had an idea. You are obviously a clever man. You would not be waiting on the platform, ticket in hand. You would buy your ticket, then leave, to watch the station for any danger, which is why I was looking for you here. Then I saw the sneakers and the new haircut. There are still hairs on your shirt. Brussels, no?"

"How did you know?"

"We simply asked in the station if any American or British fitting your description had bought tickets to Belgium in the last twenty minutes. We can spot you very easily, monsieur. The color of hair and eyes, the pale skin, the bizarre dress sense. It's not so difficult. Tell me, has anyone ever approached you in the street, and asked you a question in English?"

Montrose slowly nodded.

"Voilà! How did they know? Permit me to introduce myself. I am Detective Bonsergeant." He took another sip of his coffee then dabbed his lips with a napkin.

Montrose shifted in his seat. "You don't look like a policeman."

"No, I don't look like an American TV policeman. They seem to sleep in their clothes. This is Paris, monsieur." Bonsergeant settled into his seat. "I heard about the armed robbery in Zurich." He tapped his breast pocket. "Twitter. Very useful for a policeman. And then I hear of the robbery in Rue Lamont, where someone tries to sell a diamond! I spoke to the owner of the pawn shop. Of course, as a policeman, I find it very intriguing."

"Yeah, and I find it fucking ridiculous." *I've had some shit ideas, but that had to be the gold standard. After the Zurich gig, the word would have gone out to the whole trade. Anyone trying to sell diamonds was going to stand out like a bulldog's balls. And I had to pick a Jew.* "I did what I had to do."

"You make it sounds like a Western movie, monsieur!"

"Maybe, but there's no happy ending. If the sheriff arrives, I'm the one he's going to shoot."

"Ah, the shooting. Very strange, this Zurich business. Amateurs, I thought. An armed hold up? Professionals don't open fire at the drop of a hat. I checked the witness messages on Twitter. And they didn't match up with the police bulletin. So, diamonds are stolen in Zurich and then someone turns up in Paris trying to pawn one? The pawnbroker was very reticent about what you were trying to pawn until we examined his security camera. Now the intrigue starts to blossom. It becomes addictive. The detective's nose, it scents . . . merde!"

"Yeah, there's a lot of it about."

"Also, the police report tells me that the suspect is armed and dangerous. Do not approach. Really? If the man in Zurich and the man in Rue Lamont are the same, why are they behaving so differently?"

Montrose couldn't resist a wry smile and saw a corresponding amusement in Bonsergeant's eyes.

"Are you armed, monsieur?"

"No. Apart from a Swiss Army knife."

Bonsergeant blew out his cheeks. "I don't want to ruin your reputation as an armed robber, monsieur, but a penknife doesn't really count." He waved his hand dismissively. "I watched you in the café. You do not have a gun. So, why would they say that a man like you is armed and dangerous? The kind of phrase that makes a policeman shoot first and ask questions later? Eh?"

"Because they want me dead."

"Voilà! Tell me, monsieur, who are they? Who did you steal the diamonds from?"

"You really don't want to know. They stole them many years ago. All the original owners, they're all dead."

"Dead? All of them?"

"They were from Antwerp. In 1941." Montrose watched Bonsergeant's face change, his blue eyes clouding over and lips tightening as the dates and location clicked home. Montrose held out his hands. "There are things I cannot tell you. The less you know the better. But they will come for me." He leaned forward, his elbows on his knees. "Can I trust you?"

Bonsergeant rolled his eyes. "Who else have you got?"

"They tried to kill me in Zurich. I was in the car, with the diamonds. Check the witness reports. The shots came from the car in front. I escaped, but they won't stop. They'll try again. I just have to stay away from them as long as possible."

Bonsergeant stuck his chin in the direction of the station. "The crimes of the Gare du Nord are well known, monsieur, but this café? Do you know its history?"

"No, I don't."

"This was a restaurant and hotel before the war and then it was taken over by the Gestapo. Very convenient for the station, you see. They took people straight from the train and into the cellars below us. They tortured them. Or sent them to Germany for slave labor, to die in the camps. I know all this because my grandfather kept a diary. He was a policeman, just like me. In those days, it was the police who did the dirty work in Paris. He had to arrest many people, most of whom were never seen again. Of course, like most of the police, he let some escape when he could. But, he did it once too often and was brought here. In the rooms below your feet, he was tortured and beaten to death." Bonsergeant sat silent for a moment, then looked up. "I am proud of him because he saved lives where he could. And it is ironic, monsieur, that I am here now, to tell you something that could save your life."

Montrose leaned forward.

"If you come with me to the police station and plead guilty to the charge, then you will be under my personal control, and the control of the Department of Justice. You will be remanded in custody until an appearance before a judge." Bonsergeant looked over at the station. "If you do not, if you try to run, then I have no hold over you and you will be 'armed and dangerous'. I have no doubt that they will try to kill you."

Montrose stared into his coffee. "Why are you telling me this?"

"I am a policeman, monsieur. I live by the law." Bonsergeant jabbed a finger towards the station. "The men in there. They have been told to take no chances. I have seen their orders. That means the likelihood is that you will be shot. Someone is trying to use the Paris police to do the dirty work they failed to do in Zurich."

Montrose let his head drop and felt his legs weaken. *This guy just saved my goddamn life. I should be face down on the platform, lying in my own blood and shit.* He looked up and saw the intensity in the man's face. "I know. You can't let me go. I'll take what's coming to me."

Bonsergeant pulled a slim notebook from his jacket. "Your name, monsieur?"

No way. I might as well slit my own throat. "I cannot tell you." He felt the passport in his back pocket. *Fuck. I should have left it in the station with the wallet.*

"Ah, monsieur, you have the right to remain silent, but your fingerprints will be more revealing."

Montrose slumped forward. *I've sat in his seat. I know how it works. Strip search and inky fingers. Then it's over. Even if I somehow ditch the passport, my prints will be on the system tonight. The Interpol database will pick them up tomorrow morning. And then a whole world of shit is going to come down.*

A blue police van pulled up at the curb. The driver's door opened, but Bonsergeant held up a hand. The policeman closed the door and sat patiently behind the wheel.

When I appear before a judge, the feeding frenzy will start. If this guy is right, I'll be safe until then. Maybe that's all I need. Like I've got a choice. Montrose took out his passport and penknife and held them under the table. "Destroy the passport if you wish, but please take it. It might buy me some time before they come for me."

"Monsieur, the Paris police won't kill you for a bad French accent. On the other hand, whoever owns the diamonds . . . "

"If my name remains unknown, I will confess to the robbery in Rue Lamont. But the people who are looking for me make the Gestapo look like boy scouts."

Bonsergeant shrugged. "I'm not surprised, monsieur. You seem to lead an interesting life." He closed his notebook. "If you choose not to tell me your name, that is your affair." Bonsergeant took the passport and penknife and slipped them into his pocket.

"Thank you."

"Come with me."

CHAPTER 22

The van slowed then came to a halt. He tried to lift his hands, but the shackles were too heavy. Fatigue washed over him and he leaned against the metal wall of the van. *There was no way out of this one. I should have run. Taken the shot.*

His head dropped forward and he looked down at the heavy chains, dragging his arms to the floor. *Game over.*

The doors opened and the guard pulled him to his feet. A floodlight lit the interior of the van. Montrose shielded his eyes, but he could see a brightly lit doorway and a uniformed guard approaching.

"Welcome to *La Prison de Haute Surveillance de Versailles*," said the guard as he unlocked the chain. "I am Superintendent Corbeaux." He grabbed Montrose's handcuffs and pulled him from the van.

Montrose shuffled behind him into the office.

"Stand on the line in front of the desk," said Corbeaux. "Listen carefully."

Montrose dropped his head.

"I said, listen carefully," repeated Corbeaux and sat down at the desk.

Montrose looked up.

"You are being detained for armed robbery. Since you have failed to identify yourself, you will forfeit all rights. Other than the arresting officer, no one knows you are here and there is no name on any records. Until you tell us who you are, you will be kept in solitary confinement. When you have something to say, you will speak only to me. We will become better acquainted later." The door of the office closed behind him and Montrose heard the van drive off.

"*Bon*," said Corbeaux. "We are alone." He examined a sheet of paper in front of him, then pushed it aside. "I don't know who you are, but I can tell you're not the usual scum we have here. However, I have my instructions, and I shall follow them to the letter. An armed robber? You look more like a travelling salesman. And not a very good one. Keep yourself clean, eat your food and do what you are told. And when you've had enough of our hospitality and delightful French cooking, I am here to listen." He drummed his fingers on the table. "Because you give me a big problem, monsieur." He pulled open a drawer, and lifted out a laptop. "You have no name. Or are at least, not one which you are willing to share with us. And that upsets me." Corbeaux pointed to a dark corner of the room.

Behind a smoked glass door, the lights from a rack full of blade servers twinkled in the gloom. Montrose felt his mouth drop open. *All the shit I've been through and this asshole is worried about his computer records.*

"Every prisoner is here," said Corbeaux. "Every personal detail indexed. Family, friends, visitors, cell mates. Any entry can be cross-referenced." He tapped the laptop. "Knowledge is power. My relational database is the envy of the French Prison System."

Montrose let out a low whistle. "Yeah. I can see why they'd be jealous."

"Then you turn up with no name? *Mon dieu!* What do I do?"

Get a fucking life.

"*C'est impossible!* So where do you go?"

"A for anonymous?"

"*Très drôle.* No, but I have an idea. I am a big fan of the American movies and your TV cop shows." He pointed a thumb and forefinger towards Montrose. "*Eat the earth, you fucker of mamas!*"

I'm going to lose it. Montrose clamped his jaws together.

"Therefore, I shall call you *Jean* Doe. Clever, eh?"

"I see what you've done there. Outstanding."

"*Bien.* You've already had the haircut. When was the last time you had something to eat?"

Montrose shook his head. "I can't remember."

"Then go through to the office next door. You will be given a uniform. I'll have some food sent down. When you want to tell me your name, I will be here. Understood?"

"Understood."

The air was thick with the reek of disinfectant although it couldn't mask the underlying stench of piss and stale sweat. Montrose stepped into the cell. He checked the bunk and decided against bouncing on the thin mattress.

A small, cracked sink with a bucket below seemed to be the only en-suite facilities. The barred door clanged shut behind him as the guard walked away without saying a word.

Montrose stared at the small window near the ceiling. *Once my fingerprints hit the system tonight, I'll have to get a PA to handle my calls.*

He turned as a tray slid under the bars. He managed to get a glimpse of the food before the lights went out. The smell made him salivate despite his thirst, and he gulped down the water from a plastic jug. He picked up a forkful of meat and shoved it in his mouth, savoring the taste.

A beam of moonlight entered the corridor outside his cell. *The names. The accounts. The victims of the death camps. Stripped of their wealth and sent to die.*

The world would know. I'll make damn sure of it. But not yet. Reinhard would have to wait. It would be worth it. This wasn't over.

The chandeliers rattled as the office door burst open and Kessler threw his briefcase to the floor. "Where's Kurt Reinhard?"

Jacques Kessler jumped up, knocking a pile of papers across the desk. "Father! I didn't hear you arrive."

"There are a lot of things that seem to have escaped you. Like the fact that Montrose looks nothing like Erwin Reinhard!"

"Father, please, the ID photo was over seventy years old."

"I don't want excuses." Kessler thrust his finger

towards his son, his face creased with anger. "Listen to me very carefully. There are men in London and Moscow who are holding me personally responsible for Montrose. I accepted an assignment to get rid of him and I have failed to do so. We have a very short time to get this right or they will withdraw all their business. And that includes any deal in Afghanistan. We'll lose millions of dollars in commission." He didn't mention what would happen next. No country in the world would be safe from their vengeance.

"But, don't they understand . . .?"

"All they understand is that Montrose is killing their chances of a trade deal. The Afghans are stringing them along. They want Montrose dead and they want blood money. It's the way these savages do business. They're not going to sign anything. And then the Chinese will keep us out of Afghanistan for fifty years." He bowed his head, shoved his fingers hard through his thinning hair. He looked up at his son. "We have one last chance."

"What are we going to do?"

"I am going to go to the Afghani ambassador in Rome to convince him I am in control of the situation. What *you* are going to do is go to Paris. Get the team. Kill Montrose. Then hand over a briefcase full of diamonds to the Afghani ambassador in Paris. Take the jet and fly him to Kabul. He can distribute the favors and then the Afghanis will be satisfied. Then they'll sign the deal. Do you understand?"

"Of course, I . . . "

"Where's Kurt Reinhard?"

"He's in Paris, as you instructed. He left this afternoon with the two English guards. But why Paris?"

"Montrose. He's locked up in a Versailles prison, nine kilometers west of Paris."

"Versailles?"

"He rode his luck a little too far." Kessler strode over, kicked the office door shut. "Thanks to the Paris police, his fingerprints are now on every system in Europe. Including the Swiss." He picked up his briefcase and pulled out a small envelope. An object rattled around inside.

"What's that?" asked Jacques.

"This is what Montrose desires. A video that exonerates him from the murders in Rome. Tomorrow we'll see how much he really wants it."

"A video?"

"Just do as you're told. Where's the Swiss team?"

"They're at the border, waiting for instructions."

"They'll need paperwork. Tell them to meet me at the Zurich Police Headquarters. I'm about to pull in a few favors."

"I'll tell them." Jacques picked up his cell phone and began to text.

He thrust the envelope under his son's nose. "Take this with you. Montrose is locked up for the night. We can't get access until the prison office opens. The French and their bourgeois bureaucracy won't let us near him until then."

"I'll do it, Father."

"And when you get to Paris, don't get involved with Reinhard. Let him do the dirty work. Then you can clean up." Kessler stood in the middle of the office, staring out into the courtyard. "Jacques. Look out of the window."

In the courtyard, security lights shone down on

the rear of a panel van. A line of bank staff unloaded document boxes and carried them inside.

"That bag, Jacques, contained more than just diamonds. Locked in Erwin Reinhard's apartment were the personal details of every Jew he interrogated before they were sent to the death camps. And he only chose the wealthiest."

"Their bank accounts?"

"Christ, no! We helped ourselves to those years ago, as did every other bank in Switzerland. But in the bag of diamonds was an envelope, containing a list. Your grandfather told me of its existence. It was only years later, when we investigated Reinhard and what he kept in his apartment, that we understood its true significance. That list will unlock safe deposit boxes across Switzerland that could yield a billion dollars. We need the diamonds, Jacques, but get that list. Bring it straight to me."

Jacques didn't take his eyes from the document boxes. "My God, Father. It's all on a piece of paper?"

"Yes. The codes and locations of all the security boxes. Everything the Jews locked away before the Nazis arrived. You want to know where all the disappeared treasures are? Caravaggio? Rembrandt? Da Vinci? Those are only the paintings." He thrust a finger towards the courtyard. "Can you imagine it?" Kessler placed both palms on the window. "Take Muller and meet up with the English team. Don't fail me, do you hear? Kill anyone who gets in your way."

CHAPTER 23

A thin, grey light began to filter through the security glass near the roof of the cell. Montrose lay on his back, hands behind his head, the threadbare blankets tucked under his chin. There was no use going over all the other possibilities again. They'd been running through his head all night. Only one would work.

The faint pealing of a church bell drifted through the cell. *Maybe another hour and they would change the guard. Nothing would happen until breakfast.* The window was about six inches high and a foot long. Pulling off the blankets, he stood and stretched up with his fingers, but it was out of reach. Behind him the bunk was bolted to the concrete floor. *It didn't matter. Daylight was enough.*

He stepped over to the door and gripped the bars then let his forehead rest against the cold metal. *Nothing to do but wait.* The corridor was still dark. Closing his eyes, he heard the sounds of the prison waking up. The scraping of a chair. Rustling of paper. There had to be a guard at the end of the corridor. Probably writing the night report. All quiet.

Not for long.

Montrose lay down on the bunk. The shift change might be at seven, to allow the handover to take place before the prisoners had to be fed.

The light was stronger now and he began to make a search of the cell. Smooth walls, thin plaster smothered in whitewash. He picked away with his fingers at a crack in the plaster. Behind was solid stone. No good. The bunk was welded together in one piece. No bolts or screws, no springs. The sink was a single unit, its stained and cracked porcelain set firmly into the wall. Where the glaze was broken, the clay powdered away under his thumbnail. It would shatter if he hit it hard enough with the bucket, but there was no way he could do that without alerting the guard. *I don't need the attention. Not yet.*

There was nothing sharp enough to make an edge, except the lip of the metal slop bucket. That would take a while. And catching hepatitis wasn't part of the plan.

Nothing. Absolutely nothing. Even the buttons on the prison denims were made of wood. *There had to be a way.* He dropped down onto the bunk and leant forward, his head between his knees.

He looked up. The frosted glass was sparkling in the early morning sunlight.

After a few moments, a faint aroma of coffee penetrated the sour smell of sweat and sleep. He jumped up and stuck his face against the bars. Coffee and croissants. Adrenalin shot through his veins and his heart skipped a beat. *Time for breakfast. Shame it won't do me any good.*

*

The village was waking up. She cut the engine on the motorcycle then leaned forward over the handlebars and glanced around the corner of the alley. The prison was at the end of the street. Too early for visitors. She'd have to wait.

An old man in faded blue denims trudged past, a baguette of fresh bread tucked under his arm. A scrawny dog of undetermined heritage skipped alongside, eagerly looking up at the bread. From the side door of a boulangerie, a baker emerged, shaking the flour from his stained white apron. He leaned against the wall, eyes closed, dragging on a cigarette.

She sat back on the Norton, the tips of her toes barely touching the ground. Prison visits didn't start until 09:00. If they let her see him. She flicked out the stand and gently leaned the bike over to the side, skipping on one foot as she hauled her leg across the seat. She stood for a moment, stretching the muscles in her calves.

It was getting easier. The old British superbike had been her dream, ever since that day she had stood, eyes wide open and her arm high in the air, reaching up for her mother's hand.

'C'est Grand-père!' her mother had said.

Her grandfather, astride the Norton and dressed in an immaculate Italian suit, waved as the bike thundered down the Avenue des Champs-Élysées. She felt the power bouncing off the windows of the fancy stores.

The first words she learned in English were easy. *'Eight-Fifty Norton Commando.'*

She looked down at the engine, ticking as it cooled. The bike was far too heavy for her. If she dropped it she doubted she could ever pick it up, but once on the move, the famous Isolastic frame was perfectly balanced.

The smell of fresh bread from the boulangerie was driving her crazy. She peered around the corner. A car sped through the village. She stepped out onto the street and watched a long, black Citroën pull up beside the prison. A man got out and pressed the intercom. She couldn't be sure, but it looked like there were two other people in the car.

The church bell rang seven times. The man at the intercom took something from his pocket and held it up to the intercom camera. The gates opened and the Citroën disappeared inside.

Quiet returned to the village and the sun edged higher above the trees. She pulled a pair of Ray Bans from her pocket and leaned against the wall of the boulangerie.

CHAPTER 24

A clatter of crockery came from the corridor. The squeak of a service cart wheel. *It started now.*

A guard appeared with a tray in his hand. Montrose ran up to the bars and bent over, clutching his stomach. "Monsieur! I need your help!"

The guard ignored him and slid the tray under the bars.

"Wait!" said Montrose, between gritted teeth. "I need medication. It's my stomach ulcer. It's killing me. Can you get me a doctor?"

The guard shrugged. "Eat," he said, and walked away.

Bastard. Montrose looked down. The tray was a plain wooden board. *No knife. No surprise.* The coffee cup was chipped and missing a handle. The plate was plastic and flexible. They were all useless. He stood for a moment, head bowed.

The tray. It might work.

He lifted the tray onto the bunk and sipped the coffee.

It was good. Grabbing the bread, he tore it into pieces and stuffed them in his mouth, then gulped down the croissant and finished off the coffee.

Water would help. The faucet creaked as it turned. He wasn't sure whether it was drinkable. France had a reputation. Not that it mattered.

The reek of chlorine stung his nostrils. Three cups was enough. He cleared the tray and held it up to examine the edge. It was smooth from a thousand hands, but the wood was old and brittle. Holding it before him, he searched around the cell. The plaster on the wall would be useless, but the concrete on the floor could work. Kneeling down, he tore the edge of the tray across the floor. He put his whole weight onto his arms and dragged the tray back and forward. The wood powdered under the force and cracks sprang up along the grain. Digging his fingernails into the wood, he pulled back a sharp splinter and ripped it from the tray. He touched the tip. It was dry and sharp.

He dropped onto the bunk and placed the empty cup by his side, then poked a finger under his tongue, searching for a pulse. The spongy feel of a bulging blood vessel throbbed against the end of his finger. He brought up the splinter and placed the sharp tip against the blood vessel. *No hesitation. Just do it.*

He jabbed the splinter in hard. Tears burst from his eyes with the pain and his mouth flooded with blood. Grabbing the cup, he leant forward, filling it halfway with one mouthful, then held the cup aside as blood spilled from his lips, splashing in fat drops on to the floor.

In for a penny. He took a deep breath, opened his mouth and rammed his fingers down his throat. His stomach slammed back into his spine and he vomited over the filthy floor and through the bars into the corridor. Wiping away tears, he grabbed the cup and emptied the blood onto the vomit. He took a few deep breaths and retched at the stench. The vomit stuck behind his nose and the back of his throat was raw with stomach acid.

"Help me!" He threw the cup through the bars. It smashed against the wall. Pieces of china bounced and scattered along the corridor. He stood for a moment, blood dripping from his mouth.

Footsteps. Boots, running.

In for a pound. He collapsed into the pool of blood and vomit.

A guard slid to a halt in front of the bars. "Merde!"

Montrose tried to speak and let the blood gush from his mouth, then dropped his head into the vomit. Out of the corner of his eyes, he could see the black boots of the guard. *Do something, you prick.*

He heard a slow hand clap. Another pair of boots appeared at the bar. And then a deep belly laugh. "Alors, monsieur! That is a good effort! What do you think, Henri?"

Montrose looked up.

The other guard nodded in approval. "Best I've seen for some time. He really went for it."

Are you serious? He tried to grab the bars and drag himself towards them. "Please, get me a doctor!"

"Back off, you idiot. I'm not getting covered in your shit." He turned to the other guard. "So, what do you think? Did he go for biting his own tongue or cutting his cheek?"

"Tongue," replied the second guard. "Got to be. Very impressive. Oscar-winning performance."

"Putain!" The first guard saw the blood oozing towards his boot. "There's always one. Henri, get a hose to clean him up. I'll find him some clothes. I'd leave the idiot naked for a week, but he's got visitors."

The other guard reappeared with a fire hose in his hand. "Do you think it's Steven Spielberg?" *Visitors*? Montrose looked up as a jet of water caught him full in the face.

Corbeaux stood with his arms wide as Montrose stepped into the office. "Mr. Connor Montrose of Interpol! At last I have a place for you on my database!"

Montrose tugged the front of his shirt, peeling the cloth from his soaking skin. *I'm CIA, you asshole. And you know where you can shove your database.* Two figures leaned over Corbeaux's desk, signing several sheets of paperwork.

Corbeaux took each one and filed it in a separate pile. "Now I understand why you were so reticent about your name. If I was a policeman, I would keep very quiet if I was invited to stay in this particular hotel. You would win no popularity contest."

One of the men at the desk gave him a sideways glance.

Montrose shivered.

"These men are from the Swiss Justice Department, Mr. Montrose. Your fingerprints were very illuminating. Given the seriousness of the allegation against you, they have arranged with the authorities to have you transferred immediately to Zurich for questioning. You must be very popular. These orders come straight from the top."

Yeah, I'll bet Kessler has got friends in high places. One of the men approached with handcuffs. Montrose held out his hands and the steel bands clicked into place.

Corbeaux placed the paperwork in neat rows in front of him. He stood up and crossed his arms. "I hope you understand, Mr. Montrose, that it is a good thing if I say that I hope to never see you again."

Montrose nodded. They were ready. He walked forwards towards the door and the two men fell in behind him.

The door opened into bright sunshine and Montrose bowed his head and half-closed his eyes against the glare. He caught the shape of a black Citroën.

One of the men whispered in his ear. "Get in the back, you piece of shit."

Maybe 400 miles. They'll have to stop for fuel. Or food. Maybe by plane. Whatever, I'm out of that cell.

A man's hand enveloped the back of his head and shoved it down hard, then bundled him into the back seat.

She lifted the Ray Bans and pushed them through her auburn hair. The prison gates opened and the Citroën pulled out. She glanced up when the car flashed past, then pulled out her cell phone and brought up the grainy photo from the pawn shop. *Was it him?*

She pivoted on the ball of her foot and threw her leg over the seat, then grabbed the handlebars and hauled the bike upright. The side stand shot back into place and she jabbed the starter button. The bike coughed into life and thrummed beneath her.

The Citroën disappeared around a bend. She paused for a moment then edged out on to the road. The front of the Norton rose up as she dumped the clutch and twisted back the throttle. The roar of the exhausts bounced off the houses of the village. She squeezed the tank between her legs and held on tight. *It had to be him.*

CHAPTER 25

The blood was starting to slow. Montrose kept his tongue pressed firmly down into his jaw. *I'm out. Not the way I wanted, but I'm out. Time to lose the Zurich pigs.* He could feel the heat from the men on either side as their legs pressed against his. He lifted his cuffed hands.

"You can take these off, guys. You know I didn't shoot anybody in Zurich." The car slowed for a junction and stopped before the main road. A stream of commuters flashed past. "C'mon, I was in the Mercedes. They were trying to shoot me! Are we going to go all the way to Zurich for me to be a witness? You don't need to cuff me for that."

"Zurich?" said the man on his left, his mouth drawn into a thin sneer. He pulled a snub-nosed revolver from his raincoat and jabbed it into Montrose's stomach. The rush hour traffic slowed and the Citroën came to a halt. "Don't even think about it. The doors are locked." He smacked the barrel of the gun against Montrose's cheek.

A cold shock of fear shot through his body. *These ain't cops.*

"You've made a lot of enemies," said the man, "The Italians, the French police and Interpol for a start. But when they heard what we had in mind, they were only too glad to help." He thrust a bunch of official-looking papers in Montrose's face. "The Prefét of Police was very helpful. Says here you're being transferred to Zurich. Before that, we're going to have a little chat. Can you guess what we want to talk about?"

Montrose's breathing became ragged. *They're Kessler's men.*

"Listen to me, I knew Shechter. We served together in the army. And believe me, I'd rip your fucking tongue out just for fun, but you'll need it to talk."

The traffic cleared and the Citroën accelerated towards Paris.

Montrose dropped his eyes for a moment. *Snub-nosed revolver. Handy for concealment but shit for accuracy. If the trigger was pulled, the shooter might take me out and the guy sitting next to me. A .38 slug would make a big hole and they couldn't talk to a dead man. Helluva gamble. They might go for a flesh wound, but if I make it out the car, I'll take my chances. The way the guy in front was driving might help. Make a grab for the door. Hitting the road would be a damn sight better than what these guys have in mind.*

He squeezed his eyes shut. *Do it. And do it fast.*

The car turned onto a two-lane blacktop. *A sharp corner would work. Dive and roll.* Montrose glanced to the right. The door locks were down. The gun was hard against his guts. *The bastard might be a professional, but he was holding the weapon too close. Go for the gun with the right hand, then roll over, throw the locks and out the door. If the goons want to follow me out, that's their problem.*

The driver began cutting up the traffic. Montrose was thrown to the left and put out his hands to stop himself falling, holding on to the edge of the front seat. He braced his feet against the transmission tunnel. *Next corner. It had to be the next corner.* A hand grabbed him around the throat and pushed his head back over the edge of the rear seat.

The man with the gun hissed into his ear. "I've had enough of your fucking tricks."

The butt of the revolver flashed past his face and a sharp pain shot across his skull. Then nothing.

Everything was black. Montrose felt his head being thrown from side to side. He opened his eyes and saw an open hand just before it slapped him across the face.

"Wake up, you piece of shit! Listen to me. We're getting out of the car. If you try to run, I'll shoot you in the ass. You'll live long enough to tell us what we want. Remember that."

The car stopped. Montrose's arm was pulled sharply to the right, dragging him across the seat. Tall white terraced buildings towered above him. *Paris. Maybe south of the river. Invalides or Montparnasse.* He flinched as the gun was pushed against his spine.

"Down the steps. Go."

Basement apartment. Harder to see from the road. Montrose stumbled to the bottom of the steps. The man grabbed Montrose's collar and pushed his head down, dragging him along. A door slammed. The man spun him around and kicked him behind the knees. Montrose dropped onto a chair that creaked under the strain.

"Hands behind your back."

His arms were tugged together and thick rope tightened on his wrists, then around his waist.

The man leaned forward, pushing his face so close that Montrose could feel flecks of spittle against his cheek. "You'll be glad to know that Mr. Reinhard is on his way, especially to meet you. I don't think he's going to be in a very good mood. Funnily enough, neither am I."

Montrose saw the man pull back a fist. *Shit, not again.* Then the lights went out.

CHAPTER 26

His eyes took a while to focus, but at least his sight had returned. Followed by the pain. Dried blood crackled in his nose as he gulped down a breath. He tried to move his hands and felt the ropes holding them hard against his back.

Montrose looked down. The ropes were bound around his waist and tied to a gilt chair. Lifting his head, he gazed around an opulent *salon* decorated in the nineteenth century style

Where the hell am I now? Have I died and gone to rococo heaven?

At the end of the room, two French windows faced onto a paved terrace, leading to a carefully tended garden, bordered by a high stone wall.

Around him, antique furniture was crammed into the room, displaying more wealth than taste. A whirring of cogs made him look up at a carved marble mantelpiece where a lacquer and gold-covered horologe chimed the hour. It was the ugliest clock he had ever seen. Silence returned to the room.

A muted voice came from behind the door.

Kurt Reinhard.

Montrose blew out a breath. *Tell it like it is. You're up to your neck in shit. Reinhard will be desperate, but I've got to stall them. Talk, and I'm a dead man. But it was Kessler's men who picked me up. Who's pulling the strings here?*

Whatever. Either bastard will kill me. Time for a little bargaining. Maybe lead them back to Stein's. Tell them I need my ID. And I'm the only one who can get the diamonds. Then somewhere along the way, lose them. Old Reinhard will have to wait until I'm clear of these psychos. There's got to be a way. Play your cards.

The carved rosewood door swung open and smacked against the wall. Kurt Reinhard strode into the room, his face twisted with rage. He ran towards Montrose and jumped with his foot high, catching him flush on the jaw. Montrose heard a crack and flew backwards, crashing to the floor. His head thudded against the carpet and his vision swam before him. He focused in time to see Reinhard's shoe above his head before it stamped down, the heel grinding into his ear. He gasped as the pain seared through his brain.

Reinhard stood over him. "Where's the bag?"

Montrose tried to open his mouth. A grating sound came from his jawbone.

White puffs of saliva spread from the corners of Reinhard's mouth. "Where's the fucking bag?"

Looked like Nazi boy wasn't in the bargaining mood. Montrose tried to flex his jaw. It hurt like hell, but it wasn't broken. *Got to turn the tables.* "Yeah . . . We should talk about that."

"You think so?" Reinhard stepped back then turned

quickly and booted Montrose in the guts, knocking the chair onto its side.

Montrose pressed his forehead into the carpet and retched. *Good answer, hotshot. You have to slow him down. If Reinhard let loose with his boot, it would be game over.* The words came out in a rush. "I want to talk to your father. I'll only deal with him."

Reinhard grabbed a poker from the fireplace and swung it in a high, wild arc. Montrose pushed his face into the carpet and twisted away, straining against the ropes. The blow whacked the side of the chair and thumped into his shoulder muscle.

"My father is dead!"

Christ, another great move. You're on a lucky streak. Reinhard is going to beat the shit out of me whatever happens. Just as well he's losing it or he'd have damn near killed me with the poker. But the old man was dead? "Listen to me, I've got nothing against your father, even if he was a fucking Nazi. I don't care."

Reinhard stood up and lifted his chin. "He was an officer of the *Wehrmacht*. Not a Nazi."

"Yeah, whatever. Nazis, Wehrmacht. Same shit, different hats." The poker cracked across Montrose's knees. A howl burst from his mouth and he twisted his wrists against the rope to fight the pain. *Stay focused, you have to take control. And less of the smartass.* "You'll never get those diamonds without me and the security video."

Reinhard stared at him. "What security video?"

Is he serious? He doesn't know? "Don't try to bluff me. Get the video and you'll get the diamonds."

Reinhard dropped the poker and threw his hands in the air. "Who gives a fuck about diamonds?"

What the hell was he talking about? Montrose unscrewed his eyes.

"There was an envelope in the bag you took from Zurich. Where is it?"

"An envelope?"

"Don't try to fuck with me. Is it in the bag?"

The names. He spat blood onto the carpet. "I'm not sure . . ."

Reinhard dropped his knee onto Montrose's head then took a Zippo lighter from his pocket and pulled off the brass case. He jammed a thumb into Montrose's right eye and dragged back the eyelid, then pushed his finger into the cotton wad of the Zippo, squeezing the lighter fluid into his eye socket.

The fluid burned like a bastard. Montrose screwed his eyes shut then blinked hard to try and wash his eye.

"What you did killed my father, so I'll take great pleasure in burning your eyes, one after the other. You'll still be able to talk, so I'll ask you once again. Think very carefully about the answer." An almost imperceptible tremor crossed Reinhard's face as he reassembled the lighter and flicked open the lid, his thumb on the flint wheel. "Is the envelope with the diamonds?"

Through a blur of tears, Montrose could see Reinhard playing with the Zippo. S*hit,* he thought, *I can't get out if I'm blind. It was time to play the game.* "Yeah. It's there."

Reinhard stepped back and dropped onto the edge of a sofa. He leaned forward and bowed his head.

A picture of the thin, yellow sheets, the list of names, flashed through Montrose's mind. "You'll never get access to those accounts."

"The accounts?" Reinhard laughed and looked up. "They're empty! The Swiss banks helped themselves a long time ago. After the war, relatives couldn't get access unless they produced a death certificate. I don't remember Auschwitz handing out too many of those. Easy pickings."

It didn't make sense. Without the diamonds there were no more cards to play. What the hell was in the envelope? Christ, I have to know. It's the only thing that could keep me alive, and Reinhard wasn't going to volunteer the information. Unless he was really pissed. Yeah, so how many beatings would it take before Reinhard revealed the real deal? Just make it fast. "You're talking out of your ass. No diamonds? What's a parasite like you going to live on? You're after dead men's money, you fucking leech."

"Money?" Reinhard leapt forward and stamped on Montrose's neck. "You think all I'm after is some dead Jew's cash?"

A searing shock of pain flashed down his spine. His legs began to spasm and his arms went limp in the ropes. *For fuck's sake, spit it out. The next one might be my last.* "It's . . . Holocaust money. You're lower than . . . snakeshit."

Reinhard stepped back.

Montrose saw it coming and tried to clamp his thighs together but Reinhard's boot caught him hard in the balls. Nausea swept over him and he retched uncontrollably, his stomach pinned against his spine.

"The Jews saw what was coming. They knew their accounts would be raided. It had already happened in Germany. So they moved all their money into gold, got together their most valuable possessions and stashed them all in safe deposit boxes. Guess where? Zurich!"

Montrose raised his head, fighting to clear the mucus and vomit from his throat. "They're numbered boxes. The Swiss will never let you near them."

"Are you serious?" Reinhard stared at him in disbelief. "It took the Swiss thirty years to admit the bank accounts even existed. So you think they're going to own up about the boxes? There is untold wealth in those boxes. Completely untouched. From families going back generations. Have you any idea what I'm talking about?"

"You can't . . . "

"In my father's apartment are the files of all the wealthy Jews from Antwerp. He interviewed them before the SS sent them to the camps. They were very forthcoming, for a number of reasons. Mostly to do with a gun being pointed at their children. I think you get the picture."

"We have their names." Montrose spat green bile onto the carpet. "They will be remembered."

"Not for long. Yes, I know, we didn't kill them all. So much for German efficiency. But, we can provide the correct documentation to open the boxes. And the Swiss don't ask too many questions, especially when you are being represented by Kessler."

"They'll find out – they won't . . . "

"It's not going to happen. Think about it. Gold, jewelry, lost art works. There are currently around three hundred Old Masters and Renaissance paintings unaccounted for since the war. But I know where they are. We're talking maybe . . ." Reinhard shrugged. "A billion dollars. Picasso, Leonardo Da Vinci, Caravaggio, Rembrandt. And the combination numbers are in the envelope."

Montrose let his head drop to the floor.

"So now you get it. Bank accounts? You fucking idiot."

The list. The names of the dead. Everything they owned. All waiting to be taken. His voice croaked as he spoke. "It's not over, you sick bastard. What happens to me doesn't matter. They'll hunt you down like a dog."

Reinhard grabbed the poker. "I'm protected by the Swiss banking industry. They make the CIA look like fucking Greenpeace." Reinhard hefted the poker in his hand and flexed his shoulders. "One last time. *Where's the bag?*"

A pulse hammered behind his eyes. *There was no choice. Got to string it out.* "Far away from here, sucker, and you need me to get it." *Here it comes.* He squeezed his eyes shut and buried his chin on his chest, twisting his body to the floor.

Reinhard roared and smashed the poker down onto Montrose's kidneys.

His body snapped into a rictus of pain, his back arched and his mouth opened in a silent scream.

"I'll leave this to the professionals." Reinhard threw the poker to the floor. "Kessler's men are betting you'll tell them *everything* you know in thirty minutes. They want to get it done before the specialist arrives. Professional competition, you see. He's a consultant urologist from a Zurich hospital. He has a special steel catheter that he sticks in your dick. Apparently, it's for taking tissue samples. It opens up like an umbrella and the blades scrape the sides as he pulls it out. But this one's a *little* bit bigger. And sharper. They tell me he has a one hundred percent success rate. By the time he's finished, you'll be able to piss an eight ball." Reinhard made towards the door.

Shock crashed through Montrose and he sagged in the ropes. The words came in a high pitched whisper. "I'll . . . kill . . ."

Reinhard marched from the room, slamming the door behind him.

Montrose pressed his forehead into the carpet. *The only man who could give me an alibi is dead. They are going to tear me apart.* He slumped down in the ropes. He heard footsteps on stairs. He knew what came next. And he'd tell them. Everything.

The first sobs racked his body. He lay face down, rocking back and forth as he wept.

His eyes opened. Rage tore through him like a savage bolt of lightning. A guttural roar burst from his chest and his head thumped the floor as he thrashed and strained against the ropes. His breathing became fast and ragged and he jammed his mouth shut to stop himself hyperventilating. "*Focus,*" he croaked, "*fucking focus!*" The pain in his jaw was incredible, but it cleared his mind. He blinked away the tears, looked up and heard the rumble of water pipes behind the walls.

They were running a bath. For me.

"No!" He twisted his wrists, the rope burning and tearing his skin. The chair creaked under the strain. Montrose shot a glance down at the antique frame. *Maybe two hundred years old.*

Rolling onto his knees, he threw himself back and balanced on the balls of his feet. He hopped across the room and hurled himself towards an overstuffed leather sofa. The legs of the chair cracked when they hit the sofa, but were muffled by the cushions. Struggling upright, he jumped into the air and dropped down hard. The legs splintered and folded and he tugged the rope under the chair seat and past his feet. The knots were wound tight around his wrists, but the rope was loose and he wrestled free and ran to the French windows.

Locked. No key in sight. The window panes were about the size of his hand, framed in thick wood. *I'll never get through in one go. If I smash the glass, they'll be on me in seconds. Maybe seconds are all I've got.* The garden outside was about twenty feet long. *Too long. I'll never make it.*

He ran over to the door. *Guard outside?* He placed his hand on the handle then snatched it back. *Too risky.* He knelt down. Through the door jamb he could see two bolts. *Locked.*

Do something. Do it now. Or you're a dead man.

He spun around. No other windows or doors. He grabbed the poker from the floor. *Wait until they came through the door? No. Too many guns.*

The panic began to rise in his gut. *No, godammit! Fight it! I'm not gonna die. Not today. No fucking way.*

An ancient gas fire stood in the grate. Candles on the mantelpiece. Matches beside them. To the right, a six foot tall Normandy armoire. Solid oak.

If I'm going down, some of these bastards are going with me. He pulled open the doors of the armoire and stifled a cry of despair. Every shelf was covered in delicate crockery. His mind raced. *The shelf. Take out the shelf.* The crockery chinked together as he slid out the shelf and laid it on the floor, followed by two others.

Grabbing the candles and matches from the mantelpiece, he ran to the door and listened for a moment, but there was nothing. They were upstairs. He rubbed the candle hard into the jamb of the door below the hinge. Wax flaked and fell to the floor, but some stuck to the wood. He ripped the sandpaper from the side of the matchbox and wrapped it around the head of the matches, then gently pushed them into the wax, until they were wedged together in the door jamb.

Water. I need water. A drinks tray sat in the corner of the room. All of them contained spirits. *No good.* The handle of a soda siphon stuck out from the back of the tray. He lifted it clear and squeezed the handle, spraying it in his eye to wash out the lighter fluid, then sprayed the curtains and ripped them down. Beside the window lay a length of cord for the curtain.

Something to make a noise. The clock. The goddamn fucking ugly clock.

He threw one end of the curtain cord to the fireplace. It was long enough. He ran over and looped one end around the clock then dropped down to the gas fire.

He found the controls and twisted them around until he heard the hiss of gas. A flame burst into life and he bent to blow it out. He was breathing so fast he could hardly keep the air in his chest. He slowly turned down the control and blew hard. The flame sputtered and died.

He spun the controls to full and stepped back, listening to the escaping gas. *It's not enough.* Water pipes rumbled and banged in the wall, then stopped. *The bath was full. It was time.*

At the side of the fire was a copper pipe and he stamped on it with all his weight. It didn't budge. Sweat stung his eyes and his tongue stuck to the roof of his mouth as he tried to breathe. He held on to the fireplace, then jumped and dropped down hard.

He heard a sharp crack as the fitting came away from

the side of the fire. The hissing increased. He grabbed the pipe and tugged with all his might. It snapped back, sending him tumbling onto the carpet.

Gas spewed out and he snatched up the curtains and ran to the armoire. He jumped in, pulled the curtains over his head then picked up the cord and pulled the armoire door closed.

In the darkness he could see a faint sliver of light from the bottom of the door. *They made these old cupboards well. Just how well, I'm about to find out.* He crouched, his arms wrapped hard around his leg. He lifted his head for a moment and sniffed the air. *It won't take long. The gas was under pressure. Unless they came in first. Then I'll know. Yeah. I'll know.*

The stench of gas was getting stronger. They could come in at any moment, but if he waited any longer . . . *No. It had to happen now.* He pushed the armoire door open a crack and jerked the cord, hauling the door closed before the clock crashed to the floor.

Voices. They were coming. He pulled the curtain tight over his head and pressed his hands to his face.

The force of the blast slammed the armoire against the wall. The doors burst open and he tumbled out onto the floor. The whole room was alight. Two men were lying by the door, screaming and beating flames from their clothes and hair. A long tongue of yellow flame spewed out from the broken pipe, fed by gusts of air pouring in from the shattered windows. Fumes and smoke scorched Montrose's lungs. One of the men got to his feet, his clothes ablaze and his scalp covered in black and bleeding wounds. He roared and ran across the room.

Montrose turned, but his foot caught in the curtain

and he tumbled backwards to the floor. The air exploded out of his chest as the man dropped onto him. Thick hands clamped around his throat. The flames from the man's clothes licked his face. The man rose up, bringing his full weight down on his arms. Montrose heard the cartilage of his windpipe crack. His sight began to blur and the noise around him dropped to a whisper. Weakness washed over his arms and chest. His grip on the man's arm slipped and his hand dropped onto the shelf of crockery. His fingers tightened around crystal. *One shot . . . It had to be one shot.*

He brought up a champagne flute and thrust it deep into the man's eye. Blood and optical fluid spurted from the eye socket, hissing as it sprayed the man's smoldering clothes. Montrose pushed the screaming man aside, rolled over on to his knees. He pulled his jacket over his head, dipped his shoulder and ran for the windows. He burst through the broken door frame and into the garden.

Montrose felt himself running in slow motion until he slammed into the wall. He hauled himself up, skin tearing from his fingers, then scrambled over the top. He caught a glimpse of the inferno just before he dropped to the ground.

Fuck them. He hit the sidewalk.

He spun around at the roar of a motorbike as it slithered to a halt on the cobblestones. He grabbed the handlebars and stood in front of the bike, staring into the shocked face of a girl. "I need your bike!"

She pushed up her visor and stared at his clothes. His jeans were still smoldering.

Montrose leant over the handlebars. *I've never hit a girl before. I'm not going to start now.* "Listen to me, please. I need your bike. Now!"

She gazed at him for a moment and then recovered. "What you need, Monsieur Montrose, is a ride. But if I drop this clutch, you'll get a tire mark straight up your chest."

Montrose stared at her, his mouth wide open.

"Make your mind up," she said. "I don't know what happened behind that wall, but I'm not hanging around to find out. Get on."

CHAPTER 27

"Hold tight and lean into the corners." She dumped the clutch and opened the throttle. The bike shot forward, rear wheel spinning and snaking around on the cobbles.

Montrose looked over her head and saw traffic flash past at the end of the road. He twisted his legs to take the pressure off his aching balls, but slammed into her back when she hit the brakes at the end of the alley and threaded the bike through a gap in the traffic. The only way to survive was to hold on tight. His arm could have wrapped around her entire body. She pulled the Norton down to the left and gunned the engine along the Boulevard Saint-Germain.

The twin exhaust roared as she went up hard through the gears. His chin thudded against her helmet as the bike lurched forward with each gear change. He lifted his head clear to stop the pain in his jaw. The bike weaved through the rush hour traffic. Pedestrians crossing the road heard them coming and stepped back. They knew what was good for them.

The traffic in front came to a halt and she stamped down on the gear shift, the engine shuddering in protest. Turning into a narrow street, barely wide enough for a car, she weaved past delivery wagons and bumped the Norton up onto the sidewalk to pass a dustcart, scattering pedestrians. Buildings crowded in on either side, the street lined with expensive boutiques and cheap trinket shops for the tourists. His face chilled in the blast of cold air, but it took away the pain in his face.

She stood on the foot brake at the end of the street. He glimpsed Notre Dame to their left, golden stone rising high into the morning sunshine. She pulled on to a main road, cutting up a line of cars, then took the road for the bridge across the Seine and the Ile Saint Louis.

Where the hell are we going?

The traffic cleared and she pulled the throttle wide open over the Pont Marie. Montrose caught a glimpse of the corner of Rue Lamont and the pawnbroker where he had jumped to the street. *Shit, the whole of Paris to choose from and she comes here.*

The front of the bike dipped when she braked at the end of the bridge. She threaded her way past a line of tourist buses and into the side streets of Le Marais.

The old Jewish Quarter. Maybe that answers the question. And explains who the old guy in the pawn shop was calling.

Mossad.

The thought sent a shiver through his guts. *The most ruthless agency on the planet. The fun in Zurich and Rome had probably set off alarm bells in cop shops all over Europe. Mossad would have picked it up. And the boys from Tel-Aviv were not known for their forgiveness and understanding when it came to Nazi loot.*

They were deep into the back streets of Le Marais. *No cops. They would be hitting the road junctions and train stations. But if Mossad were on the trail, it wouldn't take them long to find me.* He held on tight to the girl as she weaved between the cars. *Maybe they already had. But I'm not their enemy. No need to add them to the list.*

The bike slowed and turned up the Rue du Temple. She snicked the gears down through the box and turned the Norton into a dark alley towards Rue Rambuteau. The alley narrowed and the walls became closer around them. At the end was a wooden door.

Montrose looked behind. *Nothing.*

She nudged the front tire up to the door and pushed it open. The door sprang back and opened into a dimly lit stairwell. Feathering the clutch, she eased the Norton over the step and onto the worn flagstones of a cramped hall. The engine thundered in the tight space at the foot of a winding flight of stairs. She hit the kill switch and the engine coughed and died.

She turned her head. "You can let go now."

Uncurling his arms, he stepped off the bike. "Where are we?"

"Home." She kicked the door closed. "Come with me. Keep your feet to the side, the staircase is very old."

Montrose looked up at the dusty wooden steps. Some of them were almost worn right through. It might take her weight, but he wasn't sure it would take his. A faint light came from above. He looked up the winding staircase and saw a narrow skylight high up in the roof.

She said nothing and headed up the stairs. He began to follow. It looked about four or five flights to the top. The banister was unpainted iron, smooth and black with age. The air was clean and dry. At each landing was a small, heavy wooden door that looked as though it came straight from the middle ages. *No nameplates. These weren't apartments. No one lived here.*

He caught her eye when she turned up another flight of stairs.

"They're old workrooms," she said, "from when the building was used in the last century. The lace trade. No one works here now."

He ran his hand along the rough walls, paint flaking at his touch. The whole place had to be pre-Haussmann, the age before progress had flattened vast swathes of medieval Paris to form the broad boulevards and grand buildings so loved by the tourists.

She stopped at the top and pushed open a low door. Montrose followed her into a small attic room, one wall sloping and a large skylight showing the rooftops of Le Marais.

She pulled off her bike jacket, then lit a one-ringed gas stove. Montrose walked straight to the window.

"Yes," she said, "you can escape through the window. But we're five floors up. You'll fall through a rotten roof, or you'll end up on the street. Very quickly." She pushed her fingers through her auburn hair where it had been flattened by the helmet. Her dark eyes flashed a nervous look as he stood in the middle of the room.

Montrose rubbed his jaw. His mouth hurt like hell, and his tongue found a few loose teeth. The dull ache in his kidneys spelled trouble. He gingerly touched the swollen flesh of his lower back and knew he'd be pissing blood for a week. He lifted his head. She was looking him up and down with a mixture of shock and disgust. "Who are you?" he said.

She dumped her leather jacket on a low bed in the corner. "I'll tell you who I'm not. I'm not your enemy. I'd like to keep it that way." She blew the dust from a coffee pot and filled it from a sink.

"Okay," Montrose sighed. "Who do you work for?" From her look, he could see he'd wounded her pride.

"I work for no one. Although I help certain people."

"Who?"

"People who have been searching for something for a very long time. The diamonds, Monsieur Montrose. Now, take your clothes off."

"What?"

She shrugged. "You stink, you're dressed as a prisoner and your clothes are either burned or covered in blood. Wash in the sink. There's a towel by the bed. I'm going to get you something to wear." She stopped at the door and turned. "I'm not your jailer, Monsieur Montrose. I'm told the whole of the Paris gendarmerie are looking for you. Not forgetting the people you met earlier. But I can help you. And you can help me. So I'd appreciate it if you stayed put until I return. Make some coffee." She closed the door behind her.

Her footsteps on the stairs became faint. Montrose stood for a moment and the pain returned, shooting spasms from the back of his neck to his balls. Blood was clotted hard in the back of his nose, but the bleeding in his mouth had stopped.

He walked to the skylight and took a few deep breaths until the pain subsided. He gazed out over the rooftops. In the distance he could see the dome of the Sacré Cœur on the hill of Montmartre.

He pressed his forehead against the glass. *Whoever the girl on the bike was, she saved my life. Those bastards would have chased me through the streets and shot me down like a dog. Though the girl didn't behave like a spook. She couldn't be police. Not on her own, and not on a bike like that. But whoever she worked for, she could lead them straight here.*

He tried the door. It was unlocked. He bent over the guardrail of the stairs. She didn't look up, just squeezed past the Norton and tugged open the door to the alley. *I could get out right now. But it's going to be tricky. The police would be everywhere. And I look like a prisoner covered in shit. Not the best disguise.*

There was another door to the right, at the top of the landing. It was locked although the handle was shiny with use. Montrose moved down the stairs trying each door, but none would open. Standing at the bottom of the steps, he could hear nothing except the ticking of the engine. He caught the smell of hot oil dripping from the Norton's crankcase. A stained piece of cardboard across the flagstones told him that the bike was normally parked there. *It's not a safe house. Maybe she did live here.*

He checked the bike. The tax disc was registered to Paris Arrondissement Four. Le Marais. He flipped up the seat and saw papers wrapped in plastic, then pulled out a flimsy registration document. The owner was clearly marked. *Charlotte Marceau. Rue de Rose Croix. Seemed like she was telling the truth. Unless it was a helluva good cover. Mossad were experts at that.*

Montrose stuffed the papers back in the plastic and closed the seat, then squeezed past the Norton and slowly opened the door. People passed by at the end of the alley. He stepped out and looked up. *Maybe an eight foot jump from one roof to the other. On ancient, mossy slates. Not the easiest of options.*

He hurried to the end of the alley and stood back from the corner. No cars, the street was too narrow. Arab grocers, a video store, tobacconist. People walked past without giving him a second glance. No curtains twitched, no one looked over. He ducked back down the alley.

Whoever she was, she's the best thing that has happened to me for a long time. He climbed the stairs, keeping his feet to the side.

The coffee pot bubbled on the stove. He lifted the lid and threw in some grounds from a paper bag. The label said pure Colombian. *Yeah, if only they stuck to making coffee.*

He poured a cup, wincing when it hit his tongue, but it was hot and good. Now it was all down to her. There was nothing else he could do. He looked around the room. Nobody had been here for a while. He guessed she wasn't accustomed to bringing people back. He opened the skylight onto the roof. *She was right. It's a death trap.* Turning away, he took the towel hanging by the sink and ran it under the faucet, then wiped his face and hands. A knife and fork lay in a drawer under the sink. He slipped the knife into his pocket and left the door open as he crossed to the top of the stairs.

The girl was real. The way she had handled that big bike through the streets of Paris. She had a fire in her belly. Damn it, if she is Mossad they could have the diamonds. I'm not in much of a position to say no. Old Reinhard is dead. And the video died with him. At least the diamonds would find their way back to the families, if any of them were still alive. I just need a way out. A ticket to London in exchange for the bag. It wasn't a bad deal. Mossad had to go for it. Though I'll have to play it tight. She said they'd been looking for something. It had to be the diamonds.

She hadn't mentioned the list, or safe deposit boxes. Maybe Mossad had no idea. It didn't matter. They could have the list. Then Mossad could go after Kurt Reinhard. The bastard would get what was coming to him. If I don't get him first.

He looked back to the room. The skylight was wide open. He fingered the knife in his pocket. *Nothing to do but wait. If anyone else other than the girl comes through that door, then slippery tiles or not, I'll be out of the skylight and across the roof like a cat on amphetamines.* Fatigue washed over him again. He sat down on the top step and rested his head against the wall.

A wry smile crossed his face and the dull ache in his jaw returned. *Doesn't matter what I do with the diamonds. Mossad are going to unleash hell.* His smile faded. *Old Reinhard is dead. The chance to clear my name died with him.*

A hum from distant traffic drifted through the stairwell and the light breeze from the skylight cooled his aching face. He blew out a long slow breath as the fatigue took hold. His shoulders slumped and he closed his eyes. *Just for a few minutes.*

CHAPTER 28

The sound of a door opening. His eyes shot open. *Christ, how long have I been out?* He jumped up and grabbed the handrail.

Get ready. He held the knife in his pocket.

Peering down the narrow shaft of the stairwell, he saw the girl struggling past the Norton, her arms full of store bags. She began to climb the stairs. The door to the alley closed behind her. She was alone. *Guess I won't be doing a rooftop escape.* He turned back into the room and closed the skylight, then slipped the knife in the drawer under the sink.

She reached the top of the stairs and had to shuffle sideways to squeeze through the attic door with the bags.

Montrose watched in amazement as she dumped them on the floor, each one emblazoned with a designer name.

She shrugged. "I have friends in the fashion industry."

"You know my size?"

"My father and grandfather were tailors. I picked it up from them."

"Thank you," he said. "I don't know what I've done to deserve this."

"I do. What you've done is incredible. But I think you have no idea."

"I guess not." He extended a hand. "Connor Montrose."

She looked down, struggling with a decision. "Charlotte Marceau."

Her hands were tiny, but her grip was warm and firm. "Charlotte?" he said. Her hair hung over her shoulders. She was beautiful. Though he got the impression it was singularly unimportant to her. "Why you? And, if I have to be honest, why me?"

She shrugged. "You are not important."

Montrose grinned before she held up a hand. He thought she was in danger of actually smiling.

"You know what I mean," she said. "You have the diamonds. Who you are is irrelevant."

Maybe, but Mossad might think differently. "Is that the only reason you're helping me?"

"Yes. Because I want you to give the diamonds back."

"Back? So they're yours?"

"No. To the families that lost them. To their children."

Montrose heard the passion in her voice. She didn't have to be told about how the diamonds were taken. For her, this was personal. "Charlotte? Who are you?"

She tossed aside her hair with a hand. "You have my name. That's all you need to know."

"Can you prove it?" He gave her a wry smile. "Perhaps we can take a walk to the Israeli Embassy?"

"I'm French. I'm not a spy for Israel. I have no

business at their embassy. Not even the French government know about me. Not that they care. Of course, I report back to a contact. And it would be quite naive to think that they are anything other than some . . ." She looked up at the low ceiling, searching for the words. "Well, intelligence agency, I suppose. So if it's Mossad, or another part of the Israeli government, I don't know. But the operation is global."

"I'm sure." *Mossad had been clever. Just set up a network of contacts, keep them talking, keep them watching, and then the results would come in. Mossad never give up. They must have been waiting over seventy years for this moment. But her poker face was slipping. She was practically skipping with excitement.* "So, how did you know?"

"We heard someone had stolen a shipment of diamonds from Zurich. From someone called Kessler. A big shipment. For us, it could mean only one possibility."

Montrose shook his head. *They were way ahead of me.*

"And an Interpol agent goes missing. Your name was all over the Swiss police radio."

He began to laugh, but his jaw hurt like hell. "Yeah, I'm sure."

"I couldn't work it out. Why would Interpol try to steal diamonds from the Holocaust? Besides, you don't look like a diamond thief."

"So I've been told."

She moved closer to him and held her head to one side. "Why did you steal them? Is Interpol working with Mossad?"

"No. Charlotte, the diamonds . . . Well, I can't tell

you why, but Interpol are not with me on this. I work for someone else. I stole them for my own reasons. That's why I went to Zurich."

She stepped back. "You did this yourself? Who do you work for?"

Montrose could see it written all over her face. "Relax, I don't want the diamonds. You can have them. I don't care. I just want to get out of France." *And the rest of the world can go to hell.*

"Where are they?"

"They're here. In Paris."

She threw back her head. "I can't believe it. We've been looking for so long. For me, all my life. This means everything. *Mon dieu!* I haven't told my grandfather!"

"Your grandfather?"

"He's from Antwerp. He lost everything in the war. It nearly destroyed him. He's spent half his life looking for the diamonds. When he became ill, it fell to me." She looked up. "Where exactly are they?"

"Not far. They're in a safe deposit box. First we have to get to Gare du Nord. I've left my ID there. I'll need it to get the diamonds."

She nodded, her chin bobbing up and down. "I picked up some more information. Every flic in Paris is searching for an escaped prisoner. It's come straight from the Prefét de Police." She took a bottle of dark liquid from a bag and gave it a hard shake. "We have to change the way you look. I'm going to stain your skin. Just your head and neck, and your hands. You look too Anglo-Saxon."

Montrose grinned. "Yeah, a flic pointed that out to me." A thought nagged at him. "Charlotte? How did you know I was in Paris?"

She shook her head and poured some of the liquid onto a soft cloth. "I wasn't expecting you to turn up here. We heard about the pawn shop. He was supposed to keep you busy until someone arrived, but he panicked."

He wasn't alone.

"He said you could have killed him, but that you threw away the bullets."

Maybe that's why I'm still alive. I owe that old nutjob a beer.

"Then some of Kessler's men were tracked to Paris and I was told that a thief had been taken to a prison in Versailles. No trial. No name. Why? So I was sent to observe. I followed Kessler's men to the house in the seventh arrondissement and found you."

Montrose had to laugh. "I'm glad you did."

"Coming over the wall was quite a surprise. Now, take off your top."

His shoulder ached when he tried to he removed his shirt. He caught her cheeks reddening.

"I'll color your hair and eyebrows." She dabbed the cloth against the dark stubble on his jaw and neck, then smoothed it across his cheeks. "My friends in the fashion industry use this for photo shoots."

He flinched as she wiped the cloth across his nose.

"Excuse me," she said.

Montrose held his arms out in front of him and she brushed the liquid over his hands, then stepped back. "It'll dry in a few minutes. Then we'll do your hair." She looked up at his buzz cut. "That won't take long."

The breeze from the window felt good on his skin. He stood, arms outstretched, examining the color of his hands.

"Was it bad?" she said. "In that house?"

He could see the concern in her eyes. She had no idea. "It could have been worse." *Being repeatedly beaten and half-drowned, face down in cold water, for hours on end. It broke the strongest men. I don't want to think about the urologist. I might never sleep again.* "It was a lot worse for them."

"Kessler's men?"

"Yeah." Montrose looked away.

"All that time," she said. "We had no idea. Switzerland? I couldn't believe it, but then it all made sense."

"Kessler was just the banker." Montrose waved his hands around to help them dry. "He was holding the diamonds for a man called Reinhard."

Charlotte's eyes narrowed. "*Lieutenant* Erwin Reinhard?"

"That's him."

"We know he was involved in the Antwerp interrogations, but he died in battle, no?"

Montrose shrugged. "Apparently not."

"Where is he?"

"Well, this time he really is dead. It's a long story."

Charlotte threw up a hand. "Yes, some other time." She stroked his cheek. "It's dry. I'll do your hair. Bend over the sink."

The blood rushed to his face when he bowed his head and a trickle of blood came from his nose. He wiped it away before she noticed.

She rubbed the liquid into his hair. "It's a black dye, but it only lasts a day or so. Stand up."

Montrose felt light-headed as she smoothed the liquid over his eyebrows.

She stood back and admired her handiwork. "I should

have brought a razor. I didn't think. It's not too bad. In a few moments you can change. Pick what you want. I've gone for brighter colors. More Mediterranean, and less . . . "

He could see she was searching for the right word. "Anglo Saxon?"

"I was going to say *Rosbif*."

Montrose remembered the name. What the French called the English. Roast Beefs.

"Oh, and I got you this." She held out a white tube. "It's medical cream. For your skin."

He glanced down at the raw bands around his wrists where the rope had burned the flesh. "Thanks. Have you got any painkillers?"

She thought for a moment, and then fished around in her purse. "Only these." She held out a large pink pill. "They are for . . . monthly pains."

"That's roughly where it hurts."

"You can change now," she said. "I'll leave you."

Montrose nodded. "You had better change too, if you're coming."

She looked down at her jeans. "Me?"

"Someone may have heard the motorbike when we got out. I mean, I like the biker chick look, but you know . . ."

She stood for a moment, and pulled on her lip. "I'll think of something," she said, then turned and left the room.

Montrose tried to see his reflection in the window, but the sun was too strong. The fake tan felt slightly tacky though it was dry enough. If it was the same color as his hands, it was the best tan he'd ever had.

He pulled a shirt and suit from the bag. It was top

quality and a long way from what he normally would have chosen. She'd gone for a caramel suit with padded shoulders. The shirt was electric blue. *Must be a French thing. With this tan, it'll work.* He kicked off his sneakers and pulled on a pair of brown Gucci loafers. *The girl had friends with taste.* At the bottom of the bag lay several pairs of sunglasses. He chose a pair of Ray Ban Aviators and slipped them in his pocket.

The water from the sink was icy cold. He rubbed himself down with a cloth, then pulled on the shirt. It fitted well and since he was going continental, he didn't need a tie. He took a slug of coffee from the pot to wash down the pill. He could feel his knee stiffening where Reinhard had hit it with the poker. The joint would fill with fluid and swell up. *I'll have to keep moving. Yeah, no shit.* There was a knock at the door.

"Come in."

She stepped in, wearing a mid-length cotton dress covered in a delicate floral pattern. She'd pinned up her hair. Montrose thought it made her look like a teenager, but it worked. She was gorgeous.

Charlotte took in his suit. "Very good. *Très chic.* I've ordered a taxi to take us to the Gare Du Nord. The police won't be looking for a well-dressed, handsome man."

"Or his beautiful companion."

She blushed and turned away.

"Wait," he said. "You ordered a taxi? From your home address?"

"Of course. Why?"

This girl was genuine. An amateur. "Nothing. Let's get my ID before the cops lock the place down. And pick up the code for the safe deposit box."

"You don't know it?"

A sudden pain in his jaw made him wince. The painkillers only seemed to be working from the waist down. "Remembering a number wasn't top of my list at the time. I just wanted to put them in a safe place."

She shrugged. "We'll go to the Gare du Nord. Then the diamonds. But first, there is someone I want you to meet. This way." She opened the door at the end of the landing.

Montrose grabbed a light raincoat from a bag and followed her into a narrow corridor where the décor changed completely. No more dusty old attic. At the end was a stairwell. Thick carpets covered the steps and the banister was rich, dark wood. The walls were lined with watercolors and small, iridescent oil paintings. He didn't know much about art, but they looked damn expensive. At a turn in the stairs the sunlight filtered in through a long, stained glass window, and color dappled the walls. Around him, Montrose recognized the swooping curves and stylized flowers of the Art Nouveau period. Little expense had been spared. The wood became more carved and ornate as they descended, every inch seemed to be covered in an intricately patterned design.

They turned into a wide corridor and stopped before a heavy oak door. "Grand-père can't talk," said Charlotte. "A stroke robbed him of most of his powers. But not his mind."

She opened the door into a salon. The decor became more outrageous, although still of exquisite taste. Bookcases covered with leaded glass doors lined the walls, facing a polished marble fireplace, the stone an almost light, translucent blue, carved with rose motifs. Chaise longues covered with embroidered throws sat in the middle of the room, beside an inlaid cherry wood table. Montrose walked over to the wide window, his shoes sinking into a thick Persian rug. He caught a shock of white hair just above the edge of a wing-backed chair, facing away from the room, onto the street.

"*Grand-père?*" She placed her hand delicately on the old man's arm. Montrose couldn't stop himself and crossed to the window. An old man sat, impeccably dressed in a grey woolen suit. His shoes gleamed and the creases in his pants were razor sharp. A glittering gold fob watch hung from his vest.

Charlotte knelt in front of him. "*Grand-père?*"

The old man stayed completely still. Piercing dark eyes turned towards her, then across to Montrose. The old man might be as still as a statue, but his eyes burned. The mind still keen, trapped inside a frozen body.

"This man," she said, "has found the diamonds! He's found them, Grand-père! They're here in Paris. He's going to give them to us."

The old man's pupils widened and his lips trembled.

She held onto his arm. "I'm going to get them now."

Montrose could see a million questions in the old man's eyes.

"He's an American," she said, holding on tight to her grandfather's arm. "He stole them from Switzerland, where the Nazis had hidden them."

Her grandfather's eyes glistened.

Charlotte's voice began to shake. "I'll bring them back here for you to see, then I'll call our contact. They'll know what to do." She pulled a white linen handkerchief from his top pocket and dabbed at the corner of his reddening eyes. "I'll return soon," she said and kissed his cheek. She took a deep breath and walked towards the door.

Montrose stood for a moment. The old man's eyes burned into him. Unsure of what to say, Montrose bowed his head and followed Charlotte out of the room.

The staircase became wider and they descended into a spacious hall.

"The taxi will be here in a few minutes," she said as she sat down on a carved wooden bench. In the corner an ancient grandfather clock chimed the hour. Montrose looked around at the paintings and hanging tapestries. He could have stepped back to the turn of the century and the Belle Époque. The entire floor was inlaid with small marble tiles in pastel colors.

Through the frosted glass of the door, he saw a black car pull up. Charlotte got to her feet. "I've been looking forward to this for so long. Sometimes it seemed impossible we would ever find them. Now, it's time."

"Wait." Montrose pressed his face against the glass of the door and saw the taxi light on top of the car. "It's good. Let's go."

The narrow street was quiet. Montrose held the door for her and she swept her skirt to one side and got into the taxi. *Maybe it was safer this way.* He sat down beside her. *We can get out somewhere south of the station then check for police. It would be better to take a side door or blend in with the crowd. If it was like the last time, the cops would be waiting at the main entrance.*

She leaned over to the driver before he could stop her. "Gare du Nord," she said.

Montrose sighed and sat back. *I'm going to have to take control. We're leaving a trail for the cops a mile wide.*

She turned her head and was about to speak when Montrose held a finger to his lips and pointed to the driver. They sat in silence and the taxi headed west onto the Boulevard Sebastopol.

He could see she was burning with questions. She sighed and tucked her dress behind her legs, shifting on the seat to get comfortable. Montrose guessed she didn't have too many dresses. He could still see the marks on her legs where the leather bike boots had been tight against her calves. "You look great," he said.

"*Merci*." She smoothed her hands across her thighs, and arranged the pleats. "The dress belonged to my mother."

"She had marvelous taste."

Charlotte shrugged, but he could she was pleased. "She was an artist and a collector. Many of the paintings you saw in the apartment were chosen by her."

Montrose reckoned that what he knew about art could be written on the back of a postage stamp. With a marker pen.

She glanced at the driver then leant over and spoke quietly in Montrose's ear. Her hair brushed the side of his neck as she spoke. "My mother was wearing this when they escaped to France. They were still at school, but their age was no barrier to the Nazis. Friends here helped them get the right documents. Then my grandfather joined the Résistance. After the war, the Israelis asked him to use the old network to look for the diamonds. But there was no trace of them. After a while my father and mother sold up and moved to Israel. Grand-père tried for a while, but I wanted to come back to Paris. So did he. Unfinished business, he would say. So we came back and now I look after him. But when illness overtook him, they gave me training and showed me how to watch and listen."

Montrose turned, just as she tilted her head towards him and his lips brushed her cheek. "Like a sleeper?" he whispered.

"With those people out there, I don't sleep very well." She sat back in silence and the taxi turned on to the Boulevard de Magenta.

The station was dead ahead. CRS vans were crowded around the entrance. There was no way to avoid them. The steps to the Métro were to the right. *Down there and go through the tunnels into the station.*

The taxi pulled up behind the CRS vans. Charlotte handed the driver the fare.

Montrose got out and slipped on his sunglasses. The line of vans blocked the view of the station entrance. "We'll go in through the Métro," said Montrose. "There are too many cops around."

She stood for a moment.

"Don't look at them," he said. "Try and be natural." Montrose offered his arm. "We're just a handsome couple."

She took his arm and they turned into the tunnel for the Métro. At the end were steps leading up into the station.

"Where are we going?" she said.

"Ticket booth."

They emerged onto the platforms. Groups of heavily armed CRS milled around the main concourse. Montrose stopped for a moment to check the exits. *Looks like they had the place sewn up tight.* He turned and saw a cleaner, broom in hand, pushing the dust and litter towards the ticket booth. *He's going to push all that crap underneath.* "Follow me. Move!" he hissed. Montrose strode over to the side of the booth and held up a hand as the cleaner approached. "Wait! Have you swept this bit yet?"

The cleaner shrugged. "No. Not since this morning."

"Look, give me a few minutes. I've dropped a contact lens. It's got to be here somewhere."

The cleaner gave him a skeptical look, then turned away. "Bonne chance, monsieur."

"What's wrong?" she said.

"Stand here." He gently pulled Charlotte to the side of the booth then knelt down and grabbed his shoelace. His eyes scanned from side to side, along the line of litter and dust. He blew out a breath when he glimpsed the edge of the wallet. "It's there."

Charlotte glanced across the concourse. "Make it fast, Mr. Montrose."

"Please, call me Connor." He looked up at her and saw two policemen looking in his direction. *I'm the right height and build. Nothing I could do about that.*

"Then make it fast, Connor. There are too many flics around for comfort."

The policemen began walking towards them. *Good move, that's what I'd do. See what the target does next.* He stood up and smoothed down his suit.

"I can see them," said Charlotte. "Remember, it's not a Hollywood movie. So don't grab me in a romantic clinch if they get too close."

He let out a nervous laugh and she flashed him a look of indignation. "Don't worry," he said, "I never kiss on a first date."

Her face melted into a smile. "Well, I do." She stood

on tiptoes then gently took his face in her hands and kissed him full on the lips. She stood back before he had a chance to recover. "Thank you," she said. "You don't know what this means to me."

From the corner of his eye he could see the policemen moving off. "Well, I think I do now."

"It was for the benefit of the police. Mostly."

Montrose grinned. She had style.

She raised an eyebrow. "The code?"

"Yeah." He bent down and shoved his hand under the booth. His fingers found the lighter; he pulled out the wallet and watch and slipped them into his jacket. "Let's go," he said and stood up. A group of policemen hung around the side door. "We'll have to go out the main entrance to the taxi stand. They'll be watching for people leaving Paris, rather than coming from the station."

They turned away from the platforms. Montrose slid to a stop. Outside the station, a man stood in the middle of the plaza, arms folded across his chest. He turned towards Montrose. *I know that face. Bonsergeant.* "Take the Métro."

"What is it?"

"The man in the suit. On the Plaza. He's the flic who arrested me. Back to the booth. We need some Métro tickets." He took her by the arm and led her away from the entrance.

"I have some in my bag," she said. "Where are we going?"

"Rue des Rosiers."

She stopped, and her lips fell open. "Mon dieu! That's not far from my apartment!"

"If Bonsergeant saw me, then we can't lead them straight there. We have to go another way."

"I know where to go," said Charlotte.

"You sure?"

"I'm Parisian. If you need to hide, there's no better place than where we're going. I have contacts."

Of course you do. "Okay, which line do we take?"

"Châtelet. Line 4."

You could be taking me straight to Mossad. "Then we'd better move. The cops are right behind us. Make sure we don't give them any room for suspicion. Look happy."

She linked her arm into his. "I am happy."

They descended the steps into the subway and followed the signs for Line 4. Tourists and travelers struggled past them with suitcases.

"Take off the sunglasses," she said. "It looks like you're trying too hard to be cool."

Armed soldiers stood at every corner. Heavy automatic weapons hung at their sides. "They've called out the troops," he said.

"No, they're usually at the major stations, just a show for terrorists. They don't have magazines in their weapons."

They were only boys. But they were wearing bulging ammunition pouches.

Charlotte skipped down the steps to the southbound platform then glanced back. "There's no one behind us."

"Find the busiest spot," he said. They weaved past the tourists on the crowded platform. A train rattled into the station, brakes squealing. The doors slammed open and passengers fought their way onto the platform while others pushed their way onto the train. It was chaos. Montrose took her hand and brushed people aside.

They attempted to stand in the middle of the carriage, but were maneuvered into a corner by a family of noisy Italians barging onto the train and lifting kids onto their suitcases.

Charlotte was pushed up against him. The train took off with a jolt and she almost fell backwards over a suitcase.

Montrose grabbed her around the waist and hauled her towards him. She couldn't reach the handrail above her and was forced to put her hands around his waist. "Hold on tight," he said.

"Don't get any ideas."

"Nothing could be further from my mind." He caught her delicate perfume. A flower and citrus scent. She smelled good. He remembered how perfume affected him. He felt her tiny hands holding onto his waist. The rocking of the train forced them together in waves. For a moment he was transported, holding on to the handrail of a swaying Métro carriage with one hand and a beautiful French girl with the other. He caught sight of the nape of her neck when she turned her head. Her skin was like caramel silk. He felt himself involuntarily opening his lips. *Yeah, dream on buddy. Your next romantic tryst might be with the bad boys from Tel Aviv.*

"What's wrong?" she said.

"Nothing." He smiled. "Just a dream. A good dream." The rolling carriage was bumping them together in all the wrong places. *Jeez, if this keeps up she's going to know exactly what I think about her.* He looked over the heads of the passengers, searching for uniforms. *Keep your mind on the job. Did the cops get on? Maybe the other carriage? I can't see a damn thing.*

The train rattled through the tunnels, slowing as

signs for Les Halles flashed past the window. Crowds lined the platforms. Montrose took her by the hand and pushed his way to the exit. Les Halles was a busy station, scores of lines coming together in central Paris and a constant stream of people filled the subway corridors.

Montrose glanced up the stairs to the street entrance. *No sign of the cops. They'd need fifty men to cover a station this size and they'd concentrate on the junction points.*

"Nearly there," she said.

They emerged into the sunshine on Rue Ballard. She headed north and onto Rue Montmartre, skirting the faceless buildings of the shopping centre built on the site of the old Paris market of Les Halles, where for centuries, produce had come from the surrounding countryside to feed the city. Then the seventies happened and regeneration for Paris. The whole market, an intricate web of wrought iron, glass and five hundred years of history, was flattened. In its place grew dull blocks of concrete and a shopping centre.

"Wait." She slowed to a halt and ducked into a dingy alleyway. "Follow me. Quickly!"

"What's going on?"

"I'm not sure. Run!"

She pulled him to a halt as they rounded the corner at the end. "Look!" She pointed to a shop directly across the road. In the reflection of the window he watched the alleyway. She was right. Two men stood at the far end of the alley then began to jog towards them.

"Where now?" said Montrose.

She looked left and right. "We keep going. We can make it."

"To where?"

"The Bar D'Raymond. The worst bar in Paris."

She tugged his arm and hauled him across the street and down another small alley which wound around the buildings.

Montrose kept his head low, avoiding pipes and cables. "The worst bar in Paris?"

"*Mais oui!* It's not been cleaned since Napoléon was a very small boy. But it has a history. There's nothing you can't buy there. Besides, we won't be bothered by the police in that bar. The patron can smell them a mile off. Though I'm surprised he can smell anything."

They turned into a tiny, dark square lined with bags of trash. The walls of the surrounding buildings were damp, lichen-covered stone, dotted with filthy windows stretching up around ten floors. Montrose arched his neck up and saw a patch of sunlight. At the far wall was an entrance to a courtyard and, almost hidden in the corner, a low door led into a bar.

A rusting 'Les Routiers' sign was pinned to the wooden lintel. Montrose had to laugh. "Isn't that for places that are recommended?" He followed her through the door and they stopped for a moment while their eyes adjusted to the darkness. Montrose caught a weird stink. *Jesus, who the hell would want to drink here?* "What's that smell?"

Charlotte smirked. "You'll find out."

Men sat around tables, a glass of beer or wine in their hands. No one looked up as they squeezed past the tables.

"We've lost them," said Charlotte.

Montrose eyed up the bar taps. *A beer wouldn't hurt.* "Let's give it ten minutes. We can plan a way out of here." He nodded at the barman who was pulling a draught lager, and held up two fingers. "Though I wouldn't fancy buying a new jacket from these guys. It might be still warm from its last owner."

"Don't worry. That's not why we're here."

The barman pushed two beers towards them and waited while Montrose pulled a few euros from his pocket. *No tab. Yeah, it's that kind of bar.*

A telephone rang. The patron picked it up from below the wooden bar top. He listened for a few moments and looked over at Montrose. "There's two flic at the end of the alley. Something to do with you, monsieur?"

"Christ, we've got to get out of here!" said Montrose. "Where's the exit?"

"The door you came in." said the patron. "There's one way, in and out."

Montrose picked up the beer glass. "I'm going to start a riot. You ready?"

"No!" Charlotte leaned over the bar. "Patron! We need the key!"

The patron shrugged. "What key?"

"You know what key. My grandfather is Emile Marceau. Your own father helped him escape from the Nazis. Now it's your turn."

"The Nazis?" The patron glanced at the door. "The war's over, mademoiselle."

"No, it's not. Not for my grandfather, and not for me."

The patron picked up a grubby bar towel and began to polish a glass. "Even if I had this key, what would you do with it?"

"I'd turn the handle the wrong way."

The patron grinned and fished around in his pocket.

"When I was a kid, I thought your grandfather was the best dressed man in Paris. Give him my regards."

Charlotte grabbed the key and pulled Montrose by the arm. "Connor, come with me. Right now!"

He followed her as she swerved around bar stools to a door in the corner. It was open and they ran down the steps into a cellar.

"Charlotte, they'll find us, we have to run."

She didn't turn. "Follow me!" She flicked on the light. The room was littered with beer kegs and boxes of wine. "Over here!" she said and ran to the far wall.

Two small doors faced them. Montrose turned the handle of the first and pulled it open to reveal a cupboard of shallow shelves, littered with old bottles and bar cloths. "Charlotte. This isn't going to work."

CHAPTER 29

Charlotte twisted the handle of the second cupboard, but it was locked. "*Idiote*!" Her hands shook as she tried to push in the key and it fell from her grasp.

Montrose grabbed it from the filthy floor. "I'll do it. He slotted in the key and grasped the handle, then pulled open the door. It was an identical cupboard.

"No!" she said. "Close it!"

"What?"

"Do it!"

Montrose slammed the door shut.

"Give it to me." She turned the key in the opposite direction then twisted the handle to the left and pushed the door. "It's stuck. Help me!"

Montrose put his shoulder hard against the door. The whole cupboard swung inwards on squealing hinges to reveal a dark passageway cut into the stone.

"Go first," she said. "Find the lights."

Montrose jumped in and covered his face from the stench of raw sewage. He ran the palm of his hand up the clammy wall and found a switch. Low wattage bulbs fizzed into life. A line of wet stone steps opened up before him, descending into the gloom.

She shoved past him and hauled the cupboard back into place.

Montrose tried to pinch his nose, but it hurt too much.

"Take your time." She blew out a breath. "They won't find us now. Connor?"

He turned towards her and could see the fear in her eyes.

"Were they the police? They didn't look like policemen."

"Maybe." *Hard to tell. The list of people wanting my head on a plate is getting longer.*

"I can help," she said. "My contact, when they get the diamonds. I can ask them to protect you."

"Yeah, that would be good." *Mossad would be grateful. Dammit, they had to help. I've got no more cards to play.* The fetid smell became stronger as he descended the steps. "Where does it go? No, don't tell me. I've got a pretty good idea."

"*Les Egouts*. The city sewers. My grandfather told me of this place. The family of the patron have always been famous for smuggling. The police could never catch them. During the war, the patron's father hid British and US airmen down here, then passed them down the line of escape routes to Spain. There was a whole network in France dedicated to getting prisoners to safety. Or at least out of Nazi-occupied territory. Of course the network also worked in reverse, for contraband wine and brandy. The Gestapo never found out. But then the Résistance had the sewers booby-trapped. You had to know what you were doing. The ones that didn't, well, their filthy German bones were washed out to sea."

"Nazis, not Germans."

She stopped and turned. "What?"

"Have you ever heard of the S.S. Saint Louis?"

Charlotte gave him a puzzled look.

"It was one of the last ships out of Germany before the Nazis closed the ports. Packed with refugees. My grandfather was on that ship. Otto Heffel. An English teacher from Berlin. Just passed his exams and on the run because he spoke out for the Jews. He sailed to America, but they wouldn't let them in. Neither would the British Colonies. Then they ended up in Cuba. Same thing. He got the message. It wasn't hard to steal a sailor's uniform and slip ashore then disappear."

"Your grandfather was German?"

"Yeah. Once he'd mastered the accent it was easy to get to the States and turn up at a recruiting centre. He said he was a country boy. No papers. Then he joined the fight against the real enemy. Not the Germans. The Nazis. He landed with the US Rangers at D-Day. He wasn't alone. There were tens of thousands of Germans who stayed behind and fought for what was right."

Charlotte shook her head. "I didn't know. Maybe they should have done more."

"Their life expectancy was measured in days. But they made a difference. It's not all black and white."

She shrugged, but said nothing.

Montrose looked down at her dress and pulled off his raincoat. "You'd better take this." He could hear the water. At the bottom of the steps was a thickly-barred iron gate. A heavy padlock and chain hung around the bars. "It's locked."

"Only if you try to open it." She stood on a small stone at the foot of the bars. The gate clicked and the whole frame and padlocked gate swung away from the wall.

"Something your father told you?"

"That and other things."

They stepped through and turned a corner. Thin shafts of light from the street appeared through openings in the gutters, barely piercing the gloom. A dark river flowed at his feet, leading into darkness. A narrow pathway hugged the wall, inches above the water.

"This way," she said.

"You know where you're going?" Montrose peered into the tunnel.

"The water always flows to the Seine. So, we go in the other direction."

"To where?"

"Rue des Rosiers, no? For the diamonds?"

"Absolutely." *The sooner the better. They were closing in.* "You know the way?"

"I don't have to." She pointed up to where the channel joined the main stream. "All the main sewers are as wide as the roads above, and they have the same street signs. You wouldn't want to get lost down here."

Montrose kept his head down and fell in behind her. The low roof was arched in cut blocks of stone, supported by carved columns. It reminded him of a crypt.

"I think we can get pretty close," she said. "I know there's an entrance not too far from the Rue des Rosiers. It would take us about ten minutes above ground. This will be quicker. And safer."

"It goes all the way?"

She didn't turn around. "Sewers like this cover most of the city and there are thousands of old mining works, even from the Roman age. Paris is built on a warren of tunnels. They used to have tourist boat trips down here until 1974. The sewers even have their own museum."

Montrose shook his head. "Only in Paris."

She stopped before a large metal grill in the wall. "We have to take a detour. Not all of the sewer walkways are passable. And it's a shortcut."

Montrose edged forward towards the grill where the empty eye sockets of a human skull stared back at him. He flinched, just stopping himself from slipping into the water. "Holy shit!"

"Don't worry Connor, they're all dead. Probably about six hundred years ago."

He peered through into the darkness. "This is the catacombs, right?"

"No, this is an ossuary for the medieval church above. The grill is a run-off, in case there's a flood."

"Jeez. Don't they bury anybody in Paris?"

"Of course, but space is tight. They had to empty the city cemeteries in the sixteenth century or they would have had no room to bury anyone else. Thousands of unmarked graves, mostly the poor and homeless. There are catacombs and ossuaries all over Paris, containing the bones of over eight million people. You can take a guided tour at the Denfert Rocherau catacomb."

"Yeah. Absolutely. Maybe some other time."

She leaned through the grate and placed her hand into the eye socket of a skull. "But this one is not open to the public." She pulled her hand back slowly, an iron key between the tips of her fingers. She turned it in the lock and pulled hard on the grate. It swung noiselessly towards them.

She smiled at him. "You first."

This is freakin' spooky. Where's Scooby Doo when you need him? "Scared, eh?"

"No. I have to lock the gate behind us."

"Ah, yeah, right." He stepped through and his vision became a monochromatic nightmare of femurs and skulls. His eyes began to adjust to the darkness and he saw a narrow corridor lined with thousands of neatly stacked human bones, stretching away into the darkness. A drip of water splashed on the floor. He heard the gate close behind him.

"Straight on, Connor."

He kept his arms tight by his side and walked down the line of skulls. Endless empty eye sockets watched his progress. The gloom was getting worse. He pulled the lighter from his pocket. The flame flickered eerily against the yellowing, dusty bones. "I can see better, but that's not necessarily a good thing." He stepped forward. "How many people are down here?"

"No one knows. They estimate the wall of bones may be fifteen deep. Either side."

He noticed there was no echo and resisted the urge to turn around and look back towards the sewer. His feet splashed in small puddles, but all sound seemed to be sucked up by the bones. The narrow corridor began to drift left then turned a sharp right. In front was a wall of skulls. "What the hell?"

"Relax, Connor, keep going."

He held up the light in front of the skulls and twisted left, spotting a small gap in the wall, just wide enough to squeeze through sideways. "You're joking, right?"

"No, don't go down there. That is not good."

He turned around, holding up the lighter, moving his

fingers as the metal began to burn. "This isn't exactly Fifth Avenue either."

She giggled and pointed in the other direction. "We go this way. Squeeze between the bones."

He held the lighter at arm's length and saw a small strip of darkness. "You're freaking crazy." The light showed a narrow gap less than a foot wide between a towering wall of skulls. "What about the other way? It's easier."

"No. the other way is . . . dangerous. This is under the church, but the other way leads into medieval mining tunnels. The corridors go around in circles for miles and the ground is unstable. And so are the bones. You could be buried alive. And they would have to dig through hundreds of thousands of skeletons to find you. And you know, I don't think they would."

"You know that?"

"Let's just say some of the skeletons in there are not medieval."

Helluva frickin' choice. He turned to the dark strip between the bones. "Me first, yeah?"

"You've got the light."

"Yeah." He shuffled sideways into the gap, holding the lighter before him. He felt his nose brush against the bones and jaws of skulls jut into his back. The metal lighter began to scorch the tips of his fingers. He tried to bring his other arm forward, but his shoulder jammed against the bones. He tried to move the lighter in his hand, but it slipped from his grasp. The flame spiraled downwards and died with a hiss as the hot metal hit the wet floor.

"Shit!" He automatically tried to squat down to retrieve it, but his knees jammed hard into the wall. A squeak of dry bones rubbing against each other made his heart skip a beat.

"Attention!"

He could hear the panic in her voice.

"Don't move the skulls. Just . . . don't."

He looked up into the darkness. *If this lot comes down . . .*

"Let me do it, I'm smaller."

He felt her hanging on to his pants as she twisted down and her hand fumbled around his feet.

"Got it."

He blew out a breath. Her hand slid up his leg, pressing the lighter against him. He reached down as far as he could and she slipped the lighter into his palm. He brought it up to his side and flipped it open, thumbing the flint wheel. It sparked into life and he saw the tiny skull of a child directly below his cheek. *Fuck, I've had it with this place.* "Let's go."

"It's not far."

He shuffled forward and could hear the running water of the sewer. *At last. Never thought I'd be glad to see a river of shit.* The corridor began to drift in a curve and a faint, grey light appeared. They came to an iron grate. "We're here." He shuffled to a stop in front of the wet iron. The grate was locked. "Which skull?"

"On the right. Pick one and I'll tell you."

He placed his hand in the nose cavity of the biggest skull.

"Two up, one right. In the eyes."

He moved his hand along and poked into the eye sockets, felt the cold metal of a key. "Got it." He tapped the skull with the key. "Thanks, buddy."

"*Connor!* Have some respect. This is also a graveyard."

"Excuse me." He turned the key in the lock and stepped onto the narrow walkway, bordered by a fast flowing stream.

Charlotte locked the grate, then thrust her hand through and replaced the key. "This way," she said and headed to the end of the walkway where the stream joined a large tunnel. She stopped at the corner. "Look." She pointed up at a sign for Rue de Rivoli. "We're below the main road."

He heard the faint noise of traffic.

"You know that film?" she said. "*Raiders of the Lost Ark*?"

"Yeah?"

"That's where they got the idea of a giant ball rolling to crush Harrison Ford. That's how they used to clean the sewers."

Montrose looked over his shoulder.

"Don't worry, they don't use it any more. This way." She turned the corner into Rue De Rivoli.

The arched roof was higher and the water had picked up speed. "We're under the Town Hall," said Charlotte. "That's the reason the sewer's so big. They say there's more merde generated there than in the whole of Paris." Charlotte paused at a corner then headed left into a narrow tunnel.

Montrose caught a stained and rusting sign, nailed to the wall by his head. Rue Vieille du Temple.

"The old home of the Knights Templar," she said. "This leads to Rue des Rosiers. We can get out there."

"In the middle of the street?"

She scoffed at the idea. "No. I live around here. I know where they come out. I'm not going to be seen by my neighbors climbing out of a sewer."

They came to a smaller channel entering from their right. Montrose looked up at the sign. Rue du Trésor.

"Treasure Road," said Charlotte. "Many people think the Templars buried their treasure down here."

"Have they?"

"Well, it's got to be somewhere. It was never found. Though it hasn't stopped people looking."

He could see several holes in the wall that had been hastily filled with broken bricks and cement.

"Last time, they dug into someone's basement," she said. She stood at the end of the channel. "We'll have to cross, so be careful." She held up the hem of his raincoat and jumped to the narrow path on the other side.

Montrose looked across. There was hardly room for him to stand up, never mind jump. He squatted down and leapt over, landing in a crouch.

"Not far now," she said.

He kept his eyes on his feet and almost walked into her as she came to a halt.

"This must be it," she said, "It should lead into a courtyard off Rue des Rosiers."

Montrose gazed up at the rusted ladder. "Use the coat to cover your hands. I'll go first." He shoved the heel of his shoe into the ladder and hauled himself up. At the top was a thick metal grate. It gave way with a push and he shoved it to the side. The sunlight stung his eyes and he squinted across a cramped courtyard then climbed out and reached down. "It's quiet. C'mon, no neighbors are watching."

She grasped his hand and pulled herself up.

They both took a few deep breaths. Montrose kicked the grate back over the hole. He looked down a short alley to the street at the end. A bicycle flashed past. "Is that Rue des Rosiers?"

"Yes. Where now?"

"It's a small square, just off the street. Next to a café and a boulangerie."

She looked up at him with disbelief. "Are you looking for Monsieur Stein?"

"You know him?"

"I've lived here most of my life. Of course I know him. He should have told me."

Montrose said nothing. *I should have known.* They turned into the street. He glanced back and forth, but there were no cops.

"Down here," she said and led him through a winding alley between the buildings. They emerged beside a café. Stein's was on the corner.

Montrose crossed over and stood beside the door. "I didn't expect to be back here quite so soon."

She laughed and pushed the buzzer.

"*Oui?*"

Montrose was about to speak when Charlotte stepped up to the intercom.

"It's Charlotte Marceau, Monsieur Stein."

"*Entrez*, Charlotte."

Montrose held the door, then followed her along the corridor. The old man looked up as they approached.

"Charlotte! What a surprise!"

"*Bonjour*, Monsieur Stein."

The old man stood up from behind the desk. "I see you've met Monsieur Montrose. I take it you got my message."

"Ah, no, I have been out all day. Don't worry, I found him on my own."

Stein grinned. "You must excuse me, Monsieur Montrose, I suspected your recent deposit was not entirely genuine. However, if you are with Charlotte then you are amongst friends."

Charlotte kissed the old man twice on the cheeks and turned to Montrose. "My father made many friends in his life. Monsieur Stein has been very helpful."

The old man laughed. "Whatever it is, I don't want to know. Though I can see by your smile that you are going to make your grandfather very happy."

"I've told him already. You should have seen the look in his eyes. It was incredible!"

"I'm so glad. Now, Monsieur Montrose, I imagine you wish to visit your box?"

"Yes," he said and pulled out his ID.

"That won't be necessary," said Stein. He opened the barred gate and iron door.

"After you," said Montrose, holding out a hand.

Charlotte stepped into the room.

"Number 62."

He undid the Omega from his wrist and dialed the serial number. The door sprang open and Montrose lifted out the bag and placed it on the floor. "All yours," he said.

Charlotte knelt down, pulled back the zipper and pushed the clothes aside. A mass of diamonds sparkled back at them. "*Mon dieu!*"

"There's an envelope, too. A list."

Charlotte ignored him and dipped her hand into the diamonds. "*C'est incroyable!*" She made to pick up the bag, then stopped. "Connor? Did you mention a list?"

"Yes. It's in the bag."

She shrugged. "I've heard about a list, from Antwerp,

that was supposed to exist, but we were never told what it was. Have you seen it?"

"Yes. Names and numbers. I'll tell you later." *It'll blow your mind.* "Let's get out of here."

"I'll let my contact know. It might mean something to them."

"Let me carry that for you." Montrose pushed the clothes back over the diamonds and closed the leather bag.

They stepped out into the hallway. Stein was sitting behind his desk. "I hope you make this young lady very happy, Monsieur Montrose. *Au revoir.*"

Charlotte blushed. "He already has. *A bientôt,* Monsieur Stein."

Montrose stood on the sidewalk and looked over at the café. "Can I borrow your phone? I just want to check my email."

She handed over a Blackberry. "Connor, I can't thank you enough."

He shrugged. "The diamonds mean nothing to me. They never did. Until I found out where they came from. They were just a bargaining chip with Erwin Reinhard. But now he's dead."

"I'll call my contact. They'll help, I'm sure." She laid her head to one side. "Will I see you again?"

Montrose hesitated. *The clever answer was no. But this girl was different. You're crazy. Keep your mind on the job.* "I might not be back for some time." He looked across at the café. "Let's have a coffee. Then you can call your contact. I think I'm gonna need some help to stay away from the cops."

"I understand. Maybe we'll say *au revoir* instead of goodbye."

"I hope so," he replied before he could stop himself. *Wherever the hell I end up.* They crossed to the square and stood before the café. "Have you ever been to Morocco?"

"Yes, I'll let you know some good places to eat. But first, I'm going to wash my hands. I feel filthy from the sewer." She turned and headed towards the restrooms.

Montrose sat at a corner of the bar, where he had a good view of the square. He sipped the espresso and held the cup in front of him. It was the smallest amount of coffee he had ever seen, but it kicked like a mule.

No one can clear my name. No one. He downed the coffee. *Less of the self-pity. Just get out of town. Give Mossad the diamonds and list. They have the power to get me clear of Europe.*

He brought up his internet browser on her phone and logged into his email. A new message appeared on the screen.

Re: FAO Jacques Kessler.

Montrose – I have the video. It was contained on a memory stick found in the possession of my late father. I will exchange the memory stick and email the video to Interpol when I have the diamonds and the list.

This is the deal. The diamonds and the list. I will accept nothing less. You have a chance to clear your name. I suggest you take it.

Call the number below.

Kurt Reinhard

Sweet Jesus. He's got it. He looked down at the bag. *Mossad can't clear my name. Only the video can do that. If I get the memory stick, I'll damn well hand myself in. Once I'm in the clear then the Mossad attack dogs can tear Reinhard to shreds.* He thumbed the number on the screen. The call was answered immediately.

"Montrose?"

"Yeah. Bad penny and all that. I got your email."

"Good. Then let's deal with this like professionals. I have what you want. But do you have what I want?"

"Yeah. Right here with me."

"Come to my lawyer's office . . ."

"Not a chance, slimeball. I'll tell you where and when. I don't want your goons showing up and spoiling the party."

"Pick your spot. I don't have time for dramatics, Montrose. The entire Parisian police force are after you, so you'd better get there before they get to you."

He's got a point. But I'm not gonna hand myself in until I have that memory stick.

"Montrose? Are you still there."

"Shut up, I'm thinking."

"Tick tock, Montrose. If the cops get to you first, you'll be put away for life."

Yeah, and you're a dead man. This has to be done quickly, before Reinhard has a chance to prepare a set up. "I've got the place. Pont Neuf, beside Notre Dame. Middle of the bridge. You'd better be alone, or the diamonds and the list are going in the water. And so am I. You understand?"

"I understand, Montrose, that if you don't turn up with the diamonds and list, then the memory stick will be going in exactly the same place. Thirty minutes. Pont Neuf."

"Thirty minutes? You think so?" *He's running around with his ass on fire, 'cos the Mafia in Rome are waiting for their money. No point making it easy for him. Not my problem.* "Might take me longer, the traffic in Paris is murder, you know."

"My patience won't last forever, Montrose. The police aren't the only people in Paris looking for you."

"Yeah, tell me about it." *That's nothing to the hell that awaits you.* "Which means I've got other things to think about than sightseeing on the Point Neuf. I'll be there when it's safe. Why don't you get there and enjoy the view? Have an ice cream. You can watch the . . ."

"Be there! Thirty minutes!"

"Yeah. Later, sucker." Montrose cut the call and looked down at the leather bag.

The mirror was cracked and stained, but she had to admit, the dress did look good. She allowed herself a smile. He was a handsome man. Honest, too. There were not many of them about, in her opinion.

She pinched her cheeks, just like her mother used to do, then smoothed down her eyebrows. Maybe pluck them? God, she thought, you've changed. That's something that's never occurred to you before. Her mother had been forever dragging her around the chi-chi boutiques of the 5th Arrondissement, trying to turn her into a chic Parisienne. Maybe her mother had been right all along. She examined her reflection. In this dress, all she needed was a pair of ridiculous high heels and she was ready for the Ritz.

A pair of high heels was something she didn't have.

Her wardrobe was purely functional. Jeans, boots and leather coats. She looked good in those. Her father had just smiled and said she looked good in anything. But now the diamonds were safe, life was about to change.

She turned and opened the door into the café. He wasn't at the table. She ran to the bar. "The man who was sitting here. Where did he go?"

"He left a moment ago, mademoiselle. He seemed in a hurry."

She ran out onto the terrace. A taxi pulled away from the other side of the square and through the back window she could see the short dark hair of the passenger. "Putain de merde!" The taxi was around the corner and out of sight before she could move.

She stood, hands held out. There were no other taxis. She began to run then stopped. The taxi would reach the Rue des Rosiers in seconds. She'd never catch him.

An old Lambretta scooter was parked to her right. At a table sat an old man. "Monsieur!"

He looked up from his coffee. "*Oui?*"

"I need your scooter! How much?"

"What?"

She pulled a wad of cash from her bag. "Five hundred euros. Right now."

"Mademoiselle, I have to tell you, it's not worth a hundred."

"I don't care. This is an emergency."

"Do you want to sign the papers?"

"No, just give me the keys." She grabbed the keys from the table and threw down the cash.

"Ah," said the old man. "The gentleman who left in a hurry. I hope he's worth it."

She jumped on the scooter, turned on the ignition and pumped the kick-start.

The old man shrugged. "Some lovers are not worth pursuing, mademoiselle."

The motor spluttered into life and she twisted back the throttle. Not a lover. He was a dead man.

CHAPTER 30

He slid down in the seat and glanced back. There was no sign of her. He bowed his head and squeezed his eyes shut. *I've got no choice.*

The taxi came to a halt in the traffic. The driver turned in his seat. "Bad news, monsieur. The police have blocked the roads around Châtelet and all the side streets are jammed. We can go around, but it will take forever. We'll have to head down to the Bastille, then over the river."

"Whatever is the quickest way. I just have to get there. What's going on?"

"An escaped prisoner. American, I heard."

Montrose sat up with a jolt. "Is that so?"

The taxi spun a u-turn towards the Rue de Rivoli. Through the windshield, he could see the six-way junction around the Bastille. Normally cars would be speeding around the base of the monument, but everything was gridlocked.

I've thrown away my last card. Mossad were not

going to help without the diamonds. Or without Charlotte. Only one way. Get the memory stick with the video and hand yourself in. He rubbed his face hard. *Yeah. Helluva plan. Make it happen.*

"Ah, no luck, monsieur," said the driver. "They're stopping every car entering the Bastille. They must really want this guy."

That's for sure. Montrose watched policemen check cars then wave them through. *This isn't gonna work.* "Damn this traffic! I'm going to be late for my appointment. How far is it to walk?"

"About thirty minutes, monsieur."

"Looks like I'm on foot." Montrose handed the driver a fifty euro bill. "Keep the change for your trouble." He was out of the taxi before the driver had a chance to reply.

The Métro station, Saint Paul, was across the road. *That line goes along the river, past the Pont Neuf.* He was about to turn in when he saw two gendarmes just inside the station entrance. *They've locked the place down. It would have to be on foot. Back streets and fast. Head south and west, make it to the river and then down to the bridge. However long it took. Just stay clear of the cops.*

He turned off the street and slipped into a doorway. *Damn sure there's a price on my head. The taxi driver could go straight to the cops. Time for another change of clothes.* There was nothing on the street except small shops and apartments. *A department store or clothes shop would be on the main drag.*

He headed towards Rue Saint Antoine and saw the Bon Marche. *Five floors high. They've got to have something.*

The police would concentrate on the main junctions and Métro. Then they would appear on the streets when the taxi driver opened his mouth. He fought the urge to look over his shoulder and pushed through the glass doors. In front were aisles of food. A plan was pinned to the wall with the escalator to the right. *Menswear, next floor. Don't run.* He glanced back at the top of the escalator. Two gendarmes, pushing their way through the doors of the shop. The taxi driver had worked it out.

In front was the menswear department. *They're tailing a guy in a suit and carrying a leather bag. Even if I get out of the store, the suit's a giveaway. Too damn flash.*

Pulling a duffle coat from a rack, he ducked into a changing booth, tugging the curtain closed behind him. He took the duffle coat from its hanger and threw them onto a small bench at the side of the booth. His hands tore at the suit jacket. He pulled out his wallet and stuffed it into the pocket of the duffle coat. He looked down at the leather bag. *They'd spot it a mile off.*

He peeked out of the curtain. In front was a cash desk with large store bags behind the cashier. *If I buy the duffle coat then I can hide the leather bag in a store bag. That would work. Then give the gendarmes the slip and out of a fire exit.*

As he drew back the curtain, two Kepi hats appeared at the top of the escalator. The gendarmes. They'd be on him in seconds.

There was nothing in the changing booth to use as a weapon. He looked up. Above him was a sprinkler. *Now would be a good time to start smoking.*

He grabbed the coat hanger, pulling the plastic arms together and folding the metal hook into a spike. He twisted the light bulb from its socket on the side of the changing booth then tore the plastic price tag from the duffle coat and twisted it around the end of the metal hook. He pointed it towards the empty light socket and the two copper contacts. *One of those has got 110 volts running through it. Get it right or the cops will be picking up a corpse.*

He touched one side of the hook against the right hand contact. *Nothing. The other one is live. Good choice, you lucky bastard.* Holding it hard against the contact, he gently turned the hook until it was a millimeter away from the live contact. His hands jolted as a blue electric arc sparked across the gap to the hook. The plastic wrapped around the hook began to smolder. *Again. I need more.*

He widened his stance, his hands trembling as he edged the hook once more towards the live contact. A fat blue arc shot across the gap and ignited the plastic. He ripped the hanger from the socket and jammed it up into the sprinkler.

The fire alarm burst into life. Water spewed over him and he pulled up the collar of the duffle coat and peered around the curtain. It was raining in the store. The gendarmes stood there for a moment, water running off their Kepis, and then ran back down the escalators.

Montrose burst out of the booth and ran across to the cash desk, snatched up a large store bag, stuffed the leather bag inside and joined the rush of shoppers and staff heading for the fire exit. He ran past an old lady, then stopped and turned. "Let me help you," he said, grabbing her arm and bundling her towards the exit and down a flight of stairs before she could protest. He held on tight to the old lady until they emerged into an alley at the side of the store. *No cops.*

"Good luck," he said and walked off. Sweat was streaming down his back and he felt on the edge of hysteria. *Keep control, you know what you have to do. Head south for the river. West to the Pont Neuf. They're not looking for a guy in a duffle coat.*

He tried to breathe, but his chest was so tight he could only take short gasps. Lights flashed in front of his eyes as panic closed in. *Just walk. Keep it together. Run when you hit the water.*

"STOP!"

Shock slammed through him. He dropped the store bag. The leather bag spilled out. He tried to pick it up, but his hands shook so much he missed the handle.

"Hands in the air!"

Montrose turned.

A soaking gendarme pulled a pistol from his holster. "Put your hands on your head, you bastard."

I'll never make it. It's over.

The gendarme's hands tightened around the pistol. He didn't hear the scooter until it ploughed into him from behind. He flew into the air before landing head first on the cobbles and lay, motionless.

Charlotte tumbled to the ground beside him. Her face was creased with shock and anger. She looked down at the gendarme's pistol, lying at her feet.

Montrose realized his hands were still in the air.

A shout came from the end of the alley. They both turned.

Two men in suits. Shit, I've seen them before. Montrose threw the store bag over his shoulder and picked up the scooter. "Charlotte! I'll find you!" He climbed on and opened the throttle, careering down the alley until he shot out onto the Avenue des Célestin.

Got to make it south of the river. He turned onto the bridge over the Ile Saint Louis. The scooter bounced around as he weaved through the traffic. *Fuck the cops. I can make the Pont Neuf in a few minutes from the south side. Straight along the quay.* He jumped the lights and headed west.

They're looking for a guy in a duffle coat with a store bag. On a scooter. They'd guess I'm heading over the river. The Boulevard would be lined with CCTV. The scooter would have to go. Try to make it to the edge of the Pont Neuf then ditch it.

The traffic at the end of the bridge was solid. The lights were red and he bumped the scooter up onto the curb and around the corner, pedestrians scattering around him. He ran off the sidewalk and squeezed into a gap through the traffic on the Rue de la Tournelle. Glancing up along the quay he saw blue flashing lights in the distance. They were coming his way. *Go south, through the side streets then double back to the Pont Neuf.* He dragged the scooter left on a pedestrian crossing then turned down an arched street to the Latin Quarter.

The streets were close and winding as he dodged past tourists and parked cars. He was going nowhere fast. *It would have to be the Boulevard Saint Michel. Get some speed up. I'll be tracked the whole way, but there's no choice.*

He turned at the end of the street and slotted into the traffic heading west, past the tourists and the *fin de siècle* cafés. The road opened up. In this traffic they would spot him easily. It wasn't going to work.

The Métro. That would take me to the bridge. There had to be a station around here, and the line that stopped on the Ile de la Cité, where the Pont Neuf crossed the river.

Montrose squeezed the brakes and pulled into a side street, stopping behind a van. He tore off the duffle coat and dumped it on the seat of the scooter. To his left were the usual shops and overpriced cafes. He slipped his wallet into his pocket and took off down the street. He stopped in front of an Arab maroquinerie.

Leather isn't my style, but it would have to do.

The owner greeted him with arms wide. "Monsieur! You look like you need a cool drink!"

"Yeah." Montrose looked up behind the counter to a line of gaudy clocks with the Eiffel Tower painted on the dial. *I'll make it. Only a few stops on the Métro. The cops would be charging around trying to find the scooter.* "And I need a coat and a suitcase."

The owner brought out a bottle of Coke from beneath the counter and popped the lid. "Please, have one on me! I will fetch you a selection."

"Thank God for Arab hospitality," said Montrose, and drank greedily from the bottle. He examined the label. The drink was dark and fizzy, but it wasn't Coke, no matter what the label said.

"This is my finest coat," said the owner, holding up a long leather overcoat.

That's absolutely fucking appalling. "I'll take it. What's that?" Below the glass counter was a selection of cheap watches and knives. He could see what looked like a folded up toolkit, stamped with the Stars and Stripes.

"It's a Leatherman, monsieur. A multi-purpose tool. Like a very clever penknife."

"I'll take that too." Montrose pointed to a rack of luggage. "That big rolling suitcase. How much for everything?"

"Well, normally . . ." the owner began to roll his eyes.

"I'm in a hurry. Just name a price." Montrose downed the rest of the bottle

"Three hundred euros!"

He peeled off a few bills and held them out. "Put the bag into the suitcase, I've got to rush for a train."

"Of course!" The owner tucked the cash into his pocket and lifted the leather bag into the suitcase.

Montrose pulled on the black leather overcoat which reached down past his knees. He felt like a Gestapo officer. "I'll need a hat. Nothing fancy." *For chrissake, not a fedora.*

The owner grabbed a red baseball cap with "*I love Paris*" emblazoned across the front. "For you, monsieur, on the house!"

Talk about a fashion crime. Montrose held it in his hand. *If Bonsergeant catches me, he'll put me away for life.* He felt the buzz of the phone in his back pocket. *Charlotte's phone?* He pulled out her Blackberry and held it in his palm. *Do I answer it? At least I owe her an explanation. Yeah, that and a bag of diamonds. I'll tell her about the bridge. Then Mossad can pick up Reinhard, and throw his corpse in the river.* He thumbed the phone and lifted it to his ear. "Charlotte? Look, I had to . . . "

"No, it's not Charlotte, you asshole. Guess who?"

Reinhard? How did he . . .? "Where did you get this number?"

"A little bird told me. A little bird that we picked up at the department store. The police radio has been very busy. We just missed you. Pity, but we came away with a consolation prize."

It was them. The two men at the end of the alley behind the store. The Brits from Rome. Black and Grey Suit. No, they can't . . . "Bullshit."

"Really? Listen to this."

His hand began to tremble and he pressed the phone hard to his ear. *I delivered her straight to them.*

"Connor! Don't tell them . . ."

He heard her retch. *Oh, Christ, no!*

"So, Montrose, this changes things, wouldn't you say? You get your ass over to the Pont Neuf in the next ten minutes or we're going to start cutting bits off her face. Ears, nose, lips, you get the picture. I don't really have a plan, so I might go freestyle. Just hack away at anything. I'm feeling a little stressed, you know. I think I might enjoy it."

"You touch her and I'll . . ."

"You're talking, Montrose, you should be walking. Or running. I start cutting in ten minutes." The call ended.

He stared at the phone.

"Monsieur?" The shopkeeper stood with the empty store bag in his hands. "Are you okay?"

"Gotta go." *Run! No, it's too far. I can't make it.* He half turned to the door. "Where's the nearest Métro station?"

"Saint Michel." The shopkeeper pointed to the west.

"Does that line go to the Pont Neuf?"

"Oui, monsieur, Line 4." He pulled a tattered Métro map from his pocket. "The tourists, you know, they are always asking me . . ."

Montrose pulled it from his hands and scanned

the lines. *Saint Michel would be crawling with cops.* "What's the next station to Saint Michel on this side of the river?"

The shopkeeper tapped the map with his finger. "Odéon, monsieur. Straight down the Boulevard Saint-Germain, past Cluny Sorbonne."

He stuffed the Leatherman in his pocket, grabbed the handle of the wheeled suitcase and dragged it from the shop. He headed west to the Boulevard Saint-Germain. *Just get to the bridge.*

The wheeled suitcase banged against the wound on his heel as he turned into the Odéon. He stopped at the corner and saw, to his left, the classic art nouveau metalwork of the Métro entrance.

He bounced the suitcase down the steps and hurried across the ticket hall. He slotted a few euros in the machine, pulled out a ticket and made for the escalator.

At the end of the ticket hall two policemen stood, distracted by an old lady asking for directions. One of them gave him a double take. Montrose ignored him and stepped onto the escalator. Turning back would be a dead giveaway.

He fought the urge to jump down the steps. His legs twitched, ready to run. He stepped off and saw a round security mirror placed high up on the wall. *Two dark uniforms, standing on the escalator. Can I play the lost tourist? Not a chance.*

The rumble from the tunnels told him a train was coming. *Two entrances. Left and right. North and southbound platforms. The train approaching was southbound. Wrong direction. But not with two cops on my ass.* He watched the carriages flash past as it pulled into the station.

He checked the mirror. The cops were walking down the escalator. They'd heard the train. Taking the Leatherman from his pocket, he flicked out the blade, tucked it into his palm, then pulled the suitcase down to the far end of the platform for the southbound train.

The carriage doors slid open. He placed his foot inside and waited. The train was ready to go. In the corner of his eye he saw the two figures march onto the platform and stop by a carriage door. Now they were waiting for him.

If they were clever, they'd just stop the train. The alarm sounded that the doors were closing. *Guess they're not that clever.* He jumped into the carriage. The doors began to close and he booted the suitcase towards the platform. The doors slammed into the sides of the suitcase, and he grabbed the edge of the doors and pulled himself through the gap. He hauled the suitcase out and tumbled back onto the platform. The doors crashed shut and the train moved off. He caught the faces of the policemen at the window. *Yeah, I'll bet you're pissed. Even if you pulled the cord, the train would be stuck in the tunnel.*

Two down. If the cops haven't told anybody, I'm in the clear. Their radios might not work underground, but they'll be shouting for every damn cop in Paris once they get to the next station.

He sprinted along a connecting tunnel to the north platform, tore off the leather coat and stuffed it in a bin.

Another change of clothes and I'll be down to my shorts.

A northbound train pulled into the station and he checked the map on the wall. Two stops to Ile de la Cité, the station in the middle of the island. *Close enough.* The edge of the island jutted into the centre of the Pont Neuf. *I can make it from there.* He stepped onto the train.

But the train went through Saint Michel. The doors closed and the train pulled away. *No choice now. If the cops on the southbound train were fast there would be an army waiting for me. Got to get there first.* He held on tight to the handrail as the train rattled around a corner. *Saint Michel was a big station. Three or four lines met there. I could lose them in a maze of tunnels and then run for the bridge. Maybe five hundred yards. But all the cops had to do was stop the trains and cover the exits.*

No. It's not gonna work.

He ran down the carriage and through the connecting doors, jumping over suitcases and barging past passengers until he reached the driver's cabin. Taking out the Leatherman tool, he fixed the pliers around the triangular door lock. The train was starting to slow. They were close to Saint Michel. He squeezed the pliers hard and the metal bit into his hand, but the lock turned. He jumped into the tight space beside the driver and slammed the door behind him.

The driver spun around.

Montrose slid out the blade from the Leatherman. "Don't fuck with me," said Montrose. "I'm not really in the mood."

The Dead Man's handle began to slip from the driver's grasp and he looked down at the mic for the intercom.

"Don't even think about it. Listen to me. Keep going. Stop the train at the entrance to Saint Michel." The train slowed and Montrose braced his arm against the windshield. Through the tunnel he could see the platform and the passengers. *No cops. They'd be in the station, covering the exits.* "Forward a few feet. Just before the platform."

The driver pulled the train to a stop. Montrose grabbed the mic and thrust it in the driver's face. "Tell Control there's someone on the tracks. Tell them to cut the power."

The driver took the mic. "This is train 464. I'm in the tunnel at Northbound Platform 2. There's someone on the track. Cut the power."

Montrose held the knife against the driver's cheek. "It's a kid. Tell them to do it now."

"It's a kid. Cut the power."

Passengers on the platform stared at the train as it stood in the tunnel. The motor hummed beneath him, and then slowed. The cabin lights dropped. Montrose ripped the mic from the dash of the cab. "Get back into the carriage."

"Monsieur . . ."

"This train's going nowhere. They've cut the power. Move it!"

Montrose leapt from the cab and ran up the steps. He dumped the suitcase on the platform and wrenched it open. Passengers stared at him. "There's a bomb!" he shouted. "Get out of the station!"

Everyone turned and scrambled for the exit. Montrose ran to the far end of the platform and jumped down onto the track. If the cops were heading for the platform, they would have to fight their way through a mob of frightened passengers. He ran up the dark tunnel, timing his run and hitting the gravel between the wooden rail ties. The air was thick and hot in his lungs.

Through the darkness he saw the lights of the station ahead. His breath pounded in his chest and his throat was raw as he ran up onto the platform at La Cité. A sea of faces turned towards him. He was about to shout to get them out of the station but stopped himself. *No. That wouldn't help. It would only attract attention.* He scanned the faces of the passengers. *Like I'm not doing that already.*

He headed for the platform exit and took the stairs two at a time. The ticket hall was quiet. *No cops. They'd all be down at Saint Michel.* He kept his eyes fixed straight ahead, slotted his ticket and walked to the exit and up the steps to the street.

Shielding his eyes from the sun, he looked around to get his bearings. Directly in front, behind a formal garden of hanging trees, was the long gothic façade of La Préfecture de Police.

The biggest cop shop in France. Someday, I'll tell Charlotte. If she ever forgives me.

He looked down at his feet. *Lose the suitcase.* He popped the locks, pulled out the leather bag and threw the suitcase over the railings into the garden.

To his left he could see the river and he hurried to the Quai de la Corse. At the end of the street the Pont Neuf stretched across the Seine, stone mullions set into the side, where tourists sat with their guidebooks and sandwiches. Cool, damp air from the river filled his lungs as he ran.

Cops. He saw the light blue shirt of a gendarme outside a building. Above him, three small French tricolors stuck out from the wall. *Relax, official building. He's supposed to be there.* He slowed to a walk and crossed the street to the shade and cover of the trees, then picked up pace and slid to a halt at the end of the road where it joined the Pont Neuf. He scanned the length of the bridge.

She wasn't there.

CHAPTER 31

Montrose jerked his head around. A black Jaguar sedan slowed to a halt in the middle of the bridge. A man got out from the driver's seat and sat on a stone bench set into a semi-circular mullion at the side of the bridge.

Reinhard.

Montrose crossed the road and stood before the mullion before lifting the bag onto the edge of the bridge. *Let him see what's going to happen if he tries anything.*

Reinhard kept his eyes on the bag as he stood up. "I was beginning to think you wouldn't make it. I've been hearing on the police radio about all sorts of adventures. They really are very upset with you."

Montrose nodded towards Reinhard's jacket. "If you're carrying a piece, the bag is going in the water."

"Do you think I'm going to double-cross you?" Reinhard opened his jacket. "Happy now?"

"Where is she?"

Reinhard nodded towards the Jaguar.

Through the rear passenger window he saw a small figure in the rear seat. She sat very still. A tracksuit top was pulled up to just under her nose. Her eyes darted from side to side.

"Anyone you know? You must think I'm an idiot, Montrose."

Montrose shook his head. "No, that really doesn't cover it. Bring her out."

Reinhard nodded. "Good move. That's what I'd do." He stepped over to the Jaguar, opened the door and hauled her from the seat.

Behind the lip of the tracksuit top Montrose could see the edge of the thick black tape covering her mouth. He looked down and saw the same tape wrapped around her wrists. Fear and fury were in her eyes as he pulled her close.

Reinhard clapped his hands. "That's so sweet!"

"Fuck you. Show me the memory stick."

"Patience, Montrose. All in good time," said Reinhard, patting his pocket. "And of course the video is ready to send to Interpol, from my phone." He nodded at the leather bag. "Now, open it."

Montrose tightened his grip on the bag. "Let her walk away. Then we deal. Or the bag goes over the side."

"You know, I knew you were gonna be a prick about this." Reinhard pointed towards the quay. "Look over there. See the guy with the raincoat?"

Montrose looked. A man rested his elbows on the wall of the quay facing them, a raincoat draped over the stone. *That face again. Black Suit from Rome.*

"You know what he's hiding?" said Reinhard. "No? Well, if you so much as make one *fucking* move with that bag, there's a rifle trained on your friend. It's a

Heckler and Koch 417. Currently the weapon of choice for British Special Forces in Afghanistan, with a 7.62 mm round. It'll go through the human body and leave a hole the size of a basketball. But a sexy little chick like her? It will cut her in half. Just a little incentive for you."

Montrose could make out the end of a muzzle under the raincoat. *It's not a bluff.* He pulled her to edge of the bridge, shielding her from the shooter.

"Hurry up, Montrose. Think how pretty she's going to look when a 7.62 has blown her guts all over the road."

Montrose stood his ground. "I want the shooter to walk away. Or I'm just gonna lose it. And you can clear up whatever fucking mess is left."

"That's not gonna happen."

"I swear, if she goes down, you're going with me."

"You behave yourself, Montrose, and she won't. Straight swap. The bag and list for the girl."

Charlotte mumbled through the tape. Montrose pulled down the tracksuit top and eased the tape from her lips. She twisted her head to Reinhard. "*Fis de pute!*"

"Shut it," snarled Reinhard.

She shook her head. "You have no idea what you're up against. You're a dead man."

"Charlotte, start walking," said Montrose without taking his eyes from Reinhard.

"*Non!* I'm not afraid of him."

The tremor in her voice told Montrose otherwise. "Please, I need you safe. Go now!"

"No. I want to stay with you."

Montrose saw the determination in her wet eyes. She looked like a child.

Reinhard scoffed. "Oh, how touching! The drama!"

"Shut the fuck up," said Montrose through gritted teeth.

"Hurry up, Montrose. He might just shoot you first and then her. Who can say?"

Ain't no choice. He'll do it. Montrose brought the bag down from the edge of the bridge and laid it at his feet. "You've got what you wanted."

"Slide it over to me."

Montrose kicked the bag forwards.

Reinhard reached down and pulled out the envelope. He examined the contents briefly. "And now, for the finalé." He nodded towards the man on the quay.

Montrose glanced back to the quay. He stared at Black Suit. Tourists strolled behind him as he leaned against the quay. *This ain't right. He's actually gonna drop down to the scope and take up a firing position with a sniper's rifle? Under a raincoat? In broad daylight?* He turned back to Reinhard. "You know what? This is bullshit. He's not gonna shoot her. In the middle of Paris? Surrounded by witnesses? Good try, dickhead." He stepped forward to grab the bag, and edged her back towards the edge of the stone. He froze as metal jammed hard into his kidneys. He could smell the cologne. *Mr. Grey Suit.*

"So," said Grey Suit. "You worked it out. He's not the shooter. I am. And do you think I'll miss from this range?"

He felt Grey Suit angling the weapon against his back, pressing his knuckles into his kidneys. *Professional shot. In the back, through the throat and into the head.* He could feel the barrel stretching up his spine. The length told him that the weapon was fitted with a suppressor.

He saw the tears well up in Charlotte's eyes. *Silenced weapons. Soft head rounds. No exit wound. No one will know. They're going to kill us. Right here. Right now. Then walk away.* He turned his head slowly towards her. "Charlotte? Tell your friends."

Reinhard narrowed his eyes. "Don't do anything stupid."

He looked left and right down the river. *No boats. Let's hope they're not under the bridge.*

She looked at him quizzically, "But, we cannot . . ."

He reached over and held her bound hands. "Someone's got to tell them. That's you." He brought up his hand and shoved her hard in the chest. Her bottom smacked against the stone parapet and her legs flew into the air as she tumbled backwards over the bridge.

"You stupid bastard!" shouted Reinhard.

Montrose gasped as the gun stabbed hard into his kidneys. He heard her scream before she hit the water. Shouts went up from the quay. He looked over at Black Suit as people crowded around him, pointing to the middle of the river. Black Suit covered the muzzle of the rifle, stepped back from the quay and began running towards the bridge.

Reinhard's face twisted with rage. "You have an extraordinary capacity for fucking things up, Montrose."

"It's a gift." *Jesus, I hope she can swim.*

Reinhard stared at Grey Suit. "What are you waiting for? Shoot the bastard!"

People began gathering near the edge of the bridge. Grey Suit shook his head.

"Shoot him!" hissed Reinhard. "He's a fucking psychopath! We'll say it's an arrest. I mean, he just tried to kill one of his victims by trussing her up and throwing her off a bridge!"

Passers-by crowded into the mullion, pushing them aside.

Grey Suit pulled Montrose hard against him. "Get in the car. Or are you gonna try some fancy move where you spin around and sweep away the gun and then throw me over the bridge? Go for it. I'll even shut my eyes."

Montrose stood his ground. He looked over and saw a *bateau-mouche* approach, the guardrail lined with people. One man was stripping off his jacket while the other was ready with a life belt.

Grey Suit hissed in Montrose's ear. "You'll be dead before you hit the water." His hand tightened around the waist of Montrose's pants. "You're just a geek. This is what I do for a living. Now, stop being a twat and get in the car."

Montrose felt his bladder tighten. *I'm not going to piss myself in front of these guys.* "You sure you wanna do that? Shoot me right here? There's people everywhere."

"You call for the cops, I'll shoot you. You try to run, I'll shoot you. You make a move on me, I'll ... Do you see a pattern emerging here?"

The wail of a siren came from the end of the bridge. Montrose saw the *bateau-mouche* slip out of sight under the edge of the bridge. He heard shouts and then a cheer and applause.

The barrel of the gun twisted against his skin. "Enough of this shit," said Grey Suit. "Three seconds to get in the car or I'll drop you. One ... Two ..."

He'll do it.

Montrose walked towards the car. He felt Grey Suit's legs against his own, matching his steps. He slid into the back seat. Grey Suit got in beside him and closed the door. Black Suit was out of breath as he hauled open the driver's door and jumped in, his shoulders spilling over the edge of the seat.

Reinhard got in the front and heaved the bag of diamonds onto his lap. "Get the fuck out of here." The Jag pulled away onto the bridge and accelerated towards the quay. He turned around in the seat. "Just fucking shoot him!"

Grey Suit shook his head. "Don't be a bloody fool."

"You watch your mouth!" said Reinhard. "You damn well work for me."

"We work for Herr Kessler. We don't take orders from you."

Montrose realized he hadn't drawn a breath since he got in the car. He inhaled greedily. *Not such a happy crew. And these are Kessler's goons?* "Yeah, you tell him, Mr. Grey Suit. The little prick."

Reinhard tried to lean over from the front seat, but the bag of diamonds slipped from his grasp. He grabbed them and held them tight. "Give me the gun! I'll shoot him right now."

"Not in the car," said Grey Suit. "I mean, have you ever seen *Reservoir Dogs*? The young guy in the back seat when the gun goes off his face? Yeah? Well, this is my car. It's not going to happen."

Montrose nodded. "That's a good point." *Thank God for Tarantino.* "Helluva mess."

"Shut up and hands out," said Grey Suit, holding up a pair of handcuffs.

The steel clamped tight around Montrose's wrists

and cut into the raw wounds. He stared at the back of Black Suit's head. *Got to get away from these psychos.* He looked down to the steel chain hanging between the bracelets. *The handcuff chain. Black Suit's neck is as thick as one of my thighs. It would work. Wait until the car had built up some speed, then throw the cuffs over and choke the bastard from behind. The bigger the crash, the better. Running through the streets of Paris with handcuffs on isn't the worst thing that could happen to me. Not today.* He felt something cold on his thigh. He looked down to see the broad blade of a hunting knife.

Grey Suit leaned over. "You know, that might work. He could lose control of the car. But by the time you've got the cuffs around his neck, I'll cut you right *here*." The tip of the knife pressed into the top of Montrose's left leg.

Femoral artery. Colossal loss of blood. Virtually unstoppable without an artery clamp. That's if you managed to cut open the thigh and locate the deflated artery as it spewed blood and shrank behind some of the biggest and toughest muscles in the body. Combat medics have to shove their hands up into the pelvic cavity to find it. It rarely worked. Death in five minutes.

Grey Suit slit the cloth of Montrose's pants. "Your move."

"Thought you didn't want to mess up your car?"

"For you, I'll make an exception."

Whatever I'm gonna do, it's got be quick. As soon as we step out the car, I'm dead. Grab the knife with both hands and go for it. Don't think. Just do it.

The driver blasted his horn over a pedestrian crossing.

They're heading out of town. There would be no

witnesses, nobody to call the cops. Nobody to see me die. There's only one option. Wait for a corner to the left. Pick your spot.

At the end of the avenue cars streamed around the Arc de Triomphe. *The craziest junction in the world. No rules applied, just a foot hard on the accelerator and a hand on the horn.* He could see the cars jostling for position. *The driver would have to slow to find a gap. Now or never.*

Reinhard turned his head. "I know your story, Montrose. And your sister. The whore? Is that true? I heard about the porn videos. Might check it out later. Watch her taking it doggy from some junkies. Bet she loved a gangbang."

Calm. Focus. Montrose glanced at the door handle. A fist slammed down into his groin.

"You're still thinking about it," said Grey Suit. "How about I just keep the knife pressed against your balls? Do you think you could do it then?"

Montrose let his head drop back against the seat as nausea swept through him.

Grey Suit produced another pair of handcuffs and locked Montrose's wrist to the door handle. "Now try it, tough guy."

CHAPTER 32

The afternoon sun was dipping in the sky as Montrose stepped from the Jaguar. *Northern hemisphere, so the sun would be in the south. We're west of Paris.* A thick forest lined both sides of the road. He watched Grey Suit unscrew the suppressor from his gun and eject the magazine. He slipped both into his pocket and pulled out another magazine.

Grey Suit looked over at Montrose, grinned and slotted the magazine home. "I like to make a statement."

What did he just load? A black Mercedes drove past at a crawl, then pulled into the side of the road. A passenger got out. *Jacques Kessler. The whole gang was here.*

Reinhard emerged from the Jaguar and held the leather bag aloft. "You know, Kessler, if you want something done . . ."

Jacques Kessler nodded to the driver of the Mercedes. "Muller, please help Herr Reinhard with his bag."

Muller pulled a silver pistol from his coat. He walked

over to Reinhard and held out his hand. "I'll take care of that."

"I think it's better if it remains with me until we reach the vaults," Reinhard scoffed. "You didn't take particularly good care of it last time."

"Sir. Give me the bag," said Muller.

"Enough of this nonsense," replied Reinhard. "The bag stays with me."

"No really, I insist," said Muller as he snapped back his arm and pistol-whipped Reinhard across the face.

Holy shit. Montrose watched him stagger around and then drop to the ground. *The goons all work for Kessler. He's been pulling the strings all along. And the shooting in Zurich? Christ, he took out his own security staff.*

Reinhard lay on the road, gripping the bag with one hand and holding his mouth with the other, blood trickling through his fingers. His eyes said it all. He tried to turn away but Muller stepped over him. "Get away from me!"

Muller stamped on Reinhard's wrist and snatched up the bag.

"No!" Reinhard got to his knees, but Muller turned and kicked him full in the face. His head snapped back and he slumped down onto his back. Muller reached inside Reinhard's jacket and pulled out the envelope and memory stick.

"That's mine!" Reinhard stumbled to his feet and spat out a tooth.

The window of the Mercedes slid down. A voice came from inside. *"What is going on?"* Kessler leaned into the window. "Nothing to worry about, sir. Just tidying up some loose ends. The airport is only five kilometers away. I've scheduled take-off in fifteen minutes. That's plenty of time." He pointed towards Montrose. "Muller, have the English team take care of these two. We have to go." Kessler took out his cell phone. "Father? We have them. The list and the diamonds. Yes, the video too. Muller, place the list in the bag." He slipped the memory stick into his suit pocket and looked over at Reinhard as he spoke into the phone. "Not for very much longer. Montrose too. I'm leaving for the airport. Yes, I have him with me. We'll be in Kabul in three hours." He cut the call.

"Jacques!" said Reinhard. "You can't do this!"

Kessler didn't look at him. He stepped into the Mercedes. "You know, I think I can."

Grey Suit grabbed the free handcuff bracelet hanging from Montrose's wrist and tugged him forward, then slapped it onto Reinhard's wrist.

Muller placed the bag of diamonds into the trunk of the Mercedes and drove off.

Shit, this is not what I need, handcuffed to this jerk. Reinhard's face was white with shock. Montrose grinned and shook the cuffs. "Welcome to my world, tough guy." A hand shoved him hard in the back. "How does it feel?"

Black Suit stood by the Jaguar. "You need a hand, mate?"

Grey Suit grinned and held up his gun. "Not with this bad bastard." He pulled back the slide and chambered a round. "Into the forest," he said. "I don't have all day."

Montrose pushed his way through the scrub and into the trees. *There's no point hanging about. There's more cover in the forest. If I make it that far.* His arm was hauled back as Reinhard stood rooted to the spot.

"No!" screamed Reinhard, turning back towards

Grey Suit. "Please, for God's sake! I'm on your side!"

Montrose tugged the handcuffs. "What the fuck do you think this is? Cowboys and Indians? Hurry up, you yellow bastard."

"It's him you want!"

Grey Suit brought up a fist. There was an audible crack and Reinhard's nose burst across his face. "Move it, rich kid, or I'll shoot you right now."

Reinhard dropped to his knees, holding his face, blood streaming through his hands.

Montrose pulled Reinhard to his feet and dragged him into the trees. He searched around the scrub. *Grey Suit would have to go in further if they want to dump our bodies. The further the better.* The forest was thick with pine and silver birch. In the clearings, some young oak saplings and low scrub. *No paths. No animal tracks. The only cover is the trees.* He felt Reinhard stumble behind him.

No. The only cover is Reinhard. Pick your time.

Before them the ground started to become uneven. He heard Reinhard cry out. His arm was nearly wrenched from the socket as Reinhard stumbled into a dip and slammed into a tree. Montrose managed to stay upright and tugged hard at the handcuff chain. *Pick your time? Seriously? Any time now would be good. Do it from low down.* "C'mon, tough guy, get up." He squatted down and widened his stance then placed his hands around Reinhard's torso.

"Get away from me!" squealed Reinhard.

"Let's just do it. We played, we lost. Man up." He felt a tremor in his thighs as they took the strain of Reinhard's weight. *Legs, don't fail me now.* Glancing over Reinhard's shoulder, he waited until Grey Suit was directly behind Reinhard then launched himself up with all his strength and slammed Reinhard into Grey Suit.

The breath blew out of Grey Suit as he smacked into the tree.

A shot rang out and they tumbled backwards into the undergrowth.

Reinhard slid to the side and Montrose smashed his right fist down onto Grey Suit's face, then chopped the heel of his left hand down onto his throat.

Grey Suit tried to bring up his gun, but it was pinned down under Reinhard, whose left arm flailed about as Montrose hammered down with both hands. Grey Suit's head hung limp to the side and blood sprayed from Montrose's knuckles, mixing with the mucus and blood bubbling from Grey Suit's nose.

Montrose fell back, pulling Reinhard's arm with him.

Reinhard mouthed a silent scream as he looked down at his guts spilling forward over his waist. His lower chest was an unidentifiable mass of shredded meat and bone. He tried to pull his arm back from Montrose and scoop up the tattered intestines as they slipped through his hands. He began to scream in short bursts, red froth blowing from his ruptured lungs. He slumped to the side and earth and dried leaves stuck to his guts as they spilled out, his blood spreading and seeping into the ground, darkening the soil.

Montrose retched, spitting yellow bile onto the leaf litter. He tore his gaze from Reinhard and shoved his hand into Grey Suit's pockets. He pulled out a handcuff key, stabbed it into the cuffs and twisted it around. He picked up the gun and wiped the earth and blood from the pistol grip. *Black Suit would be expecting two gunshots. If he doesn't get them, he'll come looking. No reason to disappoint him.* He turned the gun towards Grey Suit.

"No, don't . . ." Grey Suit tried to lever himself up. A tooth tumbled from his bleeding lips. "No . . ."

"You said you like to make a statement. So do I." He leveled the gun at Grey Suit's chest. "And you know what that statement is?" He squeezed the trigger. "Fuck you."

Grey Suit's chest burst open and a pink mist sprayed over the bushes behind him. He collapsed back, the jagged edges of his ribs sticking out white from the gaping wound.

He weaved through the trees, keeping low. Branches whipped against his body and he held up a hand to protect his face. The ground began to rise. He dived down onto his stomach and crawled flat over a ridge, then slid down a slope into a muddy creek, filled with leaf litter and pine needles. He set off in a fast crawl, keeping his head below the ridge. Water seeped into his shoes from the soft ground and his hands were caked with mud.

The road was dead ahead. Rolling into a patch of ferns, he lay on his side, holding Grey Suit's gun to his chest. *SIG Sauer P220. Swiss issue. .30 Luger ammo. Maybe nine rounds.* He wiped his muddy hands on his shirt and slid back the top grip of the SIG and saw the shiny brass cartridge in the block. *The weapon was ready.* He let the slide return and glanced back down the creek. *Nothing.* He rolled onto his front and snaked through the ferns. The image of Reinhard's shredded guts flashed through his mind. *What did Grey Suit load?* Pushing the release catch, he dropped the magazine. The tip of the first round was cut with a deep 'X' into the tip. *Dum-dums. Just get to the Jag.*

He replaced the magazine and peeked out from the ferns to the rear of the Jaguar. Wisps of smoke burbled from the exhaust. *He's ready to go.* He turned and checked in the other direction, spotted another car parked near the forest. *Who the hell is that? BMW. Paris plates. The cops?* There was no one in the car. *Maybe spooks. Oh, man, not those bastards from Langley. That's all I need.* He pressed his face to the ground and looked under the cars. There was no one around.

With the gun held in front of him, he ran to the rear of the Jaguar. He looked up and saw the rear windshield shattered, with a hole on the left hand side. *What the hell?* Pressing his body to the side of the car, he slid around and brought the gun up fast to the driver's open window.

Black Suit's face was missing and the windshield and dashboard were spattered with blood and shredded flesh.

He heard his own breathing coming short and fast. *That explains the hole in the rear windshield. Who is driving that BMW? CIA? Whatever. Just go!* He opened the driver's door and hauled the corpse onto the road, dragging the legs clear of the door. The steering wheel was sticky with blood as he slammed the auto stick into drive. The tires screeched, trying to grip the road, then the hood rose and the Jag lurched forward.

He braked into a tight bend, keeping his right foot on the accelerator, then steered for the apex and stamped hard on the accelerator. The Jag immediately snapped into an oversteer as the back end shot out, thumping and dragging the rear wheel against the edge of the road. He steered into the skid and weaved across the road, trying to get the Jag to go in a straight line. *Christ, this thing's got some power.* He recognized the banshee wail from under the hood and looked down at the dashboard. *Boost gauge. The damn engine was supercharged.*

The tail end of the car came into line just before he hit the next corner. He stood on the brakes, but this time feathered the throttle and fed in the power. The rear end began to slide, but he brought it into line with a flick of opposite lock. A long straight opened up in front of him. Montrose braced himself against the steering wheel and hit the loud pedal.

Director Spinks stared down at the phone in his hand, settled back into the rear seat and stared out of the window as the Mercedes sped past the tree-lined edge of the Tiergarten, towards the centre of Berlin. His cell phone buzzed and he jammed it to his ear. "Yeah?"

"It's Ferguson, sir."

"Have you found him?"

"Montrose is in Paris, we sent . . ."

"Paris! What the hell is he doing there?"

"We think he fled there after Zurich, sir. But he was arrested and his fingerprints were flashed around all the European cop systems. So we sent a team to pick him up, but the prison told us the Zurich cops had got him and were taking him to Zurich."

"Thank Christ! Phone the local team. I don't care

how they do it, but I want Montrose in our custody. Or just shoot the bastard, it's all the same to me."

"Sir, we phoned the Zurich police. They don't have him."

"They don't . . . What the hell are you saying, Ferguson?"

"It wasn't the Zurich cops. But someone from Zurich got to Montrose before us. Probably the Security Services. Now all we're being told is that Montrose killed three of them and is now on the run in Paris. The French are on full alert for an escaped prisoner."

"You fucking idiot! You and the stupid cops! Is there no one in Europe who knows what the fuck they're doing?"

"Sir, I think . . ."

"Shut up! Montrose has got help. He's going to get the hell out of France. They'll never find him. That psycho is capable of anything."

"Sir, there are three police forces looking for him. We've tapped into their systems. As soon as they know, we'll know, if we don't find him first."

"You fu . . . he could be coming right here. And the Afghan he shot is still lying in a hospital bed." He thought for a moment then jabbed the driver's shoulder. "Get me to the hospital. Fast."

The Mercedes veered to the left and accelerated past the cars in front. Spinks held on to the door handle and forced the cell phone against his lips. "Ferguson, if the importance of this situation hasn't got through to you, let me put you in the picture. The reason Montrose ended up in Interpol was so that we could get him away from the Langley computer systems. He went through them like crap through a goose. He saw things that nobody should know, including you and me. Now, all he has to do is kill whoever the fuck he likes, then turn up at the door of some communist bastard South American shithole of an embassy, say he was framed by the CIA, FBI or any other Washington fucker, and tomorrow morning you and I will be starring on Wikileaks!" His voice began to rasp as he bellowed into the phone. "The whole world will be hanging on to his every word! Have you any idea what I'm saying?"

" Sir, I . . ."

"If he turns up in Berlin, I will personally fucking shoot you. Do you understand? Kill him!"

CHAPTER 33

The Jag rose into the air over a rise, the hood obscuring the road, then crashed back down. A junction appeared fifty yards ahead. Montrose stood on the brakes and hauled on the steering wheel. The tires locked and the Jag fishtailed wildly before he wrestled it to a halt.

Smoke from the tires drifted past the window. An acrid stench of burned rubber filled the car. *Left or right?* He looked south across fields of corn and sunflowers towards a low ridge of hills. No good for an airport. *It had to be north. Kessler said ten minutes. Can't be far.* Above the tree line a light aircraft pulled slowly into the sky, its engine straining as it climbed. *Kessler won't be in that piece of crap. It'll be a private jet.* A picture of Sandie flashed into his mind. *Christ, what is it with me and private jets? One thing is for sure. That bastard is going nowhere. If I get there in time.* He turned the Jag to the right. The trees thinned out and he saw a security fence tracking the edge of the road.

The end of the runway came into view. A sleek, ivory-liveried Lear Jet was heading away from him along a slipway. Four windows lined the fuselage and a face appeared at the glass. *Kessler? Swiss registration. It's got to be them.* The road turned right to track the perimeter fence bordering the runway. *Once the jet reached the end of the slipway, all the pilot had to do was turn on the taps and they were gone.*

Montrose gunned the Jag. The kickdown sent the supercharger screaming then pausing for breath each time the transmission banged up a gear. He kept his eyes on the road. Utility poles flashed past. *If I come off now, two ton Jag or not, I'll be sliced in half.*

Gripping the wheel hard, he glanced down at the speedometer. 200 kilometers per hour and climbing. He passed the Lear Jet, glimpsing it in his peripheral vision. The end of the road was ahead. He pressed the brakes hard and the Jag shuddered to a halt. There were no gates in the fence. *I'll have to do this the hard way.*

He hit reverse, the synchro whining as he careered backwards. To the right, the jet was near the end of the slipway. *They were ready to go.*

The shoulder was six feet wide with a drainage ditch. *If I'm fast enough I'll go straight over the ditch and hit the fence. Chain link ain't going to stop me. Fast enough wasn't a problem.* He floored the pedal.

The supercharger shrieked and the Jag gathered speed. He hit the grass at the side of the road. Turf flew past his window as the Jag shot across the ditch. The fence burst up and over the hood, gouging deep scars into the windshield. The Jag veered to the left as it hit the grass, then snapped back into line when the tires bit into the asphalt.

The Lear Jet was turning to face the runway. Montrose could hear the pilot wind up the engines. *Twenty meters to go.* The Jag hurtled towards the tail of the jet. *If I'm directly behind when the pilot hits the gas, I'll be right in line for the engine exhausts. It'll burn the Jag to cinders. And me.*

The tail of the Lear Jet dipped. The pilot had pushed the levers all the way.

The blast from the engines scorched the paint from the hood and rocked the Jag from side to side. The windshield glass started to bubble. A few seconds more and the temperature inside the car would be over a thousand degrees. Montrose kept his foot on the gas and swerved to the left. The rear windows exploded in a glass storm. He hauled the Jag in a tight arc to the right, swinging back towards the tail of the plane.

The rear aileron headed directly for the windshield. Montrose dived into the front passenger seat and tried to tuck his body under the glove compartment. The Jag slammed into the tail of the jet. He covered his face against the searing heat as the aileron burst through the windshield and carved open the roof. The Jag spun around and slewed to a halt.

The air was thick with the stench of burned paint and jet exhaust fumes. The back seat had taken the worst and flames licked the rear window. Montrose rolled out onto the asphalt and stuck his head around the battered fender of the Jag. The jet had ground to a halt with half of its tail section scattered across the runway.

He got to his feet and heard the jet engines start to wind up once more. *Are they crazy?* He looked down the runway, and saw the Mercedes parked by a terminal. *No, they're going for the car.* Thick smoke from the Jag drifted past his face. He brought up the SIG. *They ain't gonna make it.*

He took aim along the sights and pumped a round towards the starboard engine. The SIG jerked around in his hand and a chunk of carbon blew off the rudder. *Christ, what did that goon load this thing with?* He steadied his feet and let loose another two rounds, the first hitting the bottom of the fuselage and the second on target, blowing a hole in the engine cover. The plane shuddered as a deadened thump shook the airframe and a long yellow flame shot back towards him. He hit the asphalt. A whoosh of extinguishing gas blew over him as the engine sputtered and died.

A face appeared at a window, twisted in shock and rage. *Kessler!* The face disappeared and Montrose heard the port engine begin to pick up speed. *Jesus, don't they ever . . .?* He lifted the SIG and fired directly into the port engine. His ears rang as the turbine shattered and hot shards of metal flew past and embedded into the asphalt beside him.

Game over. He got to his feet, holding the SIG before him, scrambled under the wing and ran to the port door. *Only one way out. Let's squeeze the rats out of the hole.* He steadied the SIG and pointed it at the door. *No, wait. Sandie. What did she say about the other exit on a private plane? The day she said she had to step out onto the wing because the guy's ex-wife had just arrived. Emergency exit. Got to be.*

The handle of the port door swung down. *Let's make sure.* "Stay where you are!" He fired two rounds into the top of the door then rolled under the fuselage. Leaking jet fuel dripped onto his foot as he stood and steadied the SIG on the wing. One of the windows had the outline of a small door. *Yeah, she was right. Shoot the first bastard that comes out.*

The frame around the window popped from its mountings and fell onto the wing. A white-shirted man was pushed forward, his hands covering his face, holding onto his pilot's hat.

Okay, not the first person. "Get the fuck out of here. Move!" Montrose kept the SIG leveled at the window. The pilot stayed crouched, his arms covering his head and face as he rolled away from Montrose and dropped from the wing, then took off down the runway.

A voice came from the cabin. "Don't shoot!"

"Out! Now! Hands held high!"

Kessler edged towards the exit, the bag held before him.

"Guess who, dickweed. Drop the bag." Montrose pressed himself against the fuselage.

Kessler twisted the handle of the bag in his hand. "But . . . no. I'm not that stupid. You'll just shoot me."

Montrose lifted the SIG and looked down the iron sights into Kessler's face. "I'll fucking shoot you now if you don't."

Arms extended, Kessler dropped the bag out of the exit. It slid down the wing and landed at Montrose's feet. Montrose kicked it behind him towards the nose of the plane. "Out the door. And tell your man to throw out his gun."

Edging forward, hands held before him, Kessler crouched and squeezed through onto the wing then looked back. "Muller? You heard him. Throw out your gun."

Montrose stepped back, covering the door as Kessler dropped onto the asphalt.

"All right, Montrose. You win. How much do you want?"

Montrose stared at him, fingering the trigger, his eyes darting towards the door.

"It all comes down to business. So, how much? One million? Ten million? You're holding all the cards. Name your price."

Montrose said nothing. Blood buzzed in his ears. "Tell Muller to throw his gun out. Right now."

"You got your girlfriend back. Reinhard wanted to kill her. I changed his mind." Kessler tried to shrug, but it looked as if he'd just been jabbed with a cattle prod. "Reinhard was out of control. It had nothing to do with me, I can assure you. I'm a businessman. I have no time for such things."

Smoke from the Jag drifted across the runway. "You lying bastard," said Montrose. "You wouldn't care if she lived or died." He shouted towards the door. "Muller! Throw out the gun or your boss gets it in the head. Right now!"

Kessler nodded towards the plane. "Muller has the memory stick from Reinhard. It's the full video of the murders in Rome. So, how much is it worth to you? Think about it, you're a man on the run with a lot of enemies."

"Yeah, tell me about it." He turned to the door. "Muller! You've got three seconds. One!"

Kessler held out his hands. "If I were you, I'd get out while your luck holds. And go back to being an IT geek, or whatever shit job you do. So, can we do business?"

Montrose wrapped his hands tighter around the SIG. "You know, I'm thinking of a career change. Two!" He felt the cold steel of a gun barrel pressing into the back of his neck.

"Actually," said Kessler, "I was tempted to say '*look behind you*', but I didn't think you'd fall for that one."

His throat dried up and he saw a wide smile spread across Kessler's face. A glance at the reflection in the window showed Muller standing behind him, still wearing the pilot's hat.

Reaching into his pocket, Kessler pulled out a memory stick. "Actually, it's right here." He waved it in Montrose's face. "Muller's a very resourceful man. He knew you'd be careless. Maybe you're just an office boy after all."

"Drop the gun," said Muller.

Kessler shook his head. "Did you really think I'd deal with a piece of shit like you?"

The hammer of Muller's gun clicked in his ear and the barrel jabbed him at the base of the skull.

"I said, drop it."

It's useless. Even if I turned around in time, all the guy had to do was pull the trigger. Montrose let the SIG fall onto the concrete.

"Now," said Kessler, "let's get this over with. Muller, shoot this prick in the face then get the Mercedes. I've had enough of this fiasco."

"Walk," said Muller, pointing the gun to the side of the airfield.

"Kessler? Who is this man?" A figure crouched at the emergency exit, his dark face creased with fury.

"This, Mr. Ambassador," said Kessler, "is Connor Montrose. And it is the last time he will interfere in our affairs."

The Afghan peered at him. "Montrose? The man from Rome?"

Montrose stood still. *Keep talking. Buy me some time.* "Yeah, how ya doing, Mr. Ambassador? Sold any heroin lately, ya fucking weasel."

The Afghan shoved his hand inside his jacket and pulled out a curved dagger, the hilt studded with colored stones. "You killed my cousin," he spat. "Now I am going to kill you."

Oh, great. End of conversation. "Join the line, asshat." He tipped his head back towards Muller. "In fact, why don't you and him fight it out? Winner gets to kill me. It'll be fun." *Come on, Mr. Ambassador, come closer.*

The Afghan stepped out onto the wing, his arms thrust forward, holding out the dagger. "This has been in my family for a hundred years. It was first used to slit open the bellies of the British women who defiled our country. When I have finished with you, it will be cherished for cutting out your heart." He dropped to the asphalt and advanced towards Montrose.

"Dude, I ain't stopping you. But you can't both kill me, so why don't you two discuss it and let me know?" Montrose nodded towards the apron. "I'll be over there."

Muller smacked the barrel of his gun against Montrose's ear. "You move and I'll blow your head off."

He could feel the heat on his face from the burning Jag. Montrose shuffled his stance wider and moved his weight to the balls of his feet. "Hey, Muller, chill. Abdul the drug-dealer is your biggest customer, surely he gets to go first?" He held out his arms and opened his palms towards the Afghan. "What do you say, Abdul? Want to come at me with that fancy letter opener?" *Come closer, you bastard.* "I'll bet the last time you held a real knife was eating some rancid goat in a flea-ridden tent, waiting for Uncle Sam to turn up with some greenbacks to buy your ass."

The Afghan's eyes opened wide and his knuckles turned white around the dagger. "I will cut out your heart!"

"Don't shit me, Abdul, you couldn't cut hot cheese with that piece of tourist crap. You probably swapped your sister for it." *C'mon, run at me.* "You're just a camel-fucker in a white man's suit."

Pushing Kessler out of the way, the Afghan lunged towards Montrose, the dagger raised in his hand.

A scorching blast of heat scoured their faces as the Jag's fuel tank ignited, showering them with shattered glass. The Afghan stumbled, holding his head, blood running from his fingers where the shards had scarred his scalp.

Now! Montrose twisted around, sweeping his hand behind and palming away the gun, then hooked his leg around Muller's knee as he threw his weight towards him. The breath exploded out of Muller's chest when he hit the asphalt and Montrose landed on top of him.

Montrose grabbed the snub-nosed revolver, but Muller kept a vice-like grip, angling it towards Montrose's face. *He's stronger than me. Do something!* He plunged two fingers of his right hand into Muller's left eye, feeling his fingernails scrape the bone as he drove into the cavity and the soft tissue behind. He hooked his fingers and threw himself back. Muller screamed as his eyeball was ripped from its socket, and clamped his hands to his face.

The revolver lay on the ground. Montrose dived

towards it, his chin hitting the asphalt, and grabbed the pistol grip, his hand greasy with optical fluid. The Afghan leapt forward and stamped down on his wrist. The gun began to slip from Montrose's grasp. The Afghan forced his whole weight down, twisting his shoe and Montrose felt the bones grinding in his wrist. *I can't hold it.* Pain shot straight up his arms and his fingers flew open.

The Afghan kicked the revolver away and Montrose watched it skitter across the asphalt. He turned just as the Afghan brought down the dagger.

Montrose twisted around on his hips and booted the Afghan in the back of the knees as the dagger flashed past his face. The Afghan tumbled to the ground and thrust his leg back, the heel of his shoe catching Montrose flush on the temple. His head swam for a moment, until he spotted the Afghan reaching for the revolver. *Get the SIG!* He rolled onto his knees and scrambled towards his gun, lying under the jet. With the Afghan's screams ringing in his ear, he snatched up the SIG, rolled to the side and braced himself for the recoil.

The hammer clicked. Nothing. Misfire. He dropped to the ground and rolled away as bullets pinged around him, yanking back the slide on the SIG to eject the dead cartridge. His leg buckled under him and a burning pain streaked across his side as he turned and fired blind.

The Afghan staggered back, revolver slipping from his fingers. He choked and blood erupted from his mouth. He slumped against the side of the jet, leaving a thick smear of gore as he slid down the fuselage, then toppled face first onto the runway. His head bounced off the ground and dropped into a spreading pool of blood, a red froth bubbling from his mouth.

Montrose saw a wound the size of a dinner plate in the Afghan's back. *Fuck him.* Placing a hand flat on the wet ground, he tried to push himself up, but a bolt of pain coursed through his leg and he fell back onto his ass. A deep carmine scar across his side began to bleed, bright red spots forming on the ripped flesh. He looked down at the blood forming at his feet, when a bolt of pain arced through his body and he cried out and fell back onto the asphalt.

He heard a roar and lifted his head up as Muller got to his feet, blood and fluid running down his face, his lips drawn back tight in a mask of fury and hate. Montrose brought up the SIG. The recoil made the grip slip on his wet hand. Blood and bone spewed from the side of Muller's head as the top slide of the SIG slammed forward and stayed there.

Empty. He dropped the gun onto the asphalt. His leg began to spasm. He looked down and saw a neat hole punched through his calf muscle. *Suck it up, bitch. You ain't dead yet.* His eyes stung from the jet fuel vapors as he turned to Kessler. "Just you and me now. Asshole."

Kessler shifted from foot to foot and stared at the carnage around him. He seemed to jolt to attention and then shot a glance towards the bag, lying near the nose of the jet. He shook his head. "I could have made you a very rich man, Montrose. Richer than you could ever dream."

Montrose laughed. "Keep up, dickhead, we've done that bit. I thought you wouldn't deal with a piece of shit like me?" He watched Kessler's eyes fix on the revolver lying beside the Afghan, hot wisps of vapor curling up from the barrel where it lay in the fuel. *If it was gonna blow, it would have done it by now. And I'd be toast. But he'll get there way before me. How many rounds are left in the chamber? What the hell, enough to kill me.* "Don't even think about it, Kessler. I'm CIA. They'll hunt you down like a dog."

Kessler threw his arms in the air. "You think? They asked us to kill you! And for what you have done to my father, I'll take great pleasure in getting my hands dirty."

"You haven't got the balls. Hand over the memory stick. It's your last chance."

"You astound me, Montrose. What are you going to do? Arrest me?"

Montrose flinched as the Jag's tires exploded and the flames grew higher, sending thick black smoke curling towards them. "An arrest isn't top of my list right now." He tried to push himself up, but his leg refused to move. "I might just beat the shit out of you. Hand it over."

Kessler patted his jacket pocket. "It's safe."

"Show me. A last request for a dying man, yeah?"

Kessler reached into his pocket, and brought out the memory stick. "Last look." He waggled it between his fingers. "All for this. If you weren't such a persistent imbecile, I might have some sympathy for you."

"Yeah, you're all fucking heart. Now, throw it clear. If you kill me, that'll clear my name."

Kessler glanced towards the bag. "That's not going to happen. I need you to be remembered as a psychopathic murderer. After all, someone's going to have to take the blame for . . ." He was lost for words as he looked at the bodies around him. "This . . . What's the word? Clusterfuck?" He placed the memory stick back into his pocket. "Goodbye, Montrose." He edged towards the revolver, watching Montrose's reactions.

I'll never make it. He saw Kessler move his weight forward, ready to sprint. *Fuck it!* Montrose threw himself towards him, arms outstretched as Kessler started to run, and slapped his hand against Kessler's heel, pushing the shoe away.

Kessler's foot slammed into the back of his own leg and he tumbled to the ground, then rolled and snatched up the revolver. He stood and looked down at his suit, the damp patches of fuel spreading across his knees and chest. "You'll pay for that, you bastard!" His hands shook as he brought up the gun.

"Yeah? I've got more to think about than your dry-cleaning." *Snub nosed revolver. He'll have to come closer. The way his hands are shaking, I'm the last thing he's gonna hit around here.*

Kessler advanced slowly, steadying the revolver. "I've never killed a man before. I often wondered what it would feel like. You know, I think I'm really going to enjoy it."

One last roll of the dice. And just keep rolling. No, I need to be further away. Or I'm dead too. "You're finished, Kessler. They'll find you. Just give me the memory stick. Take the bag." *Get some distance.* Montrose pushed himself back on his hands, across the asphalt, dragging his legs behind him. *Faster.* Pain shot through his body and his arms buckled beneath him. He slipped his hand into the pocket of his pants. *There's no choice. Do it!*

Holding the revolver with both hands, Kessler stepped forward. "I'm going to empty this gun into your stomach. Then you can watch me walk away with the bag as you bleed to death. I'm told it's the most painful way to die. Or I might just fire into the fuel and watch you burn."

"Yeah? I like your thinking." He felt the soft, familiar metal deep in his pocket. "Listen, I've got something for you. To remember our time together." His fingers folded around the metal and his thumbnail found the edge of the lid. "Made in Berlin. A present from my sister." He pulled the gold lighter from his pocket and sparked the flint as he lobbed it at Kessler's chest.

Kessler's eyes opened wide as the spark lit the flame. He tried to catch the lighter, but he grabbed thin air and it dropped at his feet. A glimmer of blue light curled around Kessler's legs and flashed across the ground, then erupted into a golden inferno, edged in black smoke, enveloping Kessler in the flames.

The heat scorched Montrose's back as he rolled away, hands over his face. He heard an ear-splitting scream, and looked up as the burning figure stumbled towards the edge of the fire then collapsed to the ground.

Kessler's entire body was alight. The hair from his scalp had gone, his head blackened and bubbling with burning fat. A carbonized hand reached out, fingers clawing into the asphalt and skin tearing away, leaving bloodied, blackened stumps. Then the hand stopped and lay still, flames and smoke curling from the tips of the fingers.

A car slid to a halt beside Montrose's head. He looked up and saw the grill of a black BMW and watched open-mouthed as a man stepped from the car and grabbed the leather bag from under the nose of the jet.

The man opened the flaps and held up the letter, then ran back to the car with the bag under his arm. The BMW drove off before the door had closed.

Who the hell . . .? Montrose dropped his face to the asphalt and crawled away from the flames.

The sound of sirens came drifting down the runway.

Oh, fuck. He leaned forward on his arms and looked down. He could see the blood trail behind him. *Here we go again.* He turned his head at the rumble of a big twin cylinder engine and saw the Norton thundering up the runway.

Charlotte slid the bike to a halt.

Montrose shifted his weight to his good leg and held a hand in the air. "Charlotte! I had no choice. They promised me the evidence to clear my name. I'm not a murderer."

She stared transfixed at the charred body of Kessler, engulfed in flames, then the burning corpses of Muller and the Afghan. She snapped her head away from the sight in disgust and shock. "I understand."

He pointed to Kessler's corpse at the edge of the flames. "And now the evidence to clear my name is destroyed." He turned to Charlotte. "How did you know where to find me?"

"Mossad. They nearly caught up with you in the forest. They'd been tailing Kessler ever since he arrived in Paris."

He looked down the runway, but the BMW was gone. "I thought they were going to shoot me."

She wiped the damp hair from her face. "It crossed my mind to ask them."

"Charlotte, I didn't know it would turn out like this." He saw Muller's blood spattered across his hands.

"You can make it up to me," she said. "I know a good restaurant in Casablanca."

"Where?"

"Morocco." She wiped her eyes against the sting of the smoke. "Get on."

I ain't gonna argue. He crawled forward and grabbed the seat of the bike, hauling himself up, then swung his bloodied leg over the seat and wrapped an arm around her slender waist.

She turned her head. "Tighter, Connor. I don't want to lose you again." She dropped the clutch.

The Norton launched forward. A blast of searing heat burst across his back as the plane exploded. The bike shook and pitched sideways in the shockwave. Charlotte wrestled it straight and opened the throttle wide.

Ferguson stood at the hotel window, looking down onto the hospital. German cops flanked the door. A blacked out Mercedes SUV sat at each end of the street, loaded with GSG9 Counter Terrorism troops. He knew there was no more could be done. Every cop in Germany had Montrose's photo, but he was nowhere to be seen. The psycho must have left France hours ago. Was he crazy enough to come to Berlin?

He peered out of the window, straining his neck to the sky. It was there, but he couldn't see it. The drones were invisible to radar and there was one above every Latin American Embassy in Berlin, and above the hospital where the Afghani Trade Delegate lay in a critical condition.

He looked down to the street where two black SUVs left to change the shift guarding the Chinese and Russian Embassy. There would be no chance of asylum. They'd kill him on sight.

If Montrose showed his face on any other street the

cops would find him, if the .50 caliber rifle on a drone didn't get him first. He turned away and sat on the bed, rubbing his face hard. A knock came at the door.

"Room Service!"

Slipping back his jacket, Ferguson pulled out his revolver, and took up position. "We didn't order room service."

"Well, you're going to want this. Special Delivery."

He whispered into the walkie-talkie. "Guys? You there? In position?"

"Yeah, we're here. It's just a room service chick. She's kosher."

He heard the voice behind the door.

"Kosher! Yes, that is a good one. You are a very funny man."

Ferguson glanced through the peephole of the door, but could only see a staff uniform.

"Stop looking at my tits."

Ferguson pulled the door open.

A figure hunched over a room service cart and rattled it into the room. She stood up straight. She was easily a foot taller than himself. "I'm Rosamund. Where's your boss?"

Ferguson tried to regain some composure, taken aback by her deep voice and her guttural Bavarian accent. "Depends who you're looking for, sweetheart."

She swept aside her red hair, cut into a bob which served only to heighten the length of her neck. "I'm not a sweetheart. I have a heart as black as the coals of hell. And you're not Spinks. Where is he?"

"Here," said Spinks, closing the bathroom door behind him, hauling his belt over his stomach.

"Ah, yes," said Rosamund, looking down at his gut.

"You must be him. Jonny said you were no stranger to a plate of schnitzel."

"Jonny?" said Spinks. "What the hell are you talking about?"

"Jonny Syracuse."

Spinks looked her up and down. "You're from Mossad?"

She threw her hands in the air. "What, do I need a Star of David tattooed on my ass? Do you know anyone else called Jonny Syracuse? I'm thinking not."

"Yeah, yeah, what do you want? Jonny sent you to gloat, has he?"

"I'm here for good and bad news. You can call off the operation. Montrose is not coming to Berlin."

Spinks strode forward, tilting back his head to look at up her. "And tell me, just how do you know that?"

"Because he's dead. Connor Montrose was killed today. At an airfield near Paris."

Spinks shoulders sagged and he stepped back, holding onto a chair. "Jesus, they got him." He stared open-mouthed out of the window, down at the hospital. "Who killed him?"

Rosamund shrugged. "If Jonny knows, he's not telling me."

"Did he talk to anyone before he died? The press?"

"I doubt it." She grinned and pointed to the mute TV in the corner, tuned to CNN, the latest news scrolling across the bottom of the screen. "You would have heard by now, no?"

"Yeah." Spinks let out a belly laugh and punched a fist in the air. "It's over!" He cocked his head to one side and eyed Rosamund. "So what's Mossad got to do with this? What did he do to you?"

"What am I? CNN? So, that's the good news."

Spinks dropped down on the bed. "Yeah, believe me, it doesn't get much better than that." He waved a hand at Ferguson. "Call them off. All of it. The bastard's dead." He held his face in his hands for a moment, then looked up. "We have to get back to Rome." He nodded towards Rosamund. "Say thanks to Jonny for me."

Rosamund shook her head. "You forgot the bad news. Before Montrose died, it seems there was a firefight. The Afghani Ambassador to France took a hit. He's very dead."

Spinks stared at her, his fleshy bottom lip edging southwards.

She bent down to the cart. "I'll leave that with you," she said and headed for the door. "Goodbye, gentlemen, and good luck. I think you'll need it."

CHAPTER 34

The Moroccan summer nights were too hot for clothes. As the morning sun rose they lay jammed together, Charlotte's face tucked under his chin. He felt the rise and fall of her breasts pressing into his chest as she slept.

His eyes opened. *Only one thing could make this better.* He gently lifted her leg, uncurled her arm from his chest and rolled out from underneath her sleeping form. *Coffee.*

He placed his feet gently on the floor. The hole in his calf had closed to a hard, encrusted scar, but the muscle was tight and sore first thing in the morning. As he stood, a warm breeze pushed the gossamer-thin curtain aside and touched the damp areas where their skin had pressed together. He looked down at her on the bed. The temptation to touch her was strong. He flexed his fingers. As strong as it had been since she had held on to him in a shaking Parisian metro carriage. *No, let her sleep.*

The melodious strains of a muezzin, calling the faithful to prayer, drifted across the rooftops. Montrose closed his eyes and listened, savoring the simple, hypnotic rhythm of the words. A hum of voices came from the vast, tented market of the Medina, jammed up against the wall of the mosque. A hint of spice hung in the air. The stallholders in the small square below their window began to light their charcoal burners and a rainbow of aromas would soon flood the narrow alleys around the house. A shout came from a man in the street, chasing young boys away from his fresh bread stall.

This ain't no paradise. But it's damn close. He turned back to Charlotte. Her skin had become even darker in the Moroccan sun. *More like chocolate. No, coffee. Hell, can't I think of nothing but sex and food? Maybe this is paradise.*

He gathered his clothes from the floor and limped through to the bathroom. He turned the squeaking faucet of the dripping shower. The water sputtered and spat from the rusting showerhead, and banged in the pipes. *I'll wake her.* He twisted the faucet closed, and stood, listening to the water dripping. *She's still asleep.*

He glanced through to the bedroom. She lay face down across the bed, the thin sheet draped across her ass and her hair spread across the pillow. *What now? Where do we go from here? Mossad would take care of her. But me?* He picked up his clothes. The window of the small bathroom was jammed shut and the heat of the day was already starting to build. Rising up from his chest, he caught the intoxicating scent of her on his skin . . . *Maybe wash later.*

*

The coffee was dark, strong and sweet as candy. Montrose placed the glass on the stained wooden table then returned to reading about the Yankees taking a beating. *The Herald and Tribune* fitted neatly behind the pages of the *Le Courrier de Casablanca*.

He relaxed back in the chair, lifted the newspaper to cover his face and let the noise of the café wash over him. Arabian cafés were not known for their love of restrained debate. He'd only be worried if it went quiet.

He didn't notice that someone had sat at his table until he heard a polite cough. His grip tightened as he lowered the newspaper. A small, pink-faced man with thick glasses smiled across at him. The tight, button-down collar and pencil tie only served to make Montrose think that the man was choking to death.

The man placed his childlike, almost translucent hands on the table. "Mr. Montrose," he said, his Texan drawl longer than a football field. "Let me say at once, I am a friend."

The deal with Mossad was a passport and a promise to keep my mouth shut. No one else knew I'm in Casablanca. Until now. "That's good to know. How did you find me?"

"I have a friend in Tel-Aviv. He owed me a favor. He wouldn't have told me unless he truly trusted me."

Montrose said nothing. There was no spook agency on the planet that was completely watertight. *Mossad had been grateful, but it wouldn't last forever. Shit, it had only lasted a week. Time to move on.*

The man's intense gaze never wavered. "May I also say, I am quite alone."

"Yeah?" Montrose glanced across the café. Everyone looked local which was why he had chosen it. It was too dirty for Westerners. But the coffee was to die for. He looked down at his glass. *Not literally.*

The man closed his eyes and nodded his head, as if in prayer. "And I am a man of my word."

"Good for you, soldier. What do you want?"

The man let out a high, almost childish laugh. "I want to shake your hand, Mr. Montrose. The heroin deal in Rome. Helluva job. I mean it. You saved so many young people from a lifetime of misery. For that, I am eternally grateful."

Montrose took the man's hand. "Really? Then let me guess, you're not CIA?"

The man shrugged almost imperceptibly, then delicately lifted one finger. "Used to be. Amongst other things."

"Whatever. So, who do you work for?"

"Our organization has no name."

Montrose raised his eyebrows. "Are you fucking serious?"

"It serves a purpose. And please, I abhor foul language. My name is Mr. Pilgrim. May I say, you came with a very good reference."

"You got a reference from my old CIA boss? I don't think so, pal."

"No, in fact, the reference was from Inspector Claude Bonsergeant of the *Sureté.*"

Montrose's mind flashed back to Paris. *This guy seemed to know everything. Okay, I'm officially spooked.*

"The Inspector said you were an honest man."

"Really? How did he work that out?"

"When you were arrested there was a steak knife on the table next to you. You didn't even look at it. Policemen see these things." Pilgrim took off his glasses and carefully polished the lenses.

"So what do you think?" said Montrose.

"I think you're looking for a steak knife. However, I go by deeds. I, too, think you are an honest man, and one who is prepared to put himself in harm's way for our country."

Yeah, but I'm not planning on making a habit of it. If the guy was looking for a martyr, he could go whistle Dixie. "Just what is it you do, Mr. Pilgrim?"

"I collect lost souls. I really do."

"You're going to have to do a little better than that." Montrose sipped the coffee. "But let me help you get to the point. What do you want?"

"I want you, Mr. Montrose. I want to offer you a job."

The guy sure had some balls. Sits down at my table, scares the crap out of me and then asks me if I want a job. Probably some right-wing crazy looking for a vigilante. He may have been impressed with the heroin deal, but next on the list would be silenced black helicopters and a Soviet doppelganger for the President. Friend of Mossad or not, he'd better get the message. Montrose pointed towards the door. "Take a hike, fella. If I want a job, I'll look in the small ads."

"My offer is genuine. And I can assure you I am not from the NSA, FBI or any other august organization." Pilgrim paused, then opened his palms on the table. "All of our people are ex-security services or military. Those with a moral core that made them stand up against what is wrong with our country. Or good patriots who have been forced to retire before their time because they opposed the excesses of some of their operations. Which is why they became targets. They were prepared to speak up. They are people of honor and action."

"Fascinating." Montrose leaned over the table. "But I'm not interested."

"Oh, I think you are. You see, I can give you what you want."

A new passport and a ticket to somewhere quiet is all I want right now. And to get far away from Mossad and Mr. Texas Loony Tunes. "Yeah, and what would that be?"

"I can give you back your freedom."

"Really? That's mighty big of you. What's the price?"

"You commit yourself to my organization."

Montrose gave him a sideways look.

"I can see you are skeptical."

You're madder than a box of frogs. "Believe me, I'm more than skeptical."

"I understand. Many of our people felt the same way. In your circumstances it is quite reasonable. I know you love your country. That's why you are here today. There are, of course, things I cannot tell you. But what I can tell you is that our work is vital. And it has no place for faint hearts. We have to make tough decisions. We don't always get them right. Sometimes people die. But we don't set out to kill everyone who disagrees with us."

"Well, that's quite a refreshing approach."

"We act as a foil, Mr. Montrose, against the more zealous members of our security agencies. Politicians and their insane schemes come and go. I've been to Afghanistan. I've seen what we've done there. And

I've seen the valleys full of poppies. You saved a lot of lives, although I'd have preferred it to be settled in a less dramatic way."

Montrose shook his head. "You and me both, buddy."

"I can give you a job, a purpose in life. To serve your country as you did before."

"Yeah, right. You know, I can't work out whether you're looking for a gimp or a bitch. Whatever. I'm not on the market."

"This is a genuine offer, Mr. Montrose, though I admit there are several problems."

Your problems, buddy. Don't make them mine.

"The first of which is the CIA."

"Yeah, I'll bet I'm still on the payroll. Are they waiting for me to turn up and collect my pay check?"

"They think you are dead, Mr. Montrose. And they have very good reason to be happy about that."

"Oh, you think so? They set Kessler and his thugs on me. And Charlotte. And they nearly succeeded. I don't give a shit whether they think I'm alive or dead."

"You should. But they had no idea about Charlotte. None whatsoever. I'm not their advocate, Mr. Montrose, but try to see it through their eyes. They were convinced you were a murderer and psychologically unstable. But more importantly, you had previously uncovered information that was particularly dangerous. Information that would make the Wikileaks scandal look like a little white lie."

Montrose smirked. "I've got no idea what you are talking about. And that's the way it's gonna stay."

Pilgrim closed his eyes and nodded slowly, lost in thought. "Let me hypothesize about what you may have uncovered. A Black Ops base in Mexico for extraordinary rendition flights, where prisoners are held for interrogation. Prisoners from all over the globe. And no one knows."

Holy shit. How does he know? Who is this guy? Whatever. Play dumb. Montrose shrugged. "Couldn't say."

"And potentially, the history of flights to South American countries in the eighties, in support of brutal regimes and the torture of dissidents. Am I getting close?"

The eighties? I don't know anything about that shit. Christ, they must be crapping themselves.

"You uncovered an extremely serious security weakness. I'm told the Director was horrified, but impressed."

"It was an accident. The firewall was wide open. Anyway, I said I'd keep quiet and they sent me to Interpol to get me outta town. No big deal."

"That was then, Mr. Montrose. This is now."

You got that straight.

"The CIA were extremely concerned that, following the murders, you would walk straight into a foreign embassy and claim political asylum."

Montrose leaned over the table. "They think I'm a rat? They think I was gonna stand up on Al Jazeera and tell the world how the Great Satan is operating covert teams and kidnapping citizens all over the globe? Shit, if I was going to do that, I'd be on the front cover of *Time* by now." He pointed a finger at Pilgrim. "I'm no traitor. I was looking for the guy with a private jet that sold my sister into slavery and turned her into a junkie. And I will find that piece of shit, and I will eat his fucking heart!"

Pilgrim bowed his head. "A little quieter, please, Mr. Montrose. Walls have ears."

Montrose sat back in the chair, his face tight. *I will find him.*

Pilgrim drew a deep breath and leaned forward. "There is absolutely no doubt in my mind that you are a patriot. And that you will not reveal anything, to anyone. But you have to understand the desperation of the CIA to . . . take care of you. They don't want another Edward Snowden, who is, unfortunately, temporarily beyond my reach."

"Yeah? Well, he's a whistle-blower. Ain't he on your team? The team with no name?"

Pilgrim looked down and tapped an index finger against the table for a few moments. "Mr. Snowden's actions were not in the interests of our country. The entire Wikileaks episode could have been dealt with in a much more efficient manner. His actions have been extremely damaging. The US has lost the trust of every government in the European Union. Think what you like about what we were doing, but it was very valuable for us. His were not the actions of a patriot. His were the actions of a traitor. A simple word in the ear of a trusted journalist would have reined in some of the more excessive actions."

"So, nobody likes us and we don't care. No change there."

"If what we are doing stops another 9/11, it will have been worth it. I have no doubt."

Montrose pushed a hand through his hair and leaned back in the chair. "I'm with ya there, buddy."

"However, I can deal with the CIA. They are convinced you are dead. But they are not your most pressing issue."

"Pressing issue, yeah. What would that be? Some weirdo turning up unannounced and offering me a job?" He could see that Pilgrim was offended by the tightening of his small, rosebud mouth.

Pilgrim shook his head and resumed his placid demeanor. "Wolfgang Kessler. The man whose son died in Paris and the man who ordered your death."

Montrose sat up. "Where is he?"

"Somewhere that even Mossad can't get him."

"I thought Mossad were everywhere."

"They were, until the Iranian Revolution of 1979 and the fall of the American Embassy in Tehran. For the CIA and Mossad it was an unprecedented disaster. To this day, they have never fully recovered. When the Iranians seized the American Embassy they captured a great deal of extraordinarily sensitive information. Much of it had been shredded, but the Iranians employed women specializing in intricate weaving, to piece together hundreds of thousands of strips of paper and reconstruct many classified documents. Amongst them was a CIA dossier detailing the history of Mossad's operations across the globe. China, Europe, USSR, information that was disastrous for Mossad. Including their Iranian contacts. Every CIA and Mossad informant disappeared overnight. You can imagine their fate."

"You would have thought the Iranians would have kept quiet about it."

"They had their reasons. The things we did to that country are unspeakable. Supporting the Shah of Iran and his puppet regime against the will of the people, and plundering their oil reserves. We suppressed democracy at the very roots. The list goes on. Has it taught us anything?" He shook his head and looked down at the table. "Prior to the revolution, Mossad also trained the Savak, the murderous Iranian Secret Service. Perhaps the only place we are detested more is in Iraq. It's a close run thing."

"So? Where exactly is Kessler?"

"Tehran. He's safe. When the French police discovered the bodies of his son and the Afghan Ambassador to France at the airport, he fled the country to Iran. They struck a deal. Kessler needed somewhere to hide. Not least from the Afghanis. And the Iranians need his skills in finance. They are crippled by international sanctions and Kessler can help them a great deal. Ironically, they also have a very serious interest in Afghan oil."

"Really? I'd have loved to listen to that job interview."

Pilgrim smiled. "Kessler is also being protected by the CIA. They have been tentatively active since the revolution, though they have much to do before operations can have any real effect. I think they want to recruit Kessler as a double agent. However, I suspect the real reason is that many important men have funds held in his bank. Men who you cross at your peril. They want their money back and the Swiss are not being too cooperative."

"Yeah, right. Plus all the crooked politicians and crime bosses across the globe."

"That's reasonably accurate. You see, apart from the Israelis, nobody wants to see him dead."

"Are you kidding me?"

"Think about it. Only Kessler can get their money. They're happy for him to set up in Iran and then recover their funds. He still has many friends in Switzerland."

"Unbelievable. I would have thought he was a dead man."

Pilgrim shrugged. "Once they have their money, I'm sure Herr Kessler will be watching his back, but since he is protected by so many interested parties, your problem only multiplies."

"How?"

"The death of his son. Kessler wants you and Charlotte dead, Mr. Montrose. He is prepared to do absolutely anything to make that happen."

Charlotte. Montrose felt his chest tighten. *Kessler could call on the best muscle in Europe. He had the funds to do anything he liked. No matter how long it took.* "I can't get to him. There's nothing I can do."

"On the contrary. Mossad have a score to settle with Kessler. So do you. Where there's a will . . ."

"I'm not an assassin."

"I know. If you were, I wouldn't be talking to you. Kessler won't go away. He'll find you."

"Mossad aren't going to tell him."

"No, but I did my own investigation. The young lady is, of course, from France. Charlotte Marceau. They know you are together, and . . ."

"She's nobody's fucking business."

"Language, please. I mean that she may have left the country with you. I know she has previously vacationed in Tunisia and Algeria. Morocco is a popular destination for the French. As an ex-colony, their language is spoken and their money accepted. If I was going to look for her, this is the first place I would start."

"Yeah? So what's your point?"

"Well, if I can work it out, so can Kessler and his hired killers. I'm sure it won't take them long." Pilgrim pointed down at the newspaper. "I see you're reading *The Herald and Tribune*. Tell me, where did you buy it?"

"At a newsagents, of course."

"Was there any one watching, or any one hanging around outside?"

"Why?"

"Because they are looking for an American and it is well known we like to read our own newspapers. They have your photograph."

The newsagents had been full of tourists. French, Italian, maybe some Brits. Outside, the guy sitting on the sidewalk. A student. Could have been American. Jeans and backpack. Was he a spotter?

"Do you remember anyone?"

"No," said Montrose. "It seemed quiet."

"Good. Perhaps you are ahead of them. However, I think I can say without any undue drama, that you will never be safe. My advice would be to eliminate the problem."

"I've told you. I'm not an assassin. It's a suicide mission. I won't do it."

Pilgrim closed his eyes and inclined his head. "This is an example of the tough choices my organization face every day. But I admire your honesty, Mr. Montrose. I really do." He looked up. "Kessler will never stop searching for you. However, I'll respect whatever decision you make."

I'll have to run for the rest of my life. Charlotte too.
"I'll think about it."

Pilgrim held out his hands. "That's all I ask. Now, I have something for you. Let's hope you never have to use it." He laid a newspaper on the table.

Montrose saw the bulge in the paper.

"Don't go back to your hotel, Mr. Montrose."

He flinched as a cold stab of adrenalin shot though

his chest. His legs began to tremble. "What . . . What do you mean by that?"

"She's gone. Where, I have no idea. I'm afraid I am not party to that information." He stood up. "I'll be in the Hotel Opera for a few days. Call me anytime. I shall leave you now. Good luck, Mr. Montrose."

Montrose watched him go. Pilgrim didn't look back. He took small, neat steps around the tables then disappeared through the door.

His coffee was cold. He put the glass down. It clattered against the table and he realized his hands were shaking.

She's gone? No, Mr. Fruit-Loops was . . . Why would he lie? Mossad would take care of her. Maybe they think I'm a threat. His mind flashed back to the newsagents. *The guy in the jeans. A spotter? Shit, there's no such thing as coincidence.*

He lifted the corner of the newspaper and saw a Walther PPK fitted with a short silencer. *At least the odds had improved.* Below was an envelope with a phone number. He opened it up, and saw a wad of cash. Moroccan dirhams, euros and dollars. *I'll have to move fast.*

He pulled four pink tablets from his pocket and downed them with the coffee. *Once they kick in I'll be stoned out of my mind.* Folding the paper over his knees, he held the Walther below the table and chambered a round then pocketed the cash.

If the spotter had told his contact they would have had plenty time to get a team up. Could be outside the café right now. They wouldn't come in. It wouldn't happen like that. They'd wait outside then follow me. A bullet in the back of the head down a side street or a knife through the liver in a busy market. He rubbed his injured calf as he stood and, using the newspaper as a shield, slipped the Walther in his pocket. No one gave him a second glance. He faced the exit. *It starts now.*

He stood just inside the door and checked the square. Locals crammed the tables outside the café. Nobody was looking his way.

Above the rooftops, he could see the pointed tower of a minaret. *The apartment is one hundred yards due south from the mosque and the Medina. Keep your eye on the minaret. Take a different route. See who follows.*

He turned and skirted the edge of the square then ducked down an alley. He began to pick up the pace as the pain in his calf eased. *Drugs and adrenalin. Ditch the walking stick.* To his right, a wide, tiled doorway led into a restaurant. He could see an open door at the far end of the room, leading onto a sunlit courtyard. He stepped into the doorway and slotted his stick into a rickety hat stand by the door. His sneakers squeaked on the ancient mosaic floor as he strode past tables of tourists drinking coffee and garishly-colored pastries, and looked up at the high, painted ceiling, lined by pillars and carvings.

Jeez, what's the hurry? She's not there. Maybe Mossad heard someone is in town. Someone like Kessler. Or his goons. Did she leave a note? He emerged into the courtyard and headed for a small alley leading towards the mosque. *I have to know.*

The alley was lined with butcher shops and men carrying carcasses of lamb hoisted high on their shoulders squeezed past each other. *I can't be far.* He stopped at the corner and glanced back, but the alley was crammed with faces.

This is it. The baker's alley. A window opened by his head and a blast of hot air, carrying the scent of lemon and mint, washed over him. Shouts came from the kitchen and he made for the alley. At the end, he could see a line of workmen standing with their clay pots of tagine in their hands, ready to go into the hot ashes of the baker's oven. By midday, their lunch would be ready.

He stood behind the line and watched the baker's shop. An old man came out, wiping his flour-covered hands. His day was done. Two old men sat near the doorway of the building, shouting at kids kicking a ball against the wall. Montrose crossed the alley and into the archway of the apartment building. He ran up to the first floor where the door to the apartment stood slightly ajar. He listened for a moment and then tapped it open with his foot.

The bed sheets had been folded at the foot of the bed. The room was bare. She was gone. He stood, staring around the room. *No note. Nothing.*

On the floor, a colored elastic hair band stuck out from under the bed. He picked it up and slipped it on his wrist. The window lay open as he had left it. He leaned over to the wooden frame and blew hard on the edge. *No dust. The place had been wiped. Probably the first time in years.* A breeze blew the thin curtain aside and he caught a glimpse of a figure standing in the baker's doorway. *White sneakers and jeans. That's not a North African face. You ain't no workman. A tourist?*

He looked around the apartment. *There's only one other window. Bathroom. Too small and won't open.* He ran through the apartment door, down the steps and backed up against the archway. *Okay, let's do it. Make for the Medina. If I can make it to the cover of the old market, I've got a chance.* He slipped his hand into his pocket and gripped the Walther. *If they're out there, they're going to get a big surprise.*

As he stepped into the alley a man emerged from the baker's and took off his backpack, then sat down against the wall.

Backpack. That's the sign. Montrose shoved his hand into his pocket and flicked back the safety catch. *It's the spotter. Wherever they are, they got me now.*

The market was dead ahead. *Don't look back, just get some cover.* He quickened his pace and ducked between the tented shops, straight into a maze of market stalls and tourists.

He was immediately surrounded by young men, each trying to persuade him to let them be his guide around the Medina. Shrugging them off, he kept his head down and moved further into the crowd. The sounds and smells of the market assaulted his senses as he twisted and turned between the stalls. He dodged around baskets of pungent spices and vegetables. Traders appealed loudly, but he kept his head down. Every Westerner was a target for deals, but he knew the secret. *Don't make eye contact. Ignore them.*

Montrose batted aside a caged parakeet that was shoved in his face and made for the old city walls surrounding the Medina. *There was no way they would be able to spot me in the crowds. It was hard enough to keep your feet.* He forced his way into the seething mass. *Unless the shooters asked a guide. Then they'd track me down, just by asking their friends. Time to turn the tables.*

To his right he saw a stall packed with long white

djellaba robes. *Not the real thing, but good enough for tourists.* Montrose grabbed one. "*Combien?* How much?" he said, then instantly regretted the question. This was an Arab market. The answer could take forever.

The trader threw his hands in the air. "You are French, monsieur? Then you know, how can you put a price on such quality?"

Montrose took a sheaf of bills from his pocket. "It's easy," he said and dumped the cash on the table. He pulled the robe across his shoulders and marched off.

The crumbling old city walls towered above him. He spotted an arched doorway leading out of the market to the back streets and the stone steps to the ramparts. Charlotte had said it was a good place for taking photos. It was, but the view over the market was even better.

He lifted the hem of the robe and ran through the arch, turned to the left and climbed the worn stone steps to the top of the wall. His calf muscle was tight, but the pain was easing as the drugs kicked in. Crouching, he peered between the turrets, down into the market. He saw two heads moving through the crowds. *Dark hair. Six foot plus. And a woman? Whatever. One marker, one shooter. And the guy's got a limp. The shooter from Zurich? The one I hit with the car? Kessler's personal killers.* He saw the red sole of the woman's shoes flashing out from beneath her robes. *Gabrielle! Yeah, call me Gabby, and steal fibers from my coat to plant at a murder scene, you bitch. Who else in North Africa is wearing red Louboutins under native dress?*

He watched guides surround them and after a brief discussion, lead them towards the trader. Cash changed hands and Fleet and Gabrielle hurried to the arch.

Montrose crouched down behind the low wall. *Don't take the stairs, you bastards, just keep going.* He pulled out the Walther and held it beneath the robe.

Glancing over the wall, he saw them striding down the street, away from the market. He was about to run down the stairs and slip into the crowd, when they stopped. They stood for a moment, then turned back to the arch.

Montrose kept his head down and ran along the ramparts, then dived back into the turret. If they walked past they would see him. But he had the drop on them. *Two shots. Aim for the body mass.* His muscles tightened and the Walther started to shake in his hand. *Wait. Then turn and shoot.*

He listened for the click of the high heels on the stone of the ramparts. *Nothing. They weren't coming. They must be in the market.* The muscle began to cramp in his injured calf. He ignored it then edged forward and peeked out of the turret.

Two figures stood on the ramparts looking out over the market.

Do it now. Aim for the upper torso. Drop them and finish them off with a head shot. He looked down at his hands. The Walther was waving around like a rag in the wind. He brought the butt up hard into his face. The pain across his nose made him gasp, but his hands stopped shaking. He wiped his wet palms on the robe, steadied the Walther, then stepped out, raising it up fast as he snapped into a firing position.

What the hell? They were gone. He stood slack-jawed for a moment and then twisted around. *Nothing.* Holding the gun low, he crept forward and caught a flash of dark hair over the wall. He ran to the top of the steps and edged around. They were halfway down.

He raised the Walther and stared at their backs for a moment, then ducked behind the ramparts and slumped against the stone. *It won't work. Tomorrow there would be more. There would always be more. Kessler's money would make sure of that.* He glanced around the edge of the stone.

At the foot of the stairs the woman stopped, and began to turn.

They're coming back. He slid behind the corner. *They're too close. If I make a run for the steps they'll just shoot me down.* He scuttled along the ramparts and came to a tower at the end. He dived in and saw the narrow staircase. *It's got to go down to the market.*

The steps were worn down by a thousand years of footsteps. He kept the gun level in one hand and slapped the other off the wall, keeping himself upright as he ran down the stairs. He stopped himself before the low, stone doorway and looked out onto the street.

The robes. The limp. It's him. And he's coming my way. Holy crap, they've split up. He checked back up the steps. *If I step out of here she'll have a clear field of fire. But she's an easier target.* He ran up the steps and knelt down at the top, sneaking a look out. *Nothing. She must still be on the steps.* He stood and edged towards the door. *If I see her, I'll drop her.*

He edged out of the tower just as the red sole of a Louboutin flashed in front of his face. The shoe caught him full on the bridge of the nose. He tumbled backwards into the tower and down the steps, his head thumping into a pair of boots.

"You bastard!" screamed Fleet, holding his wounded leg. He lifted the butt of the gun high above his head. "I've been looking forward to this."

CHAPTER 35

The reek of exhaust fumes made him retch as lights flashed before his eyes. He tried to lift his hands, but couldn't move them from behind his back. A blade of light glowed from behind him. He twisted his head around, squinting through a gap in the lid of the trunk, and saw the clouds of dust issuing from the back of the car. *Where the hell am I going? Don't matter. It won't be pleasant.*

He strained at the bonds, but his legs and hands remained tightly jammed together. *They'll make me talk. They'll want it all. Death will be a release.*

He thrashed around in panic and his head cracked against the trunk lid. His head swam and he slumped onto the floor and then brought up his legs towards the lid. He kicked with all his might. *Open, you bitch!* He heard voices from the car.

"What the hell is he doing?"

"Stop the car!"

His head smacked off a steel strut as the car slammed

to a halt, throwing him to the back of the trunk. Doors opened. The car rose up on its suspension.

Daylight blinded him as the lid opened. Fleet hauled him out by the throat. He hit the earth face first, choking on dust. He rolled over, taking in gulps of air.

"Now, Mr. Montrose," said Gabrielle, "We have to go through town, so you're going to ride with me, where I can keep an eye on you. We wouldn't want you drawing attention to yourself, would we? You really are . . . a persistent bastard. But I admire that." She turned to Fleet. "Get him in the back."

Fleet picked him up by the shoulders and threw him into the rear of the car. "On the floor!"

Gabrielle got in beside him and rested a Louboutin-shod heel on his face. "Now, if you so much as move, I will shoot you in the legs. And then the balls. And then the lungs. I'm very good at what I do, so you'll live long enough to tell me what I need to know."

"Yeah, whatever. You'll get what you need. I'm no hero."

"We'll see. It's a shame, my dear Connor. In another life we might have been more than this." She moved the spiked heel over his throat and shifted forward in the seat. She hitched up the tight skirt to allow her to spread her legs and placed the other foot on his crotch. Her robes fell aside. She looked down. "Enjoying the view?"

Montrose let his eyes drift up her stockinged legs. "Going commando? Good choice in this weather."

She began rubbing his prick with the sole of her shoe. "I might be nice to you before you die."

Montrose couldn't stop himself from laughing. "Yeah, a last wish for a condemned man. You're all heart."

"Not really. Now, shut up, there's a good boy."

"Don't tell me what to do. Unless you're naked. Oh, wait . . ."

She let out a delighted laugh. "Oh, I admire your spirit!" She leaned over him, and extended her tongue, allowing a thin line of saliva to drip on to his face. "I'm going to tie you to a chair. And yes, I'll be naked. You'll try to resist, but I'll make you hard."

"Yeah. Just shut the fuck up," said Fleet.

"Oh, you're just jealous," replied Gabrielle. "He's never been the same since you nearly broke his leg in Zurich. You can imagine my surprise when I looked back and saw you in the back of the limo and not Reinhard."

"I thought you were always glad to see me?"

"Of course, but it was too late to stop someone shooting off too early." She nodded towards Fleet. "As usual."

Fleet gripped the wheel hard to control his fury then leaned back over the seat, speaking through gritted teeth. "You've got some payback coming, you fucking twat! Then I'm going to find your girlfriend. The French chick." He rolled his thumb and forefinger into a 'O' and thrust his hand back towards Montrose. "You think I'm saying it'll be okay?" He waved his hand in Montrose's face. "No." He blew through the 'O' in his fingers. "That's how big her asshole's going to be when I've finished with her."

Montrose shook his head. "You'll never find her."

Gabrielle shrugged. "Well, we found you easily enough. I hate to say it, but I'd put my money on Fleet and his massive asshole."

Fleet sniggered, then realized she was laughing at him.

"Keep your eye on the traffic," said Gabrielle. The car slowed for a junction. A policeman walked into the middle of the street and held up the traffic. Gabrielle peered down the road. "What's with the cop?"

Fleet sniggered. "Don't know. Maybe they're looking for someone."

"Did you turn your phone off?"

"Hold on." Fleet reached into his jacket. "Done. So, where are we headed? Once we get out of this shithole, I mean. You know, all that money? We could have some fun."

"Keep your eye on the road."

The car stopped in a line of traffic. Fleet pointed. "Just a copper directing the traffic."

"Why? The lights are working." said Gabrielle.

"They're not checking cars. We're good."

"Perhaps. But just in case, why don't you sit up, Montrose? Let's look normal, shall we?"

Montrose felt her grab his shirt and pull him onto the seat. *She's stronger than she looks.* He looked down at the Velcro handcuffs on his ankles. His hands twisted in the cuffs behind his back. *This could take me all day. Where's the policeman?*

"Now, Connor, I'm sure you're not going to behave yourself. I've heard about your escapades. But I think I can arrange a little deterrent." She reached into her bag and pulled out a small, green canister.

Montrose did a double take when he saw what was in her hand. *Fragmentation grenade? What the hell is she going to do with that?*

She edged towards Montrose. "These are very useful. I take most of the explosive charge out, so it's not lethal. Then I shorten the fuse to half a second.

They really are the ultimate accessory. Honestly, Gucci should make these. I might patent the design. It's the best thing I know to cool a man's ardor." She smiled coyly then slid her hands across the seat and tugged at the zipper on Montrose's pants. She slipped her hand inside and began massaging his prick. "Now, Connor, we don't want to lose this, so be a good boy. I'll need it later." She held up the grenade and let the ring of the pin drop on to her bright red lips, then hooked her eyetooth around it and jerked it from the case.

Jesus Christ, has she lost it? He looked down at her right hand, gently cupping and lifting his balls.

She brought up her left hand and slipped the grenade through his fly. She tucked it underneath his balls and gave them a hard squeeze.

"Christ!" Montrose involuntarily jammed his legs shut.

She slipped her hands out of his fly and pressed his thighs together. "Perfect. Stay just like that. Remember, half a second delay. All I have to do is open your legs. I'll be fine, but any funny business with the policeman and you'll be wearing your testicles as earrings."

Montrose sat stock still. *Mother of God. She's a psycho.*

"C'mon, c'mon," said Fleet, staring up at the red light.

The thudding of techno music made Montrose turn his head to the right, where a car full of youths had pulled up alongside them. The music was turned up so loud he could feel the car reverberate with the beat. One of the youths in the car looked over then turned to his friends and pointed at Gabrielle. He stuck his tongue in his cheek and began pumping the skin, showing her exactly what he wanted.

"How irritating," she sighed. "I wish I'd saved the grenade for them."

Montrose felt the muscles in his leg begin to tighten; his calf was on the verge of a cramp.

Fleet glared at the youths through his sunglasses. The youth in the front passenger seat let down his window. The music became even louder.

"Hey, mec!" shouted the youth, leaning out towards Fleet and tapping his window. "Mec! How much to fuck her?"

The youths in the car began to fall about laughing. Montrose turned to see that the youth beside her was now licking the window, to the delight of his friends.

"Hey, mec!" He rapped his knuckles on Fleet's window. "Do you want to watch? Maybe you'll learn something!"

Fleet looked around for the button to lower the window.

"Fleet! Keep your mind on the job! The traffic will move in a moment."

"Hey, mec!" He waggled his little finger at Fleet. "Did she turn you down?"

"I'm going to rip his fucking tongue out!" Fleet jabbed the button, and reached out of the window, but the youth pulled a Taser from below the door and fired into Fleet's face. The electrodes pierced deep into his cheek and neck and he convulsed as 50,000 volts wracked his body.

Gabrielle went for her gun, but the rear window of the car exploded in a storm of glass. Two hands appeared either side of her head and grabbed her shoulders, hauling her up and backwards. Her nose smashed into the top edge of the window, crushing the cartilage as shards of glass lanced her face. Montrose twisted round and saw her bounce on the trunk before she was slammed onto the road. The breath exploded out of her lungs as one of the youths dropped his knees onto her chest.

The youth stood and casually fixed a red armband to his jacket. *Police.*

Montrose's door opened, and a tall, dark figure regarded him with interest. "A friend sent me."

"Please, my hands." Montrose slowly bent forward and hauled his hands up his back. The man ripped off the Velcro cuffs and Montrose let his hands drift to his side and then gently pushed a hand into his pants. *Don't get this wrong. Just don't.* He slipped his fingers past the wet skin of his thigh and found the firing lever. Curling his fingers around into a fist, he opened his legs and pulled the grenade from his pants. He held it out in front of him.

The tall man laughed. "Well, that's a trick I've never seen before. Can you do rabbits too?"

"It's armed. Half second delay."

The man's eyebrows raised.

Montrose stepped from the back seat and walked to the rear of the car. A policeman hauled Fleet up against the trunk. He watched Fleet's eyes come into focus when he saw the grenade in front of his face.

Montrose chopped his hand into Fleet's throat. He gasped and Montrose stuffed the grenade into his mouth then clamped Fleet's jaw shut. Holding his thumb and forefinger together in an 'O', Montrose slowly brought up his hand and held it in front of Fleet's face, then pinged his fingers apart.

The tall figure placed a hand on Montrose's shoulder. "Walk away, my friend."

He stared at the bleeding figure of Gabrielle, handcuffed to a stretcher.

"Just walk away."

Montrose stepped up onto the sidewalk. On the far side of the road, a small man, in a tight button-down collar and thick glasses gave Montrose an almost imperceptible nod then melted into the crowd.

CHAPTER 36

The fading murals were a storey high, each painted with the forlorn face of a soldier, surrounded by roses and butterflies to show that they were now in paradise. At the street corners, where Coca-Cola posters once filled the advertising boards, the stern faces of the Ayatollahs looked down.

Montrose shifted around on the unyielding taxi seat and ran a finger round his tight collar. The morning heat was building. Sweat soaked his back and he wound down the window. They had reckoned about an hour from Tehran airport. It couldn't be far.

Lookin' good. Suit from Old England in Paris. Shirt from Pinks of London. Montrose held out the arms of his suit. The shirt cuffs protruded just enough to show off his silver cufflinks. *Let's hope they don't have to bury me in it.* The collar rubbed against his freshly shaven skin and the goatee he'd grown was damn itchy. The dark, tightly curly wig was hot on his scalp, but it had to be done. *Man, I look like an Eighties porn star.*

The briefcase and paper bag slid across the seat as the taxi turned into a wide road and pulled up at a gated compound. Ugly, grey concrete walls surrounded the building. He closed his eyes for a moment, then wiped his damp hands on his pants. There was no going back.

If I don't do this, she'll never be safe. He closed his eyes for a moment and thought of the last time he had seen her. Her sleeping body, half-covered in a thin sheet. He ran his fingers around the elastic band on his wrist. It had been the only trace left of her when he had returned to the apartment in Casablanca, lying on the ground where she had dropped it.

He grabbed the briefcase and paper bag then shoved open the taxi door.

Play the music. Bring on the dancing girls. It's showtime.

"Wait here," Montrose told the driver, "I'll be five minutes." He stepped onto the street. He stood for a moment, adjusting his tie, and risked a glance at the roof. He wouldn't hear the shooter. Even the most high-powered paintball gun wouldn't need a silencer.

Torn and defaced revolutionary posters hung in tatters along the wall, scrawled with pro-democracy graffiti. Through a thickly-barred turnstile gate, he could see an empty courtyard, stretching around thirty feet to a two-storey building. *Car bombs. No one would get near enough. If the plan worked, there was no need. Except the last part. That was always going to be personal.*

He pictured the surveillance photo in his mind. The satellite communications dish on the roof was about six feet in diameter. Any moment now, a shooter from a neighboring roof would empty a magazine of paint balls on to the dish. It didn't have to knock it out. The silver metallic paint would dry to a sheen in moments and concentrate all the sunlight onto the receiver in the middle of the dish. In this heat it would fry in seconds. Like a bug under a magnifying glass. Comms down. Then the shooter would disappear, leaving behind a cell phone disrupter.

Montrose checked his cell phone. *Three bars. Hurry up, dammit!*

He dabbed his face with a silk handkerchief and stood before the turnstile. The freshly painted bars stretched to a height of six feet. He looked up to the second floor window. It had the green sheen of reinforced glass. *No openings. And no escape. The others seemed normal. It had to be that room.* He checked the signal strength once more. *No signal. Game on.* He pressed the unnamed buzzer on the wall.

"Speak."

"This is Monsieur Jekyll of FranzGas. I am expected."

A loud clang of bolts came from the turnstile.

"Enter."

Montrose pushed up against the bars and emerged into the courtyard. In the corner was a fuel inlet pipe, surrounded by a dark diesel stain. *Mossad intel was right about the generator. Cutting the power would have been useless, and too suspicious. Especially since they had cut the phone lines a few hours earlier. Which was the easiest part of the plan, since all the utility cables were strung between the buildings like spaghetti. Not an unusual occurrence in this part of town.*

A whirring noise came from above. He looked up to the roof. Two cameras tracked him as he walked. In front, thick glass doors barred the way. They didn't open. There was no button to press. *They're still checking me out.* He stood for a moment, gazing at his reflection. *I was right about the wig.*

The door whooshed quickly aside. He stepped into a long, cool hall and felt an icy blast from above. *At least somewhere in Tehran the aircon was working.* Three guards stood before a desk. *Tall, Teutonic. Bulges under the arms of their coats. So, right address.*

A guard moved forward and lifted his hands, signaling a search. Montrose laid his briefcase and the paper bag on a desk and extended his arms. The guard ran his fingers under his suit lapels, around the collar of his shirt, then patted his coat before pushing a hand up into his crotch and smoothing down his legs.

A bead of sweat ran over Montrose's moustache and dripped to the floor.

"All metal objects in the tray," said the guard. "And the watch."

He emptied his pockets and undid the strap of his old Omega. The guard ran a hand-held metal detector across his body. Turning his head, Montrose caught the bank of video screens behind the desk. *The whole building was monitored. No surprise. Looks like I'll have an audience.*

Another guard picked up his passport from the tray. It had the obligatory stamps for a traveling businessman and some for Tehran. *If they checked the HQ of FranzGas in Paris, they would be told that Monsieur Jekyll was out of the country on business. That's what his secretary would always say when Jekyll went off for a weekend with his mistress.*

"Look at me," said the guard, holding up a digital camera. He hit the button and then connected the camera to a laptop on the desk.

Montrose felt the sweat chill on his neck. *Face recognition software. They must be dialed into Iranian intelligence. And if the satellite dish was still working, they would find out that Monsieur Jekyll was Mr. Hyde.* He watched the guard hit the keyboard a few times before his pulse slowed.

The guard murmured to the others as they crowded around the laptop.

Time to ramp it up. "Will this take long?' said Montrose. "Do I have to tell Director Kessler that I'm late because you can't use your security systems?"

The guard popped the locks of Montrose's briefcase and flicked through a folder of notes, then opened the paper bag. He lifted out a small cardboard box, embossed in gold and tied in an intricate bow.

"Chocolates," said Montrose, "from the Rue de l'Opera in Paris. The finest chocolatier in the world."

The guard didn't rise to the bait. Not a smile. He held the box in his hand for a moment. It barely covered his palm as he swept it with the metal detector. "Leave the briefcase here," said the guard. "Second floor."

Montrose slipped on his Omega and grabbed his keys and change.

"Wait," said a guard and came out from behind the desk. He stood before Montrose and examined him closely. "Don't I know you?"

Montrose looked him straight in the eyes. "Oh, perhaps you are a member of the Club de Tennis in the Bois de Boulougne? Or you frequent the literary salon of Madame Derioz in Avenue Foch? No?" He gave a shrug. "Then I do not think I know you, monsieur." Montrose pulled a folder from the briefcase, picked up the chocolates and headed for the stairs. Behind him he heard the click of a phone. The low murmur of a voice. Then the footsteps of a guard.

Shit. Company is not what I need. He glanced around the reception area. The guards were holding their phones in the air, searching for a signal. *The dish was out. The phone lines were out. The cell phone interrupter was on the closest roof, but there was no way it would work 100%. If they found 3G this could be over in seconds.*

He came to a corridor at the top of the steps. A receptionist opened a door. "This way, sir," she said and beckoned him inside.

He followed her into a small office. The guard sat down on a chair at the side of the room and Montrose caught the butt of an automatic pistol as he unbuttoned his jacket. It was holstered, but the restraining strap had been cut away. *These guys were ready. Probably had a round up the spout. If the shit hits the fan, I'll have to get close.*

The secretary walked over to two high wooden doors. "The Director will see you now."

Montrose held up the paper bag. "A gift for the Director. Don't worry, Security has checked it."

The secretary pushed open the doors. Montrose tucked the folder under his arm and stepped into a long office. He fixed a smug banker's smile on his face and crossed the room to a tall, white-haired figure hunched over a desk. The doors closed behind him.

With his left hand, Montrose reached behind his neck and pulled a small glass phial from under the edge of the wig, then flicked off the end with his thumbnail. It only held 10ml under pressure, but it would be enough. He brushed his thumb across the needle.

The bag of chocolates swung in his other hand.

Let's hope he's not a greedy bastard or he might get a surprise. "Herr Kessler! A delight to meet you!" Montrose placed the chocolates on the desk.

Kessler grunted and stood up behind his desk, offering his hand. "Monsieur Jekyll," he said, "I hope the journey was not too tiring."

"Herr Kessler, you wouldn't believe the journey that led me here today." He took Kessler's hand and held it tight then quickly brought up the phial in his left hand and jabbed it into Kessler's wrist.

"*Scheisse!*" Kessler tried to pull his hand away, but Montrose covered it in a two-handed shake and held on tight as the drug kicked in. Kessler began to stagger. Montrose relaxed his grip and let Kessler drop back into his chair.

"This won't take long," said Montrose. He made himself comfortable in the chair. "You're a big man, but your heart is pounding. It makes it easier for the drug to take effect. Do you feel it?"

Kessler sat open-mouthed, his chest heaving. He tried to get up, then slumped further down in the chair. "What . . .?"

"Don't worry. It won't knock you out, but by now you'll have lost the power in your arms, and probably your legs."

Kessler's hands sat limp in his lap. "You'll never make it out of here alive. You're on video."

"I thought I would be. So, what did they see? A warm handshake between two businessmen and you relaxing in your chair. Then they see me smiling and laughing and waving my hands around in a typically Gallic manner, and you, talking and moving your head. If they look closely, they might see you've pissed your pants."

Kessler eyes dropped to a dark stain spreading across his crotch.

"It's the muscle relaxant. I'm told it's the most powerful on the market. Every muscle south of your scalp is about to shut down. Except your heart. Don't worry, there's not enough to kill you."

Kessler's fingers twitched. "Who are you?"

"You don't recognize me? Well, I suppose we've never actually met."

"What do you want?"

Montrose leaned back. "Work it out. When I heard you were here, I just couldn't miss the opportunity. I might never find you again."

"Find me? Mossad?"

"No. Although they've been very helpful."

Kessler's face turned bright red and his words began to slur. "You're a dead man."

"We'll see about that. So, have you worked it out yet?" He stared into Kessler's eyes and watched the pupils dilate as the shock slammed home.

"*Montrose*."

"Yeah. Quite the bad penny, huh?"

Kessler breathed hard and fast through his nose, trying to fight the drug. "You got them. The ones who killed the psychiatrist. They were out of control."

"Out of control?" Montrose leaned forward. "Those bastards were professional. They wouldn't piss without permission. You told them to kill Richmond and his secretary. And then you told them to kill Charlotte."

Kessler's head jerked from side to side.

"Don't fuck with me. I know. They told me what they were going to do to her. *Charlotte*."

"No, it . . . was Fleet . . ." Kessler could barely turn his head.

"And now there's only you." Montrose pushed the box of chocolates across the desk.

Kessler's jaw began to sag.

Montrose sniffed the air. "Jeez, that didn't take long, did it?" He pulled a Mont Blanc pen from his pocket and twisted the cap around. It clicked five times. "Clockwork. Might even be Swiss." He leaned forward and punched the pen into the side of the box of chocolates. "A little gift for you. Truffles and champagne bon-bons. Well, there would be if I hadn't eaten them all. I gotta say, they were *fucking* delicious."

Kessler's mouth dropped open.

Montrose slowly got to his feet. "I watched your son burn. I heard him screaming as he tried to claw his way out of the flames. Then I watched him die." He shrugged. "Thought I'd let you know." Keeping one eye on the camera, Montrose clapped his hands together and gave a short bow. "Anyway, I'm out of here. When I think of you, I'll remember this. You sitting there helpless, in your own filth."

Montrose crossed the office and pulled open the doors. He looked back towards the room. "Thank you for your time, Herr Kessler. I do hope you enjoy the chocolates. No, don't get up, I'll see myself out."

Closing the doors behind him, Montrose smiled at the secretary. The guard stood up. "Herr Kessler asked not to be disturbed while he's considering my proposal. *Au revoir*, madame."

Twenty seconds to the hall. Montrose stepped into the corridor and moved smartly down the stairs. The guard followed. *One minute to the gate.* He felt the wig becoming detached where the phial had been hidden and smoothed it down, but his skin was wet with sweat.

Shit, it's not sticking. He tugged down the hair to cover the edge of the wig, but it sprang back into place.

The guards at the front desk had the laptop connected to a cell phone. Montrose calmly slotted the folder into the briefcase. "Goodbye, gentlemen," he said as he turned and strode across the hall. He stood in front of the doors.

In their reflection he could see the guards tapping at the keyboard of the laptop. *Mother of God, just let me out of here.* After a moment the thick glass swept aside. He stepped into the yard, resisting the temptation to look up at the window.

No rush. Walk like a man on business. The barred turnstile buzzed and clicked as he approached and he pushed his way through onto the street.

The taxi started up. Montrose pulled open the door and stepped in. "Just a moment," he said, "I've got to check something." He felt his breath coming short and fast. *Relax. Breathe. Just one more step.*

He placed the briefcase on the seat. Hidden in the liner was a passport and airline tickets for Mr. Hyde, a British businessman. Montrose had chosen the name. It was perfect. The Texan got the joke. The man had style. It had gone straight over the heads of Mossad. Monsieur Jekyll would be checking in for his flight, but he'd never make it airside. Mr. Hyde would be emerging from the washrooms, sans fancy suit, wig and beard.

He ripped back the liner and pulled out two tickets. The first was a flight to London, with a connection to JFK. The other, stamped with the Air France logo, was for Paris. *Your choice. Pilgrim had said. If it's something you gotta do, do it now.*

But she wouldn't be there. And wherever she was, he knew she wasn't waiting for him. He ripped the Air France ticket in two, then checked his Omega. *Five minutes on the timer. The old watch always ran a little slow.* He looked up at the second floor window. He could make out the back of Kessler's chair. The startled face of a guard appeared at the window before there was a bright flash and a muffled detonation. The curtains ignited as blood and gore splattered the glass.

He closed the briefcase and settled back in the seat.

"Airport."

I want to go home.

Coming in 2016

The London Cage
Another international thriller
featuring Connor Montrose